WAVES OF STONE

PETRELLAN SAGA 2

Gordon A. Long

AIRBORN PRESS

Delta, B. C.

Waves of Stone

Gordon A. Long

Published by
Airborn Press
4958 10A Ave, Delta, B. C.
V4M 1X8
Canada

ISBN: 978-1-988898-15-5

Printed by Amazon

Cover Design by Mihaela Voicu

"So, my brothers have finished telling you how to treat me. What did they say?"

Keynou shrugged. "That they love you, they're proud and they're worried but they hope this journey will be everything you want it to be."

Kendra glanced at him once, then again. "They did not!"

"Not in those words, but it came through loud and clear."

"Oh." They rode on in silence.

"But what did they really say?"

"What everybody back at Kirigata said."

"And what was that? Come on, Cheynou, you have to tell me."

"Each one of them told me how he or she treated you. The words they used don't really matter. It was the intent that counted. You should be happy, Kendra."

"I should be happy? That all my family and friends are telling stories about me?"

"No, that so many people care so much that they want me to take a little bit of them along on this voyage to care for you."

"And that my travelling companion has neatly deflected all my questions."

"I didn't give you the answers you wanted, Kendra. I gave you the answers you needed."

The swishing of their horses' hooves through the grass was the only sound for a long time.

Finally, she spoke. "I think I understand. Thank you, Cheynou."

He shrugged, grinned. "This could be a long journey. We better start taking care of each other from the start."

She shot him another glance, frowning. "You're not joking, are you?"

"Not at all."

More from Gordon A. Long

Titles Available at Smashwords, Amazon and
other outlets

"Ocean of Grass" Petrellan Saga Book 1
"Zoysana's Choice" Petrellan Saga Book 4
"The Innkeeper's Husband" Petrellan Saga Book 5

"Out of Mischief" World of Change Book 1
"Into Trouble" World of Change Book 2
"Mountains of Mischief" World of Change Book 3
"The Trouble with Tents" World of Change Book 4
"Queen of Mischief" World of Change Book 5

"A Sword Called...Kitten?" Romantic Comedy with an Edge
"The Cat with Many Claws" Sword Called Kitten Book 2
"Cloud Cat" A Sword Called Kitten story
"Sword Called Kitten: The Early Years" Short Stories

"Factory 4-80" Science Fiction

"Storm over Savournon"
A novel of the French Revolution
"Why Are People So Stupid?" Social Humour with a Point

Look for Gordon's books, selected reviews, poetry and short
stories at <airbornpress.ca>
Gordon's opinions on humanity are at the
"Are People Really That Stupid?" blog

Find his weekly reviews and his ideas on writing at
"Renaissance Writer"

Contents

THANKS TO

Cas Peace for her sharp editing eye and her continued support.

Few can handle great power, and those that seek it most avidly are the last who should achieve it.

– Cheynou Chan

"If I tell you the answer, you'll never figure it out for yourself."

– Sarasha the Lame

PROLOGUE

Cheynou regarded the former Captain who lay, wrapped in grubby furs, too weak to rise. Orrick Bren looked smaller and older, with lines on his face deep-etched from loss of weight and touches of grey in his hair and beard.

Bren regarded the three men crowding into the small tent and shook his head. His voice was harsh from lack of use and weak from starvation. He gulped from the canteen that Pers held and began his tale.

As he spoke, his demeanor changed, and his voice slid into the storytellers' tone. Had spent many hours alone, cold and hungry, with only these events swirling in his mind.

> Those boulders that came bounding down the mountain took me by surprise. They were huge and they were coming fast. Set loose from the snow by the warmth of the spring sun, I guess. It certainly wasn't a regular avalanche: no snow or mud, just bouncing rocks. I ran like all the demons were after me, but my luck was off. A smaller one caught me below the knee. Wham! It knocked me down. I just lay there for a while. It was numb at first, but when I tried to get up I knew I was in trouble.
>
> By this time the rocks had stopped. I called to Sarasha, and she came out of the tent. She hobbled over, checked out my leg, said it was broken. Of course, she made a joke of it. Said I was going to find out what it was like to be her. She went back to the tent and got what she needed, cut some sticks for a splint and patched me up, right there on the mountain.
>
> I wasn't happy about that. "What if another bunch of those rocks comes?" I said.

She just kept on working. "Then we'll dive for safety, and to hell with the pain and damage. If we can, it's better to make it steady right here, right now." She turned and gave me that look. "Trust me. I'm an expert. In doing it wrong."

There's never an answer when she looks at you like that, so I just lay back and endured the pain. She patched me up, gave me her crutch and got me back to the tent, hopping alongside, giving me instructions. The pain was pretty bad, but she had some of that tea that kills the pain. You saw her drinking it, I guess, on the trip out here.

I don't remember much of the next few days. She kept me pretty drugged up. I remember it getting cold, though. Colder than it should have been, that late in the spring.

Everything went all right for a couple of weeks. She was really careful, making sure I didn't move, making sure my splint was not too tight, that sort of thing. Soon we were able to cut back on the medicine, and I began to notice the world again. The swelling went down and the pain stopped bothering me all the time. Only when I moved it. She was pretty happy about that, and I asked her why.

She looked at me as if I was stupid. Compared to her, I guess I am. "Because that means you're lucky," she said. "Some day the pain is going to go away and never come back."

I sort of knew she was always in pain, and believe me, by that time I had a better idea of how it felt.

Once I didn't need the drug anymore, I started to pay more attention to what was going on. Namely, how much food we had. I asked her about it.

She was pretty nonchalant. "I guess we're finding out why that mountain lion was desperate enough to attack our horses."

I asked her what she meant by that.

x

"Because there's nothing to eat around here," she answered. "If you hadn't broken your leg you could have gone down to the Prairie and hunted. But now you can't, and I can't. So we're eating what we have."

I asked her if we had enough.

She gave a grin, not a very pleasant one. "Let's just hope the boys get back pretty smartly."

So that was one mistake and one bit of bad luck, but it wasn't a complete disaster. The storm was. As I said, it had been cold, and it got colder. Then it started to snow. Real snow, like in the winter. We couldn't do anything except huddle down in our furs in the tent. We didn't dare go out and light the fire. Not enough wood, anyway. So there we were. Two days of wind and snow. Sarasha had to get up every once in a while to push off the snow where it was swirling around and building up on the lee side or it would have squashed the tent. But most of the time we just lay there, conserving our energy. After a day or so, I figured she was too quiet.

"You're not your usual chatty self, 'Rasha," I said. "Thinking?"

She turned slowly to face me, and there was something in her face. Sort of like...hard to explain. A glow, like she was really happy about something. She said, "Yes. We've done pretty well, haven't we?"

After a while, you get tired of asking her what she means, but I had to know.

She didn't give me the usual pitying look. She was enthused, like she really needed me to agree. She said, "Yes. In general, you know. Remember when we ran our ships on the beach? We were in pretty bad shape, then. Worse than anybody knew, I think. We were on the verge of dissolution as a people. It wouldn't have taken much for us to fall apart into small groups of bandits and nomads, be absorbed into the local population, spread far and wide, killed.

"And look at us now. It was a tough winter, but we survived. We're a strong, unified people, able to handle any difficulty that nature can throw at us, with no help from anyone. We have good plans for the future and the ability to achieve them."

I grinned and agreed with her, but then I remembered the bandages covering my leg. "Of course, we do make the odd slip."

She laid a calm hand on mine. "Don't worry. You'll get out of this fine."

I told her I wasn't worried about me. I was thinking of her.

A dreamy look came into her eyes, then she focused on me. "When did you ever see me without a plan?"

I had to agree that it didn't happen very often. In fact, never.

"So don't worry. It's all going to work out."

I frowned at her, told her not to treat me like a sick child. "What's going on in that devious head of yours?" I asked her.

"Calculations, numbers, estimates. Timing. I have to figure it all out."

I pointed to our limited supplies and told her I had figured it out. "There's only enough food left to keep two people alive for ten days, even on starvation rations. It took our party nine days to get here on horseback. With Yong and Cheynou walking home, on short rations themselves, it will take at least twenty days for help to get back. We've used up fifteen of those. If this storm lasts much longer, builds up more snow, they'll have to wait until the drifts in the lower pass melt: more like thirty, maybe forty days. And we're already weak. We won't survive."

"Don't be so pessimistic. This is a freak storm. We could have summer any moment."

I shook my head and repeated that we still didn't have enough food, and neither of us was in any shape to find more.

"Orrick, you were always so caught up in the obvious."

She was going all 'Sarasha' on me, you know how she...did, and I was suspicious. I asked her what she had planned.

"I'm still working on the details. If this is going to work, it has to be done precisely. There are some things that have to be done at the right time or they can't be done. I'm in the final stages. When I have it all totalled up, you'll be the first to know."

"Some consolation." There was no getting any more out of her, and I folded my arms and shrugged deeper into my furs to get warm.

She stroked my brow until I stopped frowning. "I'll just go and check the wood supply." She began to crawl out of the furs.

She didn't have her coat on, and I told her not to forget it.

"You worry too much, Orrick," she told me, but it wasn't that scathing tone she sometimes uses. "I want to make sure there is enough of everything to last until rescue comes. The food is right here, there's lots of snow to make water, and the firewood is as close as possible outside the tent."

I held her gaze for a while, puzzled. Something...I don't know. I couldn't figure. I told her to be careful. I don't know why I said that. She was only going out to check the firewood.

She touched my cheek and said, "This is a time to take great care."

That should have clued me. She never did things like that. Then she slipped out into the storm, carefully tying the flaps behind her.

There was a long silence in the little tent as the others absorbed what that meant.

Orrick had finished his narrative. He looked around at those who crowded into the small space. Then he made a weak gesture towards the corner of the tent.

All eyes turned there.

"It was only then that I realized she hadn't taken her crutch."

The silence was broken only by the flap of the canvas in the ever-present wind. Cheynou swallowed, but the acid lump stayed in his throat. "She set that up well, didn't she?"

The others stared at him.

"She won't be here to tell us the answers. Now we'll have to figure them out for ourselves." He shouldered his larger friends aside, squirmed out of the tent and strode to the cliff's edge, where he watched the water shoot out and tear into mist as it disappeared into the chasm.

He stood there a long time, his mind churning. *What will we do, now that she is gone?*

1.   SELF EXILE

"You knew!" Orrick Bren's face reddened. "You saw them go."

There was nothing to say, so Cheynou said nothing.

"Do you know that makes you a traitor, just like they are?"

Cheynou started to speak, then stopped and stared at the grass. *Now is not the time.*

The former Captain raised both hands, his work-hardened knuckles clenched. "That was the last thing we needed. We barely survived the winter and we must pull together. I thought we all were agreed on that. But those two have to choose this moment to pull their stunt."

He lowered his arms. "Oh, I know Pers isn't himself since Leide died. But Yong should know better." His anger began to rise again. "Now, when we're losing people right and left, I thought at least your group would be loyal."

Cheynou raised his head. "Sarasha is gone."

"What does that have to do with it? I miss her, too. Don't think it isn't hard for me, especially the way she died. But she's gone, and we all have to pull together even closer if we're going to survive on this Prairie."

Cheynou sighed. *What can I say? Nothing that will help.*

Now the leader's attention focused on him. "And you! Helmsmen are the closest to the Captain. They're supposed to be the most loyal. Pers walked away with some of our best Crew and all our best horses, and you stood aside and said nothing?"

Actually, Helmsmen are supposed to be impartial, but there's no point in bringing that up now.

The former Captain stepped closer, towering over him and jabbing a finger into his chest. "You'd better watch

1

yourself from now on, Cheynou Chan. I'll be keeping close track of what you say and who you say it to. Anyone sowing dissention in the Crews will be dealt with."

Cheynou looked up for a moment into the angry eyes glaring at him, determined not to wince away from the jabbing finger. *Bren has certainly regained his strength quickly.*

"Do you understand me?"

Cheynou nodded once and then turned away.

"Wait a moment. I'm not finished…"

He kept walking. His shoulder blades twitched, but he kept his back turned to the angry Captain and moved on: slowly and, he hoped, with dignity. *I am not running away. There is no sense in the man, and the conversation is over.*

A shuffle in the grass behind almost stopped him, but then Orrick must have decided it wasn't worth it. He spun and stomped off.

Relieved, Cheynou went to his family tent and began to pack his meager belongings.

"Going somewhere?"

He turned at his father's voice. "Seems like a good idea at the moment. Captain Bren is not happy with me."

"Hmm. He's not happy with anyone at the moment. Why you?"

"I was there when Pers and Yong left with the horses this morning. I didn't say anything. So now I'm a traitor as well."

Qiu Chan looked down at his son. "That's unfortunate. We've been staying out of Bren's way until he calms down."

"I know. And that's why I'm leaving. You don't need me around, spoiling your reputation for impartiality. It could ruin everything for you."

His father smiled. "Don't you think you're exaggerating your importance?"

"You didn't hear him, see how angry he is. It's a side of Orrick Bren we don't notice very often, and it doesn't bode well for his leadership."

"Ah. Sarasha's line again."

"That's right. And with her gone, there is no rein on him. He's not going to listen to me. I'm too young and insignificant. Now all the others have left, and it's up to you and Uncle Sanjin. If you can maintain some kind of sanity in the Crews without directly opposing him..."

"We're going to try."

"And I'm going to get out of your way."

"Where are you going? To the Inari with Pers?"

He shook his head. "Perhaps later, but I have another task."

"What task is that?"

"I'm going to give Sarasha a proper burial."

"Hmm. And incidentally check on Bren's story, now that the snow is gone?"

"I hadn't thought of it that way, but I suppose I'll look around."

"Orrick is going to see it that way."

He raised his head. "I can't run my life on what Orrick Bren thinks. This is the right thing to do."

His father nodded slowly. "If you think you have to do it, I suppose you should." Then his head came up. "Have you informed your mother?"

Cheynou winced. "Not yet. I was looking for the right time..."

"There's never a right time to tell your mother something like that. Go find her."

"I suppose."

"Never a right time to tell me what? Are you leaving?"

They both turned like boys caught in a prank. His mother stood there, one hand pushing back the door flap, the other

3

on her hip. "Tent walls are thin." She caught Cheynou's chin in her hand and stared into his eyes. "Word is around. You're letting Orrick Bren run you out of camp?"

Anger flared through him. "I am not!" But then his shoulders slouched. "There was nothing I could say, Mother. By his lights, he was right. He's trying to keep our people together. An important group was leaving, and I just let them go. I agreed with their choice, but it wasn't the time to tell him that. So I'm going to get out of the way for a while."

"Going to the Inari as well?"

"Not right now. I'm thinking of doing some exploring."

Mahekou nodded. "That suits you, dear. Go and draw maps." She gave him a wry smile. "It will make you feel useful."

He couldn't help but grin. "Reading my mind as usual."

"I know you'll take good care of yourself. You'd better. You're the only son I have."

He threw his arms around her, sharing a long embrace. Then she turned and strode out of the tent, but not before he saw the glint of a tear on her cheek.

2. A Fitting Monument

"Go home, stupid dog."

The creature cowered back a few steps, turned apologetically towards him again.

"I'm not going anywhere that's any better than here. Not for you. Go home."

The dog looked up at him from under those strange white marks that looked like eyebrows.

Cheynou lowered his own brows and stared back.

After a brief moment, she looked elsewhere.

"So?"

Her head came up hopefully.

"Are you going home?"

Her ears came up.

"You're not?"

She moved a hesitant step towards him.

"Huh. You're as impossible as...as some other people I know." He reined his horse around and set off at a lope across the plains to the north. A flash of black and grey at the corner of his eye let him know that his new companion had taken up station beside the horse. *Just what I need. Responsibility.* Ignoring the dog, he gazed ahead, his own thoughts pouring through his mind to the rhythm of the horse's hooves. He had a long way to go and a lot to think about.

That night he wasn't so complacent. As he laid out his blankets in a hidden swale in the rolling prairie, he felt comforted by the idea of the dog lying alert beside his tiny fire. He found himself hoping she would be there in the morning.

Once in the night a soft growl jerked him awake, hand fumbling for his sword. He peered around the campsite, lit by the dying coals of the fire and the stars above.

The dog was still lying down, her head up, staring into the darkness to the north. After a moment, she glanced over at him, looked back to the darkness again, then lowered her head on her paws.

Reassured, he let himself drift back to sleep.

In the morning, he allowed her a few crumbs of the ship's biscuit he warmed over the fire, but that was all. She was ecstatic and pushed in for more.

"My, you are a persistent little thing, aren't you? Just like a lot of women I know. Well, actually, I don't know a lot of women that well, but a lot of the ones I know are like you. Persistent. Well, on this trip, you have to feed yourself."

The dog sat there, staring up at him as if she understood every word, her ears perked up, her tongue hanging out one side of her open mouth. She looked so much prettier this way instead of her usual cringing that he kept up a nonsense conversation as he stowed his gear and saddled the horse.

If he had doubted the dog's ability to keep up, the day's travel persuaded him otherwise. Lolloping easily at the horse's side, she still had energy to explore ahead, behind, to either side and once even to take a futile run at a rabbit.

Twice that night she awakened him with that soft, warning growl, and each time she soon calmed. He assumed that meant a vagrant, threatening scent had eddied past, followed by no further evidence of danger.

The third night it was different. She came to her feet in a rush, startling him out of his dreams. Her dim shadow was rigid, her nose pointing east.

He slipped on his boots and made his way out to the horse, which was also interested in whatever was out there, but not worried.

For the longest time they stood there, listening with every pore of their bodies, until finally the horse snorted and went back to grazing. The dog prowled away into the darkness, but soon returned and lay by the fire, her nose still questing.

Cheynou left his boots on, kept his sword near to hand, and rolled in his blankets again. After a while, the long day's ride got to him, and he slept again.

In daylight nothing looked different, but he breakfasted and packed quickly. Only half a glass into the morning, all became clear. The tracks of a large party, mostly on foot, crossed their trail, heading east. Twenty or more men, although some followed others and left their tracks intermingled. The three or four horses in the group were of varying sizes, and that was all his seaman's tracking skills could reveal to him.

"What do you think, Dog? Friends or enemies? I'd say anyone travelling at night this far from anywhere is suspicious. The shoe prints look like ours. Part of the lost Sparrowhawk Crew? Probably best left alone. We have our objective, and they have theirs. Any ideas?"

It seemed she had none, and with a final browse across their trail with her nose, the black-and-grey dog lined out again for the north.

He shrugged and followed. Though he kept a better watch throughout the day, he saw no more sign of anyone.

Every morning through the lengthening summer days, Cheynou followed his routine: eating, packing his meager camp, then saddling his horse and pointing its nose to the north.

And all day he rode at the horse's best travelling pace, straight as his navigating skills could aim him across the prairie towards the destination he dreaded.

One morning he pulled up, satisfied at his progress but sobered by the insignificant mound of stones piled over the body of the small, dark man they had found frozen earlier that spring. Cheynou remembered his icy tracks, raised up out of the melting snow, lined dead straight across the Prairie, coming from the north. Once again, he wondered at the straightness of that course. How could anyone dying of hunger and cold maintain a heading so direct? The secret probably lay under the pile of stones. Looking around one more time, he imagined those icy tracks up out of the drying Prairie grass and followed them.

"All right. Don't give me that look. You can come up. If you stay awake at night, you get rest during the day. "

The black-and-grey dog, her long hair flying, took a quick run and soared up onto her favourite perch atop the pack behind his saddle. The horse, used to this by now, merely snorted and continued his plodding walk.

Cheynou looked out over the Prairie in front of him. "Aye, it's been a long walk, Dog. And likely to be a lot longer. Still glad you came?"

Having attained one goal, she decided to try for more. Her nose pushed firmly under his left arm, pleading for a pat. He raised his arm, and her head wormed forward until one brown eye peered up at him from his armpit. He twisted so that his right hand could ruffle her ears. "Well, I'm happy you came, even if the pony isn't."

Again his gaze was drawn to the sweep of land before him, rising gently to the mountains that grew closer, slowly closer, day by day.

"It's supposed to be seven days on a fast horse to the mountains, dog. We've been out here for eight already. Can you think of a reason for this?"

Catching the tone of his voice, the expressive ears cringed backwards, and she nosed in for reassurance.

"No, not you, dog. Can't you take a joke?"

It seemed she could, if only he would explain it first. Her ears came up again. He sighed. He wished the dog had more spunk. She was so sensitive to his moods that he had to be careful. The merest hint of displeasure and she cowered, trembling.

Or seemed to cower. He looked down at the laughing mouth. This dog was too smart to take at face value. Raising

8

his encircling arm, he pushed her nose behind him with one final pat.

He rose in his stirrups in a vain attempt to see farther ahead. If he remembered correctly (and why wouldn't he; it was his duty) his route should cross a small creek valley well before sunset.

Within a few more chains a dark line grew out of the flat before him, and soon he was sitting in front of a cheerful fire, the dog stretched to her fullest beside him, the horse hobbled nearby, grazing contentedly on the lush grass of the valley bottom.

Soon his hunger roused him, and he reached over to open his pack. The dog's head came up, interested.

"There's not much in here for you, dog. You can have a treat once I'm finished, but that's all. There are plenty of juicy mice and other critters out there, just fine for dogs."

He placed his fry pan on the coals, added a dash of water and laid a goodly chunk of ship's biscuit over it to warm. A handful of jerky scraps followed, and soon his simple meal was warm and softened enough to gnaw through. True to his word, he gave his companion one small shred of meat. He had ample supplies, but not enough to spoil the dog. He shuddered at the thought of Sarasha and Orrick Bren, crippled and hungry, shivering and starving in the tent while that last, late-spring blizzard howled around them.

The dog sniffed around his feet, glanced one more appeal, then trotted off through the gathering dusk to find her own supper. Following his nightly routine, Cheynou wrote his journal, updated his map, then rolled into his blankets. Satisfied with his professional duties, he slept.

Two mornings later he reached the place where he was sure they had gone wrong. Once again, the inviting opening lured him forward, although now he knew the bait was false. And if the mate of that mountain lion was still wandering around...

He sat his horse at the top of a rise, poring over the mountainscape that rolled up in front of him.

There, off to the right, that faint animal trail wound upward through the rocks and stunted trees to the higher valley, which dead-ended at a sharp dropoff with avalanche paths all around. It was there that Sarasha's final drama had taken place, with the lion, the avalanche and that last, fatal, snowstorm.

If the little brown man had not come from there, where had he come from? He had camped up there. He had buried his companion there. Again, Cheynou wondered if a mountain lion or an avalanche had caused that tragedy as well.

If there was nothing up in the hanging valley, then the two explorers must have passed through somewhere down here. Looking from this angle, solid rock walls encircled him.

So choose another view. Nudging his horse ahead, he cut off the trail down to the left. The dog decided they were hunting and started to scout the surrounding area.

He happened to be looking elsewhere when she disappeared. He stood in his stirrups for a better view, but she was gone. He lifted the reins, and the horse stepped faster in the direction she had been searching.

He had almost reached the face of the wall when a narrow slit opened off to his left. It was wide enough for a horse, as long as the rider kept the stirrups in close. They clambered through the passage and up a small incline and broke out of the confining rock into a wider canyon. The black-and-grey dog was sitting farther on wearing a 'What kept you?' look. He motioned her forward.

After that, it was easy. The trail began to drop and turn back to the right. As he rode, he kept his eye on the ledge above. It soon towered over him, sheer to the top, and he knew that he was following the bottom of the cliff, just as earlier in the year they had followed the top. He reined in for a moment, knowing what he was about to find.

An impatient yap from around the next bend and he moved forward, steeling himself for whatever might appear.

Not much. It had been a lean spring, and over the past three months the scavengers had done their work. The main evidence was the gnawed remains of two saddles, still cinched to the backbones of what had once been their horses. Further over, he could identify Sarasha's pony by the tatters of the sailcloth packsaddle covering the entwined bones of a small horse and the big cat she had carried over the cliff edge above.

He peered around. That was all. Exactly as they had seen it from the rim this spring.

He walked his horse further along the cliff bottom, glancing upward frequently, trying to place himself as close to the camp at the top of the cliff as possible. He scanned the ground as he went, but nowhere could he spot what he dreaded to find. He kept moving up the valley, the dog ranging ahead.

He tried to picture what would have happened. According to Bren, Sarasha had left the tent in the middle of the storm without her crutch. If she had meant to kill herself, she would not have waited for the storm to do its work. She would have crawled to the edge and jumped. If she got lost, she could have gone some distance, but not too far to the east, because she would have hit the creek and followed it to the edge.

When he reached the spot where the feathers of mist from the stream reached the bottom, he knew he must have missed her.

Or there was something wrong with Orrick Bren's story.

He sat his horse, thinking. But if Bren's story was wrong, what could the truth be? If he had killed her, he would have been hard pressed to move her any distance, crippled as he was. So in spite of that, her body should be nearby. He turned back down the canyon, searching more carefully.

He almost missed it the second time as well, but caught it out of the corner of his eye. A narrow crack in the valley floor, running parallel to the cliff face. He wasn't looking down, because his attention had been drawn to a huge boulder that leaned out of the rock above. At its base there

11

was less of the usual rubble, and the crack looked wide enough...

Cheynou dismounted, ground-tied his horse and moved forward reluctantly. The morning sun had not reached the base of the rock, and it was dark down there in the crevasse, but there was something... He knelt and peered deep into the shadow, trying to decipher what he saw.

It was Sarasha, he had no doubt. He could see dark cloth, wisps of hair, what seemed to be an outstretched hand, bare finger bones glistening in the darkness. He stayed there, his mind not working, until the pain in his knees reminded him of the reality of the present.

How to get her out? She was wedged away down, beyond his reach. He moved to one end of the crack, then the other, but to no avail. After a lot of clambering and prying, he realized that he was just not going to be able to get to her. The cleft where she had lodged was too narrow, and as her body had dried and decayed, it had slipped farther and farther down.

He couldn't get her out, so he would have to bury her where she lay. He thought about that for a while. It felt wrong somehow, to toss rocks down upon her.

But it had to be done. He started by filling in the crack on either side of her, first dropping in the biggest rocks that would go, then adding smaller ones to fill the gaps. Soon the two piles rose above her, and the smaller rocks began to roll down on her.

He gathered a large pile of fine gravel on either side of the crack above her. Taking firm hold of himself and not looking, he quickly shoved it all over the edge. When he thought he had pushed in enough, he peeked down. She was completely hidden. With a feeling of relief, he returned to using larger stones, and soon the whole crack was full.

By this time the sun was high overhead, and he was tired and hungry. He got water from the stream and chewed a piece of jerky while he squatted, wondering what to do now. He needed to make some kind of monument. He considered a pile of rocks, but that was somehow unfitting for one of Sarasha's stature. A woman who had taken down a whole Mastership single-handed needed something bigger. Something special. He rose to explore the area.

He was off to the side, looking for a flat stone that was big enough for the job yet small enough for him to move, when he chanced to look up. Hanging out over her grave was that boulder. A huge slab of stone. He had already noted that. What he saw now was that there was a split in the boulder all the way across. It was cloven so deep that he wondered what kept the front half from crashing down on her resting-place. Peering under, he could see that the broken part was propped up by a pile of rubble. If he were just to dig that rubble away...

...maybe the whole thing would come crashing down on me while I lay there, and I would join her forever. Well, I'll just have to be careful.

It was easy at first, because the rocks were loose and he didn't have to move them far. Soon he was working farther and farther under the boulder. He left a couple of big stones so that in case it did shift, he would be protected. Then he grimly worked on.

Through the heat of the afternoon he toiled, crawling farther and farther under the overbearing weight of stone, straining his ears for a creak that might signal his death. Finally, he came to one rock that seemed to be stuck. Considering it from all angles, he wondered if perhaps it was the one that was holding it all up. He painstakingly dug out all the loose rock around it, listening for any sound of shifting in the stone. Once it was isolated, he crawled back out into the open air.

It was a great relief to be out from under the burden of all that stone, but his problem wasn't solved. After a moment's thought, he went back to his horse and got his rope. As he returned, he was surprised to hear a scrabbling sound under the boulder. Sure enough, a bushy black tail lay across the

13

rock, and the dog's front paws were shooting a stream of small rocks out behind her.

He had a sudden stab of fear. "No! Dog! Get out of there!"

The animal backed out in a hurry and turned to him, her head and tail low. He knelt down and petted her. "You can't go in there, Dog. It's dangerous. You stay out here." He looked straight in her eyes. "Stay here."

She cowered down on the rock, and he returned to work, unhappy with having to treat her that way but unsure of how else to impress the danger upon her.

He wormed in and hastily knotted the end of the rope around the key stone. Then he scooted back, mounted his horse and took a twist around the twin saddle horns. The horse pulled willingly, but nothing happened. He moved to another angle and tried again. This time, he thought he heard a scraping. Changing the angle, keeping a cautious eye on the rock above him, he tried again. There was definite movement. Now that the horse had the idea, it became easier. They kept the pull on, moving first to one side, then the other, until the rock popped free. He dropped the rope and kicked the horse's ribs, lunging forward, looking fearfully back over his shoulder.

No movement.

Cheynou sighed, dismounted, and retied the horse a safe distance away. Walking slowly around as he coiled his rope, he viewed the boulder from all the angles he could. As far as he could tell, it was ready to fall. There was nothing left to dig from under it.

Looking up at the crack, he remembered dropping the rocks down on Sarasha. *What if I drop a bunch of rocks down into the crack? Maybe their combined weight...*

He scrambled up the steep slope to the top of the boulder. Sure enough, there were several rocks of the right size scattered around. He dropped one in, watched it fall until the crack narrowed and it wedged in solid. Encouraged, he found another, trying to drop it directly on the first rock. It, too, stuck tight.

14

Everything he knew about wedges told him he was on the right track. He started gathering up all the rocks he could find, dropping them into the crack, throwing them in, heaving them down on the other rocks as hard as he could. Soon he ran out of rocks and had to struggle farther and farther to bring them up to the split, but he worked on.

Then he heard it. Just as he threw one large rock down into the crack, he heard a grinding sound. He glanced around, but both animals were out of danger. He then thought of his own position, high on the top. Cursing himself for his foolishness, he found an escape route that took him off to the side onto some solid-looking rock.

He went and found a bigger stone. In spite of its weight, he hauled it up the hill. When he got it to the top, he struggled to raise it as high as he could. Then he heaved it down with all his might.

The big stone bounced once against either wall before jamming itself firmly. This time there was a definite grinding sound, and he was sure the crack widened. That last stone was fitted perfectly as a wedge. If only he could jam another one right down on top of it...

He raised a smaller rock above his head and slammed it down.

The reaction was instantaneous. The moment it hit, a grinding, creaking noise arose, and the split began to open. He scrambled up his path to safety, turned and looked back.

The mass of stone was moving, slowly, then faster and faster, toppling away from the mountain wall. The groaning was drowned by a roar and a crash, and a huge cloud of dust boiled up, hiding everything from view.

Cheynou held his sleeve over his mouth and moved forward as the dust cleared. The break was clean. The massive chunk of granite, taller than it was wide, had fallen away from the mountain, covering the crack where Sarasha's body lay.

He nodded with satisfaction. Seen from above, it looked something like a huge body, lying with its head to the cliff, its feet stretching away to the north. A fitting monument; Sarasha would be pleased. For a moment, the words she would have spoken rang in his head.

"Cheychan, you done good, kid."

He grinned to himself, but the joy faded. Sure, it looked right. But it also looked like a rock that had just fallen off a mountain. How to show that someone important lay here? He had nothing to carve with, nothing to write on the stone. He tried to scratch the rock with his knife, but the granite was too rough and hard.

That bothered him at first, but then he decided it was no problem. He would be back. When he came, he would bring a chisel and make a proper marking for her. Clambering once again over the boulder, he made sure that it covered the cleft completely. Then he sat for a while looking over the results of his labour, fatigue dragging at him.

As satisfied as he could be with his main task, he considered how to deal with the remains of the horses. Fire was the only way. Just up the valley, he found the skeletons of several avalanche-killed trees jumbled together and used his rope to tow them to the foot of the cliff. Then, collecting as many bones as he could, he made a pyre and lit it. Once it was burning brightly, he checked over the saddles. Rodents had gnawed them until they were useless. On the fire they went.

Sarasha's special riding/pack saddle gave him pause. He gathered up the tatters of sailcloth and considered them. Not only was the saddle badly torn, there was no one who would ever need it again.

With a melancholy heart, he was about to toss it on the fire when something heavy bumped his knee. Deep in one of the pockets, undisturbed by scavengers, he found a small package, wrapped securely in oiled leather. He had seen that before, in the equipment the northern scout had been carrying. Shoving it away in his coat, he shook the packsaddle once more to be sure it was empty, then carried it gently to the fire, laid it on and stood back.

16

It was only then, as the flames began to lick around the edges of Sarasha's saddle, that the tears came. He had been keeping himself too busy to think, but now that he had done everything he could, there was nothing to keep his memories from rushing in.

Sarasha and that dratted saddle. He remembered her trying it, that first day when the Priest-Admiral's ships were coming and they had fled the seashore. He remembered the day they had first explored the Prairie above the Eagle camp, learning to ride their horses together.

Folding into a sitting position, he stared into the flames, remembering all they had been through, remembering all that Sarasha had done, remembering all Sarasha had said: remembering Sarasha.

The fire had died into ashes and the shadow of the nearby rock was reaching towards him when a small, cold nose nudged under his elbow. Rousing himself, he looked around. This was really no place to camp for the night, but he was reluctant to leave.

Mounting his horse, he moved farther along the valley to where the stream poured down from the cliff-edge above. It was too damp and noisy there, so he came back along the opposite side. There he found a flat spot barely big enough for his bedroll and a small fire. There was no grazing, so he fed the gelding some of his meager grain supply and picketed him in a cleft in the rock so that no cougar could get behind him.

Placing his bow near to hand, he performed his usual evening tasks and was soon in his bedroll, staring at the stars. Once again the memories crowded in, and he did not sleep for a long time. Tonight he welcomed the warm presence of the dog, and he lay and fondled her ears absent-mindedly while she basked in the attention.

In the morning he felt better. He had done what he had come to do, and now he could leave. He ate, packed and mounted at his usual economical speed, then rode back up the valley to Sarasha's resting place. He grinned to himself.

17

At least no one could miss that rock. He was quite proud to have split such a large boulder. Oh, several thousand years of weathering had helped a bit, but it was his wedges that had finished the job.

"Things sure change, don't they, 'Rasha? We came ashore, and our bodies couldn't be sent back to the sea. So you decided we should be burned and sent back to the air. Well, I can't do that, so I'm sending you back to the ground. I guess that's sort of appropriate, isn't it, 'Rasha?" He paused to force the aching in his throat to subside. "If you were going to be Beached, you got Beached better than anybody ever did. You got yourself dug into solid rock!"

Tears streaming down his face, he reined his horse around and started back towards the open Prairie and the combined Eagle/Petrel camp.

3. RAIDERS

When he reached camp, he slipped in as quietly as he could, but he only took a few days to realize that nothing had changed. Bren still glowered at him, and the coolness spread to many of the other Crew.

He made his plans, then sat down with his father and laid them out.

"I'm going to see Kendra, first."

"The Farmer girl? Why her?"

"Kendra was a friend of Sarasha's. Her and Byaren. I doubt if they even know she's dead. I'll see if I can be useful to them. Learn about them; find ways our people can deal with them."

"A spy in the enemy camp?"

"Except we aren't enemies any more. I hope I can help persuade them of that."

His father put his hands on Cheynou's shoulders. "Perhaps you're the right one to do that. You get along with everyone and you've got a cool head on your shoulders." He nodded. "I think this is a good idea."

"What about you, Mother?"

She gave him a wordless hug, then leaned back and looked into his eyes. "I liked Kendra. She stood up to Orrick Bren almost as much as Sarasha did."

Cheynou raised his eyebrows. "Didn't do either of them much good, did it? Now she's back home and he's running amok."

Mahekou gave a sad smile and transferred her grip to his upper arms. "Well, maybe it's a good thing for you. Those Farmers will give you a hoe and put you to work. Put some muscle on those shoulders."

Once again he bid his family goodbye, saddled his horse, and started to mount.

"Cheynou, are you going somewhere?"

He started, then calmed as he recognized the voice. "Kendie, please don't sneak up on me like that!"

She grinned impishly up at him. "Seems to me you're the one sneakin' around."

"Kendie, if you're going to be a Scribe, you always must speak and write properly."

Immediately contrite, she corrected herself. "I'm sorry, Cheynou. But you do look pretty sneaky."

"Well, I am going somewhere, but I'm not sneaking. I'm going to visit Kendra."

The girl's face glowed at the mention of her namesake. "Can I come?"

"Of course you can't. You're too young to go wandering off across the Prairie with a young man."

A bit of red flushed her face at this implied compliment.

"And you also have your writing to consider."

"You're right, of course. I'm working very hard!" She looked appealingly at him. "Though I don't get much time to spend on it."

He grimaced. "I know, Kendie, but if Captain Bren doesn't think your writing is important, I'm not the one to tell him otherwise."

Her head went to one side. "Why doesn't he like you, Cheynou?"

He considered. "It's too difficult to explain."

"Is it because of Sarasha?"

"Partly. And her ideas."

She nodded seriously. "Some time you have to explain that to me. I must know everything about her if I'm going to continue her writings."

"You just keep doing your best." He reached out and ruffled her hair. "While I'm on the trail, I'll try to think of something I can do to help you when I come back."

He swung up in the saddle, and she waved happily as he rode away from the Petrel camp, hiding the guilt he felt. *There's a chance I won't be back. Ever.*

With that thought nagging at him, he set his course towards the coast. A flash of grey beside him caught his eye.

"So, Dog, you're back."

She looked up happily, her ears perked, her tongue lolling from the side of her mouth.

"Where did you get to?" The dog had no answer, but he didn't need one. Her life on the margins of the camp had been tenuous, and she had disappeared the moment he reentered. Obviously, she preferred to cope on her own in the Great Prairie rather than to accept the regimented life in the camp.

I can sympathize with that.

As he rode south, he considered his options. Bren might get over his pique, and he could return to the Petrel camp. However, something else would just come up. Orrick Bren needed absolute loyalty, complete control, and Cheynou couldn't bring himself to give it.

Maybe there's a place for me with the Farmers at Port Ternata. Kendra will know. I hope she remembers me. Of course she'll remember me, but maybe not in any way that makes her want to help me. He shrugged. If not her, maybe Byaren or someone else would find him something to do. Otherwise…

A small lift pushed at his spirits. There was always the Ocean. Risky, with the Priest-Admiral's fleet still around, broken though it might be. Still, it would be nice to feel the deck rise under his feet again, to take a shot of a star in a bright sky at midnight, touch the spokes of the wheel so gently…

Cheynou shook his head. The Ocean was too risky. At least, that Ocean. Another plan had been stewing in the back of his thoughts. A bigger plan.

He gave himself a shake and began to observe his surroundings more carefully. It wouldn't do him much good to get ambushed by some wild or human scavenger before he even got there. He glanced at the dog, trotting along beside him.

"Go on, Dog," he gestured to the left, "be useful." To his gratified surprise, the dog lowered her nose to the ground and trotted off in the indicated direction. *Maybe my training is worth something after all.*

Several times in the next two days he was reminded of the fine senses of his self-appointed guardian, as her nose reliably pointed out both danger and game.

Then one night she reacted with more fear. She rose and stalked to the side of the camp closest to the trail, her head low, the growl rising and falling.

He slipped out of his bed and into his boots and followed her as quietly as he could, cutlass in hand.

Shuffling noises ahead stopped him, and he dropped to one knee, his hand on the dog's back. She froze as well.

There was no moon, but enough starlight shone over the trail to reveal a file of men — mostly walking, a few mounted — heading south. They were all dressed in dark clothing, but the glint and clink of metal here and there showed that they were armed.

It was too dark to make an accurate count. They were moving slowly, but it took a while for them to go by. With his hand on her, the dog was quiet, so he stayed there until the last man was far down the trail. Then he straightened and turned back to his camp.

There was only one explanation: a raiding party. *Damn them! I know things are hard for the Ship people this spring, but destroying our relationship with our only source of trade is suicidal.*

There was only one thing to do. Packing his belongings as well as he could in the darkness, he saddled up and headed south, swinging wide of the trail and walking his horse over the dark plain. He sent the dog ahead, and once again she seemed to understand, disappearing into the darkness. He found that her patches of black and grey blended into the shadows of the bushes and the lighter patches of grass so that she was impossible to follow. As they paced through the remainder of the night, he caught only glimpses of her as she ranged ahead and circled back to him.

Dawn came, and he reasoned that the raiders would be hiding out somewhere for the day, to move on after darkness fell again. His main problem was to get past them without stumbling onto their camp. In order to avoid this, he swung even further away from the trail. Once he could see the dog trotting along in front of him, he was more comfortable, as the wind was blowing in their faces and he could count on her nose for warning. As the light firmed, he lifted the horse to a fast lope and they began to cover ground.

He rested the horse briefly several times, but he had to make it to Kirigata before dark. Gone was his plan for finding a place with the Farmers. After this raid, no matter what the outcome, any of his people would be seen as the enemy at best, a spy at worst. But still he had to warn them. *Drop this plan, move on to the next one.*

He galloped into the farmyard well before sunset, startling the workers going about their daily tasks. He brought his horse to a sliding halt and jumped off. Several men strolled over to see what this stranger brought to enliven their day. He grabbed the nearest by the arm.

"Where is Kendra? Where is Lord Kire? There are Raiders coming!"

Shocked out of their laziness, they began to ask questions, but he shouted them down. "Get the Lord. Get Kendra. Start arming yourselves. There is a raid coming from the north!"

The questioning began again.

"What's all this noise about?" Lord Kire's voice cut through the din, silencing everyone. "Who is this?"

"I'm Cheynou Chan of the Eagles. I was on the trail south, intending to visit Kendra, when I saw a raiding party. They were a long day's ride to the north last night. I don't know how far they came today. I circled around and made the best time I could. They're mostly afoot, some horses."

"How many?"

"I couldn't see too well. Maybe forty. About five horses."

"Are you sure it's a raid?"

"I saw forty men with weapons coming this way. What else am I to think?"

"And you're from the Eagle?"

"Yes. I'm a friend of Sarasha's."

"Oh. Sarasha. Well, if she sent you..." The lord turned to his men and began to snap out orders.

Cheynou found himself standing, the only still person in the midst of the turmoil. He turned to his horse, loosened the cinch of the saddle. His dog crouched close, worried by the bustle. Then she was on her feet, her lip wrinkling at something behind him. He turned to see Kendra striding towards him, her riding skirt swirling around her boots, loose blouse and blonde hair flowing as she walked.

"Cheychan! Good to see you! How did you manage to put the place in such an uproar?"

Greeted with such enthusiasm, he couldn't help but smile for a moment, but sobered to explain his message.

She nodded. "Yes, Father said Sarasha sent you. How is she?"

His buoyant mood collapsed. "She didn't send me, Kendra. She's...she's dead."

"Oh." She reached out, laid a hand on his forearm. "I'm so sorry, Cheynou. How did it happen?"

She took the reins of his horse and turned them both towards the stables. He stumbled along, trying to get his thoughts in order. "We were on an exploring trip to the mountains in the early spring, and a lion spooked the horses over a cliff. We walked back for help, and Orrick stayed with Sarasha. An avalanche broke his leg. There was a late blizzard, and they were running out of food. She…"

The girl stopped and stared at him a moment. "She…on purpose?"

He nodded mutely.

"So there would be enough food for him."

"That's right."

"That sounds like our Sarasha, all right. Do you think he was worth it?"

He shook his head, began to groom his horse with mindless strokes of the brush. "I don't know, Kendra. Our people are having difficulty surviving. We need strong leadership or we'll fragment into who-knows-what. If somebody doesn't keep things organized, there will be more of these raids, all sorts of stupidity."

She nodded. "I see. But that's not what Sarasha wanted."

"No. She was always able to think of a way to organize things without giving orders, but people did what she wanted. Bren isn't like that. He was a Captain. He gives orders and expects them to be followed." He turned to her earnestly. "He was a good Captain, Kendra. He'll do what's best for his people."

She smiled sadly. "You don't have to sing his praises to me."

"No, I suppose not."

"So if Sarasha didn't send you, why are you here?"

He shrugged. "I…well, I…"

She turned slowly towards him. "Cheynou, are you in trouble?"

"Aye, sort of."

They had finished rubbing down the horse by this time, and she took his hand impulsively. "Cheychan in trouble? This I have to hear. Come inside and tell me all about it."

"But what about the raid?"

She shrugged. "They may not hit us. They may see us prepared and go on to easier pickings. If they come, we fight." She grinned. "A little raiding party is not going to get you out of telling my why the most perfect Cheynou Chan, Helmsman of the first order, is in trouble."

He frowned. "Who says I'm perfect?"

"I don't know. Everybody. Sarasha."

"Sarasha said that?"

"Not in as many words, but I got the message. You were one of the few who would stand up to her, I remember that."

"I never stood up to her."

"You never knuckled under, either."

"Whatever you say."

"I do say." She glanced down at him, wistfully, he thought. "I wish I could be like that."

By this time they were entering the central block of the huge main house of the Kirigata Home. They crossed the dining hall and took a wide staircase up to what must be the lord's family quarters.

At his frown, she tugged at his hand again. "Right through here. I've got a sitting room with a window that faces east. We can keep a lookout as we talk."

Her rooms were high enough in the building that the panes, small and heavily shuttered, gave them a good view across the plain. There were two comfortable chairs facing the window, a low table between them.

"You must be tired and thirsty. Sit down a moment." She was gone before he could protest.

Dropping his saddlebags beside the chair, he gratefully lowered himself into its soft embrace. He peered out at the countryside, where the lengthening shadows could be hiding a thousand men. Safe in this stone fortress, he was too tired to care.

His eyelids had begun to feel heavy when Kendra reappeared, carrying a tray with two mugs of ale and several aromatic dishes. She set the food on the table, handed him his mug and collapsed into the other chair herself. "Great view, isn't it? If it wasn't for the morning sun waking me up, it would be perfect."

He didn't have the energy to respond.

She reached over and slapped his arm. "Come on, Cheychan. You're not going to duck out on me by falling asleep. Give."

"I got up in the dark and rode all day, Kendra."

"Right." She shook his shoulder. "And until we figure out who and where your raiding party is, you have to stay with us."

"It isn't my raiding party."

"Until it attacks somebody or we get some other reports, it is. So you have to stay awake. Tell the story."

He had the vague thought that there was something wrong with that logic, but it was too difficult. Easier to tell his story, since that's what she wanted.

"I went back last month. I found Sarasha's body, where she went off the cliff. I buried her and came back to report."

"That must have been a tough trip."

"It was a good trip. It had a difficult part in the middle, but I'm glad I went."

"I see. So what happened when you got back?"

"Orrick Bren wasn't too happy that I went. I don't know why."

"Maybe he doesn't like to think about a debt he can never repay."

He nodded. "That's the charitable interpretation."

"I gather you have another one?"

He sat up straighter. "No. That's it. I don't, but Orrick seems to think I might have. So he got riled. I told him as far as I could see my story supports his, but he still didn't seem happy. I didn't want to cause trouble. I tried to duck out of it, but he kept pushing me, and finally I told him."

"Oh, no. You didn't."

"Yes, I did. I said the only thing that looked suspicious to me was the fact that he was so upset about me going. That finally shut him up, but I could tell he wasn't happy. So I thought I'd be better off out of his sight for a while."

"I can see that."

"What's so funny?"

Her smile faded. "I guess it isn't so funny when you think about it. Orrick Bren lost the person who would stand up to him, and that's bad. Now he finds someone else who might fulfill that role, and he's lost you, too."

"Me?"

She reached over and poked his arm. "Yes, it could be you. It has nothing to do with your size. Orrick needs someone to keep him on the track. Otherwise he goes off on his own path and takes everyone else with him, for good or ill. Sarasha kept him from doing that. Sounds to me like you could have done the same thing for him."

He sank deeper in the softness of the chair. "I doubt it."

"Things didn't suit you at home, so you hit the trail. I like that. Maybe I'll do the same."

"Sure thing. Just pack up your horse, your jewelry, all your fancy clothes and hit the trail. Why would you do that?"

"Maybe you aren't the only one who doesn't have a proper place with your people."

He gazed pointedly around the sumptuous room.

She tossed her head. "Well, you're here, and that's our gain, their loss. What did you have in mind?"

"Hmph. Nothing that will work now."

"Why?"

He vaguely gestured towards the window. "There's no place for a Seaman here after tonight."

She grimaced. "That's probably true."

"So, I guess it's back to the Prairies, take my chances with Bren." He thought a moment. "I thought of joining Pers and Yong."

"Where are they?"

"I guess you haven't heard any news at all, have you?"

"No. You people disappeared into the Prairies late last summer, and I've only heard rumours ever since."

He sighed. "I can put you in the picture. We had a tough winter, but we survived. Barely. So several of the Ship's Crews have decided to band together, because we need to support each other. The Petrels and Eagles made it through the winter in the best shape, and Orrick seems the strongest candidate for a leader, so they've all gathered with him."

"But Pers and Yong..."

"Without Sarasha to guide him, Orrick has been...well..."

"...acting like Orrick."

"Something like that. Pers and Yong were part of Sarasha's group, and he's not too keen on having them and their ideas around. They weren't too keen to be around either, so they took their horses and left."

"They took their horses?"

"Of course. But Orrick didn't see it that way. He doesn't think of them as their horses. He says they stole Ship's property."

She looked out the window for a moment. "And that keeps them out of his way."

He nodded. "Pers and Yong and that bunch that hung around Sarasha were a powerful group. But with Captain Tourn gone, and Sarasha gone..."

"...and now you gone..."

"Me? I was only a hanger-on."

"Maybe at the beginning." She hitched forward in her chair. "The point is, now all Orrick's possible competition is gone, and he can take over."

"That's about it."

"So, where did they go?"

"To the Inari."

"The Inari? The natives?"

"That's right. The Inari have a lot more complex society than you Farmers think. Very tough people. They stayed away from you because you had nothing they wanted, and they don't get along with strangers.

"However, they've decided they want horses. Pers and Yong showed up with some good stock, and they were welcomed." He shot her a glance. "They took Owena."

"They took my horse?"

"Bren thinks she's his horse."

She laughed out loud. "No wonder Orrick is so angry with them. He had plans for that horse."

"He already got what he wanted."

"What? Did he breed her with that huge, clumsy black?"

"Aye. He got himself a colt that looks promising. Big, fast, alert."

"I guess I'm happy about that. Is she all right?"

"Oh, she's fine. Looked great the last time I saw her."

"When was that?"

"When she was heading out into the plains with Pers and Yong and the rest of their herd."

"You were there, and didn't tell anyone? No wonder Orrick Bren wants to get rid of you."

"Aye."

She slapped her hands on the padded arms of her chair. "Well, it doesn't look like anything exciting is going to happen. You're obviously not going to be able to stay awake. Finish your drink and come on."

He dragged himself up and hoisted his saddlebag over his shoulder. To his surprise, she took him, not out into the manor, but through another door into what must be her bedroom.

"Huh? Kendra, I can't..."

She shook her head. "I've been thinking about what you said. Once that raiding party gets intercepted, there's going to be a hue and cry all over here. They'll be looking for any Sea Raiders they can find. I think it best if you stay out of sight."

"But I can't..."

She smiled. "The one thing you can't do right now is argue. You're too tired, and you're out of your own territory." She reached out and pushed his shoulder.

Surprised, he stumbled. His heels caught the bed and he fell backwards into softness. Before he could struggle up, she had one of his boots off and was working on the other. "You sleep in my bed tonight. Don't worry about me. I've got lots of places to sleep. I live here."

He was too tired to argue, but one thing worried him; casual as she sounded, she had not suggested he take his clothes off. Perhaps she knew something he didn't...

He slept.

He was aroused in semi-darkness by loud voices in the courtyard below. Instantly alert, he hauled on his boots and slipped into the sitting room to listen at the window. There were a lot of men in the courtyard, but one voice commanded attention.

"We'd better take a look around, Lord Kire. They scattered in the night, and there could be one of them hiding anywhere. You're the last Home before the plains start. This would be a logical place."

Kendra's father answered heavily. "I suppose you're right, Byaren. I'll roust out the men to help you."

"Make sure they're armed."

More voices arose, and soon there were loud footsteps everywhere.

The door behind him opened and he spun, his dagger in his hand.

It was Kendra. "Back in bed, my boy."

"What?"

"My bed. Clothes off. Get in, under the covers." She was stripping off her cloak, revealing only a nightdress.

"What?"

"Don't go all stupid on me now, Cheychan. First, they'll never search a lady's room. If they do, they'll discover why I didn't want them to come in. They can only tell a Raider by his clothes."

"Oh."

"Finally it sinks in." She pushed him through the door.

He stripped off pants and shirt and ducked under the covers. She tossed his saddlebags into a hamper, his boots and clothes on top, and covered them with her own cloak. Then she slipped into the bed beside him.

"Do you have to…?"

"Not really, but it will look better if they burst in."

"But…"

"Shh."

Footsteps on the stairs. Doors being opened. Then a quiet knock. "Miss Kendra? Miss Kendra, are you awake?"

She laid a hand on his shoulder, got up and went through into the sitting room. "I'm awake."

"We're searching for Raiders, Miss."

"Is that you, Birden?"

"Yes, Miss."

"Well, come in." The door creaked open, and a flicker of lantern light spilled through.

Hesitant bootsteps. "No one here, Miss."

"I hardly thought so, Birden."

"Um…" The light brightened, was blocked by a shadow.

"There are no strangers in my bedroom, Birden. I think I'd know."

"Um…yes, Miss, I suppose you would."

"Have they caught any of them?"

"Not too many, Miss. They're very good fighters, them Raiders. What I hear, most of them are on the run. Figure they'll disappear back into the Prairies, lick their wounds, and come back with more next time."

"That sounds logical. Are we posting guards, then?"

"Oh, yes, Miss, you don't have to worry. Lord Byaren's men have searched this area specifically. They won't be bothering you, Miss. Don't you worry."

"Thank you Birden."

"No trouble, Miss. Glad to help. I'll…I'll just be going on with the search, then."

"Yes, Birden. I'll feel much better if you check all the other rooms on this floor."

"Certainly, Miss Kendra. Glad to."

"All right. Good night, then, Birden. And thank you again."

"Yes, Miss. Good night."

The door closed. He could hear soft footsteps crossing to the bed. Then the mattress sagged, and she was beside him, giggling.

"Poor man. Couldn't get over being in a lady's rooms in the middle of the night."

He rolled over and saw her head on the pillow in the gathering dawn. "You didn't help him any."

"I wanted to make it as natural as possible."

"You were very natural. Can anybody hear us?"

"The walls are thick in this part of the house. But we don't have to talk." She snuggled down in the bed.

"You're not staying!"

"Obviously I have to. They're searching the house."

"They've already searched this part."

"Who says they're that well-organized?"

"But..."

"You're beginning to sound like Birden. It's a big bed. Stay on your own side or you'll be sorry. I kick."

There didn't seem to be any response to that, so he stayed silent. Soon, in spite of all the excitement, his fatigue returned, and sleep overtook him again.

When he awoke he was alone, and sunlight streamed in the window. He got up, found his clothes in the hamper, dressed and sat on the bed, listening.

He could hear only what seemed to be the normal noises of a farm. Animals from the yard, a few men's voices. Women's tones inside the house.

Then there were footsteps on the stair. Heavy ones. The hall door opened, and he rose, flattening himself against the wall behind the bedroom door.

"Cheynou? You awake?"

At the sound of her voice, he relaxed some. "Yes."

"Good. Come on out for breakfast."

He heard the clink of cutlery. He relaxed more and stepped out the bedroom door.

To face Byaren.

There was one frozen moment, then Kendra's laugh reached him. "Don't look so shocked, Cheynou. I had to tell Byaren you were here. It's the only way you're going to get out."

He registered the smile on the bearded face.

"I gather you're the one who brought the warning."

He nodded, his mind working. "Yes. Those are not our people. I mean, they're Sea People, but they're renegades. They don't represent us. Not the Eagles or the Petrels."

Byaren lost his smile. "A fine distinction for a Farmer who has lost stock."

34

A thought hit him. "Was anyone hurt?"

"A few wounded. Oh, you mean of the Raiders?"

"No. I mean of your people. Any innocent Farmers?"

Byaren leaned forward, regarding him more carefully. "No. Thanks to your warning, we stopped them before they could attack any farms. Hit them with a barrage of arrows. We knew better than to go hand-to-hand with them. We killed several, wounded some. Does that bother you?"

Cheynou shrugged. "Like I said, they aren't my people. Not if they do stupid things like raiding."

Byaren steepled his fingers. "What do you think they'll do next?"

"It all depends who they are. If they're all from one Crew, we can find out by asking the former Captains. I'm sure none of them would be stupid enough to break the truce, and they know what's going on in their Crews.

"But they're more likely a group of malcontents from several Crews. Pers and Yong aren't the only ones wanting to break free. They're just smarter and more ethical. If this bunch is the kind I think, it won't be long until they turn into regular bandits and start preying on us as well. At that point, everyone will be united against them, and they'll be hunted down."

Byaren nodded. "When that time comes, call me. I'd like to help."

"It would be good for both peoples to work together on a venture of that sort."

Kendra tugged at his arm. "Come on, both of you. Enough diplomacy. Byaren, I bet you haven't eaten recently, either."

"Actually, no." The big man moved to one of the chairs, heavy fingers delicately selecting a slice of bacon.

Cheynou sat in the other chair, the smell of eggs watering his mouth. There was quiet for a while.

Once the edge was off his hunger, Byaren slowed his eating and looked at his tablemate. "So what's been happening up on the Prairies?"

Cheynou described the situation, both physical and political, as well as he could.

"So you think that Orrick Bren is the best man to be running things up there?"

Cheynou considered.

"You don't answer right away."

"It's not that simple. Actually, for you, I suppose it is that simple. Bren will be a strong leader and will keep his people under control. He doesn't want any trouble with you because he wants to keep the trade routes open. So it's actually an easy answer. Orrick Bren is the best for you."

Byaren nodded. "So why the hesitation?"

"Because I don't think he's necessarily the best man for us."

Again the bearded man nodded. "Ah. Sarasha's old theories about leadership."

"There's nothing wrong with Sarasha's ideas!"

A large hand waved placatingly. "No, no, I never meant there was. It's just that I'm not sure the world, at least not this part of it, is ready for Sarasha's ideas." He grinned. "Maybe in four or five hundred years."

Cheynou slumped back, nodding glumly. "I have to admit..."

Byaren locked his hands behind his head and stretched mightily. "So what do you do now? The door's pretty well closed against you here. Kendra says you're not exactly a welcome guest with your own folk."

Cheynou thought for a moment. *No harm in telling these people.* He looked up at Kendra, her eyes bright on him. "I had an idea."

"Yes?"

"I'm going to do what I was trained to do."

She smiled. "Navigate. Explore."

"That's right. That scout that we found frozen to death out on the Prairie. He came from somewhere. We were backtracking him when the lion hit us. We thought he might be a member of a larger party and they might need help. It turned out that wasn't the case, as far as we got. We found one grave, so I guess he only had one companion.

"But they came from somewhere, and they came straight. He wasn't wandering like he was lost. He was heading straight across the plains like a Helmsman would. He was well dressed and he had sophisticated equipment with him. Navigation equipment. There's a people somewhere across those mountains. More advanced than we are, probably." He paused. "Legend says another Ocean."

"And you're going to find them?" Byaren leaned forward with interest.

"That's right. Perhaps we could trade with them, or find another solution to our problems. I don't know. In any case, it's a chance to do something. Something I'm trained for. So as soon as I can get out of here, I'm going to head north again. I found the pass when I buried Sarasha, and I'm going through those mountains. I'm going north."

"And I'm going with you."

"No, you're not!"

"You're what?"

The two voices overlapped, but Cheynou's was stronger. "Kendra, what kind of stupidity would that be?"

"It's not stupidity, Cheynou. You can't go alone. I can't stay here. So we go together." She held her hands out, palms up, to show how simple it was.

Byaren was just getting the idea straight. "But...but...why would you want to leave here?"

Kendra sighed. "Byaren, are you going to marry me?"

His jaw dropped for the second time.

"Exactly. You're going to marry Stecia, and that's right for you. We agreed long ago that we would never marry, so it's all right with me. It does cause me a problem, however. There isn't anyone else that I'd like to marry."

"Why not? You're very popular..."

She shook her head. "Byaren, you know me well. You know what being a wife means in this land. The man who weds me, owns me. Body and soul. I have recently realized that I would never put up with that."

Byaren frowned, nodded. "I can understand that, Kendra, but what about Orrick Bren? I thought for a while there..."

"I thought so, too. But once I got to know him, I saw that he would be the same. He is too masterful. Just another man who would chain me to his needs and never allow me the freedom I need."

They absorbed that in silence. Then she grinned. "Besides, I couldn't very well marry Orrick Bren, could I? Not after the way I cursed him the day he stole my horse."

"Why should that matter?" A smile tugged at Cheynou's lip.

"Well, I cursed him, his ancestors," she shrugged, "and his progeny."

"I see."

"So there you have it. Another verse in the Saga of Kendra, in which she jumps into trouble, mouth first. As usual."

Once Byaren got on a topic, no little joke was going to distract him. "So you're running away with Cheynou instead?"

She glanced at the boy. "No threat in him, is there? Can you see Cheynou tying me to a bedpost and beating me?"

Cheynou, unsure whether to be insulted or not, grasped at the last image. "Orrick would never beat you!"

"He wouldn't. But he would hold me too tightly, nonetheless. He couldn't have any other relationship. He

38

worked too hard to be Captain and he will always be a captain in every aspect of his life, including marriage."

Byaren rose, stretched again. "I can't say I'm happy to see you go, Kendra, but I won't say I'm surprised. I've been watching you because I knew something was stewing in your head. Now that I know what it is, I feel better."

He turned to Cheynou with a grin. "There's nothing I can say that will influence how you'll treat her or how she'll treat you." He stuck out his hand. "But I can guarantee it will be interesting."

Cheynou grasped the hand in the Farmers' style, impressed at the solidity of the man's grip. Then he realized what he was doing.

"Wait a moment. I haven't agreed..."

Byaren shook his head. "Don't bother arguing with her. If it was a hare-brained scheme, you'd still be in trouble. As it is, you're much better off travelling with someone. There's too many men took off alone and never came back."

The big man stepped closer, towering over him. "And I don't know you, but from what I hear, you'd be a good one to travel with."

"Thanks, Lord Byaren." He found a bit of a grin. "I doubt that her parents will share your opinion."

"Oh, I think you might be surprised there as well."

He was.

He knew there had been tears. She made reference to it the next day as they were packing. But there hadn't been any of the expected shouting and arguing. Apparently, Kendra's family didn't work like that.

"Of course they're unhappy that I'm going. We all love each other, and we all know it's dangerous."

"So why are they letting you go?"

She grinned, one side of her mouth only. "That's the trouble with bringing up your children to be independent. They go and do things on their own." She closed a strap on one saddlebag. "Actually, my next-oldest brother would love to go. He can't, of course. He has responsibilities."

"And you don't?"

She shook her head. "Oh, they'll miss me in the kitchen and the dairy. But they have everything under control. No, I think they envy me."

"They do?"

"Of course. My great-grandfather came here to break new land, to make a place for himself. He brought his people with him, and they came willingly. My family has always been adventurous like that. Look at our Home: the farthest out from town, the closest to the Prairie. Are we going to take a tent?"

"I carry a piece of sailcloth and a scrap of mosquito netting."

"Good enough for me. You know that place at the First Drop where the Eagles made camp when the war was over?"

"Of course. We lived there for months."

"My family used to camp there when I was young."

"Camp? Why?"

"For a holiday in the summer. My father and brothers would go hunting up on the Prairie, and I would swim in the stream and climb all over those two little mountains. At least I thought they were mountains."

She was stuffing towels in a sack. "We even met an Inari once."

"Did you?"

"Yes. I'll save that story for some time when we're bored on the trail." She pulled open a cupboard, started to sort through pans. "What kind of cooking stuff do we need?"

"I have a cast iron fry pan. It's heavy, but it cooks almost everything."

"All right. I'll take a metal pot. We can do stews and stuff with that. I know a way to turn a pot into an oven."

"A frying pan full of hot coals on top?"

"Right."

"Aren't your family worried about the danger?"

"Of course. But I can take care of myself."

He looked at her slender form skeptically.

"I can! You don't think my father would let me roam around like I did if I couldn't defend myself?"

"Actually, that's a piece of information I need, if you're going travelling with me. What weapons do you fight with?"

She shrugged, concentrating on the selection of pots in front of her. "Oh, women's weapons, I guess."

"I don't mean that kind of fighting, Kendra. Be serious."

"I don't mean that kind of fighting, either. Women's weapons. The kind of stuff you find in the kitchen."

"Huh?"

She shook her head in exasperation. "Cheynou, our people don't exactly live in a safe, orderly world. We have been attacked, you know. A bunch of nasty people called Sea Raiders, for example?"

"You don't have to remind me."

"And there are always bandits as well. So everybody knows how to fight. Let me tell you; don't ever attack a woman in her kitchen. You'll have a handful of soap in your eyes, a slop bucket over your head and a boning knife between your ribs before you can say, 'What's for supper?' Some Raider comes storming into the kitchen at Kirigata, the girls will have him gutted, trussed and ready for the oven in no time flat."

"I see. So what specific weapons will you be carrying with you on this little junket?"

Her lowered eyebrows were the only response to his sarcasm. "I'll be taking, for your information, a hunting bow, a short sword and a buckler."

"Sword and buckler?"

"The nearest thing to a pot lid and a carving knife the armourer could come up with."

41

He held up his hands in defense. "Fine, fine, fine. I'm sorry I questioned your fighting abilities."

"Oh, I didn't say I was good with them. I just said I was taking them."

"What?"

She turned away, doubled over laughing. When she could speak again, she straightened. "Cheynou, you are so easy to tease!"

"But Kendra, this is serious!"

She sighed. "I know it's serious. You asked, and I told you. I can defend myself. Once we get travelling, we'll have some time to practise in the evenings and we can test each other out, all right?"

"Fine." *Why does it seem that I'm the one out of line*? He remembered Byaren's comment. *Oh, well, who wants a trip to be boring?*

"What do you feed your dog?"

"I don't. She fends for herself."

Kendra looked over at the dog curled in the doorway, her eyes on the action inside. "She looks in pretty good shape for a scavenger."

"She's very smart, a great runner and a good hunter. Wait till we're on the trail. You'll see."

"Oh, I don't doubt her worth. What's her name?"

"I don't know."

"You don't know?" Her eyebrows shot up. "You haven't given her a name?"

"It didn't start out like that. She just sort of joined me, and I didn't know who she belonged to or what her name was. I whistle or snap my fingers when I want her attention."

"But you talk to her as well, don't you? What do you call her then?"

"Um...I just call her 'Dog'."

"Well, she needs a name."

"So give her one."

"I will." She stared critically at the animal, whose ears perked at the attention. Cheynou waited for the inevitable cringe that would follow, but it didn't happen. She had definitely made progress in the past month.

"Where did you get her?"

"She just appeared at our camp. She wasn't like the camp dogs and she didn't get along with them but she hung around anyway."

"She's one of our herding dogs. You're right about the intelligence. She probably didn't like what was going on where she lived so she left. Look at her. She knows this is important." Kendra pondered a moment.

"She's grey and black, like the ashes of a fire. But there's a spark inside. She's like a dark cinder, glowing underneath. That's her. A cinder." She leaned over the dog. "Is that you? Are you a Cinder? Cinders?" The dog, unsure of what was happening but sensing that it must be good, jumped up and yapped sharply, her tail beating. Kendra grinned at Cheynou. "She seems to approve."

He laughed at the pair of them, and Cinders barked again.

Kendra stopped laughing, one finger raised. "That reminds me. There's someone else who will be coming with us. We should go and meet him."

She was out the door before he could respond. Puzzled and prepared to put his foot down, he followed her as she turned into a small pasture behind the stable. There, lazing in the shade of a tree, stood a donkey. Not a very big donkey, with light brown hair and a black stripe running down his back.

Kendra whistled, and one ear twitched. "You know I'm here. Stop pretending, wake up and come over and meet a friend."

The donkey's head came up, both ears now pointing at them. Slowly, as if to prove he was doing this of his own free will, he wandered over to the fence they were leaning on. His head came all the way over the fence, his upper lip, longer even than that of a horse, snuffling at Kendra's hip.

"Sorry, Martan. No treats today. I don't even have a pocket to put one in. I brought someone to meet you. This is Cheychan. We're going on a trip together. Won't that be fun? We're going into the mountains. You like mountains, don't you, boy?"

"You're taking a donkey?"

"We need a pack animal, don't we?"

"Yes, but can he keep up with the horses?"

"If we don't load him too heavily."

"Why not just take another horse?"

"Because we don't know if we can take the horses through the mountains. A donkey can get through places a horse wouldn't even try. And Martan's a mountain donkey."

"I've heard of mountain ponies, but never a mountain donkey."

"Donkeys are used by the shepherds who take the sheep up into the mountain pastures for the summer. They carry the loads, protect the herds, and keep the shepherds company."

"Protect the herds?"

"Oh, yes. They're very good at it. Take on a bear any day."

He looked at the awkward creature with new respect. "I suppose. You're the one that knows about livestock."

She smiled. "Why, thank you, Cheynou. This is the first idea I've had that you haven't argued with."

"I'm learning."

4.   FIRST DAYS

The next few days passed in a blur for Cheynou. He was introduced to an incredible number of people, mostly friends or relatives of Kendra, most of whom gave him some sort of warning about travelling with her, or about what would happen if any harm were to come to her. He deflected most of these with a pleasant but non-committal response, but got the general picture that she was well loved in an exasperated sort of way. Nobody had ever been able to figure her out, everyone knew she was destined for greatness or disaster, and it seemed the result was going to be Cheynou's fault, no matter which occurred.

This impression was reinforced by the two brothers who accompanied them out on the Prairie for the first two days to be sure they had no trouble with marauders or patrols. The rogue Raiders had faded back into the vastness of the plains, although no one had any illusions about a return.

But Cheynou suspected the main reason the two came was to reassure themselves on the nature and abilities of her travelling companion.

Jem, the older of the two, was straightforward about it. He took an early opportunity to pull his larger horse alongside Cheynou's pony and look down at his fellow traveller. "So, lad. You really think you're up to this?"

Cheynou hadn't expected the questioning to stop, but he was getting a bit tired of it. "Do I impress you as being rather stupid?"

The bigger man looked down from his horse and grinned. "Not at all. Perhaps a bit naive, but not stupid."

Cheynou let the horses go a few paces, his eyes never breaking contact. "Naive. Jem, how many battles have you been in?"

"Me? Well…not counting chasing these latest raiders around, not too many."

"In other words, none. How many family and friends have you lost in war?"

The man gave a puzzled frown. "Well, I knew a few of the fellows who went down in the battle last summer…"

"And where did you spend last winter?"

"At Kirigata, of course. Why?" When Cheynou did not answer, they rode in silence for a while.

"Oh."

Cheynou grinned. "So what sage advice do you have for me, over and above what I've been given by seventeen of your friends and relatives, on how to survive a trip across the continent with your dear sister?"

Jem grinned back. "Seventeen? That's all?"

"I lost count."

"You mean you stopped listening."

"Not quite. I stopped listening to the details, but I've been forming my impressions from the general drift."

"And what was the general drift you picked up?"

Cheynou shrugged. "That she's been going her own way since she was about two years old, that all of you love her to pieces but none of you have any idea how to handle her."

Jem nodded. "That's pretty accurate, I'd say."

"You know what about a third of the people said? They told me to lay down the law from the beginning, because if I let her get away with anything, I wouldn't have a chance."

Now the big Farmer really laughed, and Cheynou couldn't help but join in. "Lay down the law? With Kendra?" He dissolved in laughter again, to the point where he was in danger of falling off his horse.

"What's so funny, you two?" Kendra had slowed and waited while Jem, controlling himself with difficulty, pulled his horse back onto the trail and caught up.

"You."

46

"Me? I'm that funny?"

Her brother shook his head. "Not really. It was just the advice everybody back home gave Cheynou about getting along with you."

"What advice was that?"

"I'm not going to tell you. I value my head too much."

Her glance turned to Cheynou. He held up his hands as if to deflect it.

"I'll get it out of you later."

"I'll tell you later, don't worry."

She frowned. "Why don't I like the sound of that?"

He grinned. "Because I'll tell you when it's to my advantage and not before."

"You think so, do you?"

"I do."

He rode on, ignoring her glances and the laugher of the two brothers.

Clen, the younger brother who rarely spoke, took longer. It was near the end of the second day, with their objective, the First Drop, rising up out of the Prairie in front of them, that he finally got up the nerve.

"Cheynou, I've been meaning to talk to you."

Cheynou noted the man's distress and decided not to make it difficult. "About Kendra."

"Yes. How did you know?"

"Clen, every member of your family has taken me aside over the past three days and given me their advice, their warnings."

"All of them?"

"Pretty well."

"That's nice, isn't it?"

"I thought so."

They rode in silence for a while.

"So what do you think?"

47

"Me?"

"Yes. How do you think I should treat her?"

"I don't know, Cheynou. She's skittish, no doubt about it. Sort of like a high-strung horse, you know? Lots of people say she needs taming, but nobody's ever had much luck."

Cheynou shook his head. "I've been working with horses for less than a year, Clen, but I've got a pretty good idea how you tame them. You make them comfortable so they aren't afraid of you. Then you start controlling them, little by little, using punishment and reward, and they develop the habit of obeying you. Enough of that and you have a trained horse that you can depend on. Right?"

"That's about it. Sounds like a pretty good plan for dealing with Kendra. How are you doing so far?"

"I'm not. That would be a perfectly useless way of dealing with her. She's not a horse. She's a person. If I wanted to create a good soldier, or a good servant or a good slave, I suppose I could use those techniques. If I want to get along with a travelling companion, I can't think of a worse way to start than by trying to take control. Especially with Kendra. You've known her all your life, surely you can see that."

The young Farmer mulled that over for a while. "I can see where you're right. Everybody's been trying it on her for years, and it's pretty obvious it hasn't taken. But what are you going to do? How are you going to handle her?"

Cheynou shook his head. "You just don't get it. I'm not going to handle her. I'm going to travel with her."

"But you already are handling her. Yesterday, when she threatened you about telling her what Jem said. I thought you handled that beautifully. Set her right back, it did. Not many can do that. I'd be afraid to try."

Cheynou shrugged. "I didn't say I was going to let her handle me."

"Ah."

He nodded. "In dealing with people, you have to draw the line. They must know where they can go and where they can't. If you're very clear about your own boundaries and very careful about theirs, I find that people tend to treat you decently as well."

Clen nodded. "That's a pretty good philosophy, Cheynou. I wonder how it will work on my sister."

"I'll have to make sure I survive to tell you."

The young Farmer grinned and reached down to slap Cheynou on the shoulder. "I surely hope you do."

His horse slowed, and Cheynou was riding alone. For a moment.

"So have my brothers finished telling you how to treat me?"

He grinned. "That's why they came along. They're not real talkers, either of them."

"That's true."

"So they couldn't get close enough to me back at Kirigata. They had to wait until we were out on the Prairie with less competition."

"So what did they say?"

He shrugged. "That they love you very much, and they're very proud of you and they're worried about you but they hope this journey will be everything you want it to be."

She glanced over at him, looked again. "They did not!"

"Not in so many words. But the meaning came through loud and clear."

"Oh." They rode on in silence for a while.

"But what did they really say?"

"They said about what you think they said. What everybody back at Kirigata said."

"And what was that? Come on, Cheynou, you have to tell me."

"Each one of them told me how he or she treated you. That's all. The words they used don't really matter. It was the intent that counted. You should be happy, Kendra."

"I should be happy? That all my family and friends are telling stories about me?"

"No, that so many people care so much that they want me to take a little bit of them along on this voyage to care for you. I know what it's like. It's the same on a FamilyShip when everyone gets along."

"What do you mean?"

"You feel like you're a part of something bigger than just yourself. You're not alone. People care about you, and you care about them. It makes you strong even when you're away from them."

"Oh. Yes, I suppose it would."

"I'm not talking theory here. I'm talking about you."

"And you've neatly deflected my questions."

"I didn't give you the answers you wanted, Kendra. I gave you the answers you needed."

The swishing of their horses' hooves through the grass was the only sound for a long time.

Finally, she spoke. "I think I understand. Thank you, Cheynou."

He shrugged, grinned. "This could be a long journey. We better start taking care of each other from the start."

She shot him another glance, frowning. "You're not joking, are you?"

"Not at all."

She nodded uncertainly and rode on, lost in thought. She didn't seem inclined to talk any more so he left her to herself.

They soon pulled up at the old Eagle camp at the First Drop. It was a good campsite, and before they set up their own camp they checked it over closely for signs of other uses. No one had been there recently, although some cached emergency supplies were gone, the rocks rolled away from the niche where they had been stored.

"The Raiders."

Clen nodded. "No animals out here big enough to move those rocks. Oh, a bear, maybe. But I haven't seen one for years this close in."

They all looked at the rim of the Drop above them, and Cheynou sent Cinders out on patrol. She soon returned, calm as ever.

After supper, Kendra regaled them with stories of their camping expeditions, and her brothers tried in vain to contradict her.

"But Kendra, you couldn't have possibly climbed to the top. You were only about nine years old, and we knew what you were like. We kept a close watch on you."

She looked up at her older brother, grinned and beckoned towards the westerly peak. It was a stiff scramble for adults, and Cheynou was impressed that a child could have made it. If she had.

She led them to a nook near the top of the crag, looked around a moment, then pounced on a stone wedged in a crack. "There. Give me your marlinspike, Cheynou. I never could get it out with my fingers."

Sure enough, when the stone came out, there was a recess behind it. She slipped her hand in, felt around, gave a cry of triumph and pulled it out. She looked at her hand, and her triumph turned to dismay. "Drat! The mice got to it."

She held out her hand. It held a small leather box, well chewed and tattered. Pieces of paper, even more gnawed, spilled out of the corners.

"What was it?"

"It was a message to the next explorer coming by, telling him that I'd been here first!"

They all laughed, including her. Then she looked again at the battered box and tossed it over the edge, watching the bits of paper scatter away on the wind. Then she turned to them. "At least it served one purpose."

Clen nodded. "You were definitely up here. Dammit, Kendra, that was dangerous! What were you thinking of?"

She grinned. "I was thinking of how mad you'd be if you ever discovered I'd been up here. Guess I was right."

Cheynou sent a meaningful glance at Jem, who just shook his head and started down the mountain.

* * *

The next morning, with tears on both sides again, they were out on the Prairie waving good-bye to the two stalwart Farmers fading forlornly into the haze behind them. There was no trail, so they travelled side by side. To Cheynou's surprise, the donkey was still walking loose.

"Won't he wander off?"

"Won't your dog wander off?"

"Aye, but she always comes back."

"Martan is better trained than that. As long as he has a pack on, he'll follow us closely. He may wander a bit at night but he'll come when I whistle."

"What if I want him to come?"

"I guess you better learn to make that whistle."

"I guess I better."

She looked out over the Prairie in front of them. "So where are we going?"

He pointed. "See that mountain, straight ahead, two points east of north?"

"If you mean that one, yes."

"Well, our course is that way for about three days. When we get to the foothills, there's a stream runs in around the base of the first peak. The old Sparrowhawk camp is there, where that stream enters the East River. They're gone, now. We ford the East River there and go up the stream for a league or so. There we'll find the Inari camp."

"How far is a league?"

"About as far as you want to walk before you take a rest. We'll make about ten leagues a day on the horses, if Martan can keep up."

She thought about that. "I'll have to start figuring out your distance and time measures. Will you teach me some navigating techniques?"

His first response was to refuse. Then he realized that there was no need for that sort of secrecy any more. "I should. Whatever you can learn. It depends on how much mathematics you know."

"I know arithmetic. I'm good at money, weights, measures, that sort of thing. I know basic areas of ground, but only small ones."

"Do you know angles?"

"I know big angles and small angles," she demonstrated with her hands. "I know what a right angle is. That's about all."

"I'll maybe teach you some of that. We have to be careful with paper, because I don't have much."

"We can use a stick and a flat piece of ground for the basics."

"I guess. Never tried it that way. We used to use charcoal on a plank when we started out."

"All right. What are your distances?"

"A fathom is the height of a tall man. A chain is ten fathoms. A league is 250 chains. As I said, about as far as you want to walk before you take a rest."

"Fathom, chain, league. I'll try to remember those."

"I'll tell you when I think we've gone a league to give you an idea."

"Right."

They rode in silence for a while. "Where are your people right now?"

He gestured off to the left. "They wintered where the Little River falls over the Second Drop. I want to get past them before they move east to their Summer Range."

"Where is that?"

"Just above the Sparrowhawk camp."

"But the Sparrowhawks aren't there any more."

"No."

"Where are they?"

"We don't know."

"You don't know?"

"That's what I said."

She rode along, slapping the ends of the reins against her leg. "Can you tell me what you know?"

Her soft tone mollified him. "Sorry to snap at you, but it bothered the rest of us a lot. The Sparrowhawks disappeared last winter. They left most of their belongings behind, and quite a few graves. Obviously they lost a lot of people, whether through sickness or fighting, we don't know. The rest just weren't there in the spring. A few of their people wintered at other camps. They don't know any more than we do."

"What could have happened?"

"We did a lot of thinking. Two possibilities: they left voluntarily or they were forced. If forced, then they were attacked by someone. There was no evidence of a fight. If voluntary, why?"

"Did you say the Inari camp near there?"

"Not in the winter. And they don't know anything, either."

"Have you lost a lot of your people?"

"The Sparrowhawks are the only full Crew. Many of the old and the weak died in the winter. Some badly wounded in the battles didn't regain enough strength to last through. We calculate, counting the Sparrowhawks, we lost about one in five of our people."

"I'm so sorry." Then she was silent for a long, long time.

He used the pause in conversation well, making his calculations, checking his reference points, enjoying the feeling that, at least this early in the trip, he knew exactly where he was.

"We've gone about a league."

"Oh. Sorry, I wasn't really paying attention."

"Thinking?"

"Yes. I've lost a few people: older family members, friends. But one in five? I was just trying to think what it would be like to lose ten people at Kirigata."

"And that was only the winter."

"What do you mean?"

"We were in constant battle for the year before that. We lost people in the final battle on the beach. Most of those were our young Raiders, but not all."

"I see." She shook her head. "It must change everything. How you feel about other people, how you look at the world."

He considered. "I never thought of it that way, but I suppose it does. I don't feel any different, but I must be. Of course, coming ashore, changing our whole way of life, that must have changed me, too."

They rode in silence again, for about another league. "Our camp is just over the horizon, that way."

"Shall we pay them a visit?"

"My feeling is no, but I really should think about it. If we go as far as we are planning on this trip, I may not be back for some time. I should probably tell my family. I should also report on the Raiders. Do you want to?"

She frowned. "I'm the same as you. I don't want to. Partly because of Orrick, I think."

"What do you think he would do?"

"I don't know. We parted as friends, although I don't think he really understood why."

"Is there any chance he would try to make you stay?"

She winced. "I'm thinking about that. From what you have told me, I think he might. He seems to be changing."

"Yes, he is. He is becoming more and more a Captain, if you know what I mean."

"Giving more orders, asking fewer opinions?"

"That sort of thing."

She shook her head. "I'm sorry to hear that, and I definitely don't want to see it."

"So you'd rather not visit."

"I would rather not. But you should."

"I should?"

"Yes. You headed off for Kirigata to make a life with my people. You can't change your mind, go the opposite direction and ride right by their camp without telling them. Are you that afraid of Orrick?"

"I'm not afraid of him, personally. What scares me about him is what he's going to do as the leader of our people. I just don't want to live under his kind of rule."

"Can't we camp for the night, and I'll stay there and you can go over for a visit? Is it too far?"

He thought a moment. "That appeals to me. If I slip in after dark, I can visit whoever I want and leave again if I don't like the situation. It's less than a league, down in a valley where we can't see it from here."

He thought as they rode, finally nodding his head. "Yes, we'll be reaching the Second Drop soon, and we can find a well-hidden campsite there. You should be reasonably safe."

"What's to harm me?"

He shrugged. "There are all sorts of people wandering around the Prairies these days. Those Raiders aren't the only ones. I'll leave you the dog, as well. She keeps very good watch."

"So does Martan. Don't worry about me. I'll be fine."

"I'll try not to be too long."

She grinned over at him. "Kind of you to be concerned."

He returned the grin. "I wouldn't be much of an expedition leader if I lost half my party the third night out."

"I'll do my best to keep your reputation sparkling."

They found a secluded spot, backed into a sharper section of the cliff that formed the drop-off where the Prairie was broken. "If you keep the fire small, nobody will see it from anywhere on the flat. You should picket your horse in close until I get back. We can hobble both of them after that and let them graze farther out. You'll let Martan go free?"

"Yes, he guards best that way." She paused in her unpacking to stare over at him. "You're taking this all very seriously. Don't you think I can take care of myself?"

"I'm sure you can, but bad luck can always bring you a problem you can't handle. I figure the more careful I am, the luckier I am."

She shrugged. "Can't argue with you on that." She pulled out a short, useful-looking sword and laid it close to her bed. She took her shield off the saddle where it usually hung and laid it nearby as well, smiling at his approving nod.

In spite of all their preparations, he rode away with a feeling of unease that he couldn't really explain. He had never been responsible for anyone before, and he was determined to do his best. He circled to the east and rode back past their campsite, reassuring himself that there was nothing to be seen. Finally, grinning at his own silliness, he kicked his reluctant pony back to a travelling lope and headed off to the west.

* * *

It was well past the eighth bell when he returned to camp. The dog greeted him warmly as he dismounted, and Martan snorted a greeting from the rocks nearby. Kendra was in her bedroll, awake.

"Did it go well?"

"Well enough. Don't get up. I'll picket the horses out on the grass."

"Thanks."

"No problem. Everything all right, here?"

"Quiet the whole evening. Boring, actually."

"Hope for plenty of evenings like that." He stripped the gear off his horse and finished his nightly chores.

Once he was in his bed, her head came up off her pillow. "So?"

"I'm glad I went. It was good to see my family again, especially my father. I talked to him about the Raiders, and he'll pass the word, including Byaren's offer to help. He thought that was a good sign."

"How are things in camp?"

"Not so good, I wouldn't say."

She waited a while but finally burst out, "What's wrong? Has Orrick done something? Is that why you don't want to tell me?"

"Yeah, Orrick has made some changes. I'm not sure if they're all bad; some of them had to happen. Some of them, I'm not so happy with."

"Such as?"

"Well, to start with, he has reorganized the Crafts. That needed doing, since our life has changed so much. He disbanded the ones that aren't needed any more. Including the Helmsmen."

"Oh, Cheynou!"

"No, we had already figured on that. My father and uncle have it covered. Some of the other Crafts, such as the Shipwrights, are gone, of course, but we still need carpenters, so they'll be taken care of."

"Which ones don't you like?"

"The Scribes."

"He disbanded the Scribes?"

"Aye. Said that since we don't have a Ship to carry everything anymore, we have to cut back on stuff like that."

"What do the Scribes say about that?"

"Not much. Some of them are old, and three were killed in the wars. Sarasha and Leide were the most vocal, and they're both gone. Poor Kendie!"

"Who's Kendie?"

"Oh, she's a kid that used to hang around Sarasha, running errands and such. She was determined to become a Scribe, you know? Follow in Sarasha's wake."

"Oh. I met her once. Sharp features, streaky blonde hair?"

"That's the one. Word got out that I was in camp, and she came and found me. That's why I was later than I wanted to be. She followed me out of camp so we could talk. She's really upset."

"I suppose she would be, if she wanted to become a Scribe."

"She's upset at more than that. She's worried that Bren is going to become an absolute ruler. According to her, the Scribe was always sort of a balance to the Captain's power."

"How could that be?"

"Apparently it was part of the official duties of the Craft. The Scribe had all the records available. So if the Captain got off track, she could bring him back by telling him what had been decided previously, how he and other Captains had acted in similar events in the past."

"So she thinks that he's getting rid of the Scribes so there's no one to disagree with him."

"It does sound logical. He's managed to get rid of the rest of us."

"What's Kendie going to do, now?"

"She doesn't know." He glanced over at her in the dim light. "She asked to come with us."

"Did she? What did you say?"

"I said I already had one feeble woman to take care of and I didn't think that even the great Cheynou was up to handling two."

"You didn't say that!"

He chuckled. "No, but it's sure fun to see how you reacted."

She lay back in her bed with a disgusted snort. After a moment, she rolled over, leaning her cheek along her arm. "What is she going to do, then?"

He shrugged. "She says she's going to become a Scribe anyway, no matter what Orrick Bren says."

"Can she do that?"

"Not really. If she isn't officially allowed into the Conclaves, she won't have any real position, and all her information will be second hand. But I didn't tell her that. I just encouraged her to do her best. It isn't my problem, fortunately. I can't solve everyone's difficulties. In the end, I had to dry up her tears and send her back into camp."

"Tears?"

"Oh, yes. And if you think that's just a kid trying to get her own way, you don't know Kendie. She's really upset about the whole situation, not just her own part of it. She's even worried we'll lose the ability to read and write."

"Is that possible?"

"I suppose so, if our life degenerates to the point where we spend all our time grubbing for food and defending ourselves so we have no energy left for extras. I doubt it, though. There are still lots of us who are literate, and we managed to save quite a few books."

"So in the end you had to send her back to camp, and that bothered you."

"Yeah. I like her. She's a spunky kid, and the things she is saying are right on course. I wish I could do something for her."

"Cheychan, you are a nice person, you know that?"

60

"Thanks, but it doesn't help either me or her much, does it?"

"I don't know. I'm sure she feels better having talked to somebody who understands."

"I understand, all right. I'm in the same boat."

"And so am I."

"At least we're doing something about it."

"We are. How about getting some sleep so we can make some distance tomorrow?"

"So stop talking."

"Yes, oh formidable expedition leader."

He refrained from rising to the bait, and soon there was silence in their little camp.

But not for long. Cheynou was just dropping off to sleep when Cinders gave her usual warning 'Whuff.'

He reached for his sword and half-rose, listening intently. In the glow of the dying coals the dog stood alert, her nose questing.

"Look at Martan." Kendra's whisper brought his head around. The donkey, too, was staring out to the south, ears up.

"There's someone out there."

She nodded. "That's how Martan reacts to people."

He tossed back his blanket and pulled on his boots. "I'll go have a look around."

"Is that safe?"

"No, but it's a long walk without horses. I'll take Cinders."

Kendra said nothing, lacing up her own boots and hefting her shield.

Bare sword in hand, he quietly left camp to the west, the dog at his knee. Utter silence greeted them. Enough starlight glowed that he could see the horses, black blobs against the lighter grass. After a while, they lowered their heads and went back to grazing. *More evidence it's a human. With a predator, they wouldn't settle so fast.*

He was just about to continue when the dog darted forward, her head low, and disappeared in the darkness. Then she began to bay, a warning howl that he had never heard before. Her voice went on and on, rising and falling, a message he had no difficulty in understanding. There was an intruder, and she had found him.

Praying to gods he no longer believed in that the intruder had no bow, he slipped forward, cursing the rattle of stones under his feet. The dog's warning continued, just ahead now.

He was about to call her when the scraping of cloth against brush and a rattling of gravel froze him in place. Cinders lowered her voice, still barking, but with a satisfied tone.

He whistled, and she quieted and soon appeared, still slinking, her head turned to the side, ears questing. She reached his side and turned her piercing look back toward the Prairie.

Cheynou knelt beside her, a hand on her ruff, and they waited in silence. A small 'click' of stone farther out was the only evidence of their intruder.

After a while the stiffness went out of her shoulders, and the fur settled. She looked up at him, then snuffled his hand.

"He's gone, is he?"

She seemed to agree.

He ruffled her ears. "You certainly put the run on him. But I think I'll bring the horses in closer, just to be safe. Away you go."

At his signal, she crouched and slipped away, on patrol as usual.

When the horses were moored on long tethers as close to camp as he could find grass, he returned to the fire. Kendra was nowhere to be seen, but on his arrival she stepped out of the shadows, sword and buckler in hand.

"There was definitely someone there."

She knelt to make a fuss over Cinders. "No doubt about that."

"I've tethered the horses closer in. Not much feed, so I'll have to let them out, come daylight."

She nodded. "A few candles of grazing in the morning will do them. And we'll want to sleep in anyway, with all this excitement in the middle of the night."

"However long a candle is, I'll defer to your expertise. I'm for bed."

She was already sitting on her blankets. "Good night, then."

"Sleep well. I'm glad we have our loyal animals to warn us."

"Me, too."

He lay a long time before his heart slowed and peace descended on the camp. Then he slept, but in short snatches, waking to raise his head, listen and check their guardians. But the night remained calm and, near morning, he slept deeply.

5.   A CHANGE OF PLANS

They had been riding for most of the morning, and Kendra was unnaturally silent. "What are you thinking about?"

"What you said about your Trade."

"You mean that there aren't going to be any Helmsmen any more."

Kendra's mouth curved down. "Why not?"

"On the Prairie, there is no ship to helm and no navigating needed." He tossed a hand in a half-circle.

"I thought you would be needed out there where there are no roads."

His mouth twisted wryly. "Turns out the Prairie isn't as featureless as we thought. There are all sorts of trails and landmarks if you can remember them, and there are always the mountains in the distance to orient yourself."

He waved a hand around the horizon. "And the Prairie isn't as big as people think, either. Seven days riding in any direction on a fast horse and you're at the other edge. Compared to the Great Southern Ocean, that's just a lake."

"Surely that doesn't mean that all you have learned in your craft isn't going to be needed any more!"

He shrugged miserably. "I don't know. They've stopped keeping the time."

"What does that mean?"

He frowned, then realized who he was talking to. "On ship, it was very important to know the time because navigation depends on it. You can't really figure out the time on a moving ship, so we had reference points along the shore every fifty leagues or so, where we knew the exact position and we could use the exact moment of mid-day to check our time. Then we would adjust the glasses on the ship to match."

"The glasses on the ship?"

"Yes. You've seen the small ones our people use?"

"Of course. We use sun dials."

"Right. On each ship, in the Helmsmen's Quarters, there was a bank of twenty big sand glasses. Very expensive, very accurate. One of our tasks every day was to turn them and check them against each other to average them." He shook his head. "All the gods defend the poor apprentice who forgot to turn the glasses."

"Was it that serious?"

"If it meant the Ship went up on a reef because our navigation was off, it was serious, yes. It would be the deepest of shame to have to go to another ship to find the time. Of course, we checked with other ships regularly to make sure we weren't off for some other reason."

He paused a moment, then sighed. "I suppose I can tell you this because it doesn't matter any more. It was one of our Craft Secrets. The reason our Fleet had its Yearly Rendezvous where it did was because that was the zero position on our charts. All our navigation points were mapped out from there.

"You see," he reached out with his arms. demonstrating, "the angle of the sun tells you how far north or south you are. The amount of time difference at noon tells you how far east or west you are from the zero point. But you have to keep the time."

"It sounds like a very difficult process."

"Yes, it was. I took a lot of training and I know all about it and now it's completely useless, because any fool can jam a stick in the ground on a sunny day and watch until the shadow is the shortest."

"Like a sun dial."

"That's right." He paused. "Oh, I'm sorry, Kendra. I didn't mean..."

She laughed. "No, you're right. Any fool can read a sundial." Then she became serious. "So what are you going to do?"

"Well, my father and my uncle have decided to make maps."

"I see. Where there are landmarks, you can make maps."

"That's right. They can spend the rest of their lives making maps. Of course, they're working themselves out of work."

"I suppose. Once an area is mapped, you don't need a mapmaker any more. Just someone to copy it."

"Exactly. But they have that figured out, too. When Sarasha and the rest of us were looking at the rules and laws and deciding which were good for us and which were not, my father was very interested in our progress. Always checking to see which rules we had discussed. Sometimes he had ideas for us. I thought it was just because he was keen on what I was doing.

"Turns out he had more in mind. He and my uncle figure that once our Crews start living on this land, we are going to have to lay out areas of the Prairie that belong to specific Crews. There are going to be arguments over who gets what. My father and uncle think that if they have made the maps, they will be the ones who are asked to judge these disputes. Helmsmen have always stood aside from on-Ship rivalries. We have a reputation for fairness, impartiality. My father thinks he can make a place for himself as a judge or justice, solving disputes and interpreting the laws."

"What a good idea!"

He grinned. "I think so too. My old man is no slouch when it comes to brains."

"So will you follow him?"

He laughed shortly. "Can you see me in a long white beard, dispensing justice?"

"Well, maybe not for thirty years or so."

"Right. And while I'm waiting, I've got other things to do."

"Which we are doing right now."

"Yes, and we're making progress."

"We are?"

"Yes. We'll be off the real Prairie this afternoon. It's more broken up near the eastern edge. It makes travelling more difficult, but at least the landscape is more interesting."

"And easier to navigate."

"Any time you want to take over."

"I'll apprentice a while, first."

* * *

"Will you look at that water!"

The pair sat their horses, staring in wonder at the tiny pool before them. Nestled in rocks, crystal clear to the bottom, the tarn invited them with respite from the scorching summer sun.

"I'm for a bath!" Kendra slipped off her horse as she spoke, moving alongside the animal as it surged towards the water.

Cheynou scanned the surrounding rocks. "I guess it's safe enough."

"Send Cinders on patrol if you like."

"Good idea." He snapped his fingers for the dog's attention. She was standing in the water up to her stomach, lapping without lowering her head. He made a waving gesture and, happy to be given a task, she bounded out of the lake, shook herself and trotted off into the rocks.

He glanced at Martan, but he, too, was standing knee-deep, drinking noisily.

Then he turned back.

Kendra, facing the pool, was just slipping out of her trousers. She straightened and he was suddenly aware of how stunningly beautiful she was. She turned, caught him staring.

"Come on! What are you waiting for?"

"Um…it's too cold, I think." He looked to the side, to the water, to anywhere else.

She walked over to him, stood close enough that he had to face her. He kept his eyes determinedly on hers. "Cheynou, I stink. We both stink." Her face took on a sly look. "I have soap!"

He turned away again. "I don't know…"

"Cheynou! Look at me!"

His face burning, he turned.

"If you don't get your clothes off pretty quick, I'm going to get embarrassed. I've been in this position before, and I have bad memories."

"You do…you have?"

"Yes. When I met Captain Bren. And you remember how that turned out."

He struggled to remember.

"He stole my horse!"

"Oh. Aye." He smiled sheepishly.

"So, since I don't think you're going to take the horses and ride off, I'm going for a swim in that nice, cool water. You can do what you like." She turned and stepped in, shivering with the cool shock as the water rose up her legs. The curve of her back was as lithe as her front view.

"But if you don't get clean, you're going to be sleeping a long way from the fire tonight."

Once she was submerged it was easier, and he shucked his clothes and dove in. The water was not that cold, and it felt wonderful. The pool was long enough for several strokes in either direction, and he swam back and forth swiftly, not stopping until she had finished soaping herself and was back under water rinsing off. Then he swam over to her to get the soap, still worried about where he looked. The water was very clear.

She snorted and splashed a bit of water at his head. "Make sure you wash your hair. You've still got spider webs in it from last night."

"You never told me."

"I didn't think it was important. I have a mirror, if you want to borrow it."

"No, that's all right. Just tell me if I look a complete dolt, all right?"

"All right. You look like a complete dolt."

"What do you mean?"

She sighed. "I guess this isn't much fun for you, is it? Do you want to get out of the water first, or should I?"

"It doesn't matter."

"I guess that's progress."

They towelled off with their shirts in silence and pulled on trousers and shoes. She was about to throw her shirt over a bush when she stopped, looked at him and put it on, damp as it was.

"I guess we'll camp here."

He gazed around. There was good grazing near the water. The dog, lying sentry on a rock overlooking the pond, seemed relaxed.

"Yes, I think we should move a bit away from the water, though. There might be others who want to use it."

"Others? Oh, you mean the wild animals."

"I hope so." He wandered around, scouting the terrain. "Look. This is the spot." A circle of rain-beaten ashes beside an overhang of rock showed where others had camped. "A good spot, but no one has been here for a while."

"Great." Her enthusiasm sounded forced. "This is a beautiful place. Better take advantage of it while we can."

There was silence while they set up camp. Kendra gave him an evil smile as she laid out their bedrolls precisely the same distance from the fire, at a friendly gap from each other. Once everything was in place, Cheynou looked around.

"I think I'd better take a wider circle. Just check things out." He stood, and the dog, her eyes always on him, darted to his side.

"In a moment. Come over here, first."

She led the way to a low rock ledge that gave a view of the lake. They sat, and Kendra leaned back in silence for a moment. "It certainly is beautiful."

"Yes."

She sat up, looked at him. "So, we have a problem to solve."

He did not meet her eyes. "I guess so."

"Yes, I guess so."

He turned to her. "I'm sorry, Kendra, I can't help it. That's just how I am. I just realized...that..." He couldn't say it.

"You just realized that I'm a woman? You're a bit slow, Cheychan!"

Something burned up inside him. "Only Sarasha called me that!"

She sat back, startled at the force of his feeling. "I'm sorry, Cheynou. I didn't realize...."

"Aye, but it's all right." He slumped again.

"But that has nothing to do with our problem."

"Aye."

"So what, exactly, is the problem?"

He looked at her for a moment. "You surely aren't that stupid, Kendra. Or do you just want me to say it out loud?"

"You're catching on, kid."

"Yeah. Kid. That's me. Well, I always thought, since we started out, that there wouldn't be much of a problem. Then, today, when you...took your clothes off, I realized..." the words came in a rush, "...how beautiful you are."

"Oh." She paused, eyebrows arched. "Well...thank you, Cheynou. That's a nice thing to say."

"It's the truth, I'm sure you know. And there's the problem."

"I see." She looked out over the water for a while, then back at him. "Do you think it would help if we were to...lie together?"

"What? No! We can't! We shouldn't..."

"Why not?"

"It isn't right! And what if...what if you had a baby? No, that's not the solution. You don't lie with someone just because you happen to be travelling together."

"I thought we were more than just fellow-travellers, Cheynou. I thought we were friends."

"Well, you don't just lie with your friends, either. You lie with someone you love. No, it wouldn't be a good idea."

She smiled at him. "I didn't think so, either. I'm relieved that you agree."

"But...what do I do now?"

"What do you mean, 'now'?"

He shrugged miserably. "You know. Things have changed. I don't see you the same way, any more."

She placed a hand on his knee. He tried not to move, to accept it casually. "So things aren't the same way. I didn't expect them to be. We just have to find a new way of looking at each other. I'm sure we'll figure it out."

"But how do I treat you?"

"I don't know. Treat me like a sister."

"I never had any sisters," he held up a hand, "or brothers, either."

She shrugged. "How did you treat Sarasha?"

He snorted a laugh. "With a great deal of respect."

"And you're not going to treat me with respect?"

"Of course, but it's not the same, believe me."

"I suppose it isn't." She turned to face him squarely. "She was very important to you, wasn't she?"

"Yes." There was silence for a moment.

"Were you in love with her?"

"No. I was just a kid, and she was...you know. She was Sarasha."

"But you loved her."

"Oh, yes."

"Weren't you afraid of her?"

"Not really. None of her friends were, you know. Oh, she had a tongue that would rip sailcloth, but she only used it if you said something really stupid. And, of course, there was the pain. You can forgive someone a lot when they're in pain."

"Was she?"

"All the time. I don't think it ever went away. Sometimes it got worse. She never let on to everyone, but she told me."

"You were a favourite of hers, weren't you?"

He grinned sadly. "I guess I was the one who wasn't afraid to tell her off when she was wrong."

"Wrong? I didn't think she was wrong that often."

"Oh, not about things." He leaned back, the setting sun gentle on his face, and tried to put it into words. "Sarasha had a mind like a breaking wave: powerful, fast-moving, swept all before it. When it came to planning, to something like warfare, she was unequalled. But that sort of thing doesn't work with mere humans, and it doesn't work with yourself."

He glanced over to receive her puzzled look. "Aye, with herself. Sarasha was hard on people, and sometimes I had to tell her to back off. But she was worse on herself. When her father was there it was better, because he balanced her, like. But after he was killed, there was only her mother, who provided a different type of balance. Captain Bren filled in on the planning part, but in her personal life there was nobody. She had a deep wound there, like a part of her was taken

72

away. I tried to fill in, but of course, I was only a kid...." There were tears on his cheeks. He let them fall.

"I wasn't surprised when she didn't come back. She had that possibility in her always. She would just get sad, you know."

He wiped his nose on his sleeve, straightened. "I used to get mad at her, tell her to stop being so hard on herself. Then she'd try to smile and make some effort to get up and do something. Sometimes it was enough to snap her out of it. Not usually, but I always tried, and she knew it."

"It sounds like you were important to her."

"Sure. Like a friendly dog that comes around and cheers you up."

"Don't be ridiculous. I saw you together. It was more than that. She had respect for you, too. I'm sure it's like you said. Everyone needs someone that isn't afraid to tell her when she's off track."

He turned to her. "Or when he's been riding around all day with spider webs in his hair?"

She smiled back. "Stuff like that."

He nodded. "Well, I suppose."

There was a long, companionable silence while the sun slipped below the horizon. Small, sharp-winged birds soared overhead, swooping and fluttering. "What are they doing?"

"Catching bugs, I think." She stared at them. "I always wondered what it looks like to them."

"What do you mean?"

"You know. If you were a bird, flying that fast. How would a bug look, and how would you be able to catch it? Did you ever think of that?"

He shook his head, then grinned. "I remember wondering once what went through a big marlin's head when he was chasing one of those little flying fish, and suddenly it disappeared up through the roof of his world and never came back. Is that what you mean?"

"I suppose." Kendra jumped up. "We'd better get supper on, or we'll be washing up in the dark."

He rose more slowly, and they made their way back to the fire. "So, have we settled anything?"

She shrugged. "Not yet. I don't think you can just make a pact or a treaty and settle something like this. You just have to talk about it. Sometimes it just goes around and around and you don't think you really said anything new, but it helps in the long run."

"I hope so."

"And if not..."

"If not?"

She chuckled. "I suppose we could always lie together."

He tried to make it sound cynical. "I'll save that for my dreams."

6.   FRIENDS

"Are we being followed?"

Cheynou did not react immediately, but took a slow glance around them as he rode. "We could be. What did you see?"

"I couldn't be sure, but I thought I saw movement in those bushes over there." She did not point, but her head moved slightly to the left.

He watched the bushes out of the corner of his eye until they were long past, but saw nothing.

"Could have been an animal." He glanced at the dog, trotting comfortably beside him. "Downwind of the trail. I don't want to send Cinders out looking. If it really is someone, she might catch an arrow."

"What do we do?"

"Keep riding and choose our path very carefully."

"And if they attack?"

"We run if we can. If we can't, put the horses nose-to-tail and cover each other's backs."

She slipped the thong off her sword hilt. "Should I string my bow?"

"Not yet. This terrain is too rough and they could be close. If we make any hostile moves it might trigger an attack."

They rode on, all senses alert. The dog picked up their tension, and the hairs rose on her neck.

After half a glass, Cheynou looked around. "I haven't seen any place better than this. String your bow. If it is someone, they'll have to approach in the open. If they attack, the horses will be rested."

They sat their horses and waited. It was the donkey who gave first warning. He snorted and his ears went back. They looked around but could see nothing. "Might have been an eddy of wind. Keep looking."

Then the man appeared. He was much closer than they had expected but his bow was casually held in one hand, the other empty. Cinders growled, low in her throat, but Cheynou snapped his fingers and she crouched, unmoving.

The man approached slowly but without fear. He was stocky, dark-skinned and dressed only in calf-length leather pants. He wore a knife at his belt and a quiver of arrows over his shoulder. Two large birds hung beneath his left arm.

"He's been hunting. Good sign."

The man stopped a chain away, waiting.

Cheynou took one more careful look around, shrugged. "Time to be polite, I suppose."

"How do you know what that is?"

"It seems to me that when a man is on the ground, to sit on your horse shows either poor manners or fear. Don't watch me. Keep a weather eye."

She nodded, her head twisting slowly left and right. He slipped off his horse and stepped forward evenly, his hands clear of his weapons, the dog gliding at his side. When he was close enough, he stopped and regarded the man opposite him.

The impression of stockiness remained. The man's shoulders and neck were corded with muscle, and his hands looked thick and strong. The bow seemed light, but he was hunting birds. Cheynou held out open hands and waited.

The man spoke several words in a guttural tongue that sounded vaguely familiar, but no meaning came through.

"Sorry, I don't speak that language."

The dark man nodded. "Sailor." Then he frowned. "Petrel?"

Cheynou shook his head. "Eagle."

The face lightened. "Eagle? Eagle Crew?"

"Yes. Eagle Crew. I look for Pers and Yong. Pers. Yong. Eagle Crew."

Now the man smiled. "Pers, Yong. Eagle Crew. Yes." He slapped his chest. "Choti. I Choti."

"Cheynou, Kendra."

"Eagle Crew." He turned on his heel and marched away, waving a hand. "Come."

Cheynou watched him stride along, shrugged and turned back to his horse. "Seems all right. He knew Pers and Yong's names, seemed happy to know we were Eagles, not Petrels."

"So do we follow?"

"What else? That's who we're looking for."

They kneed their horses ahead and soon caught up to the walker. The man glanced over his shoulder once, then ignored them.

"We're not following a trail."

Cheynou glanced at the ground. "You're right. I wonder what that means."

"Maybe he was out hunting, and there isn't one."

"Maybe he's not leading us straight to his camp."

"Nothing to worry about..." She stopped as their guide held up a hand. They halted their horses, and sat silent, watching.

The man gave a 'stay there' gesture, his eyes fixed on something off to the left.

Cheynou glanced at Kendra, nodded when she lifted her bow. She nocked an arrow on the string and held it ready. They tried to see what he was staring at, but nothing moved. Cheynou signalled to Cinders, who remained on guard silently. She seemed alert but not upset, testing the wind. He glanced at Martan, but the donkey was ignoring them, cropping cheerfully at a clump of grass. *It's prey, then, not danger.*

The Inari glided forward at a half-crouch, his bow ready. He moved smoothly, placing his feet with care, his eyes never seeming to leave his quarry, whatever it was. Finally, he stopped, aimed carefully, and shot.

There was immediate pandemonium as a large flock of birds burst from the grass and whirred away over their heads in several directions. Kendra had her bow up, but held her hand.

Watching the flock curve and rejoin to land several chains farther away, she shook her head. "Not a chance. I'd just lose an arrow at that distance."

"Our friend had more luck."

The Inari strode forward, but the bird he had shot was only winged. As he approached, it lumbered into the air, flew a short distance, then disappeared in the grass. The hunter muttered something and moved ahead. Then, to the man's obvious surprise, the bird rose again, blundering straight towards him. He made a grab for it, and the bird, realizing its mistake, tried to reverse directions, ending up in the jaws of the dog who was rushing up behind.

Cinders shook the bird once, and it went limp. Then she carried it proudly, making a large detour around the Inari, to come and stand in front of Cheynou's horse.

He laughed and gestured towards the other man. She hesitated a moment, then made a doggish shrug and turned, trotting over to place the bird on the ground at the Inari's feet. Then she backed up and sat down as if awaiting her well-earned praise.

The hunter looked at the bird, then at the dog, then up at Kendra and Cheynou, an expression of awe on his face. Then he joined in their laughter. Picking up the bird, he wrung its neck and added it to the game already slung across his shoulders. "Good hunt." He nodded to the dog as if she were another person, then turned back to his path, cleaning his arrow as he walked.

Cheynou whistled to Cinders, and they followed, the dog's tail high, and her own version of laughter on her face.

Soon they cut onto a well-used trail and the hunter's pace quickened. While he remained alert, his cautious movements were gone. Hunting was over, and he was headed home.

They were completely off the Prairie now, and the path met a small stream, following along beside the water and up the valley towards the mountains. The foothills closed around them, and soon they joined another trail, even better trodden than the first.

"Horse tracks."

Cheynou nodded. "That way must lead to another pasture or something. There's been a bunch of them go through, all in the same direction."

She leaned down to peer at the trail. "A mixed bunch. Even a few colts. Somebody's brood herd."

"That's got to be Pers and Solen. I don't know of anyone on the Prairies who has that many horses."

"That's good, then."

"If they're in camp, it will be perfect."

The valley widened, and there were signs that horses had been grazing along the creek bank. Bits of worn ground, more trails, a small holding pen of light poles, and other evidence clued them they were nearing human habitation.

Sure enough, around the next bend the Inari camp opened up before them. It was not large: big enough for two Crews perhaps, and it spread along the south-facing hillside above the stream. Tents of animal hide were pitched wherever the ground was flat, with various tools, laundry, and the other paraphernalia of life hanging and perched between them. A considerable herd of horses grazed on the valley floor downstream of the camp, and someone was working on an anvil, the ringing strokes of the hammer drifting like bell notes on the evening air. Smoke from the smithy and the cooking fires rose, then drifted away to the south, bringing the smell of roasting meat and bread. There were people working and relaxing all around, and even some children playing by the stream. Heads began to turn as they approached.

"Nice place."

Their guide looked up at Cheynou and grinned. "Nice place." Then he lowered his head and whistled, a long, quavering sound that rose and echoed around the whole valley.

Kendra's eyebrows went up. "That's some door bell."

Cheynou glanced a question at her, but there was no time. The whole population of the camp seemed to be headed their way. The blacksmith's hammering stopped, and a tall figure with blond hair appeared at the smithy door. It was Pers, with Yong close behind him.

"Cheynou!" The former mast'n strode forward, almost pulling his fellow Eagle from his horse in the enthusiasm of his embrace. Yong's greeting was almost as rough, and Cheynou scrambled to keep his feet on the ground.

Then there was a brief silence as the two, backed by the whole village, looked up at Kendra.

"I'm not getting off this horse until I'm reassured that somebody has some manners down there."

Yong laughed. "If my Lady will deign to descend, I would be honoured to welcome her to our humble abode."

Kendra rose on her left stirrup, somehow slid her right foot over the saddle and turned so she was sitting across the horse with her feet together. She held out a graceful hand, which Yong reached up to take. She then slid, slowly and with dignity, to the ground. Cheynou could tell that she put almost no weight on Yong's hand, so she must have slipped her left heel into the stirrup to control her slide. When she was standing, Yong bent over her hand briefly, and she inclined her head graciously in return.

"Thank you, sir."

"My duty and my pleasure, my Lady."

She turned to Pers and stared at him, as if daring him to break the spell. Grinning, he took her hand and bowed over it as well.

Cheynou glanced around to see the villagers standing in silent awe at this masquerade. Kendra turned to him, winked and tossed her head towards the two Eagles. "I like your friends, Cheynou. They got class!"

Then she turned to receive a proper greeting, complete with hugs and backslapping. The villagers, released, cheered wildly, not sure what was going on but willing to join in anyway.

Pers turned to the Inari who had brought them in and spoke rapidly.

Yong slipped between the two travellers. "He's asking Choti where he picked you up, out of a sink-hole somewhere, maybe? Choti just answered that he found you wandering around lost on the Prairie, and thought you might like to meet some real people for a change."

Pers was laughing and clapping the Inari on the back, spinning him to face Cheynou and Kendra. "You've met Choti, I see, one of the prime hunters of the Clan." He indicated the birds across the man's shoulder.

Choti shook his head, indicating the biggest bird. "Not my hunt, Pers."

"No?"

The man spotted Cinders sitting at Cheynou's feet. "Smart dog. Good hunter."

Pers raised his eyebrows. "Choti is pretty picky who he hunts with. Your dog's made a good impression. What's her name?"

"Cinders."

"How original." He turned to the Inari, and the word 'Cinders' appeared in his speech.

The Inari nodded, spoke the name carefully. Cheynou motioned the dog forward, wondering what would happen next.

The dog stood, looking up at the stocky man with curiosity. He said her name, then laid a hand across his breast and said his. He extended the same hand towards the dog, and she stepped forward to sniff it. He said her name again, turned to his people and spoke some other words, seriously, it seemed. They burst again into wild cheering.

"What was that all about?"

"According to Inari custom, Choti and Cinders are now Hunting Brothers. It's considered a great honour."

"Cinders is a she."

"I don't think that makes any difference, somehow."

"I suppose not."

Then the crowd pressed forward, and they were surrounded. Several important people in the camp had to be introduced, the dog had to be exclaimed over, an honour she accepted with dignity, and everyone slowly made their way back to the camp, talking and laughing and generally enjoying themselves.

Cheynou found himself walking beside Pers. "Everyone's glad you showed up. Excuse for a party."

"That's all they need?"

"Sure. They've been working hard; any excuse will do."

"Thanks. Build a man up, then cut him down."

"I'm not worried about you, Cheychan. I'm just darned curious as to what you're doing way out here with a Farmer Lord's daughter in tow."

"Long story."

"I'll be interested to hear it."

"If we get any time."

"No problem. Now everyone has to go prepare for the party. I'll take you two to our tent and we can talk. Come far today?"

"Six or seven leagues. We've been making ten."

"Good. Plenty of energy for dancing, then."

"Dancing?"

"Don't worry. They do their type, but they love to watch us do sailor dances as well."

Cheynou shrugged. "Sounds like fun. I'll put on my best shirt."

"You're loaded pretty heavy. Pack animal and all."

"We're on a long trip, Pers."

"This gets better and better."

"Nothing so wonderful as reality."

"Why a donkey?" He caught a glower from Kendra, striding along on his other side. "Not that he isn't a perfectly decent donkey, I suppose."

"That's part of the story. Why don't you hold your questions until you hear it."

Kendra looked straight ahead and spoke casually. "Yes, I have a question of my own that comes first."

"You do? Ask away."

"Where's my horse?"

"Your horse?"

She gave him a level stare. "Don't play stupid, Pers. I know you have Owena. Where is she?"

He shrugged. "Out in the pasture with the herd, of course." Then his demeanour changed. "You just have to see her foal."

"I'm counting on it. When?"

"As soon as we stow your stuff. Come on. Our tent's just over here."

A glass or two later, they were strolling through the camp down to the meadow where a large number of beautiful horses grazed: long-limbed riding beasts, a few smaller, shaggy ponies, and one or two of the huge draft horses of the Farmers.

"Spoils of war?"

Pers looked down at Kendra intently before he answered. "You did ask for it."

She shook her head impatiently. "Probably, but with good reason. Misunderstanding, to be forgotten as soon as possible."

"I'm glad you feel that way."

"Except for my horse."

He winked at Cheynou. "Spoils of war. Best forgotten as soon as possible."

"But she's my horse."

"Not any more."

"You don't think so?" She put two fingers in her mouth and whistled. The mare's head came up and she trotted over to Kendra, snuffling her hand and pushing her head into Kendra's shoulder, overjoyed to see her. The girl, in turn, looked her over in detail, running her hands from nose to tail, checking everything. The horse accepted this with good grace, turning her head now and then to look with soft eyes on her mistress.

Then Kendra turned to go over the foal, a sturdy little black with some of his father's bulk already. He was less sure of this intrusion, but faced with the combined wills of his mother and her mistress, he soon succumbed.

Finally, Kendra was finished. She stood, dusting her hands off, and the horse thrust her nose firmly against the girl's back. "They're both in good shape, I'll give you that. He's a corker, isn't he?"

Pers nodded. "Spunky as all get out. I'm surprised he let you handle him like that. Nobody else does that to him, even at his age."

Kendra grinned. "It's because I'm his mother's chosen mistress, and he could tell. If I want her, I take her, and you'd be hard put to keep him. Fortunately for you, I can't use her right now."

"You can't?"

84

"No. Where Cheynou and I are going, we can't take horses. Especially a mother with a foal. I'll tell you what. You don't want her. You want her offspring, right?"

"I suppose that's true."

"So why don't you keep her for me? As long as you take care of her, you can have any foals she drops. But she's my horse."

He thought a moment. "You're saying the horse is mine in all respects, until some day when you want to take her back. I've never heard of anything like that before."

"It's a fact of life, Pers. She's mine. Both she and I agree, and there's nothing anyone can do about that. You don't care about ownership, I can tell. You don't think that way about horses. This way we're both satisfied. What do you think?"

"Seems fine to me. As far as anything important is concerned, she's still mine. I get what I want, and I'm not worried about you taking her away, at least not for a while."

She nodded. "It's a deal, then."

"Deal."

"There is something else you can do for us, though."

"What's that, Cheynou?"

"We don't know what to do with our horses when we go North over the Rim. We don't want to turn them loose, because they are valuable animals. If one of your people will come with us and take them back when we go into the mountains, you can have them on the same deal."

Pers chuckled. "Not quite. Kendra's riding a gelding, I notice."

"And I'm riding a stallion. Quite a nice one, you may have noticed. Fine length of leg on him. Smooth gait. Quiet for a stallion. I think it evens out."

"Who gets the donkey?"

"He's going with us."

Yong nudged Pers. "Does the one that brings them back get to keep the foals?"

85

"That's for you to figure out. Sounds fair to me."

"In that case, I'm coming with you!"

"Ah, but so am I."

The two glared at each other in mock ferocity.

Kendra grinned. "I'm sure you can work it out."

"Even if we have to do it in the Circle."

"What's the Circle?"

Yong beckoned and led them to the stream bank where a wide circle of white rocks surrounded a beaten ground.

"This is where the Inari solve their disputes."

Cheynou looked over the ground carefully. "What's that dark spot?"

"Blood."

He looked sharply at Yong, but the man was completely serious.

"I doubt if a horse is quite worth that."

Pers shrugged. "It's the principle of it."

Kendra made a snorting noise that reminded Cheynou of Sarasha at her most sardonic. "And why does your voice seem to be coming from the region below your belt?"

Pers grinned and turned to Cheynou. "And you're going to spend how long with her?"

He shrugged. "Until I find an appropriate way to get rid of her."

"We'd better come with you a ways, help you with some of our ideas."

Kendra was smiling; she had grown up with older brothers. She could hold her own.

Cheynou felt warmth blossom in his chest. It would be good to travel with some of the old bunch again, with their sharp comments, their quick minds and radical ideas. Then the cold reminder of Sarasha's absence dampened his spirits. He looked around to see if the others had noticed, but Pers and Yong were chatting away, Kendra listening carefully. You had to, with those two, or you were sure to miss something. If it was Yong, it might be a joke. If it was Pers, the joke would be on you. That thought quickened his steps, and he joined them.

"So, how are things in the Petrel camp, Cheynou?"

He outlined the changes Orrick Bren was making, finishing with, "...he's even stopped calling himself 'Captain,' to be fair."

Yong exploded into laughter. "What's he going to call himself? King?"

"You can't be a king if you don't have a kingdom."

"I'm sure he's working on that, too. Tell me more about Kendie."

Pers glanced over. "She's that kid that used to hang around Sarasha, isn't she? The one who talks?"

Yong nodded. "That's Kendie, all right. She does talk. Kept me listening three whole glasses once on the history of somebody-or-other who tried to change the Craft responsibilities on the Eagle, years back."

"And you listened for three glasses?"

Yong shrugged. "She was enthused about it. It was pretty interesting, actually. Orrick Bren should have heard her."

"He probably has."

"So what's she going to do?"

Cheynou explained the girl's solo plan to keep her skills up.

Yong shook his head. "She doesn't have a chance. Game kid, though. I'll think on it."

"Will you? I hated to leave her there, but what could I do?"

"Aye, you've already got a female. Not fair to get two."

Cheynou suppressed a grin, as he noticed Kendra's mouth firming in a straight line.

"Oh, did I say something wrong, Kendra?"

She stared up at the taller man, raised her eyebrows, said nothing.

Yong grinned. "Yep. I guess I did." He turned to Cheynou. "Note the technique. Got her completely at a loss for words. Bet it doesn't happen often, right?"

"If I answer either way, I'll suffer the consequences for days. Fight your own battles."

Yong guffawed and slapped his young friend on the shoulder. "You're learning, kid."

7. TRAVEL

They left the next day because there was no reason to wait, but they didn't hurry. Pers and Yong had a long trip there and back, and they didn't want to tire their horses. The other four had an even longer trail ahead.

So they cantered across the Prairie, then walked, then cantered some more, took long noonings where there were streams, and camped early. At night, Cheynou told them about the stars: some facts, some legends. It felt strange at first, giving the lore of his Trade to outsiders, but as the days wore on, their active minds took more and more interest, and it was a pleasure to teach them.

It was also pleasant to have two fine swordsmen in camp at night. They kept a sharp eye out as they travelled, and both Pers and Yong, now alerted, agreed that there were more tracks of larger parties of men than usual. But they met no one.

Pers and Yong were also interested in pumping Kendra for her knowledge of breeding and bloodlines. They had made up their minds to follow Captain Tourn's idea of breeding the biggest, fastest, fighting horses they could. There was a great deal of discussion about what direction their program should go.

One night in camp, Kendra stated it flatly. "You all noticed what happened when our people tried to use their farm horses in the war. Only the black that Captain Tourn stole had any real potential, and he was much too slow."

"Which is why Orrick and Captain Tourn wanted his foal out of Owena."

"Right, but that was as far as their thinking got."

Pers leaned forward. "Your thinking has gone further?"

"Not yet, but I know it has to. When you are breeding any animal, you first have to decide exactly what use you will put it to. If you were breeding war horses for the lords in my area, you would breed, as you are discussing, a horse big enough to carry a man with a lot of metal hung about him, and some protection for the horse as well."

"But...?"

"But I can't see your people using that sort of horse."

"Why not?"

"Because of the resources you need to have that kind of armour."

Pers and Yong looked at each other.

She caught the look. "You hadn't thought of that because you haven't lived off a ship for long enough. You have to get used to the nomad life. I saw your little smithy. Where's the storage for all the iron you would need? What happens when you move camp?"

Again that glance.

"You're catching on. Do you realize that Byaren has one blacksmith whose only duty is to take care of armour? He has his own, special workshop, and he works all his time on weapons."

"So you're telling us we don't want to breed horses that are too heavy, because we won't be able to use them in fighting."

"I'm not telling you anything of the sort."

Yong regarded her, then nodded. "We have to make up our own minds."

"That's right. If you, in your juvenile male minds, have decided to breed war horses, you have to first decide what type of war you are breeding them for."

"If we want to sell them to the Farmers..."

"...then Captain Tourn was on the right track."

"But for ourselves..."

She shrugged. "I don't know. How do you like to fight? I assume that you do like to fight?" She smiled sweetly.

"Well, we don't actually like to fight that much, but..."

90

"Oh, I'm sure it's often necessary."

"That's right."

"I would guess that, with the kind of life you are going to live, you want your horses to be light and fast, quick-turning."

Cheynou had a sudden thought. "Like the Eagle!"

The two men turned to him, their faces glowing. "That's right. The Priest-Admiral was upset because our ship could out-sail his big, clumsy Masterships. We can do that on land as well!"

Yong nodded. "And the one point that came very clear to me in the war against the Farmers was the mobility the horses gave us. If we hadn't had the horses, Haskel's mercenaries would have caught up with the Osprey, we would have had to give them straight battle, and who knows what would have happened?"

Kendra laughed dryly. "I thought it was the losers who usually fought through the battle over again, trying to figure out how to win it."

Yong grinned. "Just our natural modesty showing through."

Pers leaned forward. "We're off topic. Let's figure out what kind of horse we really want, here."

"Wrong."

Three sets of eyes turned to Cheynou.

"You're missing Kendra's point."

"We are?"

He knew what Sarasha would have done. He waited.

"Oh. Right."

"The kind of warfare."

"So what do we do about that?"

He raised his eyebrows. "Sit and talk about it?"

Instantly, both of them were on their feet, heading for their horses.

Cheynou glanced at Kendra. "Don't plan on travelling very far tomorrow."

She shook her head in amazement. "You sure know how to motivate people."

"Me?"

She turned to him. "Yes, you. 'Sit and talk about it.' Five words, and look at them."

He shrugged. "I always figured, you find out what people really want to do, give them an excuse, and ..." He pointed to the two men, who were vigorously attacking each other from the backs of their horses. "Do you think we ought to stop them before they hurt each other?"

She shuddered delicately. "I don't really want to start sewing up wounds so soon after eating. Do they have to use real swords?"

"That's an idea." He strolled over to the stream, where a row of willows and alders took advantage of the water and shelter to grow to a considerable height. He hacked off a couple of stems of about the right size. Cleaning them up, he interrupted the two combatants.

"You're not trying hard enough."

"What?"

"You want us to hurt each other?"

Wordlessly, he handed up the practise wands. They thanked him, sheathed their real swords and were soon back at it more fiercely than before.

He wandered back into camp. "That ought to keep them occupied for a while."

"For the rest of their lives."

"I suppose it might."

8. EAGLE's CRY

The long, hot days spun out behind them, and they ate up the Prairie distance. Cheynou began to watch his companions to see whether they were recognizing the landmarks that were imprinted in his brain. He coached them, stimulated their memories, made sure Kendra absorbed it all.

In turn, they helped Cheynou with the training of his horse. He was working on getting it to strike out with its rear hooves. Staying on the horse during the maneuver was his main problem. They also let him join in with their sword work, which he had neglected recently.

Pers nodded as he and Cheynou finished going through some of the pairs practise drills. "Your speed is impressive. You don't have much wrist strength, though."

Cheynou held up his arm. "About as much as I'm ever going to get out of that."

"Then we'd better work on your speed. That long, light cutlass works for you, that's for sure."

Cheynou grinned. "There was some advantage to being a Helmsman. I got the best equipment. I had that made specially when I realized I had stopped growing."

Another voice entered the conversation. "When is it my turn?"

Pers turned in surprise to be confronted by Kendra, sword and shield at the ready.

He glanced at Cheynou, ready to smile, but then he looked back to the girl. "Now that your partner has worn me to a frazzle, you think you'll finish me off, do you?"

"I have no illusions about finishing you off, but I need the practice as much as anyone, maybe more."

Pers nodded and stepped away, inviting her to attack.

93

She didn't. She held her ground, knees bent, shield up, sword back, ready to strike.

"Hmm. I see." He slipped forward, jabbing with the tip of his cutlass.

She shrugged it aside with a flip of her shield.

He quickly twisted his weapon back to a defensive position, but her sword stayed up, merely threatening. He attacked again, and once more she led with her shield. Over and over he attacked, but always the shield was there, deflecting his sword away. Once in a while she would parry with her short sword, but then the shield would swing back, catching his blade on the flat with a firm rap.

After a bit of this he stepped back, lowering his point, and grinned over at Yong. "It's like fighting a dratted turtle!"

Yong smiled at Kendra. "You're left-handed, aren't you?"

She shrugged. "Mostly."

"I wondered, because you always hold your reins in your right. At first I thought it was a Farmer style, but nobody else does."

Pers frowned. "Why didn't you learn to use the sword with your other hand?"

"I come from a rather rigid society. Some things just aren't done. It wasn't worth the battle. I just found a way to use my abilities to advantage."

"Hmm. It's not so great, having only a defence, though."

"Who says I only have a defence?"

His head swivelled quickly, and he stared at her. "What do you mean?"

She tilted her nose up and looked down at him. "Some day you may find out."

When the laughter had died, Yong and Cheynou took to the practise area, and the mast'n began to work the boy through some more complicated drills. When they had finished, Yong frowned. "Who taught you those? I thought only the Raiders learned them."

"What do you mean? You were teaching them to me just now."

"You had never done them before?"

"No. Oh, I watched you lot working on them, but as you say, I wasn't allowed. I was too small and weak anyway. But I got the general idea."

"I'll say you did. You picked those up quickly. What else do you know?"

Cheynou shrugged. "Same with all the other work. I've seen it all, but never actually done the formal training. Helmsmen train differently, because it's assumed that we won't go into real battle, but we might get caught up at any time. So I'm trained to fight hand to hand with a belaying pin, or an oar, even a pen or a ruler. We fight with whatever we can pick up." He grinned. "The element of surprise is our best asset. Nobody expects to have a set of dividers shoved up his nose."

Yong winced. "That would be effective, I'd say."

"Straight into the brain."

"Well, if you'll promise not to brain me with the next rock you pick up, I'll give you some pointers on the standard techniques, all right?" He turned to Kendra. "And I'll look for an opportunity to hone your offensive skills."

"Sounds like a bargain."

So an evening training session was added to their daily routine, and they ate up the leagues of Prairie, slowly approaching the distant mountains.

Finally, their journey came to a close.

Cheynou stopped his horse on the same rise he had used before. "Well, Pers, here we are."

"That's right. There's the trail up to the valley where we camped. Where the northerner buried his companion. Where Orrick Bren and Sarasha..."

"That's right. But this is where we made the wrong turning."

95

"It is?"

"Yes. It isn't obvious, and what fooled us is that the northern scouts went up there. I don't know why. They didn't come down from there, they went up. They camped there for some reason. Then something happened to the man's partner, just like it did with us. Avalanche, lion, cold. Who knows?"

Yong was looking around the sheer rock walls. "I know you, Cheychan. You're setting us a puzzle. The real trail leads out from here somewhere."

He laughed. "Look around. I solved it and I didn't have the advantage of your brilliant character judgement."

It was simple, with that hint. After a ride around the perimeter of the valley, Pers discovered the opening. He yelled gleefully and pushed inside, the others following.

When they were all through, they waited for Cheynou. "Where from here?"

Cheynou reined in his horse and looked at them. "For you, this is the end of the trail. We take the donkey from here, and you take the horses and go home. But we won't be leaving right away. I have a job to do."

"What's that?"

He said nothing, just started his horse up the valley.

"That's it?" They all sat in their saddles, staring at the huge slab of stone that covered Sarasha's resting.

Yong moved his horse ahead. "You split that off the wall? How?"

He shrugged. "I just cleared out underneath and jammed rocks into the split until it overbalanced."

"Just." Pers put a lot of feeling into the word. "So she's under that?"

"Yes. In a crack in the valley floor, like I told you. You'll have to take my word for it."

"Oh, we have no reason to doubt you, Cheychan." Yong swung out of the saddle, resting both his hands on the rock. "It's just that...well..."

"...this is it. This is where she lies..." Pers joined him. "I never sort of..."

"...aye..."

A long silence. Finally, Pers came out of his trance and turned to the two who still sat their horses. "So, what's this job you have to do? Looks to me like you did pretty well for her already."

Cheynou gestured with his chin towards the raw face of granite towering above them. "What do you see, just below half-way up?"

They stood back, craning their necks upwards.

Yong was first to notice it. "There's an outcropping up there," he pointed.

"That's right. Looks like an eagle's head."

They turned to Cheynou, and he nodded. "That's it. That's why I borrowed your chisel. I'm going to work that over until it stands out more."

"That's all? No words?"

He grinned. "Nope. Words were Sarasha's job. She wrote enough of them, and Leide took down even more. Kendie is going to put them all together, make sure they don't get lost. I'm doing rock."

"That's going to take a while."

"I've got time."

Pers paced around the base of the boulder. "You're going to need some scaffolding."

"I thought so."

"Fine. So where are we going to camp?"

"We?"

Yong frowned. "You don't think we're going to leave you alone to work on Sarasha's monument, do you? We were her friends, too!"

97

"Oh...I never thought you would want to stay. You have to ride all the way back to your camp..."

Pers grinned. "We've got time."

"Fine. The best campsite is still up there." He gestured towards the rim above them.

"Well, that will make it easy to get to work in the morning. Just jump over."

"I think Sarasha would disagree."

That sobered them. The two others remounted their horses, turned with one backwards glance and rode out the way they had come.

Once their camp had been erected in the familiar hanging valley, Cheynou noticed Pers strolling back and forth in the area above them. He went closer, watched for a moment. "Checking Bren's story?"

"Aye. Now that all the snow is gone, I thought I'd just...you know."

"Look for evidence that something else happened. I did that already."

"And you didn't find anything."

He took in Cheynou's silence. "Of course you didn't." He gestured up the avalanche path. "The rock that broke his leg must have come from there. Think there's any danger?"

"Not at this time of year. We're still pretty safe, now that we moved our camp in behind those big boulders."

Pers laughed. "Never say the Sea People don't learn from experience."

They strolled back to their tents under the darkening sky, the tall mountains leaning in around them.

After they had eaten, Pers and Yong seemed lost in their thoughts. Cheynou gestured to Kendra to follow him.

They walked out into the open, lighted by the stars. "You've been very quiet."

"Enjoy it."

"Seriously. Why?"

She made a sweeping gesture, taking in the plateau, the camp, the mountains. "This is your moment. The three of you, but especially them. You don't need me intruding. What could I say? She was wonderful. She was your friend, your leader, your inspiration.

"And here she lies. Whatever she achieved, whatever she built, she has finished. It's all up to you, now. Your friends understand. That's why they are so quiet."

"I suppose."

"So I've been quiet to give them their moment."

"Thank you."

She punched his shoulder gently. "So enjoy it. It won't last. I'm not capable of keeping it up for long."

For three days, he worked on the rock. It was painstaking, careful work, because he only had one chance. If he broke off too large a piece, he might spoil the whole effect.

So he chipped away, using a smooth stone for a hammer, sharpening his chisel on the hammer stone. He had made it clear that he wanted no help, and Pers and Yong never asked. Once they finished the scaffolding, they used their rudimentary carpentry skills to create a more permanent campsite nestled in the protection of the clump of larger boulders. When that was finished, they spent their time hunting and exploring down the trail and up the surrounding mountains. They discussed their progress around the fire at night.

"I think you're right about the trail, Cheynou. It leads down through that deep pass just west of north. A couple of places the ledges are too narrow for a horse, though. Looks like they were once wider, but they've eroded away. Steep as well. They're pretty scary for a human. I hope your donkey can make it."

"If we have to, we'll take his packs off and lead him through bare. Then we load up on the other side."

Yong laughed. "And then if he goes over, he doesn't take your supplies with him...all right, I'm sorry, please don't throw the frying pan at me."

Kendra gently replaced the pan beside the fire. "Martan will make it."

"I hope so. I sort of like the beast. He's smart."

"Ah, but you're a horseman. You appreciate that kind of animal."

Pers glanced at Cheynou. "Unlike some others?"

Cheynou held up his hands defensively. "I can deal with horses. I learned to ride sooner than most. They just aren't the same sort of people as I am. Our minds don't work the same way, like yours do."

"You prefer dogs."

He shrugged. "I get along pretty well by myself. I find people a distraction a lot of the time."

The two men laughed. "And you're going off into the mountains alone with this guy, Kendra? I suspect you're going to wish you'd stayed home."

She shot Cheynou a glance. "He doesn't know how much he needs me."

Cheynou managed to look unconcerned.

This byplay brought another gust of laughter. "Hey, Pers, maybe we ought to hang around for a few days."

"Yeah. In case one of them comes hiking back up the trail in need of a horse."

"Which one do you think it will be, Pers?"

"My money says Kendra. Nothing ever stopped Cheychan when he got going."

"Are you boys trying to send me a message?"

They both turned to her, chuckling. "Probably." Pers nodded. "You have to realize what you're getting into, lady."

"What do you mean?" She looked half-serious. So were they, but there was nothing Cheynou could do about it.

Yong shrugged. "It's nothing specific. Just don't expect to get your way all the time."

"I never expect to get my way all the time."

Pers leaned back, his hands behind his head. "I have observed that people, and I include all of us, often think that about themselves. They don't want to get their way all the time." He grinned. "Only when it's important. Unfortunately, the time when it's important is the same time for all the other people."

Cheynou could see Kendra glancing at him, assessing. He had to say something.

"Don't get the idea that I want my way all the time, either. In fact, I find it rarely happens."

Pers nudged Yong. "That's right. He doesn't get his way often."

The two spoke together, "Only when it's important," and went off into gales of laughter.

He rolled his eyes at Kendra, and she smiled. Sort of.

"You sure you don't want to come back with us, Kendra? There'd be a place for you with the Inari."

She snorted. "What kind of place?"

Yong was serious for a change. "The women have pretty good status, especially the Wise Woman."

"Who's that?"

"Next time you're in an Inari camp, look for a small, white tent. That's the Wise Woman's tent. It's the place the women gather to exchange their lore, teach their daughters," he shrugged, "I dunno...talk about the men in privacy."

"I see."

Pers nodded. "They keep the history, too."

"History?"

"Yeah. They remember the history of the tribe. Who is descended from who, when the famines were, all that sort of thing."

"They remember...?"

"Aye. Formidable memories. The Wise Woman knows the whole history of the tribe, and she teaches all the women. When she dies, someone else takes over, and the rest of the women get together and make sure she has all the stories right. It's some kind of a gathering, they tell me, the initiation of a new Wise Woman. The whole tribe gets to listen to the main stories, being told all the way from the beginning."

"Sounds interesting."

Cheynou grinned. "Sounds like they could use a Scribe."

Yong did not laugh. "Now, that's a thought."

"What is?"

"Oh, nothing." And he would say no more on the subject.

9.   DOWN THE MOUNTAINS

Finally, the sculpture was carved to Cheynou's satisfaction, and one morning they packed their belongings on Martan's back and started down the animal path that led from their campsite to the trail. Pers and Yong followed as far as Sarasha's resting.

The riders dismounted, and they all stood and gazed at the monument. Yong finally broke the silence. "I don't think there's any doubt."

"No. Someone special is buried here. That will be known for generations."

"Pers, do me a favour?"

"Sure, Cheynou."

"If you ever go back to the Petrel/Eagle camp, find Kendie and tell her about this."

"Kendie?"

"Aye. She'll want to know."

Pers winked at Yong. "Sounds like our kind of girl. Maybe she shouldn't be stuck with people who don't appreciate her."

Yong nodded. "Yes, I think when we get back, I'm going to have to do a bit of raiding."

"Raiding? What do horses have to do with this?"

"Not horses, my friend." Yong shook his head. "Scribes."

Cheynou grinned. "Do you realize what you're letting yourselves in for?"

"What do you mean?"

"Kendie takes that stuff about the Scribe being the Captain's conscience very seriously. Are you ready to have Kendie looking over your shoulder for the rest of your life?"

Yong chuckled. "A darn sight better than having Orrick Bren looking over my shoulder. I think I can handle it."

"And we'll handle Orrick Bren if we have to." Pers was smiling, but Cheynou could hear a serious note in his voice.

"I can see you two are going to keep yourselves busy while we're gone."

"When do you expect to be back?"

Cheynou shook his head. "Who knows? We may be back before winter, but I doubt it. If there is a pass through the mountains, and I'm guessing this is it, we'll go down there, contact the people, learn their language and stay as long as it takes to...I don't know...map their area, learn their skills, whatever comes up. I'll be looking for ways to help our people up here, as well. Trade, mechanical things. Again, I won't know until I get there."

Pers nodded.

"And Pers?"

"Yes?"

"If you want to make peace with Orrick Bren?"

"I probably will. At first, anyway."

"Just tell him he can have Owena's foal. It's important to him."

Kendra stepped forward. "Tell him I've taken my horse back, tell him about our deal. He'll accept that."

"And tell him you're not coming back to the Crew."

"Why tell him that?"

He glanced at Cheynou, slapped the side of his own head mockingly. "All right. I'm not that stupid. I'll tell him."

They all stood in silence then, regarding Sarasha's grave once more. Cheynou looked up, pointing; high above, an eagle with white head and tail soared on the updrafts.

Pers spoke quietly, almost to himself. "Die like the Eagle."

They all nodded somberly and turned away.

Back up at the main canyon, each rider shared an embrace with the two travellers, unspeaking in the knowledge that it might be the last time they met.

Then two swung up on their horses and rode away to the south, and two stepped out on the rocky trail north, farther into the mountains.

They were silent for a long while. Cinders, glad to be moving again, ranged ahead and behind, and Martan plodded calmly in their wake. The sun and the exercise warmed them and soon they tossed their coats over their shoulders. Cheynou glanced back, and Kendra smiled. He turned to the front and strode on.

10. THE PROBLEM WITH LIFE

"I don't know, Kendra. I sometimes wonder whether I've ever made a real decision in my life."

She stared at him, her mouth open. "Whatever are you talking about?"

"No. You tell me. Tell me one real choice I made."

Her hand flapped helplessly around. "You are here, in the middle of a foreign land, exactly where you said you wanted to go, and you don't think you chose to be here?"

"Yes, but was that an independent choice, all my own, or just a reaction to what was going on around me?"

She pondered that a considerable time, and he waited. Finally she spoke, starting slowly, then speaking more firmly as the ideas cleared in her mind.

"I think I see what you mean. I said it myself when I left Kirigata. There wasn't anything for me to do. You came along and offered this journey, so I took it. That's not much of a decision, when you come to think of it." She looked up at him. "Do you really consider your planning of this expedition in the same way?"

"How am I different from you? I came ashore because my Crew was Beached. No decision there. I went to give Sarasha proper rites because I needed to, in order to deal with her death. No decision there. That got me into trouble with Captain Bren, so I left. Not much need for decision there."

"How about deciding to warn us about the raiding party? That was a meaningful decision."

He grinned. "Thanks for the loyal defence. It may have been meaningful to you, but when you consider the right and wrong of it, what else could I do? It wasn't any big deal. I didn't put myself into much danger and I did what any decent person would. No, thank you all the same, but I won't claim to be a hero for that one.

106

"And that brings us to the big decision. Why did I come here?" He knitted his fingers together stared at them. "Well, I discovered that there was no more need for Helmsmen. I'm a Helmsman. So I went looking for a way to keep being a Helmsman. Not much virtue in that. Not much creativity, either. I just tried to keep things as they had always been. Very backward-looking, it seems to me."

"I know your problem."

"You do? Please tell me. I can't wait to find out."

"I'm serious. Your problem is that you want the war hammer."

"What?"

"You want the big solution. The grand gesture, set up perfectly. You want to see it all in front of you and make the great and marvellous choice, so that ever after you can look back and say, 'Yes, at least one time, I did it. I made a real choice.' The one big blow with the big hammer that solves everything. Isn't that it?"

"So what's wrong with that?"

"Only life."

He rolled his eyes. "Only life."

"Look, Cheynou. Everybody would like to be able to take a big hammer to all of their problems and break them open and smash them down and have them all over with."

She shook her head. "It's not going to happen, my friend. Life isn't like that. Life only gives you a whole lot of little ways to solve your problems. A little pick, to scratch away. You get to be proud of yourself by doing all the little things, day by day."

"Give me an example."

"All right. You see a coin lying on the floor. You pick it up. What do you do with it?"

"I don't know. I never saw a coin on the floor. We didn't use coins very much, only when we went ashore."

Her palm collided with his shoulder, causing him to wince. "What?"

"You're ducking the point. Do you pick it up and keep it, or do you find out who owns it, and give it back?"

"And this is an example of...?"

"Of a choice, a decision. It's all those little decisions you make, every day, that are practice for when the big ones come along. You have to practise with the tiny little hammer and chisel, so when you really need to use the big one, you have some kind of idea how."

He slouched down, his fingers laced behind his head. "Did you ever just sit and think about life and what you're doing here? I have. For hours, sometimes. And you know, I get going over the same point, round and round, and I can't get rid of it. I try to find something that makes my life important, and I just can't find anything.

"I've done good things in the past, but they're over now, and I look ahead, and nothing seems very important. You know, we threw away the gods, and for the most part that was good. But the gods gave us purpose, too. We were there because we fitted into their hierarchy. Sure, our place was pretty low. We seemed to be there to serve the Masterships and not much else. So we got away from that.

"The problem is, now we have to find our own purpose, with nobody telling us whether it's right or wrong, or even showing us where to look for something to do. I'm not doing so well at that at the moment."

She laughed out loud. "I think we need Kendie here to write down all the profound thoughts of Cheychan the Philosopher."

He rose. "Yes, well, all that thinking is making me hungry. Who's cooking tonight?"

After supper, as Kendra was cleaning the last dish and packing it away, she paused, frowning. "You know, Cheynou, it would never ever occur to me to talk about stuff like that."

He looked up from his notebook. "At least you listen. Most people just get that blank look and nod and say, 'U-huh,' at the right times, but they don't really hear what I say." He shrugged. "Of course, I can see why. All they're going to hear is what's going on in my thick head. I don't know why I even bother people with it."

108

"But you should! Everybody has thoughts like that. They just don't know how to put them into words. You help people by talking about it."

He gave a doubtful sniff. "If you say so. I usually figure I'm just boring them to death."

"Did they bore Sarasha to death?"

He frowned. "What has she got to do with this?"

"Did they?"

"No, of course not."

"Aha!"

"And what is 'Aha!' supposed to mean?"

"Just that what the wonderful Sarasha thought about anything seems to have had a great effect on you. So take her advice."

"What advice is that?"

She flung her hands up helplessly. "It's not really advice. I mean, if she thought your ideas were good, then they probably were. So don't be hard on yourself."

"I used to tell Sarasha that."

"Didn't work any better on her, did it?"

"Not often. But I tried."

Her hand rested on his shoulder. "And sometimes it did work, and so you kept trying. You're a good friend, Cheychan. When I talk about doing the little things, day by day, that's one you're very good at."

She pulled him around. "What was the huge sigh for?"

"Oh, I can just see it. There they will be, everyone who comes to my funeral, saying, 'One thing you can say about Cheynou, he was a good friend.'

"And they all agree, 'Yup, he sure was a good friend, all right.' I'd sure feel good to know they were saying that."

"Why not? What's wrong with being a good friend?"

He grinned up at her ruefully. "It's not exactly the kind of epitaph a young man dreams about, Kendra."

"Huh! I don't think many young men dream about their epitaph."

"I wouldn't be so sure."

"Right. So when you lads get going over the campfire with a bottle of wine or three, is that what you talk about? I can just hear you:

"'I dunno, Pers, what do you want to be when you die?'

"'Gee, Cheynou, I always thought I'd sorta like to be a good friend.'

"'Is that so? If you're a good friend, pass the bottle. I was thinkin' about bein' a hero, myself. What about you, Yong?'

"And Yong, being Yong, would say, 'You know, gentlemen, I believe I would like to be known as the man who snorted thirty worms up his nose.' Which would be about the most practical comment in the whole conversation."

"So what do you want to be when you die, Kendra?"

She stared at his face, which he kept dead serious. "You aren't even going to laugh, are you?"

"What? Laugh and encourage you?"

"I could promise not to take it too seriously."

"Seriously, Kendra, what do you want to accomplish in your life?"

"Dammit, Cheynou, why do you always have to make me think?"

"Because it's better to have you thinking than trying to be funny?" He ducked the slap that was aimed in the general direction of his head. "Come on. Tell."

She sighed and slipped down beside him. "All right. When I think about it, I don't really know."

"Come on. Everybody has dreams. What about when you were a kid?"

She shrugged. "That's it. Of course I had dreams, but they weren't based on anything that really mattered to me. They were based on what I expected to happen in my life."

She squirmed around to face him. "Give you an example. Of course, I always thought I was going to marry some local lord and be a lady. So, I used to dream about that. Having the most handsome man to marry, doing the best job of being a lady, raising the most wonderful children. All that sort of stuff."

"Nothing wrong with that."

110

"Yes, there was! Once I grew up enough to start really thinking about it, all I was doing was rationalizing what I thought was going to happen to me, so when it happened I wouldn't be upset. In fact, it's exactly wrong for me, as I finally figured out."

"I see. So when Orrick Bren came along..."

"You know my family has always been adventurous. Marrying Orrick and going off to lead his people to an empire in the wilderness; that was the next dream."

"Once again, a good dream."

"Yes, but once again, completely wrong for me. Do you see me as a leader, Cheynou? Sarasha was a leader. It came as naturally to her as talking. I don't think I'm that sort. And as I told you, I soon figured that Orrick wasn't the man for me."

"So then I come along and offer you an escape."

"That's right. And here I am, escaping. An escape is, of course, a sort of choice. A negative one, but a choice. Like all the other choices my life." She reached out, trickled dirt from her fist onto the ground. Suddenly, she scattered the rest away from her. "Which always leave me in a big mess."

"You're young yet. You'll figure out something."

"And this is Cheychan of the long white beard talking."

He shrugged. "You're only three years older than me. Doesn't give you the edge on wisdom or maturity."

She looked into his eyes keenly for a moment, then slumped back against the rock beside him. "No, it certainly doesn't."

11. SLIDE

The next morning, Cheynou was swinging down a particularly clear part of the trail, his mind on the conversation of the night before, when he came around a corner and there it was.

"Well, now we know why the trading stopped."

They stood on solid ground, but everything in front of them was a mess. A huge jumble of broken rock and gravel stretched ahead. To their right, far up the hill, the whole face of the mountain looked as though a huge shovel had scraped down, exposing the bare rock. To his left the slide dropped steeper and steeper, finally tumbling over a ledge and out of sight into a canyon far below.

Cheynou peered at the terrain in front of him. Huge boulders balanced atop each other, and a jumble of smaller rocks filled the spaces in between. "The path does keep going. Sort of."

Kendra nodded. "This is old. Look at the vegetation in the slide path. I come from sea level; I have no idea how fast trees grow at this altitude, but some of those look like they've been here a long time."

He caught sight of grey, weathered tree trunks and roots sticking up. "It's been here a while, all right. You think it's safe to walk on?"

"Walking is the problem, all right. Look how narrow the trail is. That's made by small animals. Maybe mountain goats or sheep, but no larger. Getting Martan through will be rough."

He shucked off his pack and stepped out into the mess. "You stay here. I'll see how hard it is to get across."

"I have a better idea. I'll go up that ridge over there to get a look from above. I want to see how stable it is. Look for recent slips, slide paths, that sort of thing."

"Good idea. Back here in a glass?"

"If I can figure out how long that is, sure."

"Well, nobody's going anywhere in a hurry." He peered ahead, plotting a course through the boulders.

It was tough going as the heat of the sun increased, reflecting off the rocks. Once he heard water, trickling deep below him, but he could not get near it. He took a small swig from his canteen and moved on. Several times he mounted larger boulders and recorded the angles back to the end of the trail where Martan and Cinders waited patiently in the shade. He had been bashing himself through this maze for a long time, and they seemed to be distressingly close every time he checked.

Several times he looked up and caught sight of Kendra's bright shirt, moving at a snail's pace along the hillside. When she reached the top of the ridge, he whistled and waved. She waved back and, after a moment to look around, they both started their return journey.

He made his crossing a bit farther down the slide, but the chance of finding a path the donkey could get through didn't look good there, either. Finally, he was back with the animals, but to his surprise, Kendra wasn't there.

"Hey, Cinders, where's Kendra? She was coming down hill. It shouldn't take her as long to come down."

The dog looked up at him and whined, unsure of his instructions.

Why not? I bet she can. "Go find Kendra." He pointed up the hill. "Go find her. Good girl, Cinders. Find Kendra."

The dog turned in the direction their companion had gone and moved to the edge of the clearing, pausing to look back.

"That's right. Find Kendra. Away you go."

Cinders turned and scrambled up the bank, disappearing into the stunted trees that cloaked the hillside. Cheynou occupied himself by removing Martan's pack. *We aren't going anywhere in a hurry.*

Then up the hill he heard the dog bark. It wasn't her usual herding yip or her warning howl. It was something else: a continued, staccatto yap.

A pang of fear shot through Cheynou's chest. *Somebody's in trouble!*

He loosened his cutlass in its sheath and sprinted up the bank and into the brush. It was hard, hot work pushing his way up the mountainside, and he soon slowed. There was no sense in exhausting himself when he didn't know what he would meet when he reached her. Once in a while he would pause, and the dog's yap would spur him on.

He broke into the open farther up the hill and paused, panting heavily. He whistled, and a faint whistle answered from above. Relief washed through him. He shouted, but received no answer besides more anxious yapping. He pushed on, faster now but carefully over the loose rocks. *No sense having two of us in trouble.*

Again he stopped to whistle, and this time her answer was closer and louder.

"Kendra! Are you all right?"

"Sort of." Her voice was faint.

"Is there more danger?"

"Only from...my own...stupidity."

"Stay still, I'll be there in a moment."

"I'm not...going anywhere."

He scrambled higher, and the dog's barking trailed away.

Soon, Kendra's voice came from his left. "Over this way."

He looked up. Cinders was standing atop a boulder, her tail thrashing, her ears rising and lowering in anxiety.

He clambered up to her and looked down between two boulders.

Kendra sat there in a narrow crevasse, looking up at him.

"Are you hurt? What happened?"

She wriggled her shoulders. "Not seriously, I don't think. Not sure what happened. I felt my ankle twisting, and I let

114

my knee collapse to minimize the damage. That threw me off balance, and I took a header down here between these boulders. I think I need a hand to get out."

He peered around her, then clambered down outside the rock pile, looking in through the crack. "I can see you, but there's no way out this side."

He circled around and looked at the other end, but a third rock blocked access. He climbed back to the top. "Looks like you have to come out the way you went in. I'll try to climb down."

"Be careful. I don't feel like being fallen on right now."

He didn't answer, peering down for footholds. It was a bit of a climb, but he made it, carefully placing his feet so he didn't step on her.

"Don't come too close." Her voice was sharp. "I don't want you stumbling around."

"Can you stand up?"

"If you'll get out of my way." Wincing, she rose to her feet. "Aye. No problem."

"How's the ankle?"

She tested it. "Better than my hip."

"What happened to your hip?"

"How should I know? There's a whole lot of very hard rock around here. I suppose I hit some of it."

He regarded her, deciding now was not the time to set boundaries. "Do you think you can climb out if I boost you?"

She looked up. "Now that I've seen you climb down, I can hardly refuse, can I?"

He tried for a grin and a joke. "It's that or I drop your supper down in pieces."

"If you're volunteering to cook, I guess I better get going." She reached up and began to climb. "Just don't push on my left hip."

It took a lot of effort, and he was sure Kendra was in pain, but finally she scrabbled up into the open, to be smothered by kisses from the anxious dog.

"All right, girl. I'm fine. You found me, didn't you? What a good dog!" Kendra lowered herself to the boulder, wincing again as she bent her leg.

Now that she was in the light, Cheynou checked her over. Scrapes marred her left cheekbone and jawline, and her shirt was torn along the left sleeve, abraded skin and flecks of blood showing through at the elbow. Blood seeped through her pants over the hip she was favouring, but very little. *That's positive, I suppose.*

He sat beside her. "What do we do now? Can you climb back down to the trail?"

She peered down the hill. "I have to try." She pounded the rock with her fist. "This is a lousy place to camp, and the beds are too hard."

"Whenever you're ready, then."

She clambered to her feet, her breath quickening, and started down the rock. It was tough at first, but then she seemed to figure out how to favour the bad leg, and she made better time. Cheynou couldn't find any way to help her, and after a while she stopped and glared at him. "You two stop buzzing around me! I'm more worried you'll fall on me or the dog will trip me than I am about slipping again."

"We're trying to help."

"You're getting in the way."

He put on a grin. "All right. I'll go first and you can fall on me if you have to."

"Much better idea. Away you go, and keep Cinders in front of you."

They didn't go any faster with this new order of march, but Kendra sounded more cheerful, and they worked their way down steadily. Once they got to the trees, Cheynou had an idea. He cut her a staff long enough to get both hands on, and trimmed and smoothed it with his cutlass.

"Thanks. That helps a lot, especially with these dratted trees so close together I can't see where I'm putting my foot."

"I'll cut a path if I have to."

She paused and faced him. "Thanks, Cheynou. I'm sorry I was sharp back there. I don't like that helpless feeling."

He grinned in relief. "Don't worry. I can take it. Anything that helps."

Kendra reached out and ran her fingers down his cheek. "I know. I appreciate it." She turned, gripping her staff firmly. "Now hack off that limb right there, and I can get past this rock."

By the time they made it to the trail, her face was white and the hand holding the staff was shaking. Cheynou laid out both bedrolls and got her lying down, her head pillowed on her packsack.

"Do you want a drink?"

"Definitely. That was hot work." She took a slug from her canteen, then shook it. "Is there water nearby?"

"I heard some down in the rocks, but I don't see any on the surface."

"Well, I'm fine here, but I doubt that I'm walking farther today. Why don't you look around for water and a good campsite? We could stay here, but it's pretty narrow, and there's little food for Martan. I don't remember crossing a stream lately."

"Just a moment." Cheynou pulled out his notes. "Yes, there's a stream runs alongside the trail only a couple of chains back. I'll go down there and have a look."

"Huh. You mean those maps you make actually have a purpose? And here I thought you were just trying to look important."

He grinned. "Glad you're feeling better. You keep the dog. If you need me, send her and I'll come running."

She smiled in return, but her face was still pale. "Sound planning. I'm going to let you be leader for a while." She raised her nose a bit and waved her hand in a graceful gesture. "Off you go now, my man. Find us an evening bivouac."

He bowed and headed down the trail.

* * *

Once she had covered the painful journey down the trail to the camp he made, he got her comfortable and brewed her a cup of medicinal tea from her pack, then sat back to watch her drink it.

"What happened up there?"

She ducked her head, then looked at him. "I was being stupid."

"You're never stupid."

"I wish that were true. I was going too fast."

"Why?"

She looked away. "I was trying to get down the hill ahead of you."

He took that in. "Ahead of me?"

She snorted. "Yes. I wanted to prove myself. Show you that I could hold my own."

"I don't understand."

She faced him. "Yes you do. You always know what's going on."

"Well, I'm not going to try. If I get it wrong I'll make you mad again, and if I get it right I can already tell it won't be complimentary. You tell me...if you want to."

She shook her head. "And there I was, trying to do it again."

He just waited.

"Trying to get one up on you. Using Sarasha's trick to make you tell, so I wouldn't have to."

He frowned. "You mean this is all about dominance? About who's stronger, smarter, a better leader?"

Her shoulders drooped. "No, I hope it's not that bad. I was just trying to keep up."

"You're keeping up fine."

"Yes, but that's the point, isn't it? I'm the landswoman, been doing this sort of thing all my life. I should be...what's your expression...teaching you the ropes, right? And there you are, the clumsy Seaman, trotting happily up the trail, dodging every rock in your path like it wasn't there."

He shrugged. "So I've got a good sense of balance."

She shook her head. "There's no excuse, Cheynou. You're just too hard to keep up with. And I don't mean on the trail."

"But why should that bother you?"

"Exactly. It shouldn't. And in the future I won't let it."

A long pause ensued.

"Have we settled something?"

"Only in my head. There was never anything between us to settle."

He grinned. "I'm not sure I understand completely...no, I'm really not sure... but if you're happy, then I'm happy."

She twisted in her seat and made a moue of pain. "I'm far from happy, but I got that off my chest. Now cook me dinner and treat me like the high class lady I'm pretending to be."

"That won't be hard." He turned to glance back at her. "And you can take that any way you like."

She pretended to frown, and he went back to work.

* * *

The next morning, he was awakened early by a plaintive voice.

"Cheynou? Cheynou, are you awake?"

119

He raised his head. "Aye. I've just been lying here hoping your Ladyship would let me stay in bed for a glass or two more. What may I do for your Ladyship?"

She lay back with a sigh. "I can't get up."

"I didn't think the rock was that soft around here."

"No joking, Cheynou. I can't."

He sat upright. "What's wrong?"

"My hip stiffened during the night. The moment I try to bend my leg, it hurts like blazes." She looked away, then back at him. "And I really need to get to the bushes."

"Oh. I see." He was already pulling on his boots. "Well, if you can manage to get out of your blankets, I'll get your boots on you and then maybe we can use your staff..." He suited actions to his words and, after a brief scuffle, she stood, leaning shakily on her pole.

"All right?"

She stumbled a few steps. "Yes, but..."

"That's not the problem?"

She looked away again. "I'm not going to be able to..."

"Squat."

"Aye."

He was thinking. "But you could sit."

"Yes, but on what?"

"Can you hold on for a while? This won't take long."

"Considering the alternatives, I can manage."

He drew his cutlass and stepped into the forest. With quick precision, he lopped off a smooth pole and lashed it between two trees at the right height. He bounced on it a few times, then turned to go back to camp. Kendra was there, watching him.

"Pretty impressive."

"Lashing. Seaman's skill. Nothing to it." He gestured towards the pole. "You drop your pants, put the end of your staff on the other side, lower yourself down. Finish your business, do the reverse."

"Sounds easy." She hobbled forward. "Feels difficult. Cheynou, would you mind...I mean, if it wouldn't bother you too much...?"

"You want me to stick around, just in case?"

"Well..."

He took her by the shoulders and looked into her eyes. "Travelling companions, right? Whatever it takes."

"That's right. Whatever it takes." She began untying her trousers. "This is going to hurt me more than it hurts you."

"You never know. Perhaps the blow to my young, inexperienced mind..."

"Oh, shut up and stand on my right and steady me."

"Yes, your Ladyship. Hold onto the pole, now..."

After they finished breakfast, Cheynou once again piled their blankets together and settled the invalid comfortably.

"I'm going to start the day with a more careful survey of the slide. How did it look from above?"

"I couldn't see any recent disturbances. I think it was one big rockfall that started far up the hill many years ago, and that solved any problems with smaller slides, because they're all gone as well."

"Good. So if I find a path that you and Martan can handle, we continue, and I'm sure a road-building team can work a more permanent path through later."

"That sounds good. What do you want me to do?"

He shrugged. "Heal?"

"Cheynou Chan! You know better than that. You will not leave me here with nothing to do but wait and wonder when you're going to return and help me get to the toilet!"

"All right, all right. How are you at drawing?"

"Passable, I suppose. Why? Do you want a sketch of Martan for a souvenir?"

"I was thinking of my map. It would be much safer if we each had a copy, in case one of our packs got lost or destroyed."

"Do you have enough paper?"

"I'll have to make do. Here's how you set it up..." He hauled out his master copy and showed her how to lay out smaller pages to cover the whole area.

When he left camp, she was concentrating fiercely, and Cinders seemed happy to stay with her. With a lighter heart, he set about his duties.

By lunchtime he had a better idea of the scope of the problem, and by supper he was feeling optimistic.

"I'm fairly sure there's a route that you can manage, maybe in a couple of days when your leg isn't as stiff. Tomorrow I'll move further down the slide where it's a bit less steep and look for possible routes for the permanent road. The next day, we'll have to see."

She nodded. "It all depends on my leg. When I can manage, maybe the first day we could just get through the slide. Could you find a reasonable campsite close by? Then I rest up, you return for my pack, and we make whatever distance we can in the following days."

"I can't think of a better plan."

"Of course you can't. I took all day polishing that one."

He smiled. "And your maps aren't bad, either."

Her mouth turned down. "They aren't anywhere near as beautiful as yours, but they'll do the trick."

"That they will."

12. WAVES OF STONE

Five days later, Kendra's injury had faded to a slight limp, and with the aid of the staff she could make decent progress. She was toting her pack again, although Martan still carried anything heavy.

Which was a good thing, because as they climbed higher among the peaks, the weather took a turn towards summer and their path faded away on solid rock. Time and again, Kendra was glad to rest while her guide explored different possibilities.

The trail they were on at the moment was faint, and it took all of Cheynou's concentration to follow it. Cinders, her tongue lolling, panted beside him. Kendra and Martan scrambled along behind, both sweating in the heat.

"Are you sure this is the trail?"

"Not really."

"Oh. Thanks. I feel much better, knowing that."

He stopped, mopped his brow with his shirtsleeve and leaned on his staff, looking around. "I can tell you why we're going where we're going, if that would help."

"In the figurative sense, or in reality?"

He grinned back at her. "If you're thinking of the netherworld because of this heat, you should know that the purgatory of the Sea People is cold. Cold and wet. And it's up in the sky, same as heaven."

He turned and pointed. "We're heading for that gap in the mountains, there. I don't know much about mountains, but it seems to me they often look like waves on the ground."

"Waves?" She reached out. "I think the heat is too much for you."

He shook her hand off his forehead. "I mean it. If you look at these mountains, they're wrinkled in rows, just like waves, with long, narrow valleys between them, like the troughs between the waves, all running the same direction."

"And here I thought they were just lumps of rock." She peered out at their surroundings and finally nodded. "I see what you mean. Must have been some kind of wind."

He acknowledged the humour with a very small grin. "So, if they act like waves, then there are large ones and small ones, and they tend to come in groups. When you're at the helm, you try to steer a course through the waves so that you don't ride up on the high ones and you find a path through the troughs. That's what I've been doing."

"You've been steering us like a ship?"

"That's what I know how to do." He pointed again. "The other thing you do, if you have to cross a bunch of waves, is look for a low one. That low spot over there seems to be in the middle of a group of flatter mountains. Either it's the pass, or we have the best chance of finding the pass around there. So that's where we're going. So far, this trail seems to be heading in that direction, so I'm assuming it's the right trail."

"What if it takes us somewhere else?"

He shrugged. "Several possibilities. First, it takes us to the right pass. No problem. Second, it disappears, and we come back and try again. Third, we find a fork that takes us the right way."

"Or, fourth, we find some evidence that the scouts from the north passed this way."

"I've been keeping an eye out."

"Remember, way back at that pool where we swam?"

He grinned and sniffed his armpit. "I'm not likely to forget."

"Not that. I remember you walked around looking for a good place to camp. When you found one, somebody else had used it. Clen once told me that when two experienced travellers cover the same area in the same direction, even if there's no trail, they often follow the same route because that's where the going is easiest."

124

"Reasonable. So if we're on the right trail, we might find evidence of our little friends."

"We could keep an eye open."

"What a good idea. Ready to go on?"

She shook her head, once. "Any time you are."

He turned and trudged down the trail. "At least it's downhill."

"Oh, that's something I've been meaning to tell you."

"What?"

She came up beside him. "When you walk downhill, especially when it's steep, don't slap your feet down like that."

"Why not?"

"It shows that your ankles are loose. Two reasons that's bad. The first one, it means your knees are also loose, and that makes them sore quicker. Second one, if your ankles are loose, you could roll one over on a stone."

"So how are you supposed to walk?"

"Go heel-toe, holding your toe up a little as you set it down. Bend your knees and sit back if the trail is steeper than this. It really helps."

He grinned. "One of those things a seaman wouldn't know. Glad I brought you."

"Today, I'm not as glad as other days."

"Me either." He turned down the trail again. "Let's get another two leagues in before we stop."

They slogged on through the heat and the rough terrain. It was not all downhill, and they found the second league taxing, up and over the shoulder of a huge cliff. However, there was nowhere to camp and no water, so they pushed on.

"How much longer do you think we'll be in these mountains?" Kendra wiped her brow. "It's been eight days already."

"True, but if we went straight back, we'd be at the top in three."

125

"You think so?"

"The map does not lie."

She slapped his arm with the back of her hand. "But we're not so sure about the man who made it. Move on."

Finally, they reached the top, and a cool breeze blew in their faces. From the height of the cliff they looked down on a wider valley, stretching away to the northwest.

Cheynou pulled his sweaty shirt away from his body so the wind could cool him, and stared around wordlessly. The mountains ringed them in, towering high above, stretching away to east and west as far as they could see. Behind them, the pass they had just traversed was cut off by the shoulder of the mountain that seemed to lean over them. In front, the valley dropped gradually off to the left. Across from them the mountains were lower, and the pass they had been aiming for seemed near.

He stretched his arms, felt the wind push at him. "Isn't it wonderful?"

"Sort of pretty, all right."

He grinned at her understatement. "You get an idea why I want to explore? The world is full of scenes like this. Some of them are beautiful, some are terrible, but so many are different and new. I just want to get out there and see as many of them as I can, and tell people about them and make it so others can go where I went."

Kendra tilted her head, raised her eyebrows. "How can a girl compete?"

Puzzled, he stared at her. Her comment seemed to have nothing to do with what he had been saying.

She shook her head. "With all that beauty out there calling you, how are you ever going to want to find a girl, settle down with her?"

"I hadn't thought about that."

She sniffed. "Whoever she is, she'll be thinking about it, believe me."

"Who?"

"Cheychan, you dummy. The girl that falls in love with you."

"Oh. And here I thought I was talking about mountains."

"You were, my friend. You were."

"But you weren't."

She merely shook her head. "So where do we go from here?"

He shrugged out of his pack. "I'd like to take some readings. This place has a great view." He grinned over his shoulder. "And yes, I do know your last question could be taken two ways, but once again, I'm ignoring it in the hope that you'll explain what you're really talking about."

She sighed, shook her head and turned her attention to the ground. "If this place is so good, maybe the northern scouts used it for the same thing."

He looked around as well. "If they did, they would have made some kind of permanent mark so that they could use it again."

"Our people use piles of stones called cairns."

"There isn't a cairn here, so it would be something else. I'm going to use that flat slab of rock over there because it's raised up and easy to lay my tools out on..."

She walked over, looked down, "...and it has this nice pair of lines scratched onto it in the shape of a cross!"

They stood and stared at the figure carved in the stone, then looked at each other. "It's them!"

"They were here!"

"I told you!"

They embraced impulsively and danced around, shouting. Cinders, caught up in it all, circled them, yapping fiercely.

"I think we'd better calm down before the dog goes off the cliff."

Kendra looked over her shoulder. "We aren't that close."

He dropped his embrace and turned to pick up his equipment. "It's just such an obvious place. Look. I can see the pass, I can see...wait a minute. Look. One side of the cross is longer."

"Where does it point?"

He grinned at her, moved around. "Where do you think?"

"Right at the pass!"

"Right at it!" He fumbled in his satchel, pulling out a piece of paper. "I'm going to make a map of this valley with the cross in the centre and all the peaks and landmarks on it. This must be a key navigation point."

He started work, and Kendra watched, fascinated. After a while, he forgot everything else, trying to make his observations as exact as possible, getting all the angles just right...

"Cheynou...?

"Huh?"

"Cheynou, look at this." Her finger was beside the cross in the rock.

"What?"

"Moss."

"Yes, that's moss."

"It's growing in the mark."

He peered closer. "I guess it is. So what?"

"Moss grows very slowly at this altitude."

"Oh."

"This cross has been here a long time."

He regarded the marks again. "I think you're right, now that I look at it."

"So it wasn't made by our little friends."

"No. I wonder what that means."

"Probably that their people have come here before."

"Which means that we must be getting closer to their civilization."

"I'd say so."

They grinned at each other, and Cheynou went back to his work with new enthusiasm.

Later, as they started down the trail again, they kept their eyes open. Sure enough, when they were down among the trees again, Kendra stopped, pointing.

"What?"

"A blaze."

"A what?" The tree she was pointing at had a small bare spot about shoulder high, with old patches of pitch crumbling away from it.

"A blaze. Made several years ago. Look how much the tree has grown since."

"How do you know it isn't just a scar from a bouncing rock?"

She moved closer. "Because it took two swipes of the axe to make that cut, and you can see the mark of the second cut in the middle."

He peered at the blaze, and sure enough there was a straight line running diagonally across the centre of the dead, bleached wood.

"I see."

"So this trail has been used at least once, as long ago as it takes a tree to grow that much." She looked at the tree. "About ten years, I suppose. Could be twenty."

"Twenty years."

"Hmm."

"Aye. Hmm."

They continued along the trail more confidently. *We're going somewhere!*

They made better progress, now, because Cheynou felt it less important to look for alternate routes. That night they camped in a beautiful spot with an overhanging shelf, almost a cave, for shelter, and a slab of rock leaning against the opening, just inviting them to put a fire at its base to reflect the heat back into their camp. As if they needed any heat. Nearby, a stream plunged off the mountainside into a rocky pool and ran merrily away down beside the trail.

"What are you waiting for? Start the fire."

Cheynou ran his fingers over the rock slab. "Look at the black."

"Lots of rocks are black, especially near the ground. Moss or something."

"That comes off in your fingers?"

"Soot?"

"Someone has camped here before."

"I'm not so surprised. Light the fire."

"Wait a moment." He pulled out his knife and began to dig at the base of the rock.

"Ashes and blackened wood."

"You said people have camped here. We saw the blazes."

"No. Those blazes were about ten years old. Look how deep this goes."

"So people have passed here for much longer than that. Hundreds of years maybe."

He pushed the pile of ashes back into the hole, wiped his knife, and began to light the fire. "I wonder how long."

But Kendra was not behind him. He glanced up, and she was wandering around the larger clearing, looking at trees.

The fire was just beginning to crackle cheerfully when her voice, full of triumph, brought his head up.

"Cheynou, come here."

"What?"

She was standing in the middle of the clearing. "All right. If people always camp in the same places, think of this as a campsite, years ago."

"All right."

"So. Fire over there. Beds in the cave. Not much room."

"There's lots of room."

130

"For us. But not for many people. Look at this." She strode over, kicked at a mossy pile of rock.

He glanced at it, then looked closer. "This is built. A stone wall."

"That's right. Roofed over to extend the shelter of the cave, it would double the number of people who could sleep there."

"At least six."

"Right. Having found that, then I started thinking. Pack animals, right?"

"I suppose so. What about them?"

"Where do you tether them? Ask a farm girl: downwind of camp." She led the way and, sure enough, there were more mounds of fallen wall downhill from the cave.

"Last..." She led him back to the centre of the clearing. "Look at the trees."

He looked at the trees.

"Don't you see?"

"I see the trees. Those really are trees, not much doubt."

"No, no, the size of them."

"You're talking to a sailor, here. The only thing I'd care about was if they were straight enough for spars."

"Come on, Cheynou. Look at them. They're all the same size!"

He looked again. "I suppose."

"Which means they are all the same age."

"Oh."

"But there are larger trees out there."

"Oh! So at one time, the clearing was larger."

"Right, and we know how long."

"We do?" He peered up at her, then at the trees.

"Yes. You can tell how old a tree is by counting the rings."

"The rings."

131

"Yes, stupid, the rings. Stop copying me and think!"

"All right, all right. You can count the rings. What does that mean?"

"The trees grow one ring every year. So the number of rings shows how old the tree is."

"I didn't know that."

"Oh. Then I'm sorry, you're not stupid. Just ignorant."

He glowered at her. "You really are pleased with yourself, aren't you?"

"Yes, I am. All we have to do is cut half-way into one of these trees, count the rings, and we'll know how long ago it was that pack trains of supplies needing six people to tend the twenty animals, used this trail. Yes, I counted the stalls."

He looked appraisingly at the trees. "Those are pretty big trees."

"I could just estimate, but trees grow faster down on the coast than they do up here in the mountains, where there is a shorter growing season."

"Am I ever glad I brought a farm girl along."

"Don't you forget it. Now, I brought you along to do the heavy work, so cut us a tree."

"Couldn't we just use a fallen one? Can you figure out how long a tree has been dead by the decay?"

"Sort of, but it's different..."

"...I know, because of the climate."

"Yes."

"All right. There's a recent blowdown over there. Even an ignorant sailor can see when there are still dry needles on the branches. We don't have to cut all the way through, just half-way?"

"Yes. We can count some of the rings where the trunk is broken, and cut where we need to."

They attacked the splintered trunk with a will, and soon had it figured out. "Seventy-five, give or take."

"Right. And since this distraction was your fault, you can re-light the fire while I find more firewood."

13.   Rescue

"Hold."

The word came quietly but Cheynou was instantly on the alert, checking both Cinders and Martan. Sure enough, both sets of ears were up, muzzles indicating something off to the east of the trail. He regarded them a moment, raised his head to scan the immediate terrain, checked the animals again, spoke softly.

"People."

Kendra raised her eyebrows.

"If it was a prey animal, the dog would be more interested, the donkey less. If it was a dangerous animal, both would be worried. They aren't. Just interested."

"But they don't know how to tell if people are dangerous or not."

"Cinders seems to know, but let's take it real slow anyway."

They left the trail to the right, easing their way, spreading apart through the small pine trunks, half their senses on the terrain, half on their animals.

After about three chains, Kendra stopped. Before she had spoken quietly; now she whispered. "Smoke."

He could not smell it, but he nodded and they crept ahead, keeping in cover wherever they could.

Then the dog sprinted forward, disappearing behind a tight group of small spruces that blocked their view. There was a loud exclamation in a foreign language, a scrabbling sound, then silence. Then the dog yipped once, her herding bark, and a man's voice said something unintelligible.

Exchanging a puzzled glance, they pushed hurriedly through the spruces and broke into a small clearing. Opposite them stood a gnarled, open-grown bull spruce, its spreading boughs sheltering a makeshift campsite: nothing much more than a fire, a blanket, a waterskin hung close by and a hunter's bow leaning against a log. Backed up against the tree trunk was a dark-skinned man, one hand propping himself up on a crutch, the other holding a short, heavy sword. His left leg was heavily bandaged from the knee down.

In front of him, Cinders crouched in her herding position: head low, paws wide to either side, eyes steady on her prey.

When the two strangers burst into his campsite, the man straightened on his crutch, then winced in obvious pain. Kendra snapped her fingers and the dog returned to her side, spinning quickly again to face the man.

He said something that probably meant, "At least the dog is under control."

"The dog, maybe."

He looked uncomprehending.

She smiled, pointed at the dog, and nodded. Then she put her thumb over her shoulder, indicating the donkey, and shook her head, waggling her hand in a 'maybe yes, maybe no' motion.

The man made a grimace that was an attempt to smile, but his sword point did not waver.

Seeing the pain in his face, she suggested that he sit, gesturing with her hand at the same time. The sword point rose and he shook his head, talking grimly at her.

She shook her head as well, in concern. "Well, if you're going to be completely stupid about it..."

Cheynou, focusing intently on the foreign words, was shocked when Kendra walked directly up to the man, pushed the sword aside and gently forced him to sit, carefully cushioning his injured foot as he did so. As soon as he was down, she slung out of her pack and stuffed it under his leg to raise it. Her coat went behind his head and, before he had time to realize what was happening, the dark man was resting comfortably. With no other option, he chose to lie back, closing his eyes briefly. Then he spoke again, slower and with some hesitation.

135

Cheynou frowned. "That was a bit of a risk."

She snorted. "No man ever hit a woman when she was making mother hen noises. He could barely stay on his feet...foot; I bet that leg's broken."

"If you're finished mothering him for a moment, I'll try to talk to him."

"Do you think you can?"

"He's tried two different languages on us, maybe three. Some of the words sounded familiar."

"How could you pick that up so fast? All I heard was gobbledegook."

He grinned, shrugged. "You had mother hen things on your mind. This shouldn't take a moment. Keep watch."

He knelt facing the stranger and began to talk.

He knew that Kendra would scan their surroundings, depending also on the animals for warning. Everything seemed calm. She pulled a blanket from the donkey's pack and used it to replace her knapsack under the man's foot. He winced slightly as she moved it, smiling apologetically, but his attention was all on Cheynou.

As Cheynou had predicted, it didn't take long. He sat back on his heels and looked at her. "He speaks a really strange version of TradeSpeak. I suppose you could say I speak a really strange version of his trading language. He doesn't know it very well, unfortunately. Mostly single words. Which is fine, because I don't understand many of them."

"What's his story?"

"I was just getting to that. He seems in a lot of pain. Is there any way of easing him?"

She leaned forward, caught the man's attention. "Where is the leg broken? Here? Higher?"

Her gestures were so clear that Cheynou felt no need to translate.

The man indicated a point just above halfway up the shin.

"Well, that's the problem. If the break's up there, you have to tie the knee as well. Every time you move your knee," she demonstrated with her own leg, "you pull the lower muscles, and it hurts."

He seemed to get the message, nodding painfully.

"We'll have to lengthen the splint. That should help some. I'll check to see if the bones are lined up properly, if I can." She made a small face. "I've never done this kind of thing by myself before. I've helped with plenty, though."

"We won't tell him that."

"He'll probably figure it out."

It was a slow and painful process, and the patient was white-faced and shaking by the time Kendra had finished splinting his leg straight from the hip down. He lay back, his eyes closed, until his breathing calmed. Then he opened his eyes, looking around for his pack. When Kendra handed it over, he dug in and came up with a small sack of tea leaves. He made motions like drinking then sleeping, talking slowly to Cheynou all the while.

"I can figure that out. It's a pain-killer or soporific. I'll stoke up the fire and boil a kettle. I gather we're staying?"

She went to Martan, who had been waiting patiently, and mimed taking off the pack saddle, looking at the foreigner on the assumption that raised eyebrows meant a question in any language.

He responded with a shrug that said there wasn't much he could do about it if it mattered, but it probably didn't.

Satisfied, she went about setting up their camp around his while Cheynou carried on a halting conversation.

As they talked, Cheynou began to grasp the syntax of the new version of Trade, and it seemed the man was dredging up more vocabulary from his memory. By the time Kendra had made the tea, he had quite a lot of information, but the injured man's energy was flagging.

"He broke his leg when his horse slipped in a canyon back there," he pointed to show her. "His companion patched him up and got him this far before they realized it just wasn't going to work. The friend has gone for help. He says two days. I don't know if it happened two days ago, or his companion is expected back in two days. In any case, we can do our best for him until help comes."

"At least we can keep him company." She smiled gently down at the man, her hand on his shoulder as he drank the tea. He sighed and gave her a weak smile in response as he handed back the cup.

"More?"

The man nodded, showing one finger.

"I didn't know how strong to make it. I figure he'll know by the taste. I'd hate to kill him with an overdose of his own medicine."

Cheynou nodded. "Hard to explain when his friends show up."

He turned to the man and spoke, receiving a reassuring shake of the head in reply. "He says it isn't very strong."

"That's too bad. He needs it." She turned to the man, hand on his forehead in the ages-old gesture. "How do you feel now?"

Again the weak smile and the eyes closed briefly. "That word was 'sleep', I think."

Cheynou nodded. "You communicate with him very well."

"So do you. How did you pick up his language so fast?"

"Like I said, we speak different versions of the same Trade tongue. It seems to be coming back to both of us; we're finding words we have in common and I'm starting to pick up some of his."

"Already?"

He shrugged. "They say that after three languages it gets easier, and this isn't really a new language."

"After three? How many languages do you know?"

"Four. Five, if you count Helmsmen's Cant."

"Helmsmen have their own language?"

"Not really, but if you sat down with us when we were discussing our trade, you wouldn't understand one word in three."

"I never knew you could speak five languages."

"The Sea People speak the same language as most of you Coast People. How would you know?" He felt vaguely uncomfortable. "It's not a big thing, really. I started learning other languages when I was young, when it's easy, and just kept on. All Helmsmen do. Whenever a Helmsman gets a chance to talk to any traveller, it's his duty to find out as much information about the world as he can. We all learn the Standard Three Languages and Trade, of course."

"I see. And what do you call the language we speak?"

He grinned. "SeaSpeak. It's one of the Standard Three."

"SeaSpeak?"

"Aye. LandSpeak is what the interior people speak, farther east. They're related languages, which makes it easy to learn them. Same syntax, some words that sound the same. The Inari speak a really weird version of LandSpeak. I think they've been out of touch for centuries."

While this talk had been going on, their host's eyes had been drooping, and now Kendra readjusted his padding so that he was lying down more. She wrapped the blanket closely around him, checked everything she could. Just as she finished, he grasped her hand and said a word, indistinctly.

"What was that?"

"Thanks, of course."

"Thought so. What's for supper?"

"Salt pork and biscuits. What else?"

She shrugged, sighed. "How stimulating."

Cheynou clapped her on the shoulder. "Don't worry. Maybe if we're really nice to this guy, he'll take us home and feed us some real food."

She looked over her shoulder at the sleeping man. "As long as he doesn't take us home and make slaves of us or something equally nasty."

"We'll have to be careful about that." His head came up, and he looked around.

"You know, if you don't mind cooking tonight, I think I'd like to take a gander down the trail."

"It wouldn't hurt to know ahead of time when the rescue party might show up."

"Exactly. You'll be all right?"

She looked pointedly at the sleeping man. "I don't see him as much of a problem."

He felt vaguely worried. "Just stay away from him. If he grabbed you…"

"…then I'd kick his sore leg. He'd let go."

"You are truly a nasty person, Kendra."

"Only if I need to be."

"I'll keep that in mind." He rose. "I'll take the dog. We won't go far."

"Just as long as it takes me to prepare you a wonderful meal."

He snapped his fingers for Cinders and made his way back to the trail. It had grown from an animal track to a noticeable path, and he recognized more old, grown-over blazes on some of the trees. He moved along briskly, easy without his heavy pack. Cinders ranged ahead, staying just in sight, checking back with her pack leader often.

They walked until the trail broke out over the side of a ridge and he got a view. The ground sloped away steeply and he could see the path in several places where it looped down. He watched a long time, but no one moved on the trail. Satisfied for the moment, he returned to camp.

"How's the patient?"

She turned up one side of her mouth. "If the smell of my gourmet cooking didn't wake him, then that tea was stronger than I thought."

She handed him a ship's biscuit, softened by the steam of the kettle, with a slice of boiled salt pork lying on top. He finished it without comment, hardly noticing. It was what he had eaten all his life.

After supper was cleaned up, they took Martan down to a small meadow nearby and left him there, happily munching. While they were away from camp, they could talk in normal voices.

"Who do you think this guy is?"

She frowned. "His clothes are well made. Fine weave, for hunting clothes. It's a nice bow, too. Laminated horn and wood, recurve. Very powerful. I doubt if I could pull it halfway."

"So we don't know their standards, but he seems well off. Speaks several languages, good haircut, sword callouses on his hand."

"That's an interesting weapon he has."

"Short and sturdy. A real hack-and-thrust."

"For use against armour."

"I'd say so."

Cheynou considered. "So with any luck, we have a chance to do a good deed for a wealthy man. In gratitude, maybe he'll put us up at his home until we can learn the language, figure things out."

She nodded. "Unless they clap us in prison or kill us because they think we're barbarian spies from over the mountains."

"That's what we are, aren't we?"

"I hadn't thought of us that way. We're certainly not sent by anyone official."

He grinned. "Quite the opposite."

"We just have to persuade him of that."

He sobered. "We are going to have to decide what to tell them."

"In what way?"

He frowned, thinking. "Well, it's the idea of being spies, and the reverse." He saw her uncomprehending expression and explained. "We're the first recent contact his people have had with the Sea People: maybe your people as well. The Sea People are going to be a growing power up on the Prairies."

"If they survive."

"Exactly. And Orrick Bren has vowed to continue Captain Tourn's idea of breeding the strongest, fiercest, fighting horses he possibly can. Who is he going to use those horses against?"

"I see."

"That's right. So, what if we tell these people about our people, and they decide to send an army to wipe us out?"

"Do you think that's possible?"

"Possible, but not likely. Even so, I don't think I'm going to tell him too much about us until I know more of what they're like."

"If he's a reasonable man, he'll understand that."

Cheynou frowned. "And if he's unreasonable, he'll lock us in a dungeon and stick sharp things into us until we tell."

"Cheynou! Don't say things like that!"

He sighed. "I'm sorry. Sometimes I worry about having brought you into this kind of danger."

"You're worried about me?"

"Yes. This was my idea. If anything goes wrong, it's my fault. So it's my responsibility to make sure it doesn't go wrong."

She stopped walking, laid a hand on his arm. "Cheynou, I'm pleased that you worry about me like that. I'm not going to tell you to stop. It keeps us safe." She turned and resumed walking. "I worry about you the same way."

He felt a small glow in his chest. Not wanting to spoil the moment, he said nothing, merely followed her slim figure back up the trail to camp.

Their guest awoke after dark and seemed more comfortable. He caught Kendra's eye in the firelight, slapped the new splint and nodded with satisfaction. She nodded in return.

With his new comfort, the man's interest turned outward. "Who are you?"

Cheynou smiled. "Barbarians from the south."

"True?"

"I am. Sea People. Great Southern Ocean."

"Great Southern Ocean?" The man looked dubious.

"True. Great Southern Ocean. Sailors." He pointed at himself. "Helmsman. You say Navigator."

"Nav...navi...?"

"Navigator." His hand swept to the stars above, and he made a pretence of sighting, writing, measuring.

"Oh. Navi...gator. I know."

"My name: Cheynou Chan."

The man struggled to sit straighter and sketched a formal salute. "Cheynou Chan. My name: Cruzen Rochana."

Cheynou mimicked the man's salute, repeated his name, turned to Kendra and introduced her as well. She followed the ritual, then spoke sharply. "I hope we're not going to have too much more of this. He needs to stay still." She emphasized her meaning by pushing down on Cruzen's shoulder. Meekly, he slumped back down, but he looked up at her slyly, speaking to Cheynou. "Cheynou Navigator. Kendra wife?"

Cheynou hid the sudden lurch of his heart. "No, not wife." He did not have the words in this language. He probably didn't have the words in any language. "Cheynou traveller. Kendra traveller. Friends travel."

"Ah. Kendra is...?"

He turned to her. "He's pretty insistent. He wants to know what you are. What do we tell him?"

She shrugged. "I don't know. What am I?"

He returned the shrug. "I don't know if you don't know. A member of the idle rich, I suppose."

"Good enough. Tell him that."

He nodded, turned to the man. "Kendra is lady. Lady Kendra."

The man would have sat up again but for her restraining hand. Thwarted, he took her hand from his shoulder and touched it to his brow. "Lady Kendra."

She nodded regally and turned to Cheynou. "If I'm the lady and you're my guide, I guess that means I'm the leader of this expedition, aren't I?"

He snorted. "So that changes anything?"

"I will have the proper respect!"

He snorted again and turned to the stranger, who was watching this exchange with a bemused smile. "Women."

The smile widened.

Cheynou sat back. "Cheynou Navigator. Kendra lady. Cruzen...?"

"Ah. Cruzen is lord. Lord Rochana. Cruzen soldier. Cruzen farmer."

"A man of many talents." He translated this for Kendra. "He must be a mover and a shaker in these parts."

"Good luck for us, maybe."

"Hope so."

"I wonder if this mover and shaker has eaten."

"Right." He turned to the man, but Kendra's hand-to-mouth gesture had already brought a pleased smile.

"Maybe he won't be so happy when he sees what he gets."

She shot him a warning glance. "He who complains cooks the next meal."

"Yep, salt pork and biscuit is so much better when I warm it up."

However, the man, after a quick glance over the offering, ate it with apparent relish.

"No food?"

Cruzen made a 'give me' gesture to his pack, took it from Kendra and reached inside, pulling out a leather pouch with a few nuts, raisins, and other dried things in it.

"All?"

The man nodded ruefully. "Two days."

"And just that water?"

Again he nodded, lifted the skin and drank. Then he shook it, judging its weight carefully.

Kendra laughed, took the skin from him and disappeared towards the nearby stream, returning with a full, dripping skin.

He took it and drank deeper.

They made the lord a new pot of the medicinal tea. Cheynou assisted him in the difficult and painful journey for a call of nature, and as the fire died they all slept.

Cheynou woke in the early dawn with a feeling of unease. He stared around their campsite, but all was still. Bright eyes in the next bed showed that the injured man was awake and uncomfortable. Across the ashes of the fire Martan stood, his head up, ears scanning. Cinders seemed unaffected.

Cheynou rose, stretched, dressed and blew the coals up into a new fire for breakfast. Once again he helped Lord Rochana to the bushes, then lowered him onto his bedroll. By the time Kendra was rising sleepily from her blankets, he had meat on the pan, biscuit around the edges to soften.

"You're up early, Cheynou."

"Aye. We've got trouble."

That woke her, and her head came up, listening. "What?" Cruzen, sensing her worry, looked around as well.

"We've got to get on the trail." He repeated the phrase in Trade.

Cruzen smiled sadly and waved a 'good-bye' gesture.

"No. You come."

The man slapped his straight leg, shook his head. "Why?"

"Storm."

Both of the others looked at the sky. Both, in their respective languages, repeated the word doubtfully.

Cheynou nodded firmly, spoke in Trade, translating as well. "Storm. Sailor say storm? Storm comes. Maybe snow."

"Snow? It's summer."

The dark man exhibited similar doubt. Cheynou ignored him for the moment, speaking to Kendra. "I've heard stories about snow at this altitude, even in summer. I have this feeling, and I listen to my feelings. Why did you put your coat on?"

She shrugged. "It's cool this morning."

"More than that. There's a bitter chill in the air. We're going to have a storm, and it could even snow. Look at Martan. He thinks so, too. If that's the case, Cruzen's friends won't be here to get him for a week, maybe two. We've got food for that long, sure, but he needs to get some proper help for that leg. What if it isn't set right?"

Kendra scowled, turned to the man. "Snow. Storm. We go." She pointed down the mountain. Cruzen winced, shook his head slowly, unsure.

"What are we going to do about moving him? He can't even ride on Martan in that splint."

Cheynou grinned. "The first thing we're going to do is eat this hearty breakfast I have prepared. Then I have an idea."

"I thought you might."

They ate, and while Kendra packed up the camp, Cheynou went into the clump of spruces across the clearing. There, deep in the dry centre of the glade, he found two small trees that, having lost the fight for sun and nourishment, had

146

stretched upwards until they died. Now they were long and slim, seasoned dry and tough. He chopped them down and dragged them out.

"Are you making a stretcher?"

"Sort of. The Inari call it a slider. I saw one in their camp." He lashed the two thin ends together, spreading out the thick ends. Going back to the spruce grove, he returned with several short, straight sticks, which he lashed parallel to each other across the two longer sticks, forming a triangle.

"Now, if Martan will only cooperate." He lifted the small end and pulled it over the donkey's rump, laying a blanket under it to pad the animal's delicate skin. The fine ends of the poles rested against the packsaddle, and a few twists of rope secured it all. Martan waited patiently through all this, turning with interest to see what was happening at his back. When Cheynou led him around the camp in a big circle, he twitched and bucked experimentally a few times, but soon settled down.

"Your turn."

"You want me to sit on that thing?"

"If our patient is going to, we'd better practise first."

"What if he kicks?"

"The cross-poles will protect you. They're too close for him to get a good swing. I think."

Kendra shook her head and sat on the poles, gingerly at first, then with her whole weight. Again, the donkey looked back with interest, then trudged gamely around the campsite again.

"It's quite springy."

"I hope so. It isn't going to be a fun trip for Cruzen, but we have to get down the hill far enough that the snow isn't a problem."

The dark man had been watching all this and when Cheynou stopped the donkey in front of him, he was ready. All three bedrolls served as padding under him. He hoisted himself up with his hands, Kendra guided the injured leg,

147

Cheynou lifted under his arms, and they slid him onto the contrivance.

They spent some time making sure he was as comfortable as possible. Cruzen bore it all in silence, only commenting once.

"What did he say?"

"He said, 'Good donkey'."

She chuckled. "I hope he still thinks that a few chains down the trail."

They made a last check of the camp, shouldered their packs and set off. It was rough going through the forest, and Cruzen bit back moans when he bumped over the larger roots. However, once they were on the trail, the journey went much smoother. Martan moved with stolid surety and the springy stems took most of the roughness out of the bumps.

Half a league down the trail they had to stop, not for comfort, but because the first splattering drops of rain found their way through the trees that arched over them. They covered the injured man with their sailcloth tent and on they went.

It was a gentle pull for the donkey, a gradual slope that wound down through the trees. Throughout the morning they moved in easy stages, stopping often to give the donkey and the patient a rest. As they went on, the air grew colder, and then Cheynou looked to Kendra to see if she had noticed.

She had. "Snow."

"And we've dropped several chains in altitude."

She nodded grimly and they moved on through the increasing flurries of fat, heavy, flakes.

They stopped at noon for a short break, enough to make a fire for food and more of the patient's medicine. As the afternoon trek began, he seemed to fall into a half-doze, merely existing through the pain, and only the stiffest jolts brought a grimace to his face.

At one spot, the trail traversed a rockslide, and the way was so rough that Kendra and Cheynou each took the end of one pole and walked him through, counting on Martan to set the pace. It was doubly difficult, because of the width of the slider, which forced them to stumble through the loose rock on the sides of the trail.

"Good donkeys."

Cheynou translated this for Kendra as they set the poles down at the end of the slide. "Tell him 'tired donkeys.' That was tough."

Cruzen nodded. "Thank you."

They looked back up the trail, as the swirling snow blotted out the mountain above them. With grim faces, they turned downhill again.

The rain continued to fall, mixed with the snow, melting any flake that reached the ground. As the afternoon progressed and they dropped lower and lower, the snowflakes disappeared, and soon they were moving through a lessening downpour. Cheynou called a halt.

"The trail doesn't look good ahead. You take a rest while I look it over."

They stopped gratefully, and he left Kendra checking the padding over Martan's rump. Sure enough, an avalanche path intercepted the trail, which was forced to wind through a jumble of huge rocks. This was going to be a tough one.

While Cheynou was surveying the situation, Cinders' ears went up, pointing down the valley.

He stood stock still, listening, and soon he heard the jingle of harness. He turned and jogged back up to his party. He had no wish to meet these men alone.

"Friends come."

Cruzen smiled, held out a hand. "Friends here."

Cheynou grinned and met the other's clasp.

He swung Martan half around so that Cruzen could see who was coming up the trail. Then there came a relieved shout, which the man answered. Five horsemen and six horses appeared out of the mist at a gallop, sliding to a stop at a reasonable distance, the men dismounting rapidly. Three of them strode forward, puzzled frowns warring with their smiles. Cruzen greeted them casually.

They spoke in a language Cheynou could not fully understand, but he got the gist. It went something like:

"Took you long enough."

"Are you all right?"

"We thought the storm…"

"What is this contraption?"

"Who are these people?"

Cruzen waved them all to an immediate silence. Cheynou filed this sign of obedience away for future thought.

Cruzen switched to Trade.

"This Cheynou Chan. Navigator for Sea People of the Great Southern Ocean." He then translated this, going for considerably longer, saying something which drew awed stares from his followers. Then he turned to Kendra.

"This Kendra of Kirigata. Lady Kendra." Again his translation went on for some time, and serious nods resulted. The lord motioned his men forward.

"Thousand-Prime: Maksa."

The soldier bowed over Kendra's hand, repeated her name carefully, grasped Cheynou's arm firmly and repeated his name. The two travellers copied the ritual.

"Hundred-Prime: Faranos Rochana" Again, the ritual. This was a young lad, barely Kendra's age. His similarity to the lord, more than his name, marked him as a relative.

"Gottwen: Doctor." After the introduction, Cheynou saw Kendra catch the doctor's eye and wipe her brow. The man nodded, turning to his patient with a brisk change of mood.

However, his master brushed off his ministrations, speaking firmly. Then he turned to Cheynou. "Trail ahead?"

"Many rocks. Many turns." He poked a thumb down the trail at the two soldiers holding the horses. "Strong donkeys?"

The lowlanders looked surprised to hear their lord's laughter. Then he started snapping orders, and soon they were moving again, with Cheynou leading the donkey carefully through the rocks, two sturdy men lifting the poles, and Kendra walking anxiously at one side of her patient, the doctor on the other. The other men had disappeared down the trail with the horses, looking for a good campsite. At times when the rocks were close to the trail it was necessary to lift the poles higher and pass them on to the person in front, so the doctor and Kendra got a good workout as well.

Finally, they were through the rocks, and Cruzen allowed his men, sweating in spite of the cold rain, to set his poles down. They resumed their trek and soon came to a flat area where the packhorse was already unloaded, a large tent was almost set up and a cheerful fire was crackling near the shelter of another spreading spruce tree.

With a grateful sigh, the lord allowed himself to be lifted out of the slider. His men carried him, with obvious care, to the thick mattress that had been set up under the tree near the fire. Before he lay down, he gestured to Cheynou. "Donkey."

Cheynou brought Martan close, so the man could stroke his silky nose and scratch behind his ears. "Good donkey." Cruzen smiled up at Cheynou. "Good, good, donkey."

The doctor closed in, and there ensued a sharp, forceful discussion. It ended with a decision not to remove Kendra's splint. When she had re-splinted the leg, she had left the area of the break exposed, so the doctor was satisfied that he could check the injury well enough for the present.

"Good work. Army trained?"

Cheynou glanced at the man beside him. Thousand-Prime Maksa was more fluent in a much more understandable Trade. In relief, he spoke comfortably for the first time with these people. "No," he gestured to Kendra, "farm trained."

151

The soldier grinned. "Ah. Farms are dangerous. Better to be a soldier."

There was a chuckle among those who understood, and translations had to be made for the rest.

Once the doctor was happy with his patient and had administered the appropriate potions ('no pain, but no sleep'), everyone was able to relax, and they sat around getting each other up to date on their parts of the story. Maksa was pleased to keep Cheynou informed, but by the time the information got to Kendra, the story was considerably diluted.

"I've got to learn this language."

"I'm working on it already. Just listen hard. It will come."

"Just listen hard? Easy for you, man with five languages."

"There isn't any other way."

"True."

"They have many words that sound the same as ours. Listen for them."

They turned back to the conversation.

It had been a hard day; Lord Rochana, in spite of the new medicine, was soon fading, and his doctor ordered him into his tent. With a sheepish grin to Kendra and a more formal bow of thanks to Cheynou, the lord allowed himself to be carried away. The two travellers set their canvas under the opposite side of the tree, hung their damp cloaks in close to the trunk and slipped gratefully into their bedrolls.

Cheynou had just settled in when Kendra's groping hand found his. "We did well today, Cheynou."

He returned the squeeze. "I think so."

Her fingers touched his cheek lightly as she withdrew her hand. "Especially you." She chuckled softly. "Good donkey."

The next morning brought improved weather and more curious looks from the Rochana party. They had been too busy tending to their master the night before, but now they had leisure to investigate these strangers. The young soldiers were greatly disappointed that they could not communicate with Kendra, and were reprimanded mildly by their officer for their lighthearted approach to a lady.

She grinned and shrugged helplessly, and they went on with their work.

Lord Rochana would travel in considerable more style and comfort for the rest of the trip. Long poles were suspended on either side of two horses with a stretcher between them. Once he was lifted into place, propped comfortably with pillows and blankets in a semi-reclining position, his leg wedged firmly, he swung gently to the slow pace of the horses. Cheynou and Kendra and their animals followed, with Maksa and one of the soldiers as rearguard.

Forced to move slowly, they strolled down through thickening forests and increasing sunshine and warmth. Soon, their damp clothing dried and they began to enjoy themselves.

At lunch, Cheynou listened with all his concentration to everything that was said, because he knew that was the only way to learn quickly. Kendra's face held an intent look as well. He conversed with Maksa about the weather, the trail and any innocuous subject where they could practise their communication. Both cautiously avoided sensitive military or political subjects.

They camped again that night, and Lord Rochana, tired in spite of the more comfortable ride, spoke little. He went, drugged, to his bed early, his doctor in attendance. Left to themselves, Maksa and Cheynou talked more, and the officer, emboldened perhaps by Cheynou's youth and friendliness, risked more sensitive questions.

"Kendra, you want to listen in on this one."

She gave the officer a friendly smile. "What's it about?"

"You."

"Oh." She waved a hand airly. "Speak on."

"He wants to know why the barbarian doesn't treat the lady with more respect."

"And did you tell him?" A grin played at the corner of her mouth.

"I'm not sure of the answer."

"Think of something, quick. He looks interested."

Cheynou turned to the soldier.

"It is true, Maksa. I am a barbarian. She is a lady of her people. But I have status with my people. I am called in Tradespeak a Navigator."

"And this is?"

"One who tells the Captain where his ship is, and where she must go. Very important. Much training, much knowledge."

The soldier nodded. "So you treat her as an equal."

Cheynou wavered his hand. "Not exactly equal. I take small freedom. And she is a woman. Never equal."

Kendra shifted irritably. "I recognize that word. You say 'woman' and you both laugh, and I know what's going on!"

He rolled his eyes at the officer, who laughed again in sympathy, eliciting a further scowl from the lady.

Cheynou became serious. "And we are one month travelling together. We are friends."

Maksa nodded. "It is often so." He turned to both of them. "In the house of Rochana, it is not too strict, but it is more formal."

"Thank you, Maksa." He turned to Kendra. "He says we'll have to watch ourselves once we get to the Rochana home. They may not be overly mannered by their standards, but these seem like a formal people."

She nodded her thanks to the officer as well. "We'll play it as we go."

"If I have to, I'll boost you up a bit. If I show you deference, it will help you."

She grimaced. "You had better. I don't have anything else."

"Of course you do. You're a lady. What more could you need?"

"Oh, I don't know. Something I was good at?"

He turned to Maksa. "I'm sorry, but I must speak with my friend. She is worried about her place in the Rochana home, and I must reassure her."

Maksa smiled reassuringly. "She is young, beautiful, and a lady. What more does she need?"

"That's what I told her." He rolled his eyes. The officer slapped his shoulder and strolled away.

"What did he say?" Kendra was frowning.

He told her, but he could see it brought little comfort. "So I'm young and good-looking. I guess that helps. But I'm a lady from a different society. All the things I know won't be the same here. I just don't have any skills to make myself useful."

"And why do you think I brought you with me?"

"What?"

He grinned. "Besides the young and beautiful part."

She glared at him. "You're telling me that you brought me because I'm a lady? You'd better have a good story, friend."

"It's true, Kendra. I figured you for a good companion on the trail, so I didn't mind bringing you. But I knew that I would really need you when we got into civilization. Certainly, the people down here would be more civilized than me. Even more civilized than your people."

"You did? How?"

"I'm a Helmsman. I told you how we talk to everyone we meet. I've heard the stories, although you can't believe most of them. Also, some of the things that little man was carrying with him, the northern scout who died up on the Prairie. Very sophisticated metalwork. I knew that when I came up against people like that, I was going to have trouble. That's where you come in."

"I do?"

"Yes. You don't know these people's rules, but you do know about the rules of societies. You know how to act. You'll make sure I don't make a fool of myself. Spiderwebs in my hair. That sort of thing."

She sat for a long time, thinking, and he did not interrupt. Finally, she nodded. "I suppose you're right."

"Of course I'm right. I'm the leader of this expedition. I have to be."

"Just remember who you're talking to."

"Yes, my Lady."

"That's better."

"Do people really say that all the time?"

"Say what?"

"Do your servants and people like that say 'my Lady' every time they speak to you?"

She laughed. "Of course not. To the women in my household, I'm Kendra. Many of them have known me all my life. Of course, in a social situation, they would."

"Just like that? A woman who bounced you on her knee, who spanked you for stealing tarts, would suddenly be saying 'Yes my Lady, no my Lady' every time she spoke?"

"Yes. In a more formal society, where everybody really is a lord or lady, the servants would do that every day."

"I can't see liking that very much."

"What do you call your Captain?"

"We call him Captain or Sir. But we don't say it all the time. Just when we want to talk to him. After that, it's just a conversation."

"Well, you are only barbarians, after all."

"Aye. No manners to speak of."

"Well, at great risk to my reputation, bunking in with a barbarian, I think it's time for bed."

He sat a moment, thinking. "That's another thing. Once we get to the Rochana home, they're going to separate us."

156

"I suppose. We could hardly share a room."

"That could be a problem."

"I can't see how at the moment, but I suppose it could. We'll have to make sure we can get in touch with each other when we need it."

"Right. One more thing we'll have to play as it goes."

"The theme of our tale."

"Sure enough."

They rose and moved towards their bedrolls.

14.   ROCHANA HOME

The small, slow cavalcade wound down out of the mountains and into a wide valley, the trail firming under their feet, widening until two could ride abreast. Soon, the road was lined with farms: not large manors like Kirigata, but small farmsteads with thatched roofs and attached barns and sheds.

The people working the fields all waved and rushed over to see the invalid. Apparently his story had already spread, and the simple life of these peasants was enriched by the adventure of their lord and the light-skinned stranger with her barbarian guide he brought home with him.

Cruzen was happy to stop, partly for the rest and partly because he seemed truly interested in his people.

"They like him."

Cheynou nodded. "And he likes them. Good sign."

"No formalities."

"No. They just bow their heads a bit at first. Another good sign, I'd say."

"That soldier did tell you..."

"Yes. He said they were less formal than most."

The two foreigners were only introduced to one man, a traveller who was riding in the opposite direction. This individual was well armed in a metal cuirass and helmet and attended by four mounted soldiers. He treated Cruzen with deference.

His name was Orwen, and he, like Maksa, was a Thousand-Prime. His TradeSpeak was poor, so they exchanged only simple formalities. Then their host chatted with the man before sending him on his way.

"That was a good meeting."

Cheynou glanced up at Maksa, who had pulled his horse alongside. "Now the word is official that you are friends."

"I see. He is a Thousander, like you?"

"Yes, but he is active duty. Lord Rochana and I are...I think 'reserves' is the word. We fight if needed."

"Reserve sounds right to me. Lord Rochna said he was a farmer."

"Among many things."

"I gathered that. Does he own all this land?"

"The correct word is not 'own'. He is responsible."

"Oh. How does that work?"

The soldier scratched the stubble on his chin. "That requires some history."

"I am interested in history."

"Well, then. When the Kyabrans first came here, there were few people in this area. It was too well-forested for farming and too far away from settled areas to sell lumber. In order to establish control, the Emperor ceded large tracts of land to forward-thinkers like Lord Rochana's father. They do not really own the land, but they are responsible for its upkeep, development..." the man smiled, "...and, of course, its taxes."

Cheynou grimaced to himself. The FamilyShips understood taxes.

"The taxes are not onerous. The Emperor at the time of the Expansion was a wise man. He knew that if he gave the right people the chance, they would create a new civilization in this wilderness. Sooner or later, the taxes would come."

"Was he right?"

Maksa gestured at the nearest farmhouse, with its spreading outbuildings and the raw slash of newly cleared land along the field edge.

"I see."

"So the old Lord Rochana invested heavily in this area. He found the right people, set them up and supported them through the first, difficult years, earning their loyalty."

Cheynou looked up. "An interesting idea."

"Earning loyalty?"

159

"Yes. Among my people, loyalty was demanded. There was no choice."

The soldier looked pointedly at Cheynou, then at their surroundings.

"Precisely. I am here as a direct cause of that error."

"Cruzen Rochana treasures the self-reliant as his father did. The main valleys of the Rochana holdings have been cleared, but there are smaller areas that could be farmed. He still accepts new applicants, screens them carefully. Once they become his people, he supports them fully, making sure they have every chance to succeed."

"A wise leader."

"Many of us think so."

Cheynou grinned up at the man riding beside him. "I'm not likely to take up farming."

"Perhaps not. The Rochana have other enterprises where a loyal and motivated person could prosper."

"Such as?"

"You will have to discuss that with my Lord Rochana."

"I will have to do that."

They travelled on in silence. Maksa seemed satisfied that he had passed along the appropriate message, and Cheynou did a quick translation of the new information for Kendra to mull over. "This was no accidental conversation."

She nodded. "I wonder what the Rochana Home has in store for us."

As the procession moved down into the lower valleys, the fields became larger, the houses more prosperous and the animals in the pastures sleeker. While Cheynou had no idea of the level of taxation, it was growing on him that their host was a powerful and wealthy man.

So it came as a bit of a surprise when they turned off the main road down a winding lane between rough stone walls. The fields were smaller here and separated by copses of trees. Rugged, pine-clad hills rose to either side, and the lane followed the west side of the valley between.

Cruzen had his litter stop at the top of a small rise in the road, allowing Cheynou and Kendra to catch up with him. "Home."

Just below them, partly hidden in the pines, was a large, square building, rather plain, its walls dressed in honey-warm stucco twined with ivy. From this elevated view, Cheynou could see that it was made in the form of a hollow square, and that the east side was one story taller than the rest. The lighter shade of the walls suggested that this side was a recent addition. Then his eyes were drawn to the skyline of the western hill, where three large windmills spread their vanes to the breeze.

Cruzen made a deprecating gesture to Cheynou.

Kendra grinned. "I think he is saying that it is not well situated for this climate." Her gesture to the east, sweeping in towards the house, said clearly, 'Nice morning light.'

The lord nodded, once. "But not enough evening warmth in the cold seasons. My father from Inner Sea. Hot, dry. Summer, very hot. Good shade. In winter rains..." he hugged himself, shivered.

She indicated the sun, mimed basking happily in its rays.

"I am pleased to offer you to discover it yourself."

Kendra laughed when Cheynou translated this. "Tell him I'm sure I will be as impressed as I am by its owner."

Cheynou grinned and did his best.

Rochana barked a laugh, his sweeping hand indicating his leg, his mode of transportation, and his general situation.

She laughed again, her eyes scanning the surrounding fields. "Do you know the word for vineyards?"

"No idea."

She turned to the lord and began a long, involved conversation about the types of wines he produced, what

161

they tasted like, and the lack of vineyards in the south, because of the cold. All without one word of shared language.

Cheynou, finding himself unneeded, watched in amazement, as did the rest of the party. Finally, the discussion ground to a halt on their mutual lack of words, both of them laughing. Rochana reached over, clapped her on the back, and gestured to his riders. "We go home now!"

As they approached the house, or manor or whatever it was, Cheynou and Kendra faded to the rear as the people of the demesne streamed out to greet their master. Once again, it was obvious that there was a great deal of mutual respect and liking.

Kendra tugged at Cheynou's sleeve. "How do you say 'My Lady'?"

"What?"

"He's bound to have a wife. I want to say the right thing. How do I greet her?"

He told her the phrase in TradeSpeak, and she repeated it until she had it right.

Sure enough, as they approached the narrow patio that fronted the new wing of the house, a door opened and another group appeared, led by a slender, black-haired lady whose clothing, jewelry and poise all shouted her status.

As did her treatment of the patient. While everyone else seemed glad to see him, she was definitely on another course. She treated him to an absolute tirade, her expressive face and hands demonstrating her fear, her worry, his stupidity, his carelessness and the need of everyone in the demesne for him to be healthy and in charge.

Kendra struggled to keep from smiling. "I don't think we need a translation. Somebody is in trouble."

"Not much. Look."

After enduring the harangue in sheepish silence for a while, Cruzen reached out and gently trapped one of his wife's hands, the forefinger of his other hand softly covering her lips. When she quieted, he brushed what might have been a tear off her cheek and said something softly. She smiled reluctantly.

Then he spoke louder, and Cheynou caught the Kyabran word for 'foreigners.'

The lady's eyes immediately scanned the party, singling out the two travellers, her eyebrows raised in expressive surprise and delight. At Cruzen's gesture, they stepped forward.

"My new friends from above the Rim of the World, this is my dear wife, Cedenye, Lady Rochana. My dear, this is Cheynou Chan, barbarian Navigator and his mistress, Lady Kendra of Kirigata."

The TradeSpeak rolled off his tongue so smoothly that he must have been practising as they came down the trail. To Cheynou's pleasure, the lady answered even more fluently.

"Please be welcome to my husband's demesne, Navigator Cheynou and Lady Kendra. Give me leave to assure myself that he is resting comfortably, and then I will show you proper hospitality."

Kendra repeated the phrase Cheynou had taught her, and he added his thanks for the gracious welcome.

She smiled and turned back to her husband, snapping orders that were followed promptly by everyone in earshot. As the stretcher disappeared through the front door, the lady gestured to Maksa. He nodded and turned to the two travellers and motioned them to enter.

"My Lady says take care of you."

"Thank you, Maksa. She seems a powerful woman."

"Ah, yes. Quick to anger, quick to tears or to laughter, quicker still to the defense of the helpless. My master is a fortunate man."

Kendra looked around at the disappearing crowd. "Children?"

Upon Cheynou's translation, the soldier's face fell. "Ah, no. A source of deep sorrow to both." His face brightened. "However, there are plenty of children here."

"I noticed."

"Faranos Rochana is heir. A nephew. Younger son of older brother."

"I see."

Kendra's face took on an absorbed look. Suddenly, she darted forward, her hand on the arm of a young woman nearby. "Excuse me!"

The servant girl startled back, her eyes wide. "Yes, my Lady?"

"What did you just say?"

"I...I was just telling my sister..."

"...to get something for the table. Cloth or linen. Right?"

"Yes, my Lady. Was that wrong?"

"No, no, I'm sure that was fine." She turned triumphantly to Cheynou. "I understood her! I could tell what she was saying."

He couldn't help but grin at her enthusiasm. "Since you're both speaking SeaSpeak, I suppose you could."

"That's what I mean!" She turned back to the girl. "Why are you speaking my language?"

The girl was really confused, now. "I...don't know, my Lady. I was speaking my language. My home language, you know?"

"So where do you come from?"

The girl looked around for a moment. "Here, my Lady."

Kendra turned to Cheynou. "What's going on?"

Cheynou passed the question to Maksa, using SeaSpeak himself, slowly.

"Do you understand this?"

The soldier frowned and nodded, but answered in TradeSpeak. "I don't understand it that well, especially the way you speak it. You have a very strange accent, if you don't mind my saying it. You are speaking the language of the

164

native people of this area, what they spoke before we Kyabrans came."

"The local language is SeaSpeak?"

"I don't know what you call it, but they had their own language before we came. They've all learned Kyabran now, of course. At least the ones who work in the Rochana Home. I'm sure they still speak their old language in their own homes. If this girl was talking to her sister, she probably would have used their family language."

Kendra was smiling. "But that means I'll be able to speak to all sorts of people! Even you, Maksa. Why didn't you say anything before? Cheynou and I have been speaking like this ever since we met you."

The older man grinned self-consciously and spoke in careful SeaSpeak, heavily accented, as the girl's was. "I didn't know. You have a very different accent. I could understand some words, but I wasn't really trying to listen. Not polite."

"I understand. What is this language called, and who else speaks it?"

Maksa turned to the girl, and they spoke in Kyabran for a moment. "Around here it's called Frasian. All the peasants speak it, as well as anyone who deals with them."

The girl tugged his sleeve timidly, added a phrase. His eyebrows rose. "She says Lady Cedenye speaks it fluently."

Kendra fairly bounced. "This is going to be so much better." She turned to the servant. "We shouldn't be keeping you from your work, my dear. Thank you so much. You have made me so happy!"

The girl reddened at the praise, curtseyed and bustled away.

Kendra took Maksa's arm, tugged him forward. "So, show us your Home, Maksa. Obey your mistress' command. Take care of us!"

With a rueful grin at Cheynou, he complied, leading them into the main hall, which took up most of the south-east corner of the new wing.

"This is where we eat on ceremonial occasions, as tonight will be. There will be many people, with Lord Rochana's adventure to hear about and foreigners to stare at." He grinned at them. "We live a slow life, out here on the frontier of the Empire. Any entertainment brings a crowd."

"As long as they will speak to me in Frasian, they can stare all they want."

Cheynou was happy to let them chatter on. It gave him a chance to listen to the Kyabran's accent in Frasian, which he knew wouldn't be accurate, since Maksa didn't speak the language that well himself. Now that he knew to listen, Cheynou was beginning to understand what was said around him. If he concentrated for a few hours, he could mimic their accent, and in a few days he would have picked up the new words and phrases he needed. Most of the rest, the turns of phrase and colloquialisms, would take much longer.

They had only toured the dining hall when a disturbance swept in from the other side. Lady Cedenye had returned. She began to speak to Maksa, but he interrupted her, using Frasian. "My Lady, our visitors speak a version of the local people's language."

Now the lady turned her attention, and the power of her smile, on the visitors directly. "You do? Well, isn't that going to be nice! My husband was just telling me how wonderful you were to him, and how hard it would be to thank you when we couldn't talk to you. And now we can!"

Kendra nodded, once, not quite a bow, but deference nonetheless. "It is a great relief to me, my Lady. My companion is an expert in languages, and I am sure he would have had little trouble. I have only the one language, and it is so reassuring to find that others speak it."

The lady regarded Cheynou a moment. "A language expert, you say?"

He concentrated, tried to speak the way Maksa and the servant girl did. "Yes, my Lady. I have trained in languages all my life."

She frowned slightly. "And you speak the same way your lady does?"

He smiled. "I used to, before I was enlightened by your delicate enunciation."

Now she laughed out loud, including Kendra in her gaze. "If this is called a barbarian where you come from, what are the civilized people like?"

Kendra pretended to frown at Cheynou. "I'm afraid I am rather normal, my Lady, but my friend here is definitely not!"

The lady slipped between them, linking an arm in Kendra's and laying her other hand on Cheynou's sleeve. Belatedly, he realized that he was supposed to crook his arm, and she slipped her hand down into the proper position on his forearm as he did so. "Come, then, and I will complete the tour that poor Maksa was saddled with. Maksa, I am sure you have things you would rather be doing..."

He seemed to be about to protest, but she continued firmly "...such as greeting your wife and children."

He bowed slightly. "I am always at my Lady's command."

She acknowledged his irony with a smile and a small toss of her head. "Off with you. The little ones will be glad to see you."

Kendra raised her eybrows. "Little ones?"

"Oh, yes. He has a wife and lovely twin boys, five years old. That's why he is here with us and not on active duty."

"I'm sure it was your gain, my Lady."

"Oh, it definitely was. He is a stalwart supporter and his dear wife gives a note of grace and style to our backwoods life."

"I am anxious to meet her, but not enough to take her from her reunion with her husband."

Cedenye tilted her head. "Very thoughtful of you, Lady Kendra. Shall we then continue our tour? We are, as Maksa has told you, in the main hall."

"Yes, my Lady. He also prepared us for tonight's viewing."

"I'm glad he thought of that. Through here, beside the pantry, is the kitchen."

They entered a spacious whitewashed room almost as high as the main hall, its ceiling darkened with smoke. The north wall was taken up by a huge hearth, with a smaller hearth on the right-hand side. Fronting this was a long counter with pots and utensils hanging overhead. The south wall contained the wide, high windows that lit the room. Various tables filled the space between. There was a hum of activity, as cooks and their helpers slaved over pots and chopping boards. The lady of the house cast a critical eye over it all, but said nothing and turned her guests back. "They don't need us distracting them. Come out into the courtyard."

Cheynou had seen self-contained farmsteads like this one and expected the inner courtyard to be the working hub of the farm, open to the barns and sheds on the other two wings of the house. He was not expecting the stone-flagged patio which extended the full width of the southern side, complete with an outdoor hearth on the back of the kitchen chimney.

Noting his interest, Lady Cedenye gestured. "When the weather is warm we live out here. There is plenty of shade, and the cooks like it."

Their attention moved along the far wall to a further surprise. Built against the side of the barn was a small ivy-covered cottage, complete with shuttered windows, battered wooden door and gabled roof.

"A bit strange, is it not? That is the original home that my husband's father built here when he started this farm. The whole enterprise grew from this small beginning."

"It's so sweet! What do you use it for?"

"Guests. It affords them some privacy, if they don't mind the noise of the workers, early in the morning."

"You mean we could stay there?"

"If that suited you. Come and see. There is a living room and a bedroom downstairs, and two small bedrooms upstairs. Our guests usually use the larger downstairs one, and their servants stay upstairs." The lady raised one eyebrow delicately.

Kendra poked her head into the lower bedroom to the right of the doorway. It was smaller than her bedroom at home, whitewashed and simply decorated. "Oh, this would be perfect!" She turned to Cheynou. "You don't mind going upstairs, do you?"

He sketched a small, ironic bow. "I am always at my Lady's service."

She slapped his arm. "Don't be silly. I'll take the other bedroom upstairs if it will make you feel any better. I'll tell you one thing, though. I'm not taking an upstairs bedroom and letting you have this one. I love it!"

He shrugged. "I guess I go upstairs then."

He climbed the worn wooden staircase, turning to the right at the top, and looked into the room. It was a better room than he had ever slept in. *A space to myself where I can walk more than three steps without hitting a wall or piece of furniture!* He glanced into the other bedroom, which seemed about the same except it had two single beds instead of the one large one he had chosen. He went back into his room and over to the window which looked down into the courtyard, his wider view blocked by the third story of the new wing. *At least I'll see the night sky.* He tramped back downstairs.

"It'll do."

The two ladies were standing in the living room, surveying the small fireplace and the rustic wooden furniture. Kendra rubbed a hand lovingly over a polished golden chair back and frowned at him. "Cheynou, you are being positively ungracious!"

"Well, you know, it's not exactly what I'm used to."

"Cheynou Chan! You spent last winter in a tent!"

169

"And before that, in a tiny cabin where I couldn't take one pace without hitting my bed or the wall. And I thought myself fortunate. No, this will do me fine."

The lady watched this exchange with a smile. "I gather the accommodations are suitable?"

"Oh, don't listen to him, Lady Cedenye. He's just pouting because I grabbed the best bedroom. He'll find some way to make me pay him back. He always does."

"Well, that's settled for the moment, then. If you have second thoughts, we can arrange for a duel at sundown."

"Couldn't do that, my Lady."

"Oh? Why not?"

"Because it would be a shame to mar such perfect beauty by slapping its butt with the flat of a sword."

The lady met Kendra's eyes, and the girl nodded. "That's right, my Lady. A month and a half on the trail with that, all day, every day. Do you think you could find a corner of the hayloft where we could stuff him?"

"I'm afraid we don't allow strange barbarians near the livestock, Lady Kendra. They tend to eat them or run off with them."

"Well, in that case, I suppose I'll just have to put up with him."

Cheynou assumed a polite and patient expression. When they both looked at him, he smiled. "Shall I bring my Lady's luggage in?"

"If you can find it."

"It shouldn't be too far away." He stepped to the tunnel through the outer wall and whistled. Soon, a long nose and two huge ears appeared in the main doorway to the outside world, followed immediately by a streak of grey that launched itself across the gravel, almost knocking him over with her enthusiasm.

"A member of the party I have not met?"

He looked up. "Our faithful guard and companion, Lady Cedenye. Cinders."

The lady knelt and held out the back of her hand to be sniffed.

"And our other faithful guard, Martan."

By this time the donkey had ambled over, standing conspicuously near so that Cheynou would unload his pack. Once again, Lady Cedenye showed her familiarity with animals, allowing Martan to snuffle her hand before rubbing him behind the ears.

"And this is the total of your party?"

"That's right, my Lady."

"You are very brave."

"Or stupid, my Lady. We haven't figured out which, yet."

She smiled. "So far, I would say a win."

He thought of the pleasant room at the top of the stairs. "I'd say so, too. Why don't you two go inside and do lady-of-the-manor things and I'll take care of the packing. After all, that's what she brought me for."

"I brought you!"

"Well, I'm trying to be good for something. Just haven't figured out what, yet."

She drew back her fist, then pretended to remember to be ladylike, and lowered it, opening her hand gently. "Shall we retire to the drawing room, my Lady? I tire of this loutishness."

The other lady laughed. "I didn't know there was such a word as 'loutishness' in Frasian. Does it mean what it sounds like?"

"If you mean him, it's perfect."

"Thank you, Lady Kendra. I have learned today."

"It was a pleasure, Lady Cedenye."

They turned their backs and paraded across the gravel, onto the stones of the patio and into the bulk of the building. Grinning, he unloaded the donkey and lugged their packs

171

into the little house. *This couldn't be better. We won't be separated, and the lady has taken a liking to Kendra. Maybe even to me.*

By the time he had settled in, washed some of the trail dust off and changed his clothes, they had progressed past the 'my Lady' stage, and were tossing first names back and forth. He found them in the kitchen, where Kendra was up to her elbows in flour, extolling the benefits of winter wheat for its textural qualities, or something like that. To his enquiring glance, Cedenye flicked her fingers towards the outside door. "Maksa is on the patio."

He nodded, that dignified motion that Kendra used to indicate respect, and followed her directions. Maksa was, indeed, on the patio, watching two small boys tussling with a large dog over a piece of rag. The dog was winning, but the boys didn't seem to notice, throwing themselves onto the animal and grasping the rag, only to be tossed away with a shake of the creature's head.

Maksa looked up. "Ah, Cheynou. Now you can meet my family." He spoke a word in Kyabran that was either 'children' or 'attention,' because it brought them to their feet at once. Shy at seeing a stranger, they dropped their gazes and shuffled their feet.

Their father spoke to them again, and they straightened their backs and presented themselves proudly in front of him. He nodded in approval, and spoke formally, introducing Cheynou in the Kyabran manner. Cheynou responded with what Kyabran he had already picked up and grasped arms formally as the Kyabrans did. The two identical faces glowed at this, and he searched for some tiny difference to separate them. They had identical shocks of hair low on their brows, but sweeping up in opposite directions.

Once he had their names, Jodethran and Taden, he thought he could remember which was which. He also noted that Jode seemed to be the leader, speaking first, holding his hand out first.

The dog, relieved of his playmates, flopped in the shade of a nearby cypress tree and dropped the treasured rag across his paws, his tongue lolling in the heat. From the size of his feet and the awkwardness of his movements, Cheynou had him figured for about a year old. A motion caught the corner of Cheynou's eye, and he gestured for the two boys to watch.

They turned silently to see Cinders slinking along the base of the patio, her stomach close to the ground. Catching her eye, he flicked his fingers to the right. She slid away from the wall into the shelter of a bush nearby. Once around the bush, she had a clear path to the back of the puppy's shade tree. Cheynou beckoned her forward, and she crept silently towards her prey.

This was going to be interesting. Cheynou had no idea what she intended. Closer and closer she crept to the oblivious pup until she was no more than her own body length away. Slowly, she assumed her herding position, crouching, her front paws spread, head low.

"Whuff!"

It was low, but it brought the puppy straight to his feet, tumbling over himself in fear. He froze for a moment, then registered his foe. A brief stare was all it took. His tail drooped, his hindquarters tucked down, and his head turned aside.

She rose slowly, never taking her eyes off him, and stalked forward. As she approached, he settled lower and lower, finally lying down on his side, his head turned up to her imploringly.

She sniffed him over, seemed to accept him and stood back, looking around. After a moment, he lowered his head, seeming to relax.

With a sudden start, he flipped over, crouched in the 'play' position, his hindquarters high, his paws spread. She dropped into the same crouch, and they eyed each other for a moment.

He broke, running away with a long, loping stride, and she followed around the corner of the barn and out of sight.

The twins were just beginning to giggle to each other when the dogs reappeared, this time with Cinders in the lead, the puppy galloping fiercely behind, his head at her flank.

There was a blur of motion and the poor puppy found himself rolling in the dust, his elusive prey now behind him, nipping at his side. He was up and away again, the smaller dog in pursuit.

Now the boys were laughing aloud, as was their father.

Cheynou snorted. "Women. You chase them until they catch you."

"A truth, my friend." Then Maksa's laughter stopped, and he rose hurriedly to his feet. "On that topic..."

Cheynou turned to face the woman who was standing behind him. She was slightly shorter than he was and on the stocky side, but her air of command made her seem taller.

"So this is the gentleman who is causing such an uproar." This was as far as the conversation got, because the two boys mobbed her, clamouring for her attention. Cheynou assumed that each was trying to tell the story of the hunt and chase. Finally, she calmed them enough that she could speak. To his surprise, she, too, was fluent in Frasian.

"Husband! Where is the military discipline these children need? Is this display not more likely from a bunch of..." she glanced at Cheynou, "...barbarians?"

Maksa sighed. "I deeply apologize, my dear. A lack of military discipline is one of my more grievous faults."

She shook her head in sorrow. "I come to the frontier, hoping to remove my children from the decadent society of the central Empire. And what do I get?"

Cheynou wrinkled his forehead. "Barbarians, my Lady?"

She turned piercing eyes on him. "Perhaps you would know something about that?"

174

"Oh, yes, my Lady. Barbarians are the kind of people who speak to ladies, unintroduced."

"Ah, but what could be less civilized than a gentleman who would allow such a situation to arise?"

Their eyes turned to Maksa, who was standing with one hand on each boy's shoulder. "I find myself torn, since I have not had a civilized chance to speak one word since your arrival, my dear. However, now that I have been granted that boon, may I present Cheynou Chan the Navigator? Cheynou, this is, as you may have correctly assumed, my dear wife and the mother of these two ideal children, Miranra, of the august and ancient house of Rimmon."

She gently pushed down on his outstretched hand. "Miranra of the House of Dumorne. At least, I was married when you left two days ago. Has something happened since?"

"No, my dear. I see no reason to make any changes."

She smiled sweetly. "I find that...reassuring."

She turned away from her husband's rolling eyes and regarded Cheynou. Noting his concentration as he tried to understand the Kyabran, she switched back to Frasian. "Word has spread around the Home, young man. It appears you are adventuresome as well as handsome. The young ladies are sorely disappointed that you are accompanied."

"I grieve to disappoint young ladies, my Lady. It seems rather...uncivilized."

"Ah. And sensitive as well."

"I find it aids in communication to be aware of how people really feel."

A slight smile lifted her lip. "But only if one wishes to impart information."

"I beg to disagree, my Lady. It is also useful if one does not wish to make the information available, yet one does not wish to offend."

There was a definite crinkle at the corner of her eye. "So you're not sure yourself, either."

He sighed inwardly. For a while there, he had thought he was holding his own. "What man ever is?"

"That one." A nod of her head indicated her husband, who grinned comfortably.

"I am not surprised, my Lady." So she had won a point. Maybe she would cede some information now. "I am impressed that you speak Frasian so well. I had understood that you have not lived here long."

"Oh, I did not learn Frasian here." She gestured to the north. "It is the local language of the whole of the Inner Provinces. My family has holdings there, and I spent much time in that area in my youth."

"If it would amuse you, my Lady, I would be interested in more information on this subject. I have only these past few days become aware of your people's presence here, and I know nothing of what lies to the north. For a Navigator, such a situation is not to be tolerated."

"I would imagine not. Perhaps Maksa will show you some of his maps. I could be persuaded to take these small heathens off your hands."

"I am sorry to tax you with boring subjects, my Lady."

"I am not bored by geography. I live in it. I merely defer to the expert."

"Well, unless the boys wish to have a geography lesson along with me..."

The parents had one of those eye-to-eye conversations that makes a decision in a heartbeat. "Perhaps they would benefit from the language lesson as well."

Maksa nodded. "Of course. Cheynou, we will discuss geography. Come on, boys. Make a courtesy to your mother and we'll go and look at maps."

The boys seriously bowed their foreheads to their mother's hand and returned eagerly to their father's side. Cheynou watched them, then copied their gesture. As he raised his eyes to hers, she smiled and nodded slightly. Then she turned and walked away, leaving the four males standing watching her until she left their view. Cheynou was sure she was aware of it.

The Dumorne family had a spacious suite of rooms taking up half of the second-floor living quarters. The public part consisted of a delicately furnished sitting room and a more businesslike study. It was here, standing over a large, leather-topped table, that Cheynou got his first lesson on the geography of the Kyabran Empire.

The boys dragged stools up and immediately began to pore over the huge map on the table, pointing out places and details. Their father stopped them. "Cheynou does not speak Kyabran. To be polite, we should all speak Frasian with him."

The two faces turned to him, slightly puzzled that this adult would not be able to speak their language.

"That would be very good of you. Later, perhaps, you can help teach me Kyabran."

They thought that was a fine idea, and both said so, volubly, until Jode slapped his brother's shoulder with the backs of his fingers. "We must speak in Frasian, Tade."

"Right. We can do that."

They turned back to the map, and Cheynou got a chance to see it. It was difficult to tell the scale, because the map stopped just south of the Rochana Home, only indicating the mountains roughly, so there was nothing familiar to relate to. As far as he could tell, though, he was only about halfway across the continent. He had Maksa translate the distances into days of travel on a good horse. It seemed that the new province of Velika stretched from the mountains north for about seven days journey, or slightly less than the distance from the Southern Ocean to Sarasha's Resting. From there it was another seven or eight days to the Inner Sea. Kyabra was to the west from there, another two days ride.

"Show Cheynou where your grandfather lives, boys."

Two fingers immediately punched a grubby spot on the map in northern Kyabra, some distance inland.

"Very good. Tade, how would you get there?"

177

A small finger trailed across the map. "I would ride from the Rochana Home in Velika, to the Panjhali River. I would follow that river to the Inner Sea. Then I would follow the coast to the west, until I reached the town of Fontanelle. Then I would go inland to the town of Mandir. That is where Grandfather lives."

His brother could no longer contain himself. "In a big stone house on a hillside, with tall, dark trees on one side. They are to protect everyone from the wind."

Maksa laughed. "They left there when they were three years old and are very proud to remember what it looked like."

"Do you have plans to return?"

"Perhaps soon. Not permanently, though. Lord Rochana has business in the Empire that he cannot allow to slide, yet he is needed here. I have his confidence, and perhaps he will delegate me to make the journey. It would please Miranra to see her family, and it would be good for the children as well."

15.   VELIKAN IDYL

And so they settled in. Cheynou, watching Kendra, couldn't help but envy her easy adaptation to life in the Rochana Home. In spite of her language problems, she chatted with everyone, found ways to help out, laughed at her own mistakes and generally fitted in.

It wasn't so easy for him. Everything was new. In spite of his Helmsman's training, he still sometimes turned the wrong way when he came out of certain rooms. He decided, to his chagrin, that while he was adept at navigating the world, he had spent his whole life on the same ship and wasn't that good at learning a new house.

It didn't take him long to figure out that he wasn't the only uncomfortable one. The third time he noticed — and who could help but notice — Faranos storming out of Cruzen's office, harsh words following him, Cheynou came to the conclusion that the choosing of an heir hadn't been a decision with equal agreement on both sides. He strolled into the courtyard to see the Heir Designate swinging up on his horse, ready to ride away.

"Where are you headed, Faranos?"

"I don't know."

"Can I come along?"

"Why?"

Cheynou shrugged. "Nothing better to do."

"I wish I had your problems."

Cheynou grinned. "I doubt it. But I don't need yours, either."

"Maybe you should try them for a while." Faranos sat looking down. "Well?"

"Well, what?"

"Are you going to saddle a horse, or are you going to walk?"

"I think a horse would be best. Give me a moment."

He slapped a saddle hurriedly on the patient mare he had been riding lately and brought her out. Faranos was circling his horse, but the red had gone from his face.

Cheynou mounted. "So where are we going?"

"I really don't know. Sometimes I just go riding. It makes me feel better, you know?"

"I don't know that. Riding has rarely made me feel anything but inadequate."

"You ride all right."

"Sure. For somebody who had never seen the back of a horse two years ago, I ride all right. I get there and I don't often fall off. If the horse cooperates."

Faranos laughed, but there was a bitter edge to it. "If you keep choosing horses like that, you're not going to learn very fast."

With a bit of urging, Cheynou got his horse to come alongside Faranos. "What's wrong with her? She gets me there."

"Sure she does. But you're not learning anything."

"Oh."

"Unless you fall off at least once a week, you're not making progress."

"Once a week?"

"Something like that. If you always choose a horse that you can just control, but not too comfortably, you will always be learning. I'll help you pick out a better ride. One with just a little spunk."

Cheynou nodded. "My father trained me that way. He always put me on the wheel when the wind was just about too strong for me to handle."

"My father trained me that way, too. Sometimes I didn't thank him for it, but it made me a good rider."

"Everybody acknowledges that."

"It's about all."

Cheynou glanced over, caught by that bitter edge again. "That doesn't sound cheerful."

"It isn't. Sometimes I wonder why I ever came out here."

"Why did you?"

"Because I didn't have much of a choice. You have to understand how things work in a big empire. Everybody has his place. My father is the Head of our Family. My brother will be the Head after him. There was no place for Cruzen's branch, so they came out here. Likewise, there was no place for me. Not close to the centre of things. So when Cruzen and Cedenye asked me to come, it looked like a good chance to make something of myself."

"And hasn't it turned out that way?"

"That's what's so frustrating. I think it might be. I'm good with animals. All animals, not just horses. I don't know anything about farming; at least, I didn't before I came here."

"But now you're learning. What's the problem?"

Faranos took in Cheynou's innocent smile.

"I thought everyone in the Home knew. How could you have missed it?"

"You're not getting along with Cruzen."

"Exactly."

"Because he's putting you on his agenda, and not on yours."

"Exactly."

Cheynou paused to think about that for a while. Their horses paced along at a slower rate, now. "What if he's right?"

Faranos sighed. "Oh, he very well could be. I know he's trying to do what's right for the Home. That helps some. But he wants me to know everything right away. He wants me to take on all sorts of responsibility and do all sorts of work, and he gives me things to do that I can't possibly handle, and then he's angry when I fail."

181

"And he tells you exactly how to do it, and that isn't how you want to do it."

"How did you know that?"

"That's the part everybody hears."

"Oh."

"But what if you're wrong?"

"You said that before."

"Yes."

"Once again, I might be wrong. But I have to learn. I'm not him. I don't do things his way. I do them my way. If they're wrong I'll change my way, not take over his."

"Hmm."

"Is that all you can say?"

Cheynou shrugged. "I could say, 'Where are we going?' I suppose."

Faranos looked around. "No idea. Let's go back."

They turned their horses. As they rode along, Faranos looked over at Cheynou. "How do you do it?"

"Do what?"

"Cruzen never tells you how to do things. He wouldn't dare."

"You really think that? You think he's afraid to tell me what to do?"

"Not afraid, exactly. But he wouldn't tell you, because you wouldn't accept it. But he doesn't get angry at you. How do you do that?"

Cheynou shrugged. "It's easy for me. He doesn't have to care. He isn't trying to train me, to make me into something. I'm not a family member he's responsible for. Plus, I don't get mad."

"You don't?"

"I try not to. At least, I try not to show it. I've always watched people, and I think the problem many of them have is that they try to be too nice for too long. Then they feel put upon and they get angry. If they'd just tell others to stop before the situation got serious, often the others would stop and nobody would have to fight."

"So next time he's telling me what to do, I can't get mad, I have to tell him, gently but firmly, that I'd like to do it my way."

"I guess."

"And then he'll say, 'Of course, Faranos, you just do it your way. I don't mind if you foul it all up again.' Somehow, that doesn't seem likely."

"You might be surprised."

Faranos laughed. "Cruzen would be."

"And what's the alternative?"

"I don't know. We keep on fighting until he dies and I can take over and mess it up myself, or he gives up and sends me back to the capital, a failure once more."

Cheynou shrugged. "I've noticed that when people make all-or-nothing statements, they aren't really looking for a solution."

The young Kyabran's frown faded, then turned to a smile. "And I'm trying to find a solution, then?"

"I hope so." That seemed to be enough of the conversation, so Cheynou changed the subject.

"I have a favour to ask. About horse training."

Faranos brightened. "Of course." He glanced over slyly. "Fallen off yours this week yet?"

"I have a theory."

"Becoming an expert, are you?"

"Maybe. It's like this. I spend all my time watching the horse, worrying what he's going to do. What does that sound like?"

"Like he's the boss."

"Exactly. So I have to switch that around, to where he's watching me, waiting for me to do something."

"You are coming along."

"So I have to find something to do that keeps him thinking. Like training him to do something."

"That usually works for me."

"So, I remembered something from our fighting last summer. Our Captain was training his horse to rear up and fight with its front hooves, like stallions do when they fight each other. We've been trying to train our horses, up on the Prairie, but it's very difficult. It would be a great attack against infantry or bandits. Can you help me teach a horse to do that?"

Faranos frowned in thought. "It's not something I've ever done. It's easier to get them to strike out behind, because they do that more often in their own defence."

"Whatever's easiest. I have to stay on her back at the same time, remember."

"We'll work with you on the rear hooves, then. I'll do some thinking about the forehooves though…"

16.   JUSTICE

The ambush was well planned. Faranos and Cheynou had been visiting at a nearby Home and had been there for several hours, long enough for news to be brought to the Sclares Home, a message to be sent, and five armoured marshals to be dispatched from the town. As the two riders turned onto the public road, a Hundred-Prime rode into the lane in front of them with two of his men backing him, the other two closing in from behind their quarry.

Cheynou spun his horse to face the danger behind, sidled tightly to his friend's mount and waited, hand on sword hilt.

"Faranos Rochana, I am instructed by the authority of the Emperor to arrest you on the charge of theft of livestock. Please submit your weapons and follow peaceably."

Cheynou watched his friend's reaction. *He doesn't seem surprised.* "Do they have the right?"

"Yes, but I don't like who they sent."

"All the wrong faction?"

"Yes. I might not make it to town."

"In that case, I think I'll just follow along with you."

Cheynou smiled and turned his horse, moving forward to close with the leader of the troop. "We will come. We will cooperate." This submissive reaction, spoken quietly, lulled the other rider into letting him get a little too close.

Cheynou drew his seaman's cutlass, but instead of handing it over, he held it for a moment. The man was suddenly aware of the disadvantage, armour or not, of his short sword. Cheynou regarded his blade judiciously.

"But we will not, I think, submit our weapons." He sheathed his cutlass with a friendly smile and gestured the other to precede him. This involved turning his back to a potential enemy, but the man had nothing to argue against but a friendly smile and a sheathed sword. After a frowning pause, he complied.

Cheynou motioned Faranos alongside and turned in behind the leader. The others were forced to trail behind.

"What's this about? I need to know, so I can tell Cruzen."

"There is a problem between the factions of Cruzen and Lord Sclares. Some stock was taken. Someone went to take it back. The stock was retrieved, along with some other animals which should have been left behind."

"I see. So once you have been delivered to the proper authorities, you should be safe, and I can scoot home and bring help?"

"I think so."

"Fine. Don't worry. Cruzen will take care of it."

"I hope he can."

"So the charge is not completely false."

"The...incident did occur."

"I see."

They rode in silence for the rest of the trip. As the party entered the town, one of their escort galloped ahead, and by the time they arrived in front of the garrison there were several men standing around. Two reached up to sieze Faranos, but Cheynou interposed his horse between them. He looked down, fingering his cutlass hilt. "Better if you are calm."

He spoke over his shoulder at Faranos, using Frasian. "Stay on your horse until someone you trust shows up."

The lad nodded and spoke to the crowd. "I have come as requested. I will submit to the proper authority of the Emperor, not a mob of my enemies."

There were a few angry shouts, but Faranos turned his horse, closing tightly with Cheynou as they had done on the road. "I think your patrons would not like you to give me an excuse to leave."

The crowd quieted.

186

Cheynou gave them a few beats to think about their problem before he spoke, caustically. "Don't stand gaping. Get someone!"

This order, snapped with all the authority of a Captain on his bridge deck, caused a stir in the crowd. At a word from the mounted squad leader, one of the men turned his horse away and trotted up the street.

As the standoff continued, Cheynou spoke casually in Frasian. "Give me some idea who they are. If they attack, who is most dangerous, who is a hanger-on, who is likely to break and run? Tell me in Kyabran. I want them to know."

"Ah. I see. Well, that man there, the ugly one? He's a retainer of Sclares himself. Some say he's an illegitimate son. He will support his patron. He's a good swordsman, but clumsy on his feet. That one there, he's not allied with any of them, as far as I know. I don't know why he's here."

"That makes it hard, Faranos. If there's a problem, how am I going to know who not to cut down?"

The Kyabran shrugged. "I think we have to assume that if they are this close, they are allied with my enemies."

"Fine. Hate to cut down an innocent witness." He turned, jutted his chin towards the squad leader, glowering on his horse.

"What about him? He's got a nice horse."

"The horse is a good runner, all right. If you have to chase him, you'll never catch him."

There was a chuckle from the growing crowd, more evidence that there were now others here besides the original supporters of Sclares.

"Anyone I definitely shouldn't kill?"

Faranos pretended to survey the crowd. "I think that one there." He pointed. "See the one with no sword?"

"I don't usually kill unarmed people. Why is he here?"

"I don't know. I'll ask him." He raised his voice even more. "Sopuerta. What are you doing here?"

The man — a pale, slim oldster — grinned. "I'm not sure, Faranos. I thought at first your barbarian was going to put on a show, but now I think I'm at the theatre, watching the satires."

"It's a little more serious than that, Sopuerta. It seems that some of us have decided to use the Emperor's authority to play political games."

"This wouldn't have something to do with cattle thieving, would it?"

"Oh. You've heard that story, have you? We would prefer to call it an ownership dispute."

The man nodded. "The opinion of the rest of the community is that you lot had better solve your disputes soon, before someone gets hurt."

Faranos sobered. "I'm beginning to agree with you, Sopuerta."

"Yes, being arrested is a thought-inducing experience."

By the time this conversation was over, the messenger had returned, walking beside an official-looking older man in a purple robe. This individual bustled up, frowning at the confrontation that faced him.

"What is going on here, Guenes?"

The squad leader dismounted and saluted. "We have arrested the criminal as instructed, my Lord."

"Criminal? Has someone been convicted already? That was a quick trial, Guenes."

"I mean the suspect, my Lord."

"I see. If he was arrested, why is he sitting on his horse still in possession of his sword?"

"He was somewhat difficult, my Lord."

"Somewhat difficult? Have you arrested him, or have you not?"

"I would like to answer that, Justice Regada."

The justice looked up to Faranos. "It would be nice if someone could."

"Guenes and his friends did come to arrest me, my Lord, but I was concerned as to their motives, so I offered to accompany them without difficulty if I could retain my weapon."

"And your barbarian bodyguard as well, I gather."

Faranos risked a shrug. "He is learning our culture, my Lord. He wished to see how our justice system works."

"I see. And you wanted his help to make sure it worked as it should."

"It seemed prudent, my Lord."

The justice looked keenly at the crowd as if memorizing faces, and they shuffled, melting back as each man tried to slip behind someone else.

"I think you can safely dismount, Lord Rochana. There are witnesses aplenty."

"Thank you for coming, my Lord. It settled a prickly situation." Faranos dismounted, but Cheynou did not.

"Are you going to invite your scholarly friend to further experience our culture?"

"No, my Lord, I think it would be wiser to send him to inform my patron."

"That would be sensible." He glanced up at Cheynou. "You may go."

Cheynou did not move, his eyes enquiringly on Faranos.

The justice regarded him more firmly. "Doesn't follow orders very well, does he?"

Cheynou inclined his head respectfully. "I did not hear an order, my Lord. If my friend wishes, I would be pleased to take word to Lord Rochana."

"Thank you, Cheynou. I will be quite safe now."

Cheynou grinned at the justice. "Yes, I have no doubt. Now."

The official frowned, unsure whether he had received a compliment or not.

Cheynou nodded again and spun his horse, scattering the Sclares supporters who had been unwise enough to close in behind him. Ignoring them, he trotted out of town, facing straight ahead but doing his best to determine if he was being followed. As far as he could tell, he was not.

As soon as he was out of sight of the village, he pushed his horse to a gallop. Only one road led to the Rochana Home, so he kept his eyes open for a second ambush and forged ahead.

He reached the farm without incident, found Cruzen in his office and explained the problem briefly.

"Arrested? Where is he?"

"In town, under the authority of an elderly gentleman to whom I was not introduced. A justice of some sort, I think. Regada by name."

Cruzen sat back. "He's safe enough, then. You say it was all Sclares' faction in the arresting party?"

"That's what Faranos said."

"What did you do?"

"We suggested in a very cooperative manner that we accompany them, as long as they let us keep our swords."

"They agreed to that?"

"I was inside the squad leader's guard with a drawn cutlass at the time."

"You were what?"

Cheynou motioned the Kyabran to relax. "It is an old trick. When you seem to be agreeing with people, it tends to...shall we say...disarm them?"

"That can be a dangerous game, Cheynou."

"My cutlass is quite a bit longer than your swords. They are made for foot soldiers. Much too short for mounted work. Back on my FamilyShip, only those assigned to battle stations in enclosed spaces below decks would have a weapon that size."

"Are you suggesting that you would have attacked them?"

He shrugged. "I would have taken care of my half of them. Had he given the order, the squad leader was a dead man, and he knew it."

"Hmm." Cruzen eyed him with speculation. "And how do you divide a squad of five men in half?"

"With my cutlass, my Lord."

"I see. There seems to be more to you than I had suspected."

"I am, after all, a stranger to you and your ways, Lord Rochana, and sometimes I must fall back upon my own methods. However, I wish to learn yours. For example, I am very interested in what you are going to do about the problem Faranos has got himself into."

"Got himself into? Do you think this arrest is warranted?"

Cheynou winced. "It is a hard thing to say, but it seemed to me that the actual charge was the only thing that did not surprise him."

"And it was cattle thieving?"

"My understanding of Kyabran is still inexact, but I caught that clearly."

Cruzen nodded. "That explains a lot. It's that damned herd of heifers. I wish I'd never seen them."

"What herd of heifers, Cruzen?"

They both turned as Kendra and Cedenye entered.

"A few cows that one of my landholders lost last fall. One of Sclares' men found them, far up the valley. At least, he said that's where he found them. Instead of driving them down and returning them, he kept them for the winter. Then in the spring he wanted to charge the owner for the feed. That would have been fair enough, but he wanted triple the value for the feed, he says because it left him short for his own stock.

"Up until now, he has refused to return the stock, including the calves they dropped this spring, and this argument has been dragging on for months. My man's sons had been making noises about taking them by force, and I hear Lord Sclares moved them to his Home in order to protect them. So those young fools went and got them, did they?"

"That would explain most of what I heard. They also got a few extra cattle, I think."

"Well, I'm not too upset over that. But what was Faranos doing in the middle of it? A foolish move. We should not be seen to be directly involved." He heaved himself out of his chair, grabbed for his crutch.

"Have them bring out the carriage. I suppose we're involved now, whether we like it or not." He stumped out into the yard, calling orders, and soon the carriage was rattling away.

Several anxious glasses later, the carriage rolled back into the courtyard with Faranos's horse on a lead behind. The two men got down, met by a semicircle of worried faces. Cruzen waved a hand dismissively. "There is no trouble for the present. The extra animals have been returned, the true owner has the heifers, and it is now a civil matter to negotiate the price owed for the feed."

He frowned. "The problem is that the herder, Bedia, saw the theft and says he knows the riders involved. He specifically named Faranos. Sclares is pressing the theft charges because he knows it will embarrass us."

Miranra took her husband's arm as the entered the house. "When is the trial set?"

"Tomorrow."

Kendra frowned thoughtfully. "We had a situation like this back home, once. I don't know your legal system, but maybe I can help."

Cruzen spread his hands. "We will investigate any possible solution."

"Fine." She faced the young man. "Faranos, you really were there."

He looked to Cruzen, who did not respond in any way. He glanced around the room, saw no support, only interest.

"Faranos, I can't help you if I don't have the facts."

"I...I was there, my Lady."

"So, what the witness saw was true?"

"It is quite possible." He held out his hands pleadingly. "I did not want to be there, Lady Kendra. I knew it was wrong. I begged them, pleaded with them not to go."

Her frown deepened. "Faranos, when you know you are right, begging and pleading is not what you do. You tell them straight out that they are idiots and that, if they insist on continuing to be idiots, then you will not have anything more to do with them. Let me guess. You went along, hoping that somehow you could make sure things didn't get out of hand."

"Yes, my Lady."

She shook her head. "Faranos, how old am I?"

"I don't know, my Lady."

"Am I older than you?"

"Not much, my Lady."

"Then you have had as much chance as I have to learn the stupidity of such an action. If you went along with them, they thought they had persuaded you. They thought you were on their side. So will the rest of the people of the community. The deed was done, you accompanied them. Guilty."

There was a long silence. "But Lady Kendra, I didn't mean..."

Her gesture chopped off his speech. "What you mean or didn't mean gave no help to the victims. As far as they were concerned, you were one of those who did the deed."

The lad's head drooped. "I can see that, my Lady."

"Good. Now let's see if we can get you out of this."

"Pardon?"

"Whether you were there or not has little to do with the position of the Rochana Family in this community. So, guilty or innocent, we still have to get you cleared of the charge."

"Oh." The young man looked around the assembly, as if for confirmation. No one enlightened him.

Kendra frowned. "So their whole case rests on the witness who says he saw you riding away?"

His attention snapped back to her. "That's right."

"What, exactly, did he see?"

"What do you mean?"

"Just answer the question, please. What did he see? How far away was he? What was the light like? Sun in his eyes, dust from the herd, that sort of thing?"

Faranos shook his head. "It was early evening. Not dark yet."

"But after sunset?"

"Yes, I believe so."

"How far away?"

"About from here to that clump of trees over there."

"And what were you doing?"

"I believe by the time he showed up, we were galloping away. He says he saw us clearly and named the names. How does this help me?"

"My point is that, depending on what he actually saw or what he thinks he saw, we might be able to shake his confidence in his report of what he saw."

"How?"

"Well, it has a lot to do with the horse."

"The horse?"

"Oh, yes. This is what I want you to do ..."

By the time she had finished speaking, Faranos was looking less depressed, Cruzen was shaking his head, and Cedenye was positively giggling. Cheynou said nothing, but inside he was in awe of the logic of her plan.

* * *

194

Late the following afternoon, a large group of officials, interested parties and blatant onlookers crowded the lower pasture of the Sclares Home. Cheynou and Kendra kept their horses back from the action.

"These are fair people, Cheynou."

"They seem to be willing to allow a defense."

She grinned. "Even a strange one like this."

"Perhaps the authorities don't want to take sides in this dispute."

"Possibly. Back in Kirigata, they would not accept this kind of demonstration for any reason."

He grinned. "Back on the Priest-Admiral's Mastership, what he said was the law, no matter what you proved."

She frowned. "Wasn't there some kind of legal process?"

"By tradition there was, but in the end, if the ruling Officers thought you were guilty, or wanted you to be guilty or just wanted someone to be punished, then you faced about the chances of a mackerel in a school of sharks."

"Let's hope Faranos has better odds than that."

They turned to watch the proceedings. It was dusk at the Sclares Home. The Quaestor and two Justices, along with anyone who could prove he was involved, were standing where the witness had said he was positioned when the cattle were stolen.

Cruzen, as Family Head, was conducting the defense for Faranos. "So, Bedia, do you agree that this is about the time of night that the incident happened?"

The man shifted from one foot to the other, glancing to his patron for reassurance. "Yes, my Lord."

"Good. In a moment, you are going to see a group of men gallop their horses along the path there, where you said you saw my Heir Designate. All you have to do is tell us which one is Faranos Rochana. Do you understand?"

"Yes, my Lord."

Cruzen nodded to the Quaestor, who raised his hand in signal. Soon, hoofbeats sounded, and a group of riders appeared from behind the hedge, pounding away down the path.

Cheynou grinned. Each rider was clothed similarly, and each rode a bay with a dark mane. As the group galloped away, eyes turned to the unfortunate witness.

"Which one was my nephew, Bedia?"

Again, the man looked to his patron, who shook his head. No one who had viewed the demonstration could have identified any of the riders.

Cruzen turned to the judges. "I think my point is made. We tend to identify a person by the clothing he wears, his usual group of friends and especially the horse he rides. In this situation, seeing a group of my nephew's usual friends and seeing someone in that group riding a dark-maned bay, it would be natural enough to assume that it was Faranos. However, a natural assumption is not enough to convict a man of a crime."

The Quaestor faced the witness. "What do you say now, Bedia?"

"What he says is true, my Lord. After this demonstration, I cannot testify for certain that Faranos Rochana was there that night. However, I am sure he was. It was the same five young men that were here the day before, threatening to take the cattle by force. The same group we see together every feast-day, every wedding, every games day."

The official nodded. "However, you cannot identify this man specifically."

The man threw up his hands in frustration. "I cannot, my Lord. I am sure that every man here knows who these young men are, yet we have been shown that no one could truly name any one man. I..." He shook his head in frustration, and said no more.

The Quaestor looked to Lord Sclares. "Does this proceeding continue?"

The lord shook his head bitterly. "No, my Lord."

The official glanced right and left to the judges, raised his head, took on a more formal pose. "I hereby declare the action of Lord Sclares against Faranos Rochana on the charge of cattle thieving to be null and void. There is no declaration of innocence or guilt. There has been no trial."

Then he fixed his eye on Sclares and Cruzen. "I do not believe that the Emperor's Court is the place for the mediation of this dispute. It was allowed to get far out of hand, and I charge both of you with the responsibility of solving this problem without wasting the time of the Emperor's officials or creating more trouble for innocent bystanders. Do I make myself clear?"

Both nodded respectfully.

"Thank you, gentlemen. I count on you. This court is closed." Turning away, the Quaestor tugged off his official helmet and strode to his horse, shaking his head.

Cheynou leaned closer to Kendra. "There goes an unhappy man."

She nodded. "Perhaps. He knows we played a game with the law and he doesn't like that. However, if you think about what he just said, he may be less upset over the outcome of the trial than he is over the original situation."

Cruzen had limped over to them, and caught the last of this. "I couldn't agree more. This situation has been festering far too long. I was remiss in allowing it to continue." He grinned wryly and slapped his sore leg. "While I may have some excuse, I refuse to hide behind it. Best to get it over with."

Spinning on his cane, he hobbled over to Lord Sclares. Their exchange was brief, but Cruzen returned with a grim smile. "He agrees on that point as well. If the two of us throw our weight against the problem, I'm sure it will be solved. Faranos, your young friends may get away with this one and, if they're smart, they will become part of the solution. If not, I hope it will help you realize what kind of friends they are."

Faranos nodded. "I understand." He turned to Kendra. "I will never be able to thank you enough, my Lady."

She nodded. "I just want to make something clear to you."

"Yes, my Lady."

"You were there, that night."

"Yes, my Lady. I was. I told you."

"You shouldn't have been, but you were there. You made a mistake."

"Yes, Lady Kendra. I made a mistake."

"You realize that one side of me said that I should let you pay the price for that mistake, because that would be the best thing to happen to you?"

The young man gulped. "I can see that you might think that, my Lady."

"However, I decided it was the best for the Rochana Family if you did not pay, in public, for your mistake. That does not mean you do not pay. It means you do not pay in public. Do you understand the difference?"

"I think so, my Lady."

"I'm not sure that you do, Faranos. It has to do with trust. As far as the rest of the community is concerned, you were not found innocent in the court, and so you are not innocent. And they will not forget. If you should become involved in another such incident, I'm sure their memories would prove long and detailed."

Faranos winced. "I'm sure you are correct, my Lady."

"So it is up to you to make sure that you never are involved in another such incident."

"I hope I can ensure that, my Lady."

"So do I. However, that does not solve your problem with the Rochana Family."

He looked puzzled.

"You are in a position of trust, here. You have violated that trust. You have brought trouble to the Rochana name. We are charitably assuming it was out of your youth and

198

ignorance. However, that trust has been violated. Trust is a very difficult thing, Faranos."

"I am aware of that, my Lady."

"So you are in a tough position. You have to regain trust that has been lost. People here are forgiving, but they are not stupid. Your mistake has probably already been forgiven by those who love you. But they will not forget that you have made a mistake. They will be watching. In the future, when the time comes to decide whether to trust you with added responsiblity, they will be wondering whether you can handle the task. It is up to you to prove that you are able."

She threw her hands up. "I don't know how you are going to do that. It is a difficult task. How you manage is a measure of how mature you are, how ready to take over the control of such a large and prosperous estate. Do not let them down, the people who have believed in you."

"No, Lady Kendra. I will do my utmost not to let them down."

She nodded, satisfied. "I can see that your intentions are good." Then she stopped, peering into his eyes. "Do not make the mistake of overdoing it. If you are given responsibility that you feel you cannot handle, do not be afraid, because of this incident, to admit that you are unsure. If you take on more than you are able, you will fail again and lose more trust. No one wants that."

"I understand, my Lady."

"I hope so." She slapped him on the shoulder, turned him around, and walked beside him. "You are a good person, Faranos. Even good people make mistakes. Don't let it destroy you."

When they reached the Rochana Home, Cruzen motioned to Kendra and Cheynou to join him on the patio. "Those were good words you spoke, back there."

She grinned. "I borrowed them."

"Borrowed?"

"I had brothers, my Lord. I have heard my father give forth on the same subject, at greater length, more than a few times."

Cruzen nodded and pondered a moment, looking sideways at her. "You were very hard on him."

"I was."

For a moment, he stared out over the darkening land. "It was the kind of thing I should have said."

"But couldn't without preaching. It will have more effect, coming from an outsider."

"I did not hear an outsider speaking, Kendra. I heard someone who was passionately concerned with the Rochana Home and name."

She tossed her head. "I understand the situation better than he does. The honour of the Name is far more important than the welfare of any one person. If all do not do their utmost to support the Home, then the Home falls, and all are lost." She shrugged. "That is true, I suspect, in any estate in any land."

"It is certainly true of any FamilyShip."

The lord glanced to each of them, nodded. "You each have a mature grasp of the realities of running a Home."

Cheynou grinned. "I understand the problems. I wouldn't put myself forward as ready to come up with the solutions on a day-to-day basis."

"Nor should you." Cruzen turned and hobbled into the house.

Cheynou reached over and laid a hand on Kendra's arm. "This time it was you that done good!"

"High praise, Cheychan."

17. LEADERSHIP

Cheynou enjoyed sitting in Cruzen's workroom, watching and listening as the lord arranged his demesne, solved problems, and dispensed justice. He felt guilty about taking too much of this busy man's time, but Cruzen seemed happy to answer his questions and discuss the philosophies of his life. One day, over an after-lunch glass of wine, he chuckled quietly over his guest's continued probing.

"If it wasn't for the inescapable fact that you are here on your own, I would suspect you of being one of those who thinks and talks but never does anything about his grand ideas."

"I don't really have any grand ideas. Oh, certainly, I would like to be able to map the world. But that's so vague a dream that nobody, especially me, would ever expect me to actually perform the task."

"A very safe objective, then."

Cheynou shrugged. "You could see it that way. I suppose I should really find a more achievable goal." He grinned. "Of course, then I would pin myself down to something I could actually fail at."

Cruzen shrugged in imitation. "And yet you are the one who complains that he never gets to choose."

"Having a goal in life doesn't add to the number of choices you get to make. Quite the opposite, I think."

Cruzen chuckled again. "I suspect you have two quite different arguments crossing each other. You have your needs and wants mixed up with your dreams."

That brought Cheynou's mind to a halt. "Explain, please."

"Every person is making decisions all the time. You make the ones that get you what you need. I think your complaint

201

is that you don't often get to decide something that you want."

"And how is that mixed up with my dreams?"

Cruzen shrugged. "It's not that easy to explain. It happens to all of us, though. There are things we need in life. Food, clothing, family, safety. All our decisions, if we make the right ones, are aimed towards ensuring that we have those needs satisfied. Often what we want at the moment conflicts with one of those needs. So we make a decision we don't want to make, but we make it because it's better in the long run. We may not enjoy having to make the decision, but we do make one."

"I see. So while I might be really angry at the cook and want to tell him so, it isn't a good idea to give in to that impulse just before dinner."

"In simple terms, yes. Then you complain that you never get any choices."

"I do choose, but I wish I had different options."

"Something like that."

"But that just puts me back to where I started. Those needs you listed. I don't have any control over them."

"Not much. You do have control over how you fulfill them."

"I suppose. It still feels like I'm being driven downwind with no opportunity to change course." He considered that. "Maybe that wonderful choice I'm looking for is one of those things that doesn't really exist, except in our minds. More a dream than reality."

"You mean like the perfect day, the perfect wind, the perfect woman, the perfect marriage?"

Cheynou laughed. "I've met several perfect women. Just ask them."

"Precisely. In reality, none of those things exist. I think you're right. The opportunity to make a perfectly clear choice, unaffected by extraneous things, is another dream.

It's like your mapping the world. It sounds like a goal, but it's just a dream."

"So we just muddle along in our own mortal way, making whatever choices we think are best for the moment."

Cruzen swung his hand around, indicating their situation in general. "We haven't done so badly, so far."

"So if I'm going to make things the best for the moment, how can I do that, here in the Rochana Home? I don't seem to have any skills you need. Not like Kendra has."

Cruzen shook his head. "She certainly knows how to throw herself into life, doesn't she?"

"All anchors down, all sails up."

The Kyabran frowned, thinking. "I'm not a sailor, but that doesn't sound like a very productive way to run a boat."

Cheynou laughed. "You're right. It's not fair to her. She actually gets things done."

"And you aren't getting things done."

"Not at the moment. I'm learning plenty by watching you work. That is important to me, but I know I'm not contributing to the general welfare, and I don't feel comfortable about it."

Cruzen nodded. "Quite right. And since I am the one who invited you to stay, it is my responsibility to find some way to make you comfortable."

"Oh, no. That just makes me seem more of a problem!"

"Don't worry. I have some ideas or I wouldn't have asked you to stay."

"You do?" Cheynou felt his anxiety recede, just a bit.

"Yes. I was just waiting for you to settle in, to see if you fitted here."

"And I gather I have passed that test?"

"Let's not call it a test. I think I'm a better judge of character than that. No, I was rather checking to see if you felt happy here, if you would want to stay for a while."

"If I thought I was being useful, I would love to stay here. Kendra..." He flicked his fingers towards where she stood in the middle of a group of housemaids, showing them some esoteric bit of women's lore.

"No question about her." Cruzen gave a satisfied nod, then looked at Cheynou, eyebrows up. "How would you feel about going on a short journey?"

"I'm always interested in a journey. Where to?"

"East. There is some land I would like you to look at."

"Fine. What am I looking for?"

"Trails, possibility of roadways, farmland."

Cheynou winced. "I can map trails for you. I can probably figure out roadways. I know nothing about what makes good farmland."

"That's where Faranos comes in. He knows something about farmland, and I want him to have reason to learn more."

"Just the two of us?"

"I think perhaps not. We have had no trouble lately, but I think a larger party is safer. Maybe four."

Cheynou nodded. "I agree." Then an important thought came to him. "Who is going to be in charge of this expedition?"

Cruzen frowned thoughtfully. "I hadn't decided. What do you think?"

"I think that is your choice to make, my Lord. I am quite willing to take on the responsibility if that is your wish. If it would achieve your objectives better to have Faranos or one of the others lead, I have no trouble with that, either."

Cruzen nodded, grinned wryly. "Turning the problem neatly back to the man who should be solving it. Fair enough. I'll think on it. Make your own preparations. Leaving in about three days."

"Not wanting to be impertinent, my Lord, but shouldn't whoever is leading the expedition have some say in that decision?"

Cruzen shot him a frowning glance, then his face cleared. "Yes, of course." Then he leaned back in the chair, staring at Cheynou. "So if you were leading, you would want to start leading from this point on."

"I don't think I'd like to find myself out on the trail with three men under my command, suddenly in charge of a project that someone else had organized."

Cruzen nodded. "I think I have learned something about the way we have been treating Faranos."

Cheynou waited, and the lord nodded, as if to himself. "Yes, that's what I will do. I will give Faranos the leadership, but I will consider, when I am organizing it with him, how I would speak if you were leading." Cruzen slapped his hands on the table. "All right. I think I have learned enough for today. Would you go and find Faranos, wherever he is, and bring him here? We will have a discussion about this possible project." He levered himself up, stumped away from his desk, then turned back.

"I apologize, Cheynou, if I seem touchy. I sit in this room day after day, and unless people bring things to me, I don't know what is going on in my demesne. It is difficult to have someone tell me that the plans I have had so much fun making are not necessarily the best ones."

"I didn't mean to..."

"Of course you did. A good commander can't sit in his office and plan a campaign, then expect his subordinate, who had no part in the planning, to understand and follow his orders to the letter. Especially when this is not the army."

"And Faranos is definitely not a soldier."

The lord frowned. "He does have military training. He achieved his Hundred Prime with some distinction, as I recall. I will remember that."

205

"I'll go look for him. He shouldn't be too hard to find. Somewhere there are horses."

"True. Again. Thank you for being understanding, Cheynou."

"Thank you for giving me a project, Cruzen." He made a reasonably crisp salute in the Kyabran manner and spun sharply out the door.

Faranos was out in the stable yard with a filly on a long lead. Cheynou watched him, unobserved, as Faranos trotted the horse around in a circle. She was blindfolded, and he was patiently persuading her to trot in spite of her lack of sight. He was firm but gentle, and completely focused on his task, a contrast to the carefree, feckless lad Cheynou was used to seeing around the farm. A boy stood just outside the circle holding a cedar bough. Intrigued, Cheynou moved forward quietly and climbed up to sit on the fence rail.

Once the animal was moving nicely, Faranos nodded to the boy, who stepped forward. Just as the horse approached the boy, Faranos called "Halt!" sharply, and the boy touched the cedar bough to the horse's face.

She skittered, reared, then stood, trembling. Shortening the lead, Faranos urged her on. She was reluctant, but finally his soft words and firm intentions had her moving smoothly around the circle again. Once more the boy moved closer, and the action was repeated. This time the horse shied slightly at the call of "Halt!" and the boy only tapped her lightly with the branch.

The third time, the horse stopped quite quickly at the command, and the boy only tickled her nose. The fourth time she stopped dead, and Faranos and his assistant shared a grin.

Faranos took the blindfold off the horse, fondling her ears and talking lovingly to her all the while. Now, with her eyes open, the horse trotted willingly, but still stopped immediately on the command. After a half-glass of practice, Faranos gestured to the lad to take the horse and strode over to Cheynou.

"That seemed very effective. How long did it take to train her that way?"

"You have seen the first lesson."

"Then it's more effective than I thought."

"I'll have to continue for a while, but she's learned that lesson pretty well."

"I don't know much about horse training, but I've never seen anything work so quickly."

Faranos shrugged. "It works even quicker if you use the barn."

"The barn?"

"Yes. That's the way they did it in the old days. You trotted the horse so that she was just missing the corner of the barn. On the last circuit, you let out a little of the lead, and when you shouted, she ran into the barn. They learn really fast that way."

"If they survive."

Faranos nodded. "I find my way takes a little longer, but it leaves a calmer horse when you're finished. If you want a calm horse, that is."

Cheynou frowned. "I'm just trying to think of a situation where I would find running a horse into a barn to be good training."

"Sometimes the Imperial Army needs a lot of horses trained quickly." They stood for a moment, looking out over the other stock in the pasture before them. "So, have you come to learn horse handling?"

"No, I have come to take you to Cruzen, who has a project for us." He glanced at the lad's reaction. "One involving a riding trip."

Becoming more cheerful, Faranos gestured. "Lead on, then."

Cruzen glanced up as they entered. "Took you long enough. Where was he?"

Cheynou waited a moment to give the lord time to realize how grouchy he sounded. "He was training a horse, and I didn't like to interfere."

Cruzen fixed Faranos with a stern eye. "If you spent as much time training yourself on the running of this Home as you do on training that horse of yours..."

Taking his cue from Cheynou, Faranos spoke calmly. "I was working with that new mare of Cedenye's."

"Oh. I see. How's she coming along?"

"Very well. Learns fast."

"Good. What were you working on?"

"The command to halt."

"You aren't running that horse into the barn, are you?"

Cheynou glanced at Faranos. "He really is grouchy today, isn't he? Maybe we should come back when he's had his lunch and he's in a better mood."

The youth looked almost as shocked as his uncle, but Cheynou held his ground, smiling in a friendly fashion. Then Cruzen ran a hand through his hair and shook his head. "You're right, Cheynou. I know Faranos doesn't train like that. It's just that my father ruined a good horse with that trick, once. It works for big, tough, plow horses that don't trot fast."

Faranos shrugged. "The cedar bough works almost as fast. You just have to remind them a few times in the following days. You also have to run them some more with the blindfold on, or you'll never be able to blindfold them again."

Cruzen nodded. "I hadn't thought of that. I'll hand it to you, Faranos, you're good with horses."

"But Cheynou says you have something else in mind. Something for both of us?"

Cruzen nodded, and ran through a quick explanation of what he wanted. "...you know the place I'm talking about, I think. We were hunting out there last fall."

208

"Oh, yes. Where the wind makes that funny sound sometimes."

"That's right. Take our Navigator out and see how he maps a snoring mountain."

"Good idea. When would you like us to leave?"

Cruzen glanced at Cheynou. "Whenever you like. Whatever time it takes to get ready."

"How big a party?"

"Your choice. Not too big. It's pretty safe, and we don't want to make a big issue about it."

"Are you suggesting that we sneak in and out quickly?"

"I don't want word to spread that we're interested, but I'm not hiding anything."

"All right." The boy thought a moment. "Three is the minimum, but if we're running a survey we need more than that. How about five? That would be Cheynou and me, two other riders, and one to cook and handle the pack horse."

"You think you need a cook?"

"If we were just travelling I wouldn't, because we could all take our turn in camp. But if we're working once we get there and we want to get finished more quickly, having one man in camp preparing while we're working is best, I think."

Cruzen nodded. "Good enough. Choose your men and let your aunt know what you'll need."

"Is anyone else going out at the time? Anyone who might need the same men or supplies?"

The lord looked at his nephew with new respect. "No, just you."

Faranos nodded. "How long do you think it will take to get there, and how big an area do you want covered?"

"Hand me that pile of maps over there. No, not that pile, the other one." Faranos looked back, confused, and Cruzen began to rise. "Don't bother, I'll get it myself."

"Relax, Uncle. I think I can manage to find a map if you'll just tell me which one."

"Obviously you can't, because I just did…"

"And now you're both starting to sound grumpy."

The two turned and stared at Cheynou, then exchanged guilty looks. Cruzen frowned, then sat down again and spoke with exaggerated clarity. "I want a large, dark-brown map, probably folded twice. It should be in the third pile on the left. If you please."

"Thank you, Uncle." Faranos began sheafing through the piles. "I know this is hard on you, not being able to rare around the Home like you usually do. I've been quite enjoying it, actually."

"You have?"

"Oh, yes." He shot a wicked grin at Cheynou. "Without you stomping around, I have been able to do all sorts of things. I sold off several head of stock to pay my gambling debts, and I also bought a couple of fast cross-country racing horses. Cheynou is going to teach me a new navigating method so I can win all the courses this summer." He turned an innocuous smile back to his glowering uncle. "Is this the map you wanted?"

"Very funny." Cruzen snatched the map. "I've changed my mind. I'm not sending Cheynou out with you. Put your two heads together with no supervision, and who knows what strange ideas you'll come back with."

Cheynou grinned. "I don't know. I think my idea to change the arms on the windmills to canvas sails and double their power was a pretty good one." He turned to see Cruzen staring at him.

"Now I'm not sure whether you are joking."

"I'm not. I was looking at those windmills the other day, thinking how poorly a ship would sail if it just put a flat plank up to the wind, instead of curved cloth. You could probably double the power of the windmill with sails instead, treating each arm like a spar. You could also adjust them, depending on the wind, and furl them in a storm."

Faranos leaned forward eagerly. "Why don't you make up a set of them, and we'll try it?"

Cheynou shrugged. "I don't know much about sewing. Do you have a sailmaker handy?"

Cruzen frowned. "Since the nearest ocean takes seven days for an Imperial messenger to reach, I doubt it."

Faranos raised a palm, as if the answer was easy. "Why don't you get one of the sailmakers from your people to make a set for us?"

Cheynou nodded. "We'll go up there and take some measurements the next calm day. Then, when we get the opportunity, we can get some sails made, rig the spars with some blocks for the lines..."

"And maybe we should get back to planning this journey." Cruzen was unfolding the map, an uncertain smile on his face. "Now I'm really worried about you two when you get your heads together."

They grinned at each other and leaned over the map.

18. SURVEY PARTY

Two days later, Cheynou felt enthused as they trotted their horses out through the main gate. He responded to Kendra and the twins, who waved mightily at him. Cinders whined at the end of a piece of rope in Kendra's hand. The puppy had turned the tables on their relationship, and now she was pregnant.

Faranos twisted in the saddle to look back. "That poor dog really wants to come, doesn't she?"

"She's too far along for a rough trip like this, even if I let her ride behind my saddle, and there's no guarantee this blockhead of a horse would let her."

Faranos pulled aside so they could ride together, observing Cheynou's mount critically. "How's the new horse? Is he giving you trouble?"

"Not yet, but I've ridden enough horses by now to know the signs."

"Well, don't let him get away with anything from the very start."

"I know that. Somehow, though, I get the feeling that he's just waiting for an opportune moment."

Faranos grinned. "That's the kind of horse I like. So much more fun than an old plodder."

Cheynou urged his horse ahead. "If I'm still in the saddle at the end of the day, I'm satisfied."

Faranos trotted his horse to catch up, and the others followed, the cook leading the packhorse at the back. The troop rode steadily and made good time, and the land flowed by beneath them.

In camp that night, Cheynou tried to be subtle about checking what was happening in the kitchen. Faranos had mentioned that the cook was not of his choosing, being the only one available who could do the job. Beit was a wiry, older man with a bald pate and a stringy grey beard. Long hair hung down from the fringe above his ears, tied back with a leather thong. He didn't look like he should be anywhere near a kitchen, but until Cheynou started pulling grey hairs out of his meal, he was willing to wait.

He found himself impressed by the man's economy of movement. Nothing happened quickly, but all went smoothly. If the smells were anything to judge by, Beit was a competent cook. Cheynou's compliment at the end of the meal brought the first smile he had seen on the man's face, and it broadened when the others chimed in. Cheynou caught a meaningful glance from Faranos. Keeping the cook happy was a key element in the comfort of the crew.

The other two men posed no problems. Brantiran was one of the stable lads, charged with any care of the horses over and above the usual daily responsibility of the riders. He was young and enthusiastic about anything that would take him away from his usual tasks.

His companion was less easy to place. Shorter, stockier and less talkative, Gire spoke no Frasian, and his Kyabran was accented in a way that Cheynou could not place, although sometimes it sounded familiar. He seemed sort of rounded, with small round ears, full, rounded lips, and a very short haircut that accented the smooth roundness of his skull. His shoulders and arms curved as well, with muscles that bulged through the light, tight shirt he always wore. Although no one was concerned about danger, Cheynou suspected that Gire would be the man to count on if there was trouble.

The only other skill Faranos had required for this trip was basic reading and writing. Cheynou wondered how either man had attained those skills. Each seemed willing to take his share of the camp chores, and it looked like they were settling into a congenial group.

Once dinner was over, Cheynou decided it was time for a lesson in surveying. Some of it was new to him, as well, and he wanted to practise. Bringing out his compass and book, he demonstrated by laying out a baseline through the centre of the camp, exactly as Cruzen had taught him. Then he sent Faranos and Brantiran to map out the left side of the camp, while he and Gire did the other side. After a glass or two they compared maps, and Cheynou walked the area with them, discussing the ways to denote the landmarks they saw.

Then Faranos brought out a shovel to demonstrate the different types of soil they might find and how to recognize good land when they saw it. That finished as darkness was falling, so they went to bed, well satisfied with the day's progress.

* * *

Cheynou was pleased to note that no one needed prodding to get out of bed when Beit made his call in the morning. It also didn't hurt his feelings that breakfast was considerably more interesting than salt pork and biscuit.

They were soon saddled up and riding farther east, crossing a range of low hills and dipping into another valley. As they rode, Cheynou took notes and called out landmarks to the others so that they would remember them on the return journey. He took special care to train them to look back as well, a lesson that Cruzen had deemed important.

For two more days they pushed deeper into the wilderness as the farms fell away and the road became a single track, then not much more than an animal trail. The third morning, they came over another low pass and saw, stretching across their route, a range of mountains even higher than the Barrier that Cheynou and Kendra had crossed. In spite of the summer sun, huge snowfields and glaciers clung to the steep flanks of the peaks, rank on rank, that disappeared into the mist of the eastern sky. The riders, feeling small, looked up at the giant barrier that towered above them.

"I guess we don't go past that."

214

"Even a sailor can tell there's not much farming up there."

"How do you want to do the layout, Cheynou?"

He scanned the valley. "Cruzen wants us to map the river, the arable land near it, a place for a mill and a defendable townsite. He also wants to know if there are passes that might lead to other places."

Faranos rubbed his chin thoughtfully. "That's an awfully big valley. We only scheduled ten days."

"Exactly. I think we should ride up one side of the river then down the other, doing a quick sketch of the area. Then we find what looks like a good townsite and camp there. We can start a more detailed survey from that point."

Faranos nodded, turned to the men. "Everyone got that? We'll continue until we hit the river, then start our first sweep. Start looking for good landmarks as we go."

* * *

"Thank you, Cheynou, but I'll do that."

Cheynou looked up from his work in surprise. It was a long time since anyone had objected to his rope work. He stepped back and allowed Beit to see the logs he had been lashing. To his surprise, the man began to undo his work.

"I think it would be better done a little more tightly. If we were only staying overnight, your way would be fine."

Cheynou observed as the man carefully re-lashed the logs, using a technique similar to one Cheynou knew, and, in Cheynou's mind, completely unnecessary. *I wonder if he really thinks it's needed, or if he's just exerting his authority over the cooking area. Whichever, it isn't worth arguing over.* Cheynou nodded and went over to help Gire with the sleeping tents.

The man grinned at him. "Your help not needed over there?"

"No. I guess he has his own way of doing things."

215

"He's the cook."

"And he's good at it."

By the end of the evening, Cheynou and Faranos were able to congratulate each other on a snug campsite. The horses were picketed a reasonable distance from the men's tents, and the cooking area was set to Beit's satisfaction, complete with a drystone fireplace and a meat safe hung high enough in a tree to discourage even the tallest bear. The men sat around a larger fire that crackled cheerfully. As the slow summer twilight descended, they chatted about nothing in particular and generally felt ready for the work to start.

In the morning, Cheynou started the survey. Faranos watched to make sure he knew what they were doing, then started his own work.

By noon, their pattern was set. Brantiran and Gire were becoming adept at laying out baselines. Gire, due to his experience with an axe, led the way through the undergrowth clearing the right-of-way. Bran came behind, sketching and measuring. Cheynou and Faranos were now free to range the area. While they ate, they discussed their findings.

"I'm getting a lot of good soil, down in the bends of the river."

Cheynou nodded. "I thought so, by the trees growing there. How far up have you gone?"

"About five hundred paces."

"And still good soil?"

"The best part is a pretty narrow strip. All of those benches," he swung his arm to point, "like the one above camp, here, look pretty good as well. It's only after the hillside gets steep that the soil gets thinner, lighter in colour and harder. The trees get smaller, and if you go even higher, soon there's nothing but bushes."

"That still encompasses a huge area. Some of those benches are a hundred paces wide."

"Exactly. We can't survey all of that."

Cheynou looked around, frustrated by all the trees growing in the river bottom. It had looked so easy as they came over the pass. *Over the pass.* He nodded. "This afternoon, you keep doing what you have been. I've got an idea."

He collected his equipment and started up the hill above the camp.

By late afternoon, he had firmed his plans. He had found several vantage points from which he could get a good picture of the whole valley. He would relate them to the baseline that the others were drawing: a fresh, straight scar through the undergrowth. There were a couple of places where he could see the bits of cloth they were using as markers. He strode down the trail into camp, quite pleased with himself.

"How did it go?"

Faranos looked up from where he was writing. "Well enough, I guess."

"I think I have it figured out."

"That's good."

Cheynou frowned. "That sounds like an overwhelming lack of enthusiasm."

The lad rose, tossing up his hands helplessly. "This is getting to be difficult, Cheynou."

"What? As I said, I think I have it solved."

"Not the survey, Cheynou, the journey."

"I don't understand. We're not on the journey. We're here."

"Yes, but I'm still supposed to be leading."

"And you are."

"It doesn't feel like it."

"Oh."

"No. You go running out of camp, not telling me what you're doing. You're giving everybody else orders, and I'm left on my own to do whatever I'm supposed to be doing."

"I thought I was supposed to be mapping, and you were doing the soil tests."

"That's right. But how? Where? Who is going to help me? I seem to be the leader of nobody but myself. If I offer to help Beit, he waits until I finish then does it over his own way."

Cheynou could grin at that. "You, too?"

"You mean he does it to you?"

"He re-lashed some poles that I had just finished."

That brought a smile. "You mean he took apart the seaman's lashing and did it over?"

"That's right."

"I hope you told him."

"I did nothing of the sort. I was helping in his kitchen, and he wanted it done his way."

"Hmph. A sure way to end up doing it all himself."

"If you watch over the next few days, I suspect you'll find it happening just like that. I'm not sure if that's how he likes it or if he'll use it to make himself a martyr." He grinned. "That's the kind of thing the leader is supposed to be worrying about."

Faranos looked glum. "Great."

"You weren't expecting it to be all fun, were you?"

"I don't know what I was expecting. I just didn't expect to feel like I wasn't leading."

Cheynou slapped him on the back. "I've been on the trail with Kendra for a month. I know exactly how you feel. Don't worry. I'll be more careful to let you know what I'm doing in the future. That was my mistake. I wasn't really sure myself, or I would have told you."

"And you are sure, now?"

"Yes." Cheynou had been meaning to tell everyone after supper, but now realized that it would be better to let Faranos do that. "I have figured out a system of observation points, and if I can get some reference points measured out on the baseline, I can locate them quite accurately. Then we can measure the points where you are taking samples and put them in as well."

"And how do we lay out the fertility of the soil?"

"I don't know." He nudged the other ungently. "That's what leaders are for. Figuring out things like that."

"Huh!" Faranos moved towards camp, but his step was lighter and his shoulders straighter.

Cheynou followed, shaking his head. *Being a leader is easier than trying not to be, it seems. I'm beginning to understand why Cruzen is having trouble with his Heir. And why he sent us out together.*

However, once Cheynou was aware of the problem, he took more care to treat Faranos as the leader, and tried to make sure the others did as well. If they asked him a question about the survey, he told them. If they asked him anything else, he referred them to Faranos. This seemed to work well until the fourth day, when Faranos took him aside.

"We've got a problem."

"What?"

"Beit says someone is stealing food."

"Stealing food? From where? How does he know?"

"He says someone is stealing food from the kitchen. Mostly leftover stuff, but sometimes things he has prepared, and no one has even had the chance to try."

"And what does he want you to do about it?"

"That's just it, Cheynou. I don't know. I don't know how to find out who is doing it, and I don't know how to stop it."

"Faranos, I don't know why you're asking me this. My total experience of leading has been to bring a party of four over the mountains."

"A party of four?"

"Yes. Kendra, me, Cinders, and Martan. Cinders listens to me sometimes. Martan never listens to me. I take it you know Kendra by now. So don't come to me for advice. I don't have any more idea than you do."

219

"But what am I going to do?"

He shrugged. "I'm sure you'll figure out something."

"What would you do?"

"I've never had the problem before. I don't know. What were you thinking about doing?"

Faranos shrugged. "I thought about asking the others."

"Sounds like a good start. We don't even know if the thief is from inside or outside the camp."

"Outside the camp! I never thought of that."

"I'm just trying to explore all the possibilities."

"That's a good idea, Cheynou. I'll ask everybody. So?"

"So what?"

"So is it you? Are you the one who has been stealing food out of the kitchen?"

Cheynou frowned. "You're not really going to go around accusing everyone, are you?"

Faranos frowned as well. "Aha! You're not answering my question! Very suspicious." Then he laughed. "Of course I'm not. Do you think I'm stupid?"

"Well, now that you mention it..."

"All right. I'm sorry I asked. I take it you haven't been taking food from the kitchen without asking Beit first."

Cheynou shook his head. "I don't so much as stick my nose into his kitchen without first wiping my feet and asking for permission."

Faranos was about to leave, but suddenly turned back. "Do you think it's a good idea, Cheynou, to let him have so much control? Am I ducking my responsibilities as a leader?"

Cheynou shrugged. "I can't see how it would cause a problem. From my limited experience, all cooks are like that about their kitchens, more or less. Just make sure that he doesn't start getting pushy outside his area."

Faranos nodded. "I agree. Thanks, Cheynou. It's good to have someone to talk it over with."

"Even if he doesn't know anything, either."

"That makes it even better. Nobody tells me how wrong I am."

It seemed that Faranos did a very subtle job of solving the problem, because Cheynou heard nothing more about it until after supper that night, when the leader made a casual announcement.

"Beit has asked me to let you all know something."

Once they were all looking at him, he continued. "If you're hungry in the night, or some time when there is no meal available, there is a box in the kitchen, right by the counter, where he will leave any available food. Biscuits, leftovers from former meals, that sort of thing. Please feel free to take any of that, at any time."

Gire grinned wryly. "But nothing else."

Faranos nodded. "Exactly."

"Suits me. As long as there's lots."

Brantiran slapped the other's hard stomach. "And we'll soon know if you're overdoing it."

"I can't help it if I'm hungry."

Faranos chuckled. "No. But you can keep from finishing off our dinners before they get served."

"I never did that!"

"Not quite."

"It was really good, too!"

Cheynou glanced over to see how Beit was taking this light-hearted discussion, but the man looked satisfied. Well enough. He caught Faranos' eye, gave him a positive signal. Faranos grinned, and the banter continued.

* * *

Cheynou had just joined the baseline party one day when he received a surprise. He had been watching Gire slash his way through a particularly springy nest of vines, and the axe kept catching on their tough stems. After a bout of this frustrating work, the axeman threw down his tool in exasperation and burst into a frustrated stream of invective that Cheynou found he could understand.

"Is that Landspeak I hear?"

Gire turned in surprise and answered in the same language. "How do you know my speech?"

"A Helmsman of the Sea People speaks many languages. However, I don't have it solid enough to completely understand what you just said, there."

Gire grinned sheepishly. "Don't try to learn that stuff. I was just getting frustrated at those vines."

Cheynou nodded. "They're too small and tough, and the axe bounces off, doesn't it? Maybe you should try a sword."

"Huh. Typical of a Sea Raider to think of a sword."

"Do my people give yours trouble, too?"

Gire shrugged. "Sometimes. We don't live right at the shore, so we don't meet often. Sometimes for trade, sometimes for battle; you know how it goes."

As they walked back to camp to get a sword, they traded histories, but it seemed that Cheynou's part of the Fleet had never actually had contact with Gire's people, who were sheepherders in the lower foothills of the huge mountain range that loomed over the camp.

The sword did a much better job on the vines, and soon Gire was through them and back to his favoured tool, the axe. He was making good progress, and Cheynou did not want to distract him with chat.

Later that evening, though, when supper was over, they resumed their conversation in Landspeak. "So how did you end up down here in civilization?"

Gire shrugged. "The usual youngster's foolishness, I guess. I just couldn't see myself tied to a flock of sheep for the rest of my life. So I took off and followed the wool."

"What do you mean?"

"When the traders came for the wool, I went with them. When they traded it to the weavers to make cloth, I went to work for the weavers. When they took their cloth to the market, I followed."

"That must have brought you closer and closer to the centre of the Empire."

"Yes, and it was there that I discovered I would be quite happy spending my life with the sheep, out in the mountains." He tossed a hand towards the Barrier, glowing in the last rays of the sun. "I like the scenery better."

They stood staring up at the Barrier Mountains. "So your people aren't that far from here. In a straight line."

"I think so. I decided to come home, but I thought I'd try the short way. That's what brought me to Velika. Once I got here, though, I was stumped. When I heard that you came over the mountains from the south, that was the first chance I'd heard that I might make it. You came from too far south, though — a long trip around, as well."

Cheynou nodded. "Maybe you could cut through the Barrier farther north. The people of the Prairies might know of a route. Otherwise, you'd have to go all the way south to the Ocean. That would be about a month's travel from the Rochana Home, I'd guess."

Gire pointed east. "Near as I can make out from Lord Cruzen's maps, my people are right through there."

A particularly large peak rose in front of his pointing finger. "That doesn't even look possible."

Gire shrugged. "There could be passes."

"It must be frustrating to be so close and not be able to make a try."

"Oh, no. I am going to try. That's why I asked Lord Cruzen to send me out with you and Faranos. Once the survey is finished, I'm going to scout out the land to the east, see if I can find a way through. Faranos knows. Didn't you?"

"No reason why I should." He stood and took a more careful look at the mountains. "Where are you thinking of starting?"

"Lord Cruzen told me that there was a trail out to the north that would get me into the next valley, which belongs to the farthest south of the Inner Provinces. If all else fails, I'll take that trail and make another try from there. At first, though, I'll climb the valley beside the Snoring Mountain and see where it goes."

"On horse, or on foot?"

"On foot, I think. Lord Cruzen offered a horse, but I doubt if it would be much use."

"Probably not. We left our horses up on the Prairies for the same reason."

"Is there anything you can tell me about navigating through the mountains?"

"A sailor tell a shepherd about mountains? I doubt it. We can talk, if you like. Maybe I'll be able to come up with something." He thought about his conversation with Kendra about mountains being like waves. "Yes, maybe I could give you a few ideas. I would like to ask you about the places you've been, though, especially the ones outside the Kyabran maps."

"Whatever I can remember."

"Great. I can practise my Landspeak, too."

"Landspeak. Is that what you call it?"

"What do you call it?"

"The People's Language."

Cheynou laughed. "Everybody calls their language something like that."

"I suppose."

"Can you write Landspeak as well?"

Gire shook his head. "I learned to write Kyabran from the traders I travelled with. I don't think anybody writes Landspeak."

"Oh. I didn't know that."

"We travel to learn, Cheynou."

"We do."

Once Gire had drawn his attention to the mountains, Cheynou regarded them with more interest. The two took to strolling up the hill above camp in the evening to discuss what they could see and try to figure possible routes. It looked daunting from their low angle, but the lure was irresistible. Cheynou showed Gire how to draw maps and pictograms of what he could see, reminding him to keep track of what was behind him in case he wanted to retrace his steps.

"After all, you might be discovering a new trade route."

Gire shook his head. "My people have been exploring into the mountains from our side for hundreds of years. If there was an easy way, they'd have found it."

"I didn't say an easy route, just a possible one. Show a merchant the way to a new market and he'll do the rest."

"As long as I can find my way home, I'm happy. Above that, who knows?"

"Is that your plan? Just start walking?"

"Basically."

Cheynou looked up at the eastern mountains. "All alone?"

"I'm used to it. We work alone with our flocks."

Cheynou shook his head. "It would scare me. I've never done anything alone."

"Never?"

He thought about Sarasha's Resting. "Well, once, I guess. But our people are used to having several hundred other Crew around all the time."

Gire grimaced. "That, I wouldn't like."

"Well, there you are."

They sat watching the shadow of the earth rise up the mountains, until only the snow-whitened peaks remained in sunlight. Then darkness descended into the valley, and they rose without speaking and made their way down to their tents.

As the surveying became routine, Cheynou turned his attention eastward. One evening, he and Gire saddled their horses and traced the course of the little stream that ran out of the valley to the east. As they rode past the great, flat-topped peak that formed the initial buttress of the Barrier, Cheynou looked up. "So that's the Snorer, I gather."

"From what Lord Cruzen told us, I guess so."

"It has yet to perform its special act."

"I guess the wind has to be right."

"Not today." It had turned into a grey evening, with low-hanging cloud dashing itself against the walls of the mountains in front of them.

"We may not get much of a view, up at the end of the valley."

"Yes, this dratted fog moved in at exactly the wrong time. Should we go back?"

"The horses need the exercise. We'll at least see what the ground is like."

"I'm game."

Gire was leading and Cheynou's attention was on their surroundings when the stocky herdsman froze, his eyes scanning the immediate area, one hand raised in warning.

Cheynou searched as well but saw nothing out of the ordinary. He caught the other's glance and raised his eyebrows.

Gire pointed to the ground in front of his horse. There, in a patch of mud, was a human footprint. Not a boot, like they all wore. A moccasin. With a final glance around, he dismounted and bent over the trail. Then he relaxed and looked up.

"Yesterday."

"Traveller?"

"If so, why didn't he visit?"

"Recognize anything?"

Gire shrugged. "The only people I know who wear moccasins are the Inara from the Prairies."

"Do you mean the Inari?"

"Inara is what my people call them. They are a fierce people. They send their youngsters out to practise their skills of war on anyone they can find." He glanced around again. "Sometimes, they get as far as our pastures. We don't make them welcome."

"The Inari over by Ternata were pretty friendly." Cheynou explained about Pers and Yong and the horses.

Gire nodded. "The elders might be hospitable if you have what they need . The young ones just want to gain prowess in battle."

"So any Inari we meet that doesn't come openly is probably out to kill us?"

"That's my experience."

Cheynou reined his horse around. "Faranos needs to know this."

"Take my horse."

"What?"

"He'll just get in the way in this brush. I'm going to track our friend and see where he goes. I'll be back by supper."

"And if you're not?"

Gire frowned. "Get out of here as fast as your horses can gallop. Don't wait to pack the tents."

The man was deadly serious, so Cheynou grabbed the extra reins and trotted away. He looked back; Gire was already bent over the track in the mud.

19.   INARI ATTACK

Faranos took the news with more aplomb than Cheynou had expected. He immediately started snapping out orders.

"Bran, saddle the riding horses first. Then the packhorse, but don't load it yet." He turned to Beit. "Looks like we might be eating on the run. Can you pack supper to carry?"

The cook nodded.

"Right."

"Cheynou..."

"You've done this before."

The lad nodded. "Military training. You think I got my Hundred Prime by polishing my boots? Now, we need a lookout. You're a sailor. Can you climb that tree?"

"Probably..."

"Get up to that big limb. Try to stay hidden from the ground and keep watch. Not only farther out, but in close as well. We don't know what we're dealing with, here."

Cheynou slipped his bow across his shoulders and mounted the tree, climbing easily on the heavy, grooved bark. When he reached the limb, he hid himself in a position where he could sit comfortably and scan most of the surrounding brush. *If I can see them, they can see me, and I'll have to move to look around the other side of the tree. This isn't as easy as I thought.* He settled in to wait.

Dusk came, and there was no Gire. Faranos sent Bran up to relieve Cheynou so he could eat. Beit had put out the fire, and they were making do with cold water to drink. While Cheynou ate, Faranos patrolled farther out, returning to report with a mere shake of the head. "What do you think, Cheynou?"

Cheynou moved in close to speak quietly. "Gire says these are fierce fighters. The Inari I met are superior even to our

228

Raiders, and that's high praise. I wonder if we shouldn't take the tents down and stow them. We won't want to sleep in them tonight in any case."

"That's..."

"Psst!"

They looked up. Brantiran was pointing up the stream, and soon a form appeared, striding down the trail in the dying light.

As soon as he was close enough, Gire spoke in normal tones. "Found them."

"Where?"

He nodded over his shoulder. "Up the stream and over the next ridge. There's only six. All in camp at the moment."

"How do you know?"

"Counted the bedrolls. Not to say there isn't another batch somewhere else."

Faranos regarded each of them. "Any suggestions?"

Gire shrugged. "Wait till they're asleep and kill them."

"We can't just go out and murder a bunch of people in their beds."

"Believe me, that's what they plan to do to us. Maybe even tonight."

Cheynou nodded. "If one of them was that close, they know we're here. Why would they wait? Maybe a preemptive attack..."

"We can't just attack unprovoked. But we can set a trap."

Gire nodded. "I could go back and watch their camp. If they start arming, I'll hotfoot back here, and we can hide out and hit them when they attack an empty camp."

"Good idea. We only have three bows. Do you want one?"

"Just get in my way in the bush in the dark."

"Off you go, then. We'll make the camp look like we've gone to bed and set our positions for the trap. If they haven't moved by midnight, come on back and we'll rethink."

It was an agonizing wait, but unfortunately it didn't go on for long. Within two glasses, Gire was back. "They're headed this way. All six. No bows, just long knives."

Cheynou gave a humourless grin. "They're after honour. Killing face to face, hand against hand."

They banked the fire, closed up the tents and moved to their ambush positions. Cheynou, assuming he was the best swordsman, stood behind the tree closest to the tents. The others were farther out, and Gire was up the trail, planning to watch the enemy pass, follow, and pick off the last man as soon as the battle started.

Their attackers were good, but not good enough. The ground beneath the cottonwood trees was littered with old leaves and fallen branches, and soon Cheynou could hear the noises. Someone was moving directly towards him. *Of course. He plans to hide behind my tree.*

He faded backwards, his ears straining. The sounds dropped off, moving more slowly, and for a long while there was absolute silence. Then, as if his eyes just came into focus, the shadow of a man's head appeared in silhouette against the faint white of the tent canvas. Without waiting, he lunged to where he hoped the body was. A stick cracked beneath his feet and the man twisted, but Cheynou's aim was good. He struck something that gave, and there was a gurgle and a short scream of pain. The sword was nearly wrenched from his hand.

What do I do now? If I withdraw, I'll lose him in the dark!

He did the only thing he could. He kept the pressure on, forcing his enemy against the tree. The wriggling slowed, and he could hear harsh breathing. Then metal clicked on metal, and a knife slithered up his sword.

Now he knows where I am. He jerked back and, assuming a right-handed opponent, swung where the arm should be. He was rewarded by a meaty 'thunk,' and the rustle of something dropping to the forest floor. *I hope that was his knife.* He struck again.

A breathy grunt exploded in front of him, then a body dropped.

He listened, but now the cries and clashing swords of the rest of the fight drowned out anything he could glean in his area. He stepped back, circled wide, and crept towards the campfire. There was a loud tussle in the brush to his left, and he moved that way, uncertain. The sound fell away, and there was silence.

How will I know an enemy from a friend? Of course. Ask.

"One down over here. Anybody need help?"

"Damn right. Two of them!" That was Bran.

"Coming in from the fire."

"Over here. Ouch! Damn."

Cheynou moved as quickly as he could towards the noises. From the sound of it, Bran had his back against a tree, and his two attackers were stymied by the length of his sword. Cheynou stopped to listen.

"They're separating. I'll take the one on your left."

He surged towards the noises in that direction, swinging his cutlass in wide arcs in front of him, cursing the bushes and limbs that impeded his cuts. He hit nothing.

Now he knows where I am. He stopped, crouching low, trying to see a silhouette against the few stars peeping in through the branches.

"Got him. You there, Cheynou?"

He said nothing. *If he lost me, he'll go for Bran, now.* He listened.

He was still peering, trying desperately to see, when light burst from the campsite. A black figure appeared in front of him, moving towards the right. The firelight glistened on a short piece of metal. Praying that Bran hadn't broken his sword, Cheynou slashed at the arm.

He made contact, and the knife dropped. The man hissed in pain and ran, dodging into the firelight, through the camp and away. Beit threw another branch on the fire and the light

231

increased. They stood, staring at each other and listening. There was only silence.

"Call in!"

Bran stumbled out of the brush, holding his left arm with his right hand. "I'm here. It's not too bad. I downed one."

"I downed one and wounded the guy that just ran through camp. Anyone else?"

There was a crashing in the brush, and Gire appeared, his axe still hefted. "I got one. The wounded one headed up the river towards their camp."

"Two left. Anybody seen Faranos?"

A voice filtered out of the brush. "Get over here with a torch and give me a hand."

Cheynou pulled one of the branches from the fire and strode to the sound of the voice. There lay Faranos, face down on top of a dark-skinned youth, his arms wound in a strange position around his opponent's head. He looked up. "Get his knife. I didn't dare let him loose."

Gire quickly twisted the blade out of the man's hand, and Faranos eased back. "Cheynou, can you talk to him?"

"I know about ten words of Inari."

"Gire?"

"Maybe." He spoke a few words in a gutteral language. Their prisoner nodded. "I just told him not to move. I think he got it."

Cheynou was about to speak when a thought hit him. "There's one more! Beit, you help Faranos. Gire, with me."

They ran into the centre of camp and stared around, their eyes searching a darkness made even blacker by the light of the fire. Brantiran was sitting on a log, still gripping his wounded arm, his sword across his lap. "Nothing I could see or hear."

"How's the arm?"

"Not too bad. Stopped bleeding, I think."

"Don't let go. We'll deal with it as soon as it's safe. Keep your sword handy."

They patrolled their perimeter, feeling useless. Then Faranos and Beit came stumbling in, part-dragging a muscular youth between them, his hands tied behind his back. They thrust him down on a nearby log and Beit tied his legs together as well. Even in the light of the dying campfire his face looked bruised, and one eye was swelling shut.

Faranos took in the scene. "Everything fine except for the missing man?"

They all nodded.

"Can anyone place him in the battle?"

Gire shrugged. "I'd think it was the second-last one in line. When the noise started, the others ran forward. I took down the last man, but the rest got ahead of me. I snuck in close and kept still, but I didn't hear anything until that wounded one ran past."

Faranos nodded. "You all did fine, from what I can gather. That was a scary way to fight."

Gire indicated the prisoner with a toss of his head. "What happened to him?"

"He jumped me. Knocked my sword out of my hand. So I disarmed him and pinned him down." He grinned. "Then I didn't know what to do. I couldn't let him up. Had to wait for help."

Cheynou looked closer at the Inari. "He's been seriously worked over."

"He didn't give up easily."

"And you did all that?"

Faranos flexed his right fist as if it was sore. "It's a different type of training."

Beit raised his eyebrows. "Weaponless? You a Master?"

The slim lad grinned. "Hardly. But I have been training all my life." He looked around. "We have other things to worry about. We can't sleep here tonight. That last fighter could be back for his friend or for revenge. We either leave or sleep with the horses, two men on guard."

"And the prisoner?"

Faranos regarded Cheynou. "The easiest thing would be to kill him. You want the job?"

"Not particularly."

"Neither do I."

"We could let him go."

Faranos frowned. "How would that work?"

Cheynou turned to Gire. "You say they come down here looking for honour?"

"I gather."

"So he has failed. Faranos beat him fair and square. What does that mean?"

"I'll ask him."

There followed a halting conversation in the gutteral tongue, with the young Inari speaking earnestly and Gire mostly shaking his head because he couldn't understand. Finally, he turned back to Faranos. "Basically, he has been dishonoured. He is your slave. You may order him to do anything, and the only honour he has left is to obey you."

"So if I tell him to go home?"

"He will do so. But I got the impression that he would rather serve you."

Faranos glanced at Cheynou, who nodded.

"Stands to reason. If he has been bested, the only way to maintain his honour is as servant to the more powerful man."

"I don't want a slave and I don't think a savage like this would fit very well in the Rochana Home. Ask him about his friend. The one still out there."

It was a brief conversation. "He says his friend will do what he will do."

Faranos shook his head. "Fine. Untie him and tell him he must return to his home and tell his people that the Kyabran Empire owns this land. Be very firm about that." He rose and frowned down at the seated Inari. "It is ours, and we do not appreciate interference!"

Gire translated, and the youth bowed his head, agreeing humbly.

Gire untied the ropes and the Inari stumbled to his feet. Faranos faced him, staring into his eyes. "Go now!"

Again, the Inari bowed his head, then turned and limped out of camp, his left hand supporting his right elbow, gripped close to his side.

As the wounded man disappeared up the trail, Cheynou turned his frown on Faranos. "Exactly what kind of training do you have?"

"The same training that everyone of my station in Kyabra receives. It's nothing unusual. I'll tell you about it on the trail, if you like, but I don't think we should hang around here any longer than we have to."

"Do you think we should pack up and leave in the dark?"

"That's one option. The other is to move our bedrolls into the brush near the horses, post guards and wait it out till daylight. I doubt if anyone is going to sleep much."

It was now past midnight, and Cheynou nodded. "I go for the second option. We'd be an easy target, clumping down the trail in the dark. One thing I learned about night fighting is that the man who stays still and silent has the advantage."

"Fair enough." The Kyabran turned to the others and laid out the arrangements.

Soon they were nestled in their dens, hidden in the deepest brush each could find. The guards, too, were out of sight. Now only the tents showed a blur of light in the clearing. The rest was darkness.

* * *

235

With the lightening of the sky they started packing, and by sunrise they were ready for the trail. Cheynou looked at Gire, swinging up on his horse. "Are you coming with us?"

The stocky shepherd shrugged. "I'm confident but not stupid. There's still three of them out there, and I have no hold on them like Faranos does. It's not my time to go wandering in this area."

"Good choice." Cheynou looked to their leader.

Faranos reined his horse forward. "At least we learned that there are trails to the Prairies. Let's move. All eyes keen for the sign of an enemy."

They stayed on alert across the valley and up the climb to the hilltop. There they turned and looked back.

"A pleasant valley."

Cheynou tossed Faranos a sardonic smile. "Seems that way."

The Kyabran shrugged. "Our people had the same problems when they first came to Velika. If we want to expand, we have to be ready to defend our territory. Cruzen won't hold back because of a few touchy natives. It's not as if they live there, after all."

Cheynou nodded, and they hit the trail again.

* * *

Back at the Rochana Home, Cheynou and Faranos sat in restless anticipation for a long time while Cruzen perused the maps, paging from one to the next, then back through again. Then he leaned back and looked at them. "Well, you certainly fulfilled one part of your assignment. There must be trails through the mountains."

"I'm afraid so." Faranos shrugged. "We didn't stop to look for them, considering the circumstances."

"Quite right. Unfortunate, but not unexpected." He lifted the maps. "These are the maps you made?" The lord shook his head. "Of course they are. What am I thinking? I just didn't expect you would come up with anything so detailed."

"Only where I could."

"But you couldn't have covered all that ground, with those few men, in that time."

Cheynou grinned. "I cheated."

"You cheated?" The Rochana lord raised his eyebrows. "What does that mean about the accuracy of the maps?"

"Oh, they're accurate, as far as they go." He relented and came to stand over the table. "See these lines here?"

"Yes. I wondered what they were for."

"I started out like you suggested, laying a baseline up the valley. Once I had Brantiran and Gire trained to run the line, I left them at it and started looking around. Faranos was working with the soil the same way, doing some general digs, just to get an idea. We soon realized that there was much more ground available than we could cover in twice the time. That's when I decided to improvise."

"I see." Cheynou could tell that he didn't.

"So I thought like a sailor. First thing you do if you want to see anything is climb the mast."

"I see. So these are high points, and the lines go...where?"

"I had the men laying the baseline indicate certain points which were easy to spot. A tall tree, a rock out in a meadow, that sort of thing. I called those reference points, and they have letters. I tied my high points in with those reference points, then went to the reference points and took the angles back to the high points. By working from both directions, I could be accurate about where everything was. Then I sketched in the land between."

"I see. What about all these areas?"

Cheynou indicated that Faranos should continue, and the lad leaned in eagerly. "We decided that it would be even more difficult to survey areas, but it should be possible to tell what the soil was like by the plants growing there. We sketched in the main groups of trees, meadows and plant-covered hillsides. Then, anywhere that looked like it could be farmed, I went out and dug holes, to see what the soil was like."

"So this is actually a map of the plants that cover the ground."

"Yes, and those points, see the ones in green with numbers on them? They are where I did my samples."

"You did three samples in the same area, here." Cruzen's finger stabbed the map. "How did they come out?"

"Those were the first ones we did. They all came out the same. That was what persuaded us to keep going like that."

Cruzen nodded, a slow, satisfied movement of his head. "If your method is accurate, this looks to be a very fertile area."

"Only in the valley bottom, you notice. As you get farther up the hillsides, the soil gets thinner."

"Of course. It's the same here."

"It is?"

Cruzen grinned and shook his head. "You have to go tearing out across the countryside for three days' ride to learn something I've been trying to teach you for a year."

"But this was important!" Faranos stopped. "Oh...I see."

Cruzen picked up the sheaf of numbered papers corresponding to the sample holes Faranos had dug. "I'm going to have to take some time to study these. But I have another job for you."

The two looked at each other in anticipation.

"Oh, you're not going to like this one as much. I want you to go out around the Rochana Home and up and down our valley and try to find sample spots where the soil and the plant cover are similar to these."

Cheynou frowned, but Faranos understood. "So we can figure out what kind of crops we can grow on them."

"That's right. I can't really tell from your descriptions, no matter how good they are. If you show me a hole you have dug and tell me, 'The soil in sample 45 is just like this,' then I can assume that all the soil in that area is like that, and make some guesses as to what we might do with it."

Faranos nodded, then grinned. "And incidentally find out something about soil, and specifically the soil around our Home."

"That wouldn't hurt."

"All right. Just so long as we have it straight. Let's go, Cheynou."

"Where are you going?"

"To get our shovels, of course."

Cruzen scratched his head, a surprised smile on his face. "I hadn't expected you to start today."

"I have to. There's a party in Imanne on Festival Eve, and it's a full day's ride."

"I might have known."

"So, come on, Cheynou. Let's go. I want to finish this in two days."

"Why me?"

Faranos pulled him out the door. "Because this was all your idea."

Protesting mildly, Cheynou allowed himself to be dragged away.

20.   WHY ARE WE HERE?

Later that evening, Cruzen steered Cheynou aside from the group sitting in the living area. "How did it go?"

"What do you mean?"

"Well, the rest of the journey. How did things go? Everybody get along, that sort of thing."

"Hasn't Faranos told you all about that?"

"Of course, but I wouldn't mind another opinion."

Cheynou stood. "I don't think that would be fair to Faranos."

"In what way?"

"I didn't go out on this duty with the idea that I was watching over him. As far as I was concerned, he was the leader, and I treated him like that from the beginning. I hope he never got the feeling that I was looking after him. Reporting back to you would destroy all that."

"Oh."

"So I think I should decline to answer your questions. You have the results of our journey. You have declared them more than satisfactory. All of us are pleased that we have fulfilled our duties so well."

Cruzen leaned back in his chair, easing his sore leg to a more comfortable position. "So once again you give me lessons."

"Do I?"

"Oh, yes. Ever so gently, ever so politely, but ever so firmly. I get the message. Faranos must be shown trust if he is to earn it."

"If it would make you feel better, my Lord, you sent him on a duty he was capable of performing with a good group of people to help him perform it."

240

"Why, thank you, Cheynou. I am glad you are willing to indicate approval of my leadership, at least."

"I have no difficulty in that, my Lord. I now find it less important to worry about your welfare."

"Hmph. So you think I can take care of myself, do you?"

"I believe so. Unless you fall off your horse."

Cruzen laughed. "Sometimes I find you too much like Miranra for comfort."

"High praise."

"That worries me even more. Having two of you in the same house is a frightening prospect."

* * *

Kendra required a different kind of report. "You mean Faranos can fight? With his bare hands?"

"You should have seen that Inari fellow, Kendra. He was built like Gire. Solid muscle. But Faranos fought him, took him down and pinned him, and when he was finished, the man's face looked like a horse had kicked him. One of his arms was barely functioning, and he was limping as well."

"So! Our Faranos has more to him than meets the eye." She leaned forward, eyes gleaming. "Did he tell you about it?"

Cheynou couldn't help but wonder at this enthusiasm, but he answered. "He says it's standard training for people of his class. The cook said something about Weaponless, and asked if he was a Master."

"And is he?"

"Apparently not. From the look of that Inari, I wouldn't want to stand up to one of those. I did get some more out of him on the trail home. Maksa is a Master of Weaponless. You have to be to get the Thousand-Prime rank. Only the nobility practise this art." He shrugged. "That's all I know. He wasn't secretive, but it must be something sacred to them."

"I suppose. You don't think Faranos would show us a few moves?"

"Kendra, didn't you hear what I just said about sacred?"

"Perhaps. But maybe he could be persuaded. It would be very handy, you know, for travelling. I'm used to fighting with what I can pick up. Think about being able to fight when your hands were empty."

Cheynou shrugged. *I suppose there's a chance he might, if Kendra asked him. But I'm not sure I like the idea of Kendra asking him. Oh, maybe I'm just being silly.*

Or maybe not. He's handsome, he's nobility, he has a future here and he's turning out to be more competent than anyone thought. He'd be a good match...

"What? What did I say?"

"Huh? Oh, nothing. I was just thinking." He put on a grin. "It would be rather handy to be able to break people's bones with your bare hands."

She smiled sweetly. "Don't worry, Cheynou. If he does teach us anything, I promise not to use it against you." Then she frowned. "Unless you deserve it."

Then her face became serious. "Cheynou, what are we doing here?"

He just kept looking at her.

"I mean it. It took us a month to get here, we've stayed for several months, and now I realize that I don't know what for."

"I thought I told you why you're here."

"To keep you out of trouble. So why are you here?"

He gave that some thought. "A lot of reasons, I guess."

"Are we really spies, finding out about these people before we attack them?"

"Probably not. I hadn't thought about it quite like that. Helmsmen just naturally go looking for information. That's what we're trained to do."

242

"So you're just like me!" She seemed happy for some reason.

"Like you in what way?"

"When I left home, I wasn't going to anywhere. I was going away, but in my mind I was still looking backwards. Then, once we got on the trail, it was enough just to get here. That was my objective and I didn't think about anything but fulfilling it. Now that I'm here, I realize that I don't know what I should be doing."

"And how am I like that?"

"Well, it sounds to me like you just automatically go looking for information because of your training. But you have no Ship to take the information back to, so now you are gathering information for the sake of gathering information. Is that enough?"

"What you say is true, as far as it goes. I don't know what I'm going to do with this information. Maybe nothing, at the moment. But when I think about it, the answer to your question is 'yes,' it is enough. Gathering information, in the deeper sense, is an end in itself. It's called learning. We're here to learn, Kendra. To learn about other people and how they do things and how they live. To learn about their land, and what the weather is like, and where there are mountains and passes through those mountains. As far as I'm concerned, that's enough for the moment.

"Some day I will find a use for all of this. For the moment, it's good enough to just experience it."

She sighed mightily. "That sounds selfish, somehow."

"You have to think about yourself to some extent, especially when you're young."

"But if I had stayed in Kirigata I might have married someone. I could be starting a family, working to increase the value and strength of my Home. I could be creating something, not just going around doing what pleased me, what was good for me."

"But you decided you couldn't do that."

243

She tossed her hands, palms up, into her lap. "I know. What does that say about me? Am I too selfish? Should I be settling down and becoming an adult?"

He took her by the shoulders and shook her slightly. "Kendra, what you're doing is not useless, immature or selfish. You are learning about the world so that when you do settle down, you'll be much better at whatever it is you decide to do."

She nodded, but he knew she was not completely convinced. "And if that's not enough for you, remember your primary task."

She sighed again, resigned this time. "To keep you out of trouble."

"Right. That ought to be enough of a challenge for anyone."

"Hmm."

He waited, but she sat lost in thought. Shaking his head, he went back up to his room to work on the charts he was making of the trail they used to come north.

21.   THE PACKAGE

"Cheynou, there is one other point we should discuss. The Kyabran scouts."

"I meant to talk to you about them, my Lord. Have you found out who they were?"

"Yes. I have been asking around. There is a family in the next valley to the west of here. Cheolean is the name. They also came in the first wave of settlers, and we have supported each other in many ways over the years. I was vaguely aware that they were interested in the South, so I asked them. They did not wish to advertise their action, but two of their people had gone on a mission of discovery." He grinned. "Somewhat the reverse of yours, it seems. Unfortunately, they did not return, and the Cheolean family was beginning to conclude that they must give them up for lost.

"I was the unhappy bearer of the bad news. They were upset, of course, and disturbed that they knew so little of what had occurred. Is there anything else you could tell them that might ease their concern?"

"Very little beyond what I told you before. However, there was something. Will you excuse me for a moment?"

He rushed back to his room and took out the package he had found in Sarasha's saddlebag. Returning to Cruzen's study, he opened the cloth and laid the contents on the table. "These were what persuaded me that there was an advanced civilization below the Rim. Look at the precision of that protractor!"

He glanced at the Kyabran. "Of course, that won't impress you so much, as I suppose you see equipment of similar quality daily."

Cruzen shook his head. "No, these are very fine workmanship. Basuar Cheolean must have had great confidence in his scouts to send them out with such valuable tools. That compass looks fine as well. The needle is suspended in oil to dampen its movement."

"And then there was this." Cheynou laid the metal box on the table. "It has us completely puzzled. A container of some sort." He shook it. "There even seems to be something shifting around inside. But how does it open?"

The Kyabran laughed and twirled the box on his fingertips. "And now we discover how good it was that you came down the trail at this specific spot. These boxes are family treasures. They are simple to open. Just a push here and a twist there, and the secrets of the box are bared to the world."

The box lay still in his hands.

"Unfortunately, the where and how of the opening is also a family treasure. I have no idea. Only the Cheolean family can open that box without destroying it."

"So can you take it to them? We have speculated for many hours about our foreign visitors. We assumed they were surveyors of some sort, because of the equipment and the last man's ability to lay a straight line across the Prairie. But we found no records in his pack. Nothing. Writing implements, but no paper."

"And you think the record of his journey might be here?"

"It stands to reason."

"Then the proper place for this box is back with its family. It is their expedition that went out, and it is their kin who died gaining this information." He smiled. "And they will be grateful to the one who gave their men decent burial and brought the news back to them. I foresee future dealings with the Cheolean family. You must come and meet them and complete your delivery."

"If it means I can learn more about the puzzle that has picked at my brain for so long, I would be glad."

"Let us go tomorrow afternoon. I will send a message."

The lord pulled pen and paper, scribbled a note and sealed it. "Take that down to the stables, would you? One of the lads will be happy to get out on such a nice day."

* * *

The Cheolean Home was unlike Cruzen's and more like Kendra's manor at Kirigata. It was built of dark grey stone: easy to defend, with a high wall and a thick timber gate studded with bolts. The two buildings on either side of the gate had slitted windows for the protection of archers looking down on the vulnerable entrance area, and the wall encompassed all the barns and outbuildings.

The welcome for Rochana and his guests was warm, however. Once they were settled in comfortable chairs with glasses of wine poured, Basuar Cheolean regarded Cheynou. "I gather you have news of my adventurous young kinsmen?"

Cheynou nodded. "I am sorry to bring you dark tidings, my Lord."

The Kyabran nodded. "It was as we feared. Please tell us what you know."

Cheynou regarded the people seated and standing in the room, all avid for news. "We have little information, only speculation. We found the body of one man on the Great Prairie above the Rim of the World. Early last spring, after most of the snow had melted. Evidence suggested that he died late in the fall, after the first snow had come. He had a series of wounds like the claw marks of a huge cat across his chest. The tracks behind him had frozen, so they were still there when the rest of the snow melted in the spring. We were amazed at the line he was walking. Even in the weakened condition that killed him, his tracks led straight as a bowshot across the Prairie. It was our first clue that this was no ordinary wanderer.

"We backtracked him and found a valley perched above the Prairie. There we found evidence of a camp and another grave, which we did not disturb. We speculate that the second man met with some tragedy, and the first man was caught by the early snow. In any case, he gave his partner proper burial and tried to continue. The weather was cruel in those mountains this year. We lost three horses to a mountain lion, and one of our most valued leaders died in a late spring blizzard in the same valley."

He proffered the cloth-wrapped bundle. "This is all that we retained of the first man's belongings."

The lord received the gift with due ceremony, opening the cloth slowly. However, once he understood the contents, his face brightened. He lifted the box and gazed around the room, meeting several glances. Then he dropped his attention to the metal container.

His hands did not seem to move, but there were several clicks, and the lid slid partially back. Lord Basuar frowned. "The moisture has got to it. I hope..." He worked the lid gently, and it retreated the rest of the way. "Aha!"

He reached into the box, and there was dead silence in the room. With a care near to veneration, he lifted clear a sheaf of thin parchment. Everyone leaned forward as he fanned the pages out on the tabletop. They were covered with fine black writing, diagrams and what looked to Cheynou like maps.

The lord skimmed through them, then looked up at his guests. "This information is far too detailed to analyze at the moment. A lot of it will already be known to our traveller friend, because he has followed their backtrail."

"I have maps of my own. It would be good to share...?"

"Of course we must..." He hesitated. "Cruzen, with your permission?"

Lord Rochana raised a negligent hand. "Whatever Cheynou wishes. He is the agent of his own people, and owes no allegiance to me."

"...other than friendship, my Lord."

Cruzen grinned at him. "Precisely." But he turned to the other lord with a serious face. "These are complicated matters, Basuar. The knowledge of this possible new trade route belongs at the moment to the Cheolean family and to Cheynou Chan. Complicating this is the fact that Cheynou is an agent of the Sea People of the Southern Plains, whose objectives and motives could be counter to those of the Empire. We will have to tread carefully. There could be great benefit and there could be great danger."

The other lord nodded. "I agree. However, I think the greatest danger to our own ability to gain from this situation would be to compete with each other. Our two families have several generations of trust to guide us."

"And I am the unknown element."

"That you are, Mr. Chan. But, as I said earlier, the information you have is here in these documents, so there can be no argument over ownership."

Cheynou indicated the roomful of people. "Information is hard to own, my Lord."

"That is true." He turned to Cruzen. "And that is why we must act on this quickly. I will spend the next few days going over Pollente's records. Once I have the gist of them I will contact you, and we will decide what to do." His gesture included Cheynou. "All of us."

* * *

But Basuar's response came sooner than that. The following day at noon a carriage rolled into the Rochana Home yard, and the lord himself stepped out. Cheynou had seen the dust cloud and was there to greet him.

The lord waved a satchel at him. "This is more important than we thought. Where is Cruzen?"

"In his office as usual. Will you follow me?"

Lord Rochana was on his feet when they entered. "What is it? What's the rush?"

249

The other lord smiled. "It's not quite so crucial that a cool drink wouldn't be missed."

"I apologize. Please sit down, my Lord." Cruzen frowned at his friend. "And tell me what the hell brought you running over here two days ahead of schedule."

Basuar held up the satchel. "My cousin's writings, as you may suspect."

"What did he know that we don't already?"

"Cheynou, that was a good guess about the accident that doomed them. It was a lion. It killed Cervera and gave Pollente a bad clawing. The wound was infected, and he realized that his chances of making it were not good." He settled back and took a deep breath and indicated the papers. "Unfortunately, the poison in his blood began to affect his mind. For the last days he wasn't thinking clearly. There was some information about what they had found that he had not written in his journals, because it was too sensitive. When he feared he was dying, he wanted to leave us the information, so he wrote it in code. However, as I say, his mind was not clear, and I cannot make out much of what he wrote. However, I did find certain words clearly stated:" the lord leaned forward and dropped his voice, "iron, copper, tin."

Cruzen laid his hands flat on the table as if to steady himself. "You think they found metals in those mountains."

"There doesn't seem to be any other explanation. Cervera knew his metals. That's why Pollente took him along. And if Pollente was so careful to hide the information, he must have thought they were in sufficient quantities to be very important."

"I don't know. You say he was hallucinating, though."

Cheynou shook his head. "But he didn't write them down earlier, before the attack."

"That's right. He must have already known."

Cruzen stood, then cursed as his sore leg hit the table leg, and he sat down hurriedly. "This changes things."

250

"Indeed it does."

"Cheynou, you know I was talking about sending a mission to your people to investigate trading possibilities."

"You mentioned it in passing. I didn't think there was any hurry."

"There wasn't. It is too difficult a passage unless the trade was very lucrative."

"But with those metals?"

"A completely different story. Once word of that gets out, there will be expeditions from all over coming through, looking for easier passes, trying to establish trading concessions: all the usual tricks."

"So you want to get up there first."

"We have two advantages, Cheynou. Time and you."

"Me?"

"Of course. I have no illusions about the difficulty of the passage. If we go up there and discover that there are workable ore bodies, we still won't have the resources or the manpower to work them and ship the ore all the way north. But if you can ensure a good relationship with the local people, we can provide the knowledge and they can provide the labour to mine and smelt the metal on site. Transporting finished metal is much easier."

"So you want me to go with you."

"Of course."

"Oh."

"Isn't that what you came here for? To find new trading opportunities for your people?"

"Yes, yes, I did say that." He thought for a moment, then smiled. "But I now realize that was only a lie I told myself. An excuse for me to go travelling."

"So you don't want to go back."

"Oh, it's not that I don't want to go. It's just that...it's just that I'm being stupid. Of course I'll go with you."

251

Cruzen glanced at the other lord, then brought his stare back to Cheynou. "But you don't want to."

Cheynou shrugged ruefully. "Cruzen, this is the point where my dream has hit reality. The trading idea was my way of making my dream of travel realistic. How can I complain when my excuse becomes real? This could be the one thing that allows my people to survive. And I can hardly refuse to help them because I want to run away and do...something completely nebulous that I can't even put into words. How could I live with myself for the rest of my life?"

"So you'll come."

"Of course. When do we leave? Kendra will...oh. Kendra."

"Kendra?"

"Yes. I didn't think of her. We are on this journey together. I'm sorry, Cruzen, Lord Cheolean, but I have to talk to her before I make any decision. If she doesn't want to go back...well, I'll just have to ask her."

* * *

"You have to go."

"I do."

"Of course you do." She leaned forward. "For all the reasons you just told me."

The relief coursed through him. "So you don't mind going back when we really just started?"

"Oh, I'm not going with you."

His heart sank again. "You're not?"

"Of course not." She relaxed back into her easy chair. "I'm happy here. I'm not going to go out on that rocky trail again all the way to the top, just for the pleasure of turning around and coming back down it again." Her brow furrowed and her head tilted. "Because that's what you're going to do, isn't it?"

"What do you mean?"

"You...you aren't going to quit, are you?"

252

"What? Quit? Of course not." He sat beside her. "It was funny, I suppose. It wasn't until I was faced with going back that I realized what was going on in my head."

"You usually have that figured out pretty well."

"Not this time. When it came to the choice of going back or staying, it struck me that all my wonderful plans about finding trading opportunities for my people were nonsense. They were just an excuse to go travelling. I didn't want to go back."

"I see. But you will."

"Of course. I can't miss such a good opportunity. This mining could be the factor that makes the difference between survival and disaster for our Families."

She smiled. "And you're going to go up there with Cruzen and introduce him to everybody and use your usual magic to get them all happily working together, right?"

"That's the idea…"

"And then…?"

He glanced over. Her face revealed an inner tension as if this meant a great deal to her. He shrugged. "Once I have used up my excuse for travelling, I must face my real reason and decide whether it is enough to keep going."

"But you won't leave me here."

"So you are staying."

Her lip twisted. "You had two good reasons for this jaunt. I only had one, and it wasn't very persuasive. So I have no reason to return. I can't. If I go home now, I will be giving up and admitting I've wasted my time."

He swept his hand to indicate the Rochana holding. "I'd hardly call this a waste of time."

"I suppose not, but I'm not sure what it was all in aid of. My only choice is to stay until I figure out why I'm here."

He didn't dare ask her what would happen then. "So you don't mind staying here while I make a little side trip back south to save my people's future?"

"I don't have much of a choice, do I?" She frowned. "As long as you come back as soon as you're done. And I don't mean completely done. Take a lesson from Sarasha. These are grown men and they don't need you to hold their hands. You get them started and you leave them alone to work it out between themselves."

"Yes, ma'am. Right you are, ma'am." He shot to his feet and gave her his best shipboard salute. "Do I have your permission to go and tell Cruzen, ma'am?"

She jumped up and spun him with an arm around his shoulders. "I'm coming with you. I want Cruzen to understand the terms of this agreement."

"Um...do you think you could wait until Lord Cheolean is gone? I mean, it's all right if he thinks you run my life, but let him keep a bit of his respect for Lord Rochana, will you?"

22.   THE TRAIL HOME

"Deep thoughts?"

Cheynou brought his mind back to the present and turned to Faranos. "I suppose so." He swept a hand out over the emptiness before them. "This mountaintop was a real turning point in our trip north. Finding the reference mark engraved in the top of that boulder was our first real proof that you people existed."

Faranos, too, gazed around. "It's a wonderful place, isn't it? The mountains rolling off to the north over there, and this huge monolith hanging over so far it looks like it's going to fall on us. I can see the lure of exploring."

Cheynou grinned. "Losing the urge to be a farmer?"

"Hmph. I never wanted to be a farmer. I'm happy to let the tenants take care of that. Breeding and training are my strengths."

"Then I have another challenge for you." Cheynou swept a hand up the trail. "Start breeding up a line of pack horses. You're going to need them."

The other nodded ruefully. "I can't see a wagon road in these parts."

"And you haven't seen the tough stretches yet."

They strolled over to help the soldiers tighten the cinches and prepare their mounts to return to the trail.

Maksa regarded the path that led down from the knoll. "I don't suppose this is the top, or anything near it?"

"No, the top of the pass is very close to the Prairie. We'll be a couple of days, yet. We have a nice camping spot for tonight, if I read the map right."

"You'd better be reading it right. You made it."

"Yes, and I'm finding mistakes in it every day." He exaggerated a sigh. "A mapmaker's work is never done." He swung up on his horse. "Shall I lead for a while?"

The older man waved a hand towards the trail. "Why change anything?"

As Cheynou pushed his horse into a careful descent, he mulled over that last statement. *Why change anything? We have a good friendship. Why spoil it?* He glanced around, missing the familiar flash of grey and black in the corner of his vision. *I miss them both. I even miss Martan. Travelling with a mob is safe, but it has its drawbacks.*

* * *

Early the following afternoon, he was willing to admit there were other advantages to enduring a large party.

"How long do you think it will take?"

Maksa regarded the toiling soldiers. "That's a long stretch of very narrow trail with little foundation to build on."

"We had to take the packs off Martan and carry them through ourselves. Even he found it a tough squeeze, and he's a small donkey."

"With a great deal of nerve." Maksa leaned out to look down. "It's a long way to the bottom."

"And a long way to solid ground at the other end."

Maksa considered the workers. "Two days at least."

Cheynou grinned. "Good thing you brought soldiers with stonework experience."

The Thousand-Prime shrugged. "Most of our troops are locals who grew up on farms. Drystone walls are second nature to them."

"If it's going to take that long, I have better use for my time. You know that side canyon that cut west about a candle back?"

"You think it might circle around and come back to this trail further south?"

Cheynou gazed up at the mountain that towered above them. "If it does, it will be a long detour."

256

"In that case, take someone with you." He glanced at Faranos, standing watching the workers. "Someone who doesn't do stonework."

"Fine. We'll see you whenever we get back." He pointed ahead. "With any luck, we'll be coming down the trail." He caught the younger man's eye and motioned towards where the horses were tethered. "Want to take a little ride?"

"Any time. I hate watching people work when I can't help. I feel so useless." He fell into step beside Cheynou. "Where are we going?"

"Roundabout."

"That side canyon you showed me?"

"That's it."

"Lead on. Sounds like fun."

Cheynou threw the saddle on his horse. "Experience tells me that it will be tough, dangerous, frustrating and above all, hot. Grab an extra canteen."

"Nice to know we won't be shirking our share of the work, anyway."

The two mounted and trotted back down the trail.

As the afternoon faded, they weren't so cheerful. The promising canyon soon narrowed, so they left the horses where there was still room to turn them around and went ahead on foot. The chasm steepened until it was almost a chimney, where sometimes their only way to keep from slipping back was to press outward with their palms against the rough walls.

"Remind me again why we're doing this?"

"To see if there's a better way to get the pack train...yes, I see what you mean. You're the horseman. Could a horse make this grade? With a pack on?"

Faranos swung onto a ledge and regarded the rock wall beside him. "This is hard rock. Granite, maybe? But we could chisel some short passages wider and build steps in this steep part. Then a horse could climb it."

"Only if it goes all the way around." Cheynou sighted with his compass and recorded the reading. "By my calculation, we're past half way. If there isn't another shoulder or ridge or fathoms-deep canyon."

"So we should start descending soon?"

He shrugged. "One way to find out."

They toiled onward. Then the trail topped out, and they crossed a smooth ridge covered with wildflowers and moss. The buttress of the mountain was now behind them to their right, and soon Cheynou began to recognize landmarks on his map. As the sun disappeared behind the next peak, they scrambled down a steep bank onto the trail.

"We made it!"

Faranos frowned. "Aye, but we have to get the horses. Which way? Back over the mountain or down the trail?"

Cheynou grinned. "Not too much difference, but if we have to do any hiking in the dark, I don't want it to be down that chimney. Plus, it will be so much fun to come down the trail from the top."

"I bow to the expertise of the mapmaker. Let's hoof it."

They trotted down the trail and crossed the worksite, grinning at the stares of the soldiers. After a quick report to Maksa and Quasan Cheolean, the co-leader of the expedition, they continued north to bring their horses back.

After supper, Cheynou gave the group a more detailed description.

When he had finished, Maksa nodded. "So, compare the route you found to this trail for length, safety, and amount of work required to finish it."

"It's longer, that's for sure. I'll show you once I put today's information on the map. It will take serious rock work to get the chimney passable for horses. I assume much longer than the men will take to fix this path. However, I don't think this trail will ever be safe. From the look of the terrain there are frequent slides all along, and I can't see ever being able to depend on it. On the detour, once the work's done it's finished, and you'll forget this was ever a trouble spot."

"Fine. For the moment, this route is the obvious choice. Later, if we decide there is a need, we can put the extra labour into the safer option. A good day's work."

"I hate to spoil the mood, but it's a good thing the horses are getting a rest tomorrow. The pitch up to the top of the pass will take a full day, and it's steep all the way."

"But after that?"

"Half a day's gentle slope down to the Great Prairie."

* * *

They reached the flat ground two days later, and when they had all filed through the narrow opening, Cheynou waited while his companions appreciated the wide stretch of the Great Prairie before them. Then he pulled his horse up beside Quasan. "Would you like to see where the first of your kinsmen is buried?"

"I would be grateful."

"I'm also interested in why your scouts went up that dead-end trail and stayed there. Perhaps you can solve that puzzle as well."

"I will try. Lead on."

Cheynou trotted his horse up beside Maksa's and conveyed the new route, then led the way up the narrow path.

The moment they pulled into the upper valley, Cheynou noted a change in the demeanour of the two Cheoleans. Jyonar reined his horse to a halt, staring up at the mountainside. Quasan pulled his horse close alongside, murmuring a question. The response seemed to be affirmative. The younger man pointed, then pointed elsewhere.

259

Maksa glanced at Cheynou, who shrugged. "I gather something interests you, my friends."

The elder Cheolean turned. "Oh, yes. We now see the reason for the notation in my cousin's book." He pointed to a fresh stain on the rock above them, probably caused by another spring avalanche. "My knowledgeable kinsman tells me that colour is a sign of iron ore." He pointed again. "One only has to look..."

Their gaze strayed to the walls of the valley, stained in several places to a similar hue.

"That's all iron?"

Jyonar tilted a hand back and forth. "This only tells us that there is iron in the rock. It is very difficult to mine solid rock like this."

"Oh." The disappointment on Maksa's face would have been comic in other circumstances.

"However, now that we know there is iron in these mountains, we look for places where the ore may be found in a form easier to mine. Is there a headwater of a large river near here? Are there any swamps?"

Eyes turned to Cheynou.

"Yes, the Big River starts in a huge series of swamps to the west over there. We never went anywhere near them. Too dangerous for the horses. I believe the river comes out of the mountain in several springs and streams that spread out and disappear into the swamps. Farther east, it gathers and becomes a river."

"And that is where we will find our iron. Perhaps the tin, as well." Quasan turned to Maksa. "Shall we go there now?"

Once again, Maksa deferred to his navigator. "How far is it?"

"Perhaps a candle's ride, but it is difficult to approach because the land gets boggier and the foliage gets thicker. There is nowhere to camp, and in the early summer the mosquitoes are awful."

Maksa looked at the angle of the sun, now nearing the mountaintops. "It is getting late."

He glanced at his co-leader, who nodded. "I would also like time to show honour to my kinsman's grave."

Maksa looked to Cheynou. "What do you think? Is it safe to stay here?"

"We didn't see any evidence of avalanches in the summer. There is water here, and the valley is a good place to graze horses. As long as nothing decides to eat them."

"Luckily, we have several people with bows who are trained in guard duty." He raised his voice. "Perhaps some of the men would enjoy a small hunting party."

There were grins and nudges in the group of soldiers sitting nearby.

"That's settled, then. Make camp, gentlemen. We are staying. Where shall we set up?"

"We have a safe spot over there in those rocks."

"Safe?" Maksa stared around.

Cheynou waved a hand at the surrounding mountains. "From avalanches, yes. It's also easily defended against humans. We left some permanent stuff here: tables and the like that we made out of..." He stopped in dismay.

"What's wrong?"

"Look at this. Everything's been broken and burnt. They've made a complete mess of the place."

Maksa nodded. "This isn't sloppiness. It's vandalism. Who would do such a thing?"

Cheynou shook his head. "Oh, I know very well who. Those Raiders I told you about. I just wonder why they came this far." He glared around. "It gives you an idea of how they think. If they don't need it, they destroy it."

He regarded his friends again. "Well, there's nothing we can do but clean up and do it all over again. I'll tell you the tale after supper. If you're going to be trading with us, you'll have to know our problems sooner or later."

Maksa nodded and started giving orders, and soon the campsite was orderly again, the broken poles trimmed for other purposes or burning in the fire pit, and newly hewn camp furniture already in use.

After supper, Cheynou told the story of the raid and his suspicions of what the destruction of their campsite might mean.

"They are the dregs of our people. As far as I can figure, these Raiders come from the malcontents that exist in any group. On Ship, they were isolated and under control. Once they were free to go where they wanted, I assume they made contact with others of a like mind and thought they'd continue with the Raiding life. Who knows what has happened over the summer."

"Do they pose a threat to us?"

"There were forty or so in the first raid. They might have grown or shrunk. We need to be careful, yes." He glanced at the big officer. "The trail to this plateau is easily defended. I suggest that once we move down out of the mountains, we use outriders and night patrols. I'm sure you know far more about it than I do."

Maksa nodded. "It's good to be forewarned. My men know how to deal with that sort of situation." He rubbed his hands together. "But for now, we have a more pleasant task. Tomorrow will be a day of discovery."

* * *

The following day, they rode east along the foot of the mountain, then dismounted and hacked a trail through the dense brush towards the swamp. Cheynou brought them in close to the wall where he found a ledge of rock with good footing and less ground cover.

As they approached standing water, the Cheoleans slowed, their eyes scanning. The others watched, unwilling to break the concentration of the experts.

"There." Jyonar reached down, tugged up a handful of peat moss and turned it over. "See those?"

Small grey nodules clung to the roots of the moss. He gathered several and passed them around. "This is the easy stuff. It collects there, and you harvest it. A few years later, more will collect, and you can come back and harvest again."

Maksa rolled one of the little balls in his fingers. "There's not much."

"No, but that's just the start, my Lord. That spring is the source. It carries dissolved ore from inside the mountain. See the oily sheen on the standing water? That's a very good sign. For some reason, iron that comes from places with that sheen is resistant to rust." His head came up, and he looked around. "Larger deposits of ore lie under the water, or in places like that bank, that was once under water. If we dig there, we'll probably find much larger quantities."

He turned to his companion. "This is a very promising site, my Lord."

Quasan raised his eyebrows, seeming surprised at his kinsman's enthusiasm. "How promising?"

"One must dig and find samples and then refine the ore before we know whether the concentration is worth the effort." He glanced back along their trail. "And considering the distances involved..."

"We have neither the manpower nor the tools, and the trail is not in any state for heavy travel." Quasan nodded his head towards Cheynou. "And we are in the territory of another folk. We need to make contact."

Maksa glanced at Cheynou and, receiving no argument, spoke. "We must visit the Petrellan camp and discuss this situation with Orrick Bren, their leader."

"He would be the one to make any decisions."

Once more, Cheynou followed his compass across the Prairie, with a pause to do honour to the other explorer whose grave mound stood out on the flatness two days above the Second Drop.

23.   MEETING ON THE PRAIRIE

They spent their final evening camped on the north arm of the Little River, and were setting out in the morning when a hail brought their attention towards the east. Two horsemen rode out of a gully, and one dismounted with his arm up in welcome.

No, her arm. "Tonu! Good to see you!" Cheynou slipped off his horse and rushed to embrace her. The dark young man following her stayed on his mount, keeping a wary eye on the strangers.

"Cheynou! Pers and Yong told me all about your journey. Why are you back? I thought you had a continent to explore."

He grinned. "Merely fulfilling part of my task. I have brought traders with goods we may need." He introduced her to the important members of the party. Once the formalities were over, they mounted again and continued their journey.

"We'll follow along for a while. We're headed back to the main Inari camp above the East River."

He glanced over at her. "And what are you doing out here on the Prairie alone?"

"I'm not alone, Cheynou." She glanced over at the young Inari riding close beside her. "This is my..." her back straightened, "...this is my husband, Barhan."

"Husband! Congratulations, Tonu." He stood in his stirrups to give her a one-armed hug. Then he leaned across, offering his hand to the Inari. "I don't know what your traditions are, Barhan, but the Farmer's handshake is all I can manage from here."

The Inari returned his smile and grasped his hand firmly.

"So you got married. You know, I thought maybe you and Pers..."

She shook her head. "No, he took Leide's death pretty hard."

"I knew that. They were a match."

"Even if I felt that way about him, which I don't, it wouldn't have been a good thing. She'd have always been between us. Some day maybe he'll meet a stranger who won't feel it so strongly."

She straightened her back again. "Cheynou, I thought about it. We lost so many of our young men during the past two years, and I didn't want to live in the Petrel camp anyway. He's a good person, Cheynou…"

"And not so bad-looking either." He lowered his voice. "The arms on the man!"

She shot a glance at her husband, reddening. "Yes, he is strong."

Cheynou nodded. "I think it was a good choice, for what it's worth coming from me. Your life is there. Why not? Did you run into any problem with your family?"

"After the initial surprise, not much. They understand the situation. Once they got to meet him, there was no problem at all." She smiled proudly.

"So he's free to come and go in the Petrel camp?"

"Oh, yes, Bren has no quarrel with the Inari, just Pers and Yong. And the rest of us Eagles, but not so much."

Cheynou nodded, and they rode along for a while. "Nice horse. Isn't that one of Solen's?"

She smiled proudly. "Wedding present."

"She's a fine mare. I don't recognize Barhan's."

"No, we bought him from one of the Farmers with my dowry."

"So you managed to squeeze your dowry out of Orrick, even when you were marrying off-Ship?"

"Yes. He's the first to realize that things have changed."

There was a pause, and Cheynou had the leisure to observe his old friend more closely. "That's a very nice jerkin you're wearing. Do I recognize the needlework?"

She preened a bit. "You most certainly do. We Sailmakers have had to change our duties, you know. Different materials, different techniques."

"How do you like working leather?"

"I love it. It's so soft and forgiving, compared to sail canvas."

"The Sailmakers aren't turning into tailors, are they?"

"Oh, no, this is just for myself. We're the Tentmakers now."

"I see."

"Yes, my family is pleased. It's a change in our status, really."

"For the better?"

"Yes. We used to be rather specialized, you know. We were only appreciated by the mast'n and the Helmsmen. Now our work is more intimately connected with everyone."

Cheynou laughed. "Keeping the rain off their heads."

"Exactly. They appreciate our skills more, now."

"And complain more if you make a mistake."

She laughed ruefully. "There's always a price to pay for popularity."

He joined in her laughter, and they moved in companionable silence for a while.

He glanced over at her. "How would you like to do a bit of sailmaking again?"

She frowned at him. "Have you got a boat somewhere?"

He grinned. "No, it's a different use of the wind altogether."

As he explained the windmill sails, her face lit up. "Of course I can make those." She began to quiz him about lengths and quality of material, strength of wind and other esoterica of her trade. Finally he passed over all his diagrams, and she stopped asking questions as she read.

Once they were satisfied with the project, he brought up an interesting topic. "How will we pay you for this work?"

"Pay me? Why would you pay me?"

"You're no longer working for the Ship, Tonu. This is a commercial task for outsiders. They pay in the gold coins of the Empire."

She shrugged. "I suppose I'll tell you how many candles of work and what materials I used, and you can tell me what that's worth in gold coins. I have no idea. Can I trade it for a small pig?"

He laughed. "Aren't you glad you have me here to help out. I have no idea either. Don't worry. This will have to be worked out once we start trading anyway. I'll talk with Maksa; I'm sure the Kyabran traders have a solution."

She smiled and nodded, and they turned their attention to their horses, which had been slowing and wandering away from the group.

They rode along for a while, and he got the impression that she was looking at him. He glanced her way, but she would not meet his eyes. This happened several times, and finally he pulled his horse aside, edging her farther from the other riders.

"Tonu, whatever it is you want to say, why don't you just say it?"

She shook her head. "I should have known. You always notice, don't you?"

"Are you avoiding the question?"

She sighed. "I didn't know if I should mention it, but now I have to. When you see Orrick Bren again, you be careful."

He did not respond, thinking that over as they rode along.

"I mean it. You watch him like a fishhawk watches the ripples on the water."

"I'm sure you're serious. I'm just wondering why Orrick Bren should care enough about me that I should worry."

She shrugged. "I know it sounds strange, but it's not who you are. It's what you stand for."

"Let me guess. I'm the flashpoint for a mutiny that will wrest control of the Ship from his able hands."

"It isn't funny, Cheynou. Relations aren't good between Orrick and those of us that went to the Inari. Combined with the rogue Raiders wandering around bothering people, he's even more on edge. I'm on the fringes of his displeasure, but Pers and Yong are the spearpoint. Pers...he's changed. He doesn't care any more. Or maybe he cares too much. He took to heart all that stuff that Sarasha used to tell us, and he's getting more and more resolute."

"I see. Has anything happened to make it worse?"

"He speaks up louder and more often. He's adamant that Bren is bad for the Families, and needs to be put under control."

"But I thought you were all moved in with the Inari. That should keep him out of Orrick's way."

"Mostly it has. But Bren was very upset when Pers and Yong pulled out, especially when they took the horses. He was ranting about loyalty and sticking together and things like that. One day when Pers was back in camp, Orrick tried to give him a dressing down. Pers stood toe to toe with him and said he would never live under the power of a tyrant again. Then he spun around, jumped on his horse, and rode away. I thought Bren was going to explode. It was very tense for those of us watching."

Cheynou glanced at her. "How does this affect you?"

She shrugged, her mouth turned down. "I'm staying out of the Petrel camp for a while. We're hoping everything will calm down but for the moment, my family visits me, not the other way round."

"I hate to hear there's so much trouble. Our trials aren't over yet. We don't need discord in the Families." He rode awhile. "But I still don't see how that affects me."

She tossed up her hands. "I don't either, but Orrick has mentioned you a few times, and it sounds like he's really angry with you. It's all about disloyalty and running out when you're needed."

"Hmph. I never thought I was that important."

She smiled. "I never did, either. Goes to show, doesn't it?"

He grinned over at her. "Thanks for the warning. I was planning on treading softly anyway, as I always do." He nodded his head towards the rest of the party. "This ought to help."

"I hope so, Cheynou. I really hope so."

"Anything else I need to know? What happened with the Raiders?"

She shrugged. "Nobody knows much. There's a band of them around. About thirty, give or take. They've robbed a few people, stolen from food caches. Basically a nuisance and not much else. They only tried that one big raid on the Farmers, but they've been stealing stock. They could become a serious problem."

"Aren't you worried, just the two of you travelling by yourselves?"

She smiled. "Oh, they don't bother the Inari. They wouldn't dare. We'd get on our horses and run them down and destroy them."

"Really?"

Her face became serious. "Cheynou, you know how we Sea People always considered ourselves the finest fighters on the Ocean?"

"We were. Nobody ever argued that."

"We aren't the finest fighters on the Prairie. These Inari are bigger, stronger, and more fiercely proud than our Raiders ever were. Now that they are getting horses, they are unbeatable." She gestured towards her husband. "Yong and Pers take weapons training with Barhan all the time. Neither of them has ever got him to put a knee on the ground."

"A knee on the ground. Is that how they lose?"

"Yes. When they fight in the circle, if it's not a serious matter, a knee down or a foot over the line loses. If it's more serious, they fight till blood is drawn." She shivered. "It doesn't happen very often, but if it's really serious…"

"Death?"

She nodded, her face working, and Cheynou did not push it. *A very fresh, very disturbing memory, I suspect.*

They were approaching a bend in the river, and the trading party turned southerly again.

Tonu reined over beside her husband. "We'll be leaving you here, Cheynou. I'd like to travel along, but we tend to stay this side of the river, and Pers and Yong are going to want to hear about your return."

She made her goodbyes to the Kyabrans, and soon the two riders were loping off across the Prairie to the east.

Maksa watched them go. "Fine horses."

"Yes, one of the locals that we met when we first landed was a horse trader named Solen. He's helping us with our breeding program. The mare is one of his."

"That's another product you could trade for in the Empire. Good horses are marketable anywhere."

"Just give us a few years to get the bloodlines worked out, and we'll be doing that." He thought of Kendra's lesson to Pers and Yong. "What kind of horses would they be looking for?"

The talk turned to the practicality of different sizes and weights of horses, and the hours on the trail passed swiftly.

24. MEETING IN CAMP

They nooned just short of the Petrel camp to give everyone a chance to spruce up for the encounter. After they ate, Cheynou noticed their little squad of guards checking their weapons. *Hmm. Probably for the better, but there should be no need. I have to conduct this meeting carefully.*

"Maksa, I don't want to give you the wrong impression of our people, but this could be a delicate situation."

"I expected that. Something your friend said?"

"The situation is not as comfortable as I hoped it would be, and my usefulness may be hampered. It would help if you remind your men to keep their eyes on me. I may not have time to relay an order."

The Thousand-Prime regarded him a moment, then nodded and went to speak to Sergeant Yondap. There was no argument, just meaningful looks in Cheynou's direction. Maksa returned to his horse and mounted. "Let's move out. I am anxious to make this contact."

Cheynou mounted and pulled alongside. "I'm just anxious."

"Don't worry. I've been through this before, usually without the help of a knowledgeable friend and translator."

Cheynou stared ahead. "We'll soon find out how much worth my help will be."

They had breasted the break of the riverbank and stood at the top of the Second Fall, the whole camp spread before them.

Maksa raised his eyebrows. "A large encampment. Very busy."

Cheynou finished his own survey. "Sergeant, I think perhaps your men should string their bows."

The soldiers did not wait for a more official order, but went on instant alert.

"What's wrong, Cheynou?"

He stared out at the camp below them and did not turn to Maksa as he answered, his eyes still searching. "Dust. Way too much dust. Something's going on."

"Why do you think that?"

He pointed. "The horse herd over there. The stock has been pulled tight together. Look there. Same with the sheep and cows. That's for protection. And there's dust in camp."

"What does that mean?"

"The Prairie sod is delicate. Even walking breaks it down, so the paths through the camp are all packed dirt. If you ride a horse through quickly you raise a lot of dust. So we don't ride horses in camp unless there's an emergency."

"This would certainly qualify, then."

"Exactly. And another development I'm not happy with. See the mast in the middle of camp? When the Eagles and Petrels moved in together, both flags always flew there. I only see the Petrel now. Things have changed since I left." He gestured towards the trail. "And we're about to find out about it."

A squad of ten horsemen, closely packed, stormed out of the camp and galloped towards them. Cheynou kneed his horse to the front and waited calmly.

"Keep a steady hand, men. I know these people."

There was a murmur behind him, and he knew that Maksa and Sergeant Yondap were reinforcing his order.

The horses drew nearer and he could see drawn swords, but no bows. *That's something, at least.* When they got close enough to recognize faces, he moved his mount farther.

The horsemen drew up just out of bowshot, their horses blowing, dust settling around them. "Stand still and identify yourselves!"

Cheynou moved forward again. "I don't know, Kohlu. You made so much dust, I guess you didn't recognize me."

"What?" The leader peered, then urged his horse forward. "Cheynou Chan? What are you doing here?"

"What I said I would. I went down over the Rim of the World and brought back merchants to trade with. What are you doing, lathering your horses up on such a hot day? The whole camp looks like a school of mackerel with a shark nearby."

Kohlu dropped his right hand, and his men sheathed their swords. "You picked a bad time to show up, Cheynou. We've just been attacked. Strangers are not going to be too welcome."

"Attacked? By who? Those Raiders?"

"We don't know. But some people were kidnapped, and some stuff was stolen."

Cheynou frowned. "You're all riled up because somebody, you don't know who, was kidnapped, and some stuff, you don't know what, was stolen?"

The man's back straightened. "Cap...Orrick Bren sent us out. He said if there were strangers, to take their weapons and bring them in. If they made trouble, kill them."

Cheynou raised his eyebrows. "My, Orrick is in a tizzy, isn't he? Well, now that you know we're not strangers, you don't have to take our weapons, do you?"

"You're the only face I recognize, and I think I'll be taking your weapon first."

Cheynou sighed. "Kohlu, you're in too much of a hurry. These are merchants who can turn around and ride away and sell their goods, which we need, to the Farmers or the Inari. You treat them with disrespect and Orrick Bren is going to be very angry with you. And one other thing...?" He kneed his horse closer to speak softly. The other, a puzzled frown on his face, leaned in.

"I'm inside your defence on your weak side at the moment, and there are five bows behind me. You so much as twitch and you and half your little army will be dead in about one heartbeat. No, don't think about rearing your horse back. Then they really will shoot."

273

The other riders' eyes darted from side to side, then back to Cheynou's face.

"So why don't you just calm down, escort us into camp with due ceremony and let Orrick Bren make the decision. You've done your job. You have assured yourself there's no danger. Let him do his."

The man's hand slid away from his cutlass hilt.

Cheynou smiled. "Good decision, Kohlu. When you've been in a few scraps on land, you'll catch on." He pushed his horse ahead, forcing the other mount to move towards the camp.

"You know, fighting on land is not like fighting on the sea, where the Captain makes all the decisions. It's more like a raid, where you have to think for yourself more. You have to learn the tactics and apply them. Especially on horseback. Everything is so different. It happens so fast."

"Aye...aye, it does." Preoccupied, Kohlu signalled his men to form a guard.

Cheynou nodded. "For example, a packed rush like you just made would be good for dealing with footsoldiers, because it would cut right through them, break their formation. Then you could attack them from the sides. Not so good against archers, though. A pack like that, they can't really miss."

"I see what you mean. Good point."

"It was smart to pull up out of bowshot, though. We were too evenly matched."

"That's what I figured."

Cheynou chatted casually with the other rider as they approached camp, creating a mutual cameraderie to mask, in the man's memory, the fact that he had just been made to look a complete fool. *No sense making enemies if I don't need to, and Kohlu is a good fighter, just not too bright.*

As they neared the first tent, Orrick Bren himself strode out, cutlass strapped to his hip. He stood, feet planted firmly and arms akimbo, waiting for them. Cheynou stopped at a polite distance and signalled his party to dismount and walk forward.

As he approached the former Captain, he remembered their last meeting: the powerful man in a rage, and himself with nothing to say. *It will be different this time. Now I have something to offer.*

"What have we here?"

"Hello, Orrick Bren. I'm back with the merchants I went looking for."

"What merchants? I didn't send you out looking for any merchants."

"Well, I found some anyway. They have some interesting products to trade and they'd like to talk to you. It's good news, Orrick."

Bren looked the group over with a calculating eye and shook his head.

"Too much of a coincidence. Your friends have just made an all-out attack on me, and two glasses later you show up with a smile on your face and a bunch of armed strangers at your back? Something smells like five-day fish here, Chan, and I think I'm going to get myself some answers!" Bren moved forward, his hand on his cutlass. He stared at Cheynou's unyielding stance, then turned towards Maksa.

"Who are you? How dare you ride armed into my camp?"

Cheynou lowered his voice, taking care to speak softly. "Orrick Bren, with due respect, I believe you need to calm down."

The former Captain spun about, his face clouding further. "Who are you to tell me to calm down?"

Cheynou made an open gesture with his hands, inviting Bren to regard himself, and said nothing.

"You would tell me how to act? You, who ran away at the first sign of trouble, will tell me how to run my Ship...to lead my people?"

"This is not about me, Orrick. This is about those who stand in front of you. Think of the possibilities. They could be enemies here to scout you out, spies, storing this scene in their memories to describe to their general who waits with his armies, poised to attack. How does your reaction look, if that is the case?"

This brought silence from Bren, and a worried look from Maksa.

Cheynou wrinkled his forehead as if in thought. "If you were really looking for a fight, you could always assume that they are the agents of the Raiders who have been causing trouble all summer. Look at them. Don't they look suspicious?"

He softened his voice. "Of course, they could be merchants with stocks of trade goods, looking for reliable sources of iron, tin and copper. How will they take your suspicious and violent reaction, if that is who they are?"

The former Captain placed his hands aggressively on his hips. "And which are they, Cheynou the Talker? Who have you brought to me? Are you our saviour or our betrayer?"

Cheynou nodded. "Now you are asking the right questions."

Bren's brow furrowed again, but Cheynou held out his hands, palms forward, calming.

Then the Petrel leader let out a huge breath and shook his head, chuckling. "Cheynou Chan, I do not know how you survive. You were always a thorn in my side, and you seem to have learned little in the time you were away."

"Without wanting to cause disharmony, Orrick, it would seem that since I have survived, perhaps I have learned a lot. But I have not lost my loyalty. I could have taken these men to the Farmers, you know. Or the Inari. Of course, the Inari have no wish to have anything to do with the Sea People. Or anyone else, for that matter."

276

He put on a smile. "But you are concerning yourself with the packaging. Do you not wish to know what is in the parcel you have been sent?"

"Yes, Cheynou, I would welcome good news. Who are these men, and what do they offer?"

Cheynou hid his elation and turned to the Kyabrans. "This is Faranos, heir of the Rochana Family of Velika. This is Maksa of the Dumorne Family, Thousand-Prime, representative of the Military Governor of Velika Province of the Kyabran Empire. This is Quasan of the Cheolean Family, and his cousin, Jyonar. Faranos, Maksa, Quasan, Jyonar; this is Orrick Bren, former Captain of the FamilyShip Storm Petrel, now acknowledged leader of the Sea People ashore."

The five men nodded to each other, a non-committal show of respect.

Maksa spoke first. "It is good to meet the man I have heard so much about."

Orrick shot another glance at Cheynou. "I hope it has not been all uncomplimentary."

Maksa grinned. "Not at all. He has impressed me with tales of your prowess in battle and your feats of diplomacy. A firm hand on the tiller, I believe, is an expression he used."

"Hmm. Yes, he would mention that." His eyes strayed to the rocks of the Fall above them. "Thousand-Prime. A military title?"

"It is," Maksa nodded, "but I am mostly on civilian business at the moment. Of course," he gestured to the sergeant and the soldiers, "our military people have interest in what happens just outside our borders."

"It heartens me to hear that at least you consider this outside your borders."

"We have no interest in bringing an army through the passes we have just traversed. When you have seen them yourself, you will understand. Cheynou will tell you. There are places where ten men could hold off an army of thousands.

"No, Orrick Bren, my military mission is merely to assure our Commandant that there is no army of Raiders waiting up on the Prairie to pour down upon us with fire and sword."

Orrick laughed harshly. "I suppose your Commandant will be pleased at what you report, then. You find us unable to stop even a kidnapping and theft, let alone any invading army."

Cheynou felt a jolt of anger. "That was no kidnapping, Orrick Bren."

"What?" The Captain's face reddened again. "What do you know about this? I thought you said you have been with these people."

Cheynou refused to give ground. "It was Kendie, wasn't it? I'll bet Yong rode in and took her away, and she went willingly. Took all the books with her, didn't she?" He nodded, satisfied from the leader's reaction that he had hit the mark.

"It was kidnapping and theft!"

"It wasn't kidnapping and theft, Orrick. It was your biggest blunder. The only crime that occurred today is that you just drove away one of the Crew's most important resources. It just walked away from you because you didn't use it, and your people will suffer because of your error." He met the larger man's eyes. "I have a lot of respect for your talent and your leadership, Orrick Bren. I have yet to find out if you have the ability to admit to a mistake."

A feeling of freedom swept over him. *Bren can do little to me without endangering the welfare of his Crew. If he says or does the wrong thing, I will turn my back, get on my horse and ride away. I have done my duty for Maksa and for my people, and I will do no more for Orrick Bren.*

Something of this must have shown on his face, because the Petrel leader hesitated. He seemed about to speak, but then another thought struck him. He visibly relaxed, and a conversational tone crept into his voice. "You know, Cheynou, there was only one person who ever had the nerve to speak to me like that."

278

"I know, Orrick, and I miss her, but I think you miss her more. You needed her."

The shared moment seemed to remove all the tension from Orrick. He gathered himself and turned to his guests.

"I apologize for airing old grievances and private woes in your presence. Please accompany me to my tent. We have retained some of the social graces, in spite of our condition."

The Kyabrans bowed their heads in acquiescence, wise enough not to speak, and Bren turned to Cheynou. "Will you be coming with us, or have you done enough damage for one day?"

Cheynou put on a grin. "I think I'll tag along. Maksa doesn't do very well in Seaspeak, and I'd hate for there to be any misunderstanding. I'll try to be polite."

"That will be a pleasant change."

He turned and strode towards the encampment, gesturing to the bystanders to take care of the visitors' mounts. Cheynou swung in beside him, and the Kyabrans followed.

"I had no intention of causing you embarrassment, Orrick, but Kendie...well, you broke her heart, you know?"

"What? This whole problem is about the broken heart of a thirteen-year-old?" He glanced down at Cheynou. "And a lippy one, at that."

"It isn't just that, Orrick. It's what we were talking about a moment ago. She wanted to be a Scribe. She was trying, in her thirteen-year-old way, to do what Sarasha did. She could have been a great help to you. She had the nerve. Now she's gone and she won't be back. Want the truth?"

"You've never lied to me yet, I'll give you that."

"I think Yong is interested in her."

"Interested?"

"Yes. Interested. You know, Orrick? Like boys get interested in girls? There aren't many women smart enough to keep up with him. I think she'd be perfect. Especially if she gets connected with the Wise Women of the Inari. They are keepers of their lore, just as our Scribes are the keepers of ours. Or used to be."

Bren looked down at Cheynou. "I've learned more about the Inari from you in the last half-glass than anything I found out in the past year. Apparently, you were somewhere else part of the time. Why do you know so much?"

"Helmsman's skills, Orrick. I listen, then ask and listen some more."

The Petrel leader snorted. "Maybe you'll do more listening during this Conclave."

"I won't interrupt unless I think there's a misunderstanding. SeaSpeak isn't their native language, and they use a very different dialect north of the Barrier Range, as they call it."

"That sounds fair enough. And afterwards, I want to know about these Inari and their Wise Women." He paused at the door of his tent. "Come in, gentlemen, and I will offer you what amenities we have."

A few glasses later, Cheynou left the Captain's tent with his Kyabran friends, a glow of satisfaction warming him. He glanced at Maksa, who was smiling as well.

"That went even better than I had expected."

Maksa looked down at him. "Better than the beginning went, that's sure."

Cheynou shrugged. "I'm sorry about that. I guess it didn't hurt for you to experience him at his worst. I've never seen him like that, myself. Once he calmed down, he was embarrassed. He had to be overly polite to make up for it."

"And I have never seen you like that, Cheynou. Who is this Kendie you were arguing about?"

Cheynou sighed. "She is just a girl with a dream. She wanted so much to be a Scribe like Sarasha. Then Orrick changed the Trades around and decided we wouldn't need Scribes any more. Yong is another friend, one of Sarasha's original group. He's with the Inari now, and when he heard what happened, he simply came in and took her away. I have no doubt she went willingly. Wait a few years, and I'll bet they're married. They suit."

Faranos laughed. "It would be nice if the love story turned out well, just like in the romances. For a while there, I thought he was going to hit you."

"Maybe he would have." Cheynou shrugged. "So what?"

"So what? He looks awfully strong."

"I've been hit before in training and in fights, but I've been hurt more getting tossed across the deck by a rogue wave. It wouldn't have made that much difference, but he would have lost another one of his people, and he knew it."

"But hasn't he lost you already?"

"Not in the same way. I brought you here, didn't I? I could have taken you to the Inari first."

Maksa turned in the doorway of the Guest Tent. "Was that a possibility?"

He chuckled. "Not likely. As I told him, the Inari have little to do with anyone else. They only accepted Pers and his friends because they decided they like horses."

Maksa shook his head and continued inside. "Cheynou, I have never stood up to a superior officer like that, and I have never seen anyone do it and get away with it."

"You have never seen anyone with good reason to do it. You would yourself, if it was necessary."

"I would like to believe that, Cheynou. You, on the other hand, have done it."

"I had to. You can't let people make mistakes and get away with it, no matter who they are. The whole Crew suffers in the end."

"Well, the end result seems to justify it. Your Captain was very reasonable."

"Reasonable!" Cheynou pulled off his boots, tossed them against the tent wall and collapsed on a cushion. "When he found out there was iron, copper and tin in the mountains here, and you would trade food and cloth for it? Ecstatic is what he was."

"So now the Sea Raiders turned nomad herders will turn to mining, will they?"

"Some of them. Our Armorers will certainly be happy. Their Trade had a dim future until today. Now they will become heroes, and rich as well."

Maksa stretched out on the cushions. "Yes, a good day: drama and emotion relieved by successful dealing."

"And don't forget a feast at the end. Orrick will be letting out all the reefs to impress you with his hospitality."

Faranos pulled off his boots. "If that means good food, I can handle it."

"Sorry. An old sailing expression you don't have to learn. Your Farsian is getting quite good, Faranos."

The younger Kyabran grinned. "Thanks to you and Kendra." Then his face grew serious. "I never thought it was important before. I never realized that there might be important people who spoke another language..." He held his hand up to Maksa. "I know. Everyone is important, even the servants. Cedenye has been telling me that ever since I got to Velika. I'm just starting to figure out what she meant."

The lad turned to Cheynou. "You're younger than I am, aren't you?"

"Probably. Why?"

"I was just thinking. I have those friends in Velika; you know the ones. I had a bunch like that back home in Kyabra before I came out here. We all thought we were pretty tough, you know? We rode good horses, we had weapons training, some of us Weaponless, all that.

"And here you are; you're younger than me and smaller than me. You just stood up to a man twice your size, a commanding officer as well, and you gave him the truth, toe-to-toe, and didn't turn a hair. I still can't believe you did that."

"You put your finger on it, Faranos. It was the truth. He had to realize it or his people would suffer. It didn't matter if he was angry at me."

The Kyabran gave a snort. "It would have mattered to me. He's not a man to have trouble with, your Captain Bren."

"Former Captain Bren. You know, he's going to have to find a title for himself. After being a Priest-Captain, he can't just be plain 'Orrick Bren.' It isn't seemly. What do you people on land call your leader?"

"Emperor?"

Cheynou sputtered with suppressed laughter. "I think that's a bit rich at the moment. Perhaps 'Dictator for Life' would do."

Faranos laughed, but Maksa hid his own smile. "All right, let's not be impolite. There's probably someone listening."

Cheynou glanced around. "Probably not. Our people don't think that way. We're used to living close together and good at ignoring things we shouldn't hear."

"In any case, perhaps we could be serious for long enough to make some plans. Do you need to go and visit with your family?"

"I would like that. I saw several of them as we walked in but didn't get a chance to do more than wave. It didn't seem to be the moment to stop and chat."

"I'd have to agree. Why don't you go ahead? We can make ourselves comfortable here, and perhaps you could drop in just before the feast to give us any pointers on protocol we need."

"Thank you, Maksa." He retrieved his boots and pulled them on. "I'll see you just after the fifth bell."

"How will we know it's the fifth bell?"

Cheynou turned in the tent doorway, grinning. "Well, since the fourth just rang, and since the fifth rings five times, I think you'll figure it out."

Maksa rolled his eyes and made a shooing motion with his hands.

It felt strange to be walking through the camp again. True to their nature, no one intruded upon him, just greeted him politely as he passed. He saw none of his former friends, nor did he expect to in the middle of a working watch. Those who hadn't left the camp permanently were out hunting or had returned to their tasks once the excitement died down. He quickened his pace as he approached his father's tent, sure of his welcome there, at least.

Once he was seated on the cushions, a drink in his hand like a guest, he looked at his family with new appreciation. He had met such different people lately that he could see his kin as a stranger would.

First, his mother. He had never noticed her. Calm, quiet, dependable, strong. What distinguished her was her absolute competence. Nothing ever fazed her, nothing caught her off-guard. Now, when her only task was providing refreshment, she had plenty of time to join them. Her fond smile reminded him what it must be like to have her only son gone so far away. He hadn't thought of that before, at least not seriously, and he felt a pang of guilt.

Then his father. He smiled and raised his glass. Qiu was talking as usual, his hands sketching, describing, filling in between the words.

And his uncle Sanjin: more like his mother. Calm competence as well, but with that sarcastic edge that always made you think and wonder, even after what he said was long past.

He smiled around at his small family and concentrated on what his father was saying.

"...I tell you, Cheynou, when Orrick found out that Kendie was gone this morning, and with her all those books, he was furious. I've never seen him out of his own control like that."

"Neither have I, Father. He was being completely stupid."

His father stopped, his hands still for a change. "And I hear you faced him."

"I had to. He was about to insult our guests."

The elder Chan looked to his brother. "Faced down Orrick Bren, and him in a rage. What do you think, Sanjin?"

His uncle glanced at Cheynou appraisingly. "Were you scared?"

"Not at the time. I was too busy figuring out how to calm him down before he messed everything up. Afterwards, I was glad that we had a distance to walk to his tent. That's when my knees started shaking."

They smiled proudly at him, and he felt a glow: part pride, part embarrassment. "Any of you would have done the same."

His father's face grew serious. "And we may have to. Our position is a very delicate one, partly because of its newness. Also because it seems to be the only official position that could ever exercise any control over Bren."

Sanjin shrugged. "Well, we have Cheynou's example to follow. It can be done, if it is done correctly. I would not have considered the direct confrontation, myself."

Cheynou flicked his fingers. "You're not half his size, either. He knew that if he hit me he'd look like a bully and an idiot."

"And we have to live with him. You don't. At least, I assume you don't. What happened to the Farmer girl?"

"Kendra had no reason to come back. She's living with the Rochana family until I finish this task. Faranos Rochana is the younger man with us."

"Noble blood, that one."

He looked at his mother in surprise.

"The way he holds his head."

"Oh. Well, you're right. He's the heir of the family. Let me tell you about them..."

He had just finished his description and was starting to answer their questions when the first strokes of the bell rang.

"Oh! I have to go and bring the Kyabrans to the feast." He glanced ruefully at his travel-stained shirt. "And put on some better clothes."

He turned to his mother. "Wait until you see the shirt Lady Cedenye made for me. They...um...go for things a little more elaborate in the Empire."

His mother's eyebrows went up. "Well, I'll be looking forward to seeing you in all your Imperial splendour, then."

He grinned, jumped up and gave her a quick kiss. Then, with a wave to his father and uncle, he slipped out the door.

25. KIRIGATA

Their reception at Kirigata was considerably more dignified. There had been time for word of their presence to reach the Farmers, and Cheynou had sent a personal message, so Lord Kire was well prepared.

Maksa glanced at Cheynou with raised eyebrows as they rounded the last corner to see a squad of men lined up outside the gate in formal receiving order, with the lord himself and his lady waiting in the centre.

"Looks like they don't want you to see them as uncultured heathens."

Maksa's eyes scanned the high structure, the tidy outbuildings peeping over the thick stone wall. "They have a sturdy Home. Prosperous, yet easy to defend. Much better than we have in Velika."

"They need it more than you do in Velika. Life is not so peaceful out here."

"Thanks to your people, I gather."

"Partly, I must admit."

Then they were approaching; Lord Kire stepped forward, and Cheynou regarded the two leaders with a certain amusement. Like dancers uncertain of the steps, each man watched the other, each providing what clues he could as to what was expected. Cheynou, vaguely aware of the formalities of each, did his best to smooth the way and the result was a dignified, formal ceremony of greeting that a watching stranger would not realize was unrehearsed.

Once they had been welcomed formally they entered the courtyard. Tables were set out in the lord's private garden where the shade of the trees provided relief from the late summer sun. Lord Kire had chosen the format wisely, and everyone stood and mingled, allowing informal conversation to flourish.

Sure enough, the lord quickly pounced on Cheynou. "So you have returned without my daughter. Couldn't put up with her, either."

Cheynou grinned. "She told me you would say that!"

"Did she, now? And so you have had the time to prepare your answer."

"I have. It is quite the opposite, my Lord. We are compatible travelling companions. However, we have not finished our journey, and she stays with the Rochana family to work on her language skills before we venture further into the huge Empire we found below the Rim."

"Huge, is it?"

"I have no idea how big. That's what we're going to find out."

"And she would not return so soon, because as of yet she has solved nothing."

"I think there is some of that, as well."

"You must talk to her mother. She was pleased to get your note, by the way. It was thoughtful of you."

"I knew you would worry if word came that I was back and Kendra was not."

"As I say. Thoughtful. Now I must play the host. It was also thoughtful of you to bring your friends to our Home first."

"They are her friends even more than mine. Thank her."

The lord gazed at Cheynou, assessing something. "I see. Kendra is doing her share, is she?"

"She is invaluable. You can see that these are a formal people, even more than your folk are. She finds that aspect comforting while I find it confusing. Believe me, the Rochanas and Cheoleans were much more interested in meeting your people than in meeting mine. They were just too polite to say so."

The lord laughed. "Good enough. I'll keep that in mind when the trade talks start."

Eyes were drawn their way, and Lord Kire strode back to his guests, leaving Cheynou to sit by Kendra's mother.

She went straight to the point. "Is she happy, Cheynou?"

He grinned. "As happy as I've ever seen her, my Lady."

She slapped his arm as Kendra would have. "Don't give me 'my Lady.' Talk to me. How is she doing? Tell true, now."

"She is truly happy." He nodded to emphasize it. "There is no need to lie. She has found a place with a good family. It is much like here, though less tranquil. We have reached their frontier, only two generations settled, so life is rougher.

"The Rochana family, represented by their heir, Faranos, is a junior branch of a powerful family in the Capital. Maksa, the leader of our expedition, is of a lower family, but his wife, Miranra, seems to be of the highest. I don't know the story there, but there is love involved. Their twin sons, age five, are the darlings of the household."

"A love story! How romantic!"

"Well, don't say anything to him about it. It's just my speculation."

"Of course, Cheynou, I never would. Tell me more about them."

He went on for some time, trying to think of those details of the Rochana Home and Family that would appeal to a girl's mother, to comfort her when she woke in the dead of night and worried about her daughter. As he talked, he discovered how much Kendra had taught him, with her rambling conversation all those days on the trail, about the women in her family: how they felt, what they feared, what they hoped for.

Finally, his tales and her questions wound down, and they sat in mutually satisfied silence. Then the lady slapped her hands to her knees like any other farm wife would and jumped up. "Enough of this lallygagging. I have indulged myself, as I perhaps deserve, but duty calls."

Then she turned back. "This Faranos. The heir, you say? Has Kendra shown any interest...?"

A pang shot through Cheynou's chest, and he struggled for a calm answer.

She regarded him. "I understand. Sorry I brought it up."

"No, I..."

She patted his arm. "Truly sorry." Then she smiled. "I have long ago given up thinking I can influence Kendra's choice of friends. For what it's worth, you seem a fine young man. Everyone speaks well of you, and if my daughter is safe and happy in your care, I will never complain."

She stood and walked away, leaving him with no need to answer. *Which is a good thing, because I can think of nothing to say.*

Soon, she was bustling people around, settling the traders in their rooms, taking care of the soldiers and juggling the concerns of twenty people in her head. Cheynou tried to imagine Kendra at the centre of such a whirlwind. *Not difficult. She's never happier than when there's action and she's at the hub of it.*

From that point on, Cheynou found himself more concerned with his duty and less with enjoying himself. The meetings with the other Farmer Lords were crucial, and he felt it doubly important that he, as a representative of the former Sea People, should be seen playing his full role. If the situation worked out as he thought it might, the pack trains would be rolling through the Sea People's territory no matter where their ultimate destination, and he made sure, as subtly as possible, that everyone took that into consideration.

So he took pleasure in a job well done, but it was not his nature to sit in stuffy halls and talk. As soon as the meetings were over, the trade pacts signed and the last trinket sold, he took his first chance to talk to Maksa.

"So, are we done?"

The sturdy Kyabran nodded. "I think so, Cheynou. Anxious to get back on the trail?"

"Most definitely. I have work to do finishing the details on my maps, and I need to travel the route once more to find those details."

"Cheynou, I'm sure that when you have finished this trip you will find that there are more details you would like to put on the maps, and just one more trip would find them."

"I suppose so. A map is never truly finished, now that you mention it. However, the amount of detail is only appropriate to the required use. Any experienced traveller could find his way over the passes using our trail markers and the maps I have already made. That is really enough. I would just like to explore alternate routes in places where the trail is risky at different times of the year."

Maksa clapped him on the shoulder. "You'll be getting your chance soon, lad. We'll be staying at Kirigata tomorrow night, then onto the Prairie the next day."

Cheynou nodded, grinned. "Suits me fine."

"Not happy in the luxury of the settled folk?"

"Not really."

"Wait till you see Kyabrad, the Capital City of the Empire."

"I could probably stand that for a while."

"We'll have to see that you get your chance. We leave the day after tomorrow. Jyonar will want one more survey of the swamp area and then, straight home?"

"I have one small detour I'd like to make. I told you that the Inari are not interested in trade, but I want you to meet some of my friends. They might come in handy, especially if the problems with these Raiders escalate."

"I'm always interested in meeting a new culture. Also in a chance to meet the main characters in the love story."

Horror shot through Cheynou. "Maksa, don't you dare say anything! I'm only guessing."

The older man grinned. "Kendra was right. It is fun to finally break through that competent façade of yours."

"Kendra. Hmph. I might have known."

26. INARI CAMP

"It was quite easy, actually."

"I'm sure." Cheynou stretched out on the pillows of Yong's tent and favoured him with a suspicious stare. "But what did you do? Bren noticed the coincidence immediately. It wasn't luck that had you stealing Kendie two glasses before we showed up."

The tall lad looked at his feet, but Cheynou knew he was unrepentant, as usual. "Come on, Yong. You used us, didn't you?"

Yong shrugged, maybe a bit uncomfortable. *Probably not.* "Well, I had already contacted Kendie, but I was having trouble figuring how to get her out of camp."

"Couldn't she just ride away?"

"With all those books? I'm not exactly welcome in the Petrel camp anymore, so I was stuck. Then when Tonu came riding in and said you were back with a troop of strangers..."

"Ah."

"Aye. I just rode over, found a herder and told him that there was a party of armed strangers coming down from the north, and he'd better go check them out. I picked Nahar, you know?"

Cheynou leaned over to Faranos, who was following this exchange with difficulty. "I don't know the Petrel Crew very well, but Nahar is young and a bit excitable, as I recall."

Yong grinned. "That's the one. He went tearing down into camp and got everybody all stirred up. They were busy tightening in the herds and rushing around setting up defenses, all looking to the north."

"So you just rode in from the south, lifted her out and rode away with your saddlebags full of books."

"A packhorse load, actually."

"A fine stunt, Yong, and I'm sure you're really pleased with yourself, no matter what damage you've done to your relations with Bren. You realize he was about to lump you in with the rest of the Raiders that have been plaguing everyone all summer."

"Oh, no. This was personal. It isn't the same..."

"Oh, yes it is. A raid by a disaffected former Crewmember. How is that different? And you certainly caused us a lot of trouble."

Yong had the grace to look abashed. "Yes...well, I didn't plan it quite that way. You must have started earlier or got there quicker than I had figured on. And I came later, because I had a long ride. I thought they'd have settled before you arrived."

"Well, they hadn't. We hit Orrick Bren in a full rage, and I had to do some fancy footwork to keep him from estranging the merchants before they even got a chance to say 'Hello.' Ask Faranos. It was very close for a while. Thanks a lot."

Yong laughed and reached a long arm over to slap Cheynou on the back. "Now, that footwork I wish I was there to see. The story's spread all over the Prairie. You faced him down twice, the way I hear it. Hand on your sword hilt the whole while!"

"I did not have my hand on my sword hilt. That's exaggeration."

Faranos cleared his throat.

"What?"

"Actually, you did, Cheynou. Well, not exactly on it, but your thumb was stuck in your belt just beside the hilt. I remember thinking how fast you bring it out, and wondering if that man was a good enough swordsman to beat you."

"That was just habit. I'd never dream of picking a fight with Orrick Bren. He's twice the swordsman I'll ever be."

Yong chuckled. "What I hear, you picked a fight, set your own ground and weapons and forced him to his knees."

"It wasn't like that, Yong, and you know it. He was wrong, and I just made him see it."

293

Yong grew serious, placed a hand on Cheynou's shoulder. "I also heard what you said about Kendie. I'll be forever grateful that you set the record straight, Cheynou."

"It was only the truth, Yong. There's nothing to thank me for."

"You can tell it any way you like, kid. I'm taking your lesson about the truth. I know it when I see it. So does Kendie. You're her hero, now. Even more than me!"

Cheynou grinned. "I doubt that. I wish I could be around in a couple of hundred years to hear what that story grows to be."

Now it was Yong's turn to be abashed. "I didn't do that much. She wanted to come, I provided the horse."

"And the motivation. Likes you, does she?"

"Well enough."

"She's young. She'll have plenty of time to discover your true nature."

"I hope so."

Cheynou looked around. "Where is she now?"

Yong rose, opened the doorflap and gestured towards a small, white tent perched in a prime, sheltered spot near the stream. He lowered his voice theatrically. "Women's business."

Cheynou nodded. "I'll see her when she has less important things to do."

Talk turned to horse training, and Cheynou just had to take Pers and Yong to the pasture to show his progress with training his mare to lash out with her rear hooves.

"That's impressive, Cheynou. How did you teach her to do that?"

"Faranos figured it out. I just did what I was told until the horse did the same."

Respectful eyes turned to the Kyabran boy, who reddened. "It's pretty basic stuff. I'm working on the forehooves as well. Cheynou gave me the idea. I'll be using

294

that technique from now on to train the horses we sell to the cavalry units. It will increase their value."

The news that they had an experienced horse trainer in their midst brought Solen in a hurry, and soon they were drinking ship's beer and telling training stories, most of which Cheynou couldn't understand and several which he frankly disbelieved. He tipped Faranos a wink and slipped out of the tent.

* * *

As he was returning to his billet, Kendie waylaid him, throwing her arms around him and almost knocking him over.

"Cheynou! You're back from the mountains!"

"Oh." He pretended to notice. "Yes, I suppose I am. My skillful navigation tells me there are no high mountains in the vicinity."

She slapped his arm. "Don't be silly. Yong says you're interested in the lore of the Inari."

"I'm more interested in the lore of the Sea People, which I gather you continue to Scribe."

"Oh, yes. Yong has been wonderful."

He elbowed her ribs. "I'm sure he has."

She blushed, but recovered quickly. "And the Inari women..."

"So I gather. Their lore is all oral, though."

"Not any more." She tugged at his arm, pulling him towards the white tent.

Cheynou hesitated outside. "Am I allowed?"

She pulled at his sleeve. "Of course. Come in."

He ducked to enter. "Why is the doorway so low?"

She smiled impishly. "So people show proper reverence as they enter. Especially you tall men."

"Very clever." He looked around. "Coming from a girl who is now as tall as I am." The tent was quite bare except for an elaborately cushioned low chair at one side with a semi-circle of plump cushions around it. "What is that for?"

"That's where the Wise Woman sits when she tells the Tales and teaches the Lore of the Tribe. The rest sit around and listen, oldest ones closest where they can hear. She says the words, and they all repeat them like a chant. It's how they learn."

"And what's that?" A small box sat over against the wall, writing implements neatly lined on its top.

"That's where I sit," her voice held a mixture of modesty and pride. "I'm copying it all down. It works really well when she's teaching them because everything is said twice. I don't get much, because my Inari is poor, but when she goes through the cycle in the coming years, I'll fill in the blanks and I'll have it."

"They have a yearly cycle?"

"Yes. Every month they tell the stories that apply to that month. The Tales because they originally happened in that month and the Lore because it's the information needed for that month's activities. She also repeats the history of the births of that month."

"It sounds complicated."

"It takes a month to recite it all."

He gazed around once more. "Is that Sarasha's book-box from the Eagle?"

"Yes. That's all right, isn't it?"

"Of course it's all right. She'd be proud to know you were using it."

"I thought so, but it's good to hear you say it."

He nodded and turned towards the door. "This is a wonderful place, and I think you're doing wonderful things here."

As they left the tent, he had an idea. "Here's a thought, Kendie."

"Yes?" Her eyes sparkled with enthusiasm.

"Who is keeping track of the heritage of all the horses? The bloodlines and such?"

She frowned. "I don't know. I think Solen keeps track of his horses in his head. Nobody talked anything about bloodlines." She shrugged. "What are bloodlines, anyway?"

"You can breed, say, a white horse to another white horse, but you don't always get a white colt. According to Kendra, the characteristics of the grandparents and even the great-grandparents show up regularly. So when the Farmers are breeding their best animals, they keep track of the whole heritage and take it into account when they choose the mates."

"I see. And somebody has to write it all down!"

He rolled his hand with a brief bow, as if introducing her to a Conclave.

"You're right! I should do that! Oh, I'll have to tell Yong!"

"You should do that. Away you go; I saw him headed for the horse pasture as we were coming up here."

"I know. Oh, thank you, Cheynou!" She pecked a quick kiss to his cheek and ran off. He watched her go, smiling when, far down the trail, she made a couple of skips like a child, then ran on.

27.   RAIDERS AGAIN

"Company coming." Yong's head was up, listening.

"Definitely a stir." Cheynou met Faranos's eyes. "Let's go find out."

As they left the tent, the cause of the commotion appeared, trotting up and stopping at the correct distance from camp. Two destriers, one of them deep red, followed by about twenty horsemen.

Cheynou peered. "Orrick and Byaren. Together with a mixed troop. Yong, they've finally decided to do something about you."

The taller lad grinned. "More likely it's you they're after. Aren't they both connected to Kendra somehow?"

"In any case, let's get out there before your Inari friends stop being curious and start asking difficult questions."

They strode out, followed by several Eagles, including Tonu and her husband.

Cheynou stared up at the two men, towering over him on their huge horses. "A pleasant day to meet old friends. May I assume it is no social occasion that brings the two of you out together?"

Orrick swung down and strode forward, handing his reins to one of his men. "We have a problem. All of us."

"The Raiders. What have they done?"

Bren's frown deepened. "They have finally gone over the line. They attacked a small wagon train that was bringing supplies and trade goods from Kirigata to our camp. They killed two guards and stole all the goods. The merchant was wounded, but he'll live."

Cheynou tilted his chin towards the row of horses stomping behind Bren and Byaren. "What do you need from us? You have some of the best mounts on the Prairies, with your best fighters astride. Go trample them into the dirt."

"Trackers. We have the power, but we have to find them."

"Ah. Solen."

"Is he around?"

"I think so."

"Good." Bren glanced over at Tonu and Barhan, standing nearby. "And any other resources we can call in."

Tonu spoke quickly to her husband and the stocky Inari nodded. "I will come. Two friends."

Choti slid up beside him. "I come. No dog?"

Cheynou grinned. "Sorry, your Hunting Sister stalks different prey below the Barrier." He turned to Bren. "We'll saddle up and be with you before you know it. How long?"

"We have supplies for three days." Byaren shrugged. "If we don't find them by then, it will be a much longer search."

"Right." He raised his voice. "Three days food, everyone, with a battle at the end."

There was immediate bustle in the Inari camp as horses were saddled and packs tied. In a very short time, sixteen men were swinging into the saddle, including the Kyabrans from Rochana.

Cheynou slipped his horse in between Maksa and Faranos. "Do you want to get involved in this?"

The big man shrugged. "We are allies, and our pack trail is a long, vulnerable route. If we don't stop these Raiders now, they will become our problem in the future." He checked back over his shoulder. "My men will acquit themselves well."

Cheynou nodded and pushed forward.

Yong and Pers trotted up, one on either side. "Nothing like a little battle to cement a friendship."

Cheynou could only shrug his acceptance and ride on. He urged his horse to the head of the troop, where Bren and Byaren were having trouble conferring with their trackers. He waved Solen ahead, and communication went smoother.

* * *

Byaren's scouts had trailed the Raiders to the old Sparrowhawk camp, where evidence suggested they had been living. The site was deserted now, and it required the combined talents of the posse's trackers to figure out the newest movement in the mass of hoofprints.

"They're headed east."

Solen nodded. "It's difficult to hide on the plains. They've been hanging around out here all summer; they've had time to find a hideout. If we're lucky, they'll use the same trail too many times to get to it."

Byaren glanced at Orrick, who nodded. "We're in your hands, Solen. I don't know how the Inari can find tracks. It just looks like dust and grass to me."

Solen tipped a finger to the brim of his hat and joined Choti and Barhan for a quick chat. Then the three spread out walking, and everyone followed at a distance.

It didn't take long. Choti waved, and Solen strode over, nodded and turned towards the leaders. "They've taken the trail alongside that creek. Choti says there's a good campsite about half a league up the trail. Good view, defendable."

Orrick turned towards Byaren, who shrugged. "Still your choice, Solen. Your people know this area."

"Fine. I'll go up the trail, send the Inari out to either side. The moment we see anyone, we'll stop and make further plans."

Both leaders nodded, and the little army moved ahead with caution.

Cheynou kept his eyes open, but he felt at a disadvantage, down on a smaller horse and unable to read the trail because those who led messed the spoor with their huge metal shoes.

The farther up the trail they progressed, the slower they moved. Finally, they came around a corner to find Solen and Barhan waiting. The plainsman signalled a dismount, and they gathered to speak quietly. "They're in the camp, all right. About two bowshots ahead. No sentries so far."

"What's the camp like to attack?"

Solen and Barhan chatted, a conversation full of shaking heads. Finally, Solen turned back to the leaders. "It's hard to approach from anywhere except the trail. It will take time to creep around, and they're sure to see us, even if their sentries are as slack as we suspect."

Byaren nodded. "We need a distraction."

Bren scanned the group. Then he afforded Yong and Cheynou a wry smile. "What do you say, you two? You have some experience with this sort of thing."

Cheynou pushed his horse ahead, cutting Yong off before he could make a retort. "I could go."

Orrick frowned. "Alone? You can't just wander in there and say, 'Look at me.' They'll cut you down without a thought."

Cheynou shook his head. "I have an idea. Not all of those Raiders will be so enthusiastic about the life they have chosen. They got into it when times were tough, they've spent the summer on the run and now winter is closing in. I'll bet a few of them are ready to quit, maybe more. At least they'll listen, and every man I turn will be one less to fight against us."

Bren frowned and caressed his cutlass hilt. "I'm not offering any amnesties. Murder has been committed."

"They didn't all do it, and they're just acting like our people have for centuries." Glancing at Orrick's stony face, Cheynou shrugged. "The point isn't to persuade them. Just to keep their attention while our attackers get in place."

Orrick and Byaren exchanged a glance, and the former Captain shrugged. "I've seen you get away with it before, Cheynou. Take care, and get out of there the moment you feel threatened. We have enough men to take them in a straight fight, but this way will save lives."

Cheynou gave a weak grin. "Let's hope mine is one of them." He turned his horse and kneed it ahead to the scouts.

"Keep an eye on me. If I turn and run, you can assume my plan didn't work."

Solen spoke a few words to Barhan, who nodded to Cheynou and slipped into the rocks beside him as he climbed the trail.

Now that he wanted to be seen, he pushed his horse up to a trot. *All the better to get it over with sooner.* Soon, he smelled a campfire and saw a wisp of smoke rising over the ridge in front of him. When he gained the top, he looked down and saw tents scattered along the hillside, tightly surrounded by a wall of rock higher than a man on a horse.

An easily defended spot. Here we go...

Cheynou reined his horse down to a walk, placing a similar tether on his fear, which rose in the back of his throat, threatening to choke him.

"Hello, the camp."

Heads came up, and men ran for their weapons.

"Cheynou Chan of the Eagles. I wish to talk."

The mob resolved itself into a mass of lesser fighters fronted by three larger figures. One of the three stepped forward. "Cheynou Chan. I've heard of you. What do you want?"

"Hello, Kahama of the Falcons. I want to talk."

"I hear you're quite a talker." The man sneered and spat on the ground. "I somehow doubt you came to join us."

"No, I'm here to give you one last chance."

Kahama guffawed. "We're a bit past the 'one last chance' stage."

"Perhaps. But not all of you. Murder has been committed, but not everyone is guilty. We understand your problems. Life on the Prairie has not been easy. It has been different from life onboard a FamilyShip. All of us have felt it."

"Right. And all of you have settled down to be herders and farmers. Some of us like the old ways. We were Raiders, and we remain Raiders."

A positive murmur ran through the crowd, although some men dropped their eyes or looked to others for support.

"Our own people?"

"Anyone who is against us is fair game."

Cheynou used his mounted perch to scan the crowd. "I see Sparrowhawks here. Betoko, is this the life you want?"

The man shrugged. "My Ship is gone. My Family has disappeared. Where else am I to go?"

"There are Families from many Ships in the Petrel camp."

Kahama sneered again. "Living under the firm hand of Orrick Bren? I'll take my chances out here. I don't see you hanging around his camp these days."

"What would you know about that?"

"The whole Prairie knows about Cheynou Chan the Helmsman and his adventures in faraway lands. I was sort of hoping you wouldn't come back."

"Thanks, Kahama. But I am back, and I'm offering you a chance to rejoin the Fleet. Any man who wants to return to the Ship can drop his weapon and walk down that trail. Only those who actually committed the murders will be punished."

"Hah! It was the middle of a battle. How can any man say who did what?"

Cheynou grinned. "Oh, I'm sure everyone has a very good idea of what happened. I can't see a proud Raider such as yourself being shy about your deeds, once the battle was over and the bottles were uncorked. Now, my offer stands as long as I am here. The moment I turn and ride away, those who remain become guilty by their own choice."

Kahama raised his sword and stepped forward, his two henchmen a pace behind. "You're not riding anywhere, Chan who used to be the talker. You're going to be the next casualty."

Cheynou spun his mount and gave her the signal to kick. To his surprise, she did exactly that, almost unhorsing him in the process. She missed, but Kahama fell back against his supporters, and the three tumbled in a heap of swearing and sharp edges flailing in all directions. Cheynou reined his horse around and pushed her forward, towering over them. "My offer stands, but not for long." He raised his gaze, focusing on the Sparrowhawks. "Anyone coming with me?"

Betoko shared glances with two others, then stepped forward. "If you don't mind, Cheynou, we will keep our swords for the moment."

"A good plan. Away you go. I'll follow."

The three stepped towards the path out of camp, and two more men trailed them. A general stir eddied through the mob, some edging forward, others pushing back.

"Don't let them go!" Kahama scrambled to his feet, sword waving. "Take them!"

Cheynou backed his horse away as three more men sprinted free. All the escapees were running now. He spun his horse and started after them, but the other Raiders were moving too, racing to cut him off. One of them made a desperate lunge and caught his offside rein, hauling the horse to a standstill.

Cursing his inability to teach the animal to rear on command, Cheynou pushed the horse to the right, trying to run the man down, but he clung fiercely, and two others were reaching in, trying to grab any part of the harness they could. He drew his cutlass and chopped down, biting to the bone on his assailant's shoulder. The man fell back, screaming.

But the other two had taken advantage of the moment to draw their own weapons, and the rest were circling, waiting for a chance to move in.

Cheynou kicked his horse to a trot, pushing the ring of men outward, but they began to run in behind him. His only chance was to blast his way out and hope no one got hold of the reins or bridle or a good cut at his mount.

304

He circled once more, looking desperately for a weak spot in the wall, but bared swords reached for him from all directions.

Then a burst of shouting brought everyone's attention outward. A wave of Kyabrans, Sea People and Inari flooded into the campsite, swords slashing. The bandits turned from Cheynou and ran to defend their position, leaving him alone for the moment in the centre of the melee.

After one breath to assess the situation, he began his own attack, using his mounted height and mobility to lend a hand to any who needed it. Now Byaren and Orrick stormed up the trail on their destriers, with Pers, Faranos and the other riders close behind. They crowded in beside Cheynou, and he pointed to where they were needed. The troop split up and and fell on the enemy.

That was the end of the fight. The centre of their camp commanded by fighters on horseback, the Raider defence crumbled, every man striving to reach the perimeter and disappear into the rocks.

Soon, quiet descended, broken only by the panting of the fighters and the moans of the wounded.

Pers slid his mount alongside. "Nicely done, Cheynou. That was some distraction."

"Took you long enough."

Yong came up on the other side. "We got delayed down the trail. A bunch came running down, said you'd offered them amnesty. Did you?"

"I did, and you'd better back me. Most of those were Sparrowhawks who spent the winter visiting and came back to an empty camp in the spring. Others were just hangers-on; didn't realize what they were getting into, but too scared to quit."

He scanned the camp. "Anybody seen Kahama and his two backers? I'd bet good money they're the ones responsible for the murders."

Orrick Bren raised his voice. "You heard him. Bring in all the captives. Don't let them talk to each other."

Byaren and Faranos directed their men as well, and soon order was restored. Kahama and one of his men had escaped; the other was dead.

"What do we do with this lot, sir?"

The leaders turned, not sure which of them had been addressed. Sergeant Yondap looked up at them, gesturing towards seven former Raiders crowding back up the trail.

Maksa deferred to Orrick Bren. "They are your people."

Bren glanced at Cheynou. "They said you offered amnesty. On whose authority?"

Cheynou grinned. "On my own, of course. You sent me in to negotiate, so I took the initiative."

Bren's face worked, but ended up in a wry smile. "Once again, you go too far. I sent you to cause a distraction. I gave you no authority."

Cheynou glanced sideways at the Captain. "And on whose authority would you have given me authority?"

Bren buried his face in his hands, then straightened to look at the other leaders. "What do I do with him?" He shook his head.

Maksa grinned but said nothing.

"I have the perfect solution for the lad, Orrick."

"Please, Byaren. Tell us all."

"Send him back to Kyabra to deal with Kendra. It's the only fitting punishment."

The two men's eyes met, and both smiled. They turned as one, looking down on Cheynou from their big mounts.

"There you have it, lad. Your sentence has been pronounced."

Cheynou stared up at Orrick, remembering that bond the three of them shared. His heart gave a lift. "Since I chose it, I suppose I'll have to accept. Even now I know what it's like."

The brief scream of a man whose dislocated shoulder was being set attracted their attention, and the lighthearted moment was over. Bren pointed to the Sparrowhawks and made a shooing motion.

Cheynou nodded, rode over to them and dismounted. "Looks like you're my problem, now. Stay close to me until we get to the Petrel camp. You'll be safer that way. There'll be a big Conclave there to straighten this all out, and after that you'll be free to go or stay. I suggest you remain there. If you disappear, any bandit problems that come up in the next ten years will be automatically laid at your feet. Agreed?"

They all nodded, relief on their faces.

"All right. Let's get this camp rolled up. There are no spare tents for prisoners with the Petrels. Did you have any pack horses?"

Three glum nods answered him. "Aye. Us. Kahama and his mates were always out patrolling or doing something else that kept them from working." The man glanced at Cheynou. "You know, we rebelled against the Fleet because of that sort of thing."

Cheynou slapped him on the back. "You're going to do just fine in the Petrel camp. Orrick Bren needs someone to keep reminding him of that."

* * *

At times, Cheynou wished he had never stuck his nose into the whole situation. It was pleasant to be treated as the hero of the battle, but his rash promise to the Sparrowhawks meant that he had to stay for the Conclave to make sure his word was kept. Maksa and Faranos went with Pers, Solen and the Inari back to their camp and joined with the other Kyabrans to wait for him.

Finally, Cheynou was free to go. One late summer morning, he and Yong were lining up a small pack train of goods for the Inari when Orrick Bren pulled him aside.

"You know, I've been thinking, lad."

Cheynou read the man's relaxed face and decided he could chance a joke. "That's good, Orrick. Sarasha would be proud of you."

Bren refused to smile. "That she would, because of what I've been thinking about." He faced Cheynou directly. "I never thought I'd be saying this, but do you really have to leave?"

"What do you mean?"

"I'm finally agreeing. There is a place for you with the Petrels. You have proved beyond doubt your use to all the Crews. Look at us. The Sea People, the Inari and the Farmers all sitting around chatting happily with each other, sharing stories and making friends. Strangers from the Empire of Kyabra lining up to trade with us. I have no idea how much of it you managed, but everywhere I look I find evidence of your fingers, nudging and twisting everything into place."

"Orrick, you know I didn't really plan any of this. It just sort of...happened."

"More evidence that your way of doing things is the right way. I freely accept that there are areas of diplomacy where I do not have the right temperament." He cocked his head and regarded Cheynou. "You have a strange sense of confidence that sways people to trust you. Sarasha had it, too. I don't know where it comes from."

Cheynou grinned. "You have it as well. Yours just comes from a different source."

"And what source is that?"

"We all take strength from our belief in what is true. Sarasha and I know what is true for our people. You believe in your own version of the truth, which revolves around what is good for your Ship...now your Tribe, or whatever you choose to call yourselves. Unfortunately, your truth involves you being in charge."

Orrick shrugged. "Somebody has to be."

"That's where we differ. But we both have the good of the Sea People in our hearts, and that's where we can come together."

Bren laughed aloud. "And again we see Cheynou Chan at his finest, finding ways to agree with people." Then his face became serious. "But I noticed your turn of phrase. 'Whatever *you* choose to call *yourselves.*' Does that mean what it sounds like?"

"I...have other loyalties, other duties, now. I have done what I can for the Sea People, and as Sarasha would have suggested, it is now up to you to make of that what you can."

"Other loyalties. The Kyabrans?"

"No..."

"Ah. Kendra of Kirigata."

Cheynou's face warmed. "Yes, but it's not just that. I started a journey, and it is not complete."

Again, the former Captain eyed Cheynou. "You in love with her?"

Cheynou shrugged. "Maybe. Who knows? But I have other dreams to follow. Maybe they're just dreams, maybe not, but that's where I'm going. If she fits into them, that's great. The day she doesn't..." He shrugged. "I'm not looking forward to that choice. But it's a long way off right now."

Bren nodded, then grinned. "That puts me closer to understanding you than I ever have in the past. I wish you the best of fortune." He reached out and they grasped forearms. "And if you should happen to chance upon any good trading opportunities, remember where your second loyalty lies."

"Is that official?"

Orrick tossed his hands up. "As official as I have the power to make it. Nothing around here is official anymore."

Cheynou stared into the taller man's eyes. "And when you get around to making it official, consider that the man who follows you in whatever position you create may not have the good of our people in mind as much as you do.

Remember what Sarasha said. Few can handle great power, and those that seek it most avidly are the last who should achieve it."

"Did she really say that?"

"Perhaps not in so many words, but..."

Orrick's eyes took on a faraway look. "It would be an appropriate way to remember her." He focused on Cheynou. "Wonderful. Now every decision I make, I'll have the voice of Cheynou Chan in my ear saying, 'Would Sarasha have approved?'"

Cheynou grinned. "And now my duty here is really done."

"I suppose it is. You've manipulated us all into cooperation and harmony without making anyone do anything. Sarasha would be proud of you."

He slapped Cheynou on the shoulder, turning him towards the gathering pack train. "Fare well in your journeys, and come back some day to tell us all about it." He glanced down. "And to make sure we're following your plan."

Deciding there was no answer to that, Cheynou slapped the bigger man's shoulder and turned to his horse.

28.   BACK TO ROCHANA HOME

It was a pleasant ride back over the Barrier Range. Hard, dangerous work as well, but relaxing all the same. They paid tribute at the graves of the three heroes who had made much of their progress possible, each in his or her own way. They made further repairs to the trail, scouted and assessed alternate routes, and updated Cheynou's maps.

Maksa and Faranos spent the evenings preparing him for what he might discover as he plunged farther into the Empire, and he repaid them with stories of his own people.

But no one mentioned Kendra. Cheynou tried not to think about his main problem, which tended to pop into his mind as he lay awake, staring at the stars. *Will she come with me?*

He had no answer.

It was too much to expect their return to be a surprise. As they approached the Rochana Home, a mob of brightly dressed people spilled out of the main entrance and poured around them, talking and laughing.

Cheynou joined in the merrymaking, but his eyes were drawn to the three women standing with dignity at the edge of the patio. He rode forward to a polite distance, then dismounted.

There was a flurry of movement on the patio, and Kendra seemed to stumble on the step. With a quick frown back at Miranra, she turned and flung herself at him, staggering him against the shoulder of his tired horse, who turned his head to give his rider a reproachful look.

"Careful! My faithful steed has borne me over mountains, across plains and through battles. We can't have him trampling me on the doorstep when I get home."

Kendra trapped his hand in hers and dragged him back towards the patio. There, she towered over Miranra.

"You! You pushed me down the steps."

Miranra laughed. "And what did you have planned? Stand there all cool and dignified until the moment was past?"

"Well…"

"And look what you would have missed. There is a time for decorum, and a time," she turned to Maksa, who strode towards her, "for affection."

She ran to her husband and threw her arms around him. He lifted her high, swinging her while the twins danced about, screaming in joy. Soon, Maksa set her down and knelt to gather the boys into a squirming hug.

Kendra had not let Cheynou's hand drop, and they stood, regarding this scene. "Barbarous bunch, aren't they?"

He grinned and, twisting around and going to one knee, kissed her hand. "My Lady is so much more refined."

She jerked him to his feet and gave him one more fierce hug. "There. Now you have been truly welcomed."

They separated, staring at each other for an awkward moment, and then the rest of the crowd swarmed around them. With everyone talking and laughing, they stumbled into the main hall, where drinks and food waited, and the tale had to be told.

Faranos and Maksa carried the brunt of the storytelling, much to Cheynou's embarrassment. In their eyes, he had planned everything, controlled everyone and carried the day with his wit and courage. Finally, he had to put an end to it.

"Don't listen to them. I went on a mission with a competent group, and each man did his share. In fact, I didn't do that much at all."

Faranos laughed. "He's right. He doesn't actually do much. He's just there, and people act differently when he's watching."

"I don't do it on purpose."

"Yes, you do." Kendra gestured like a showman presenting his star act. "You stand there glowing with the Truth, and everyone knows they can't argue."

"May I remind you of that, some day in the near future? The day you forget to argue with me is the day I start to worry."

The continuation of their usual banter warmed him, but he could not help but notice the change in Kendra and her position in the Rochana Home. Except for her fading accent, no observant stranger would be able to tell that she was an outsider. Cheynou watched as she took charge of the serving of the meal while Lady Rochana sat at ease with her husband.

Cedenye looked up and caught his eye. "I suppose you think I'm shirking my duties."

"Oh no, my Lady. Why exert yourself when there is someone who seems so eager to fill in?"

"You never noticed how bossy she is?"

He shrugged. "Not particularly."

"Hmm. Well, the rest of the world notices, whether they like it or not."

Kendra returned to her seat. "You're talking about me. I can tell by the meaningful looks."

Cedenye waved a languid hand. "Yes, I was just observing how you were ducking your responsibility in whipping the lad here into a serviceable prospect for marriage."

Kendra regarded Cheynou with a frown. "It's not up to me. The poor thing who marries him will have her work cut out for her, that's certain."

He tried not to blush. "If sitting there sizing me up like a quarter of beef for the spit is good for my development, you're doing a fine job." He inclined his head in a courtly gesture. "On behalf of my future wife, I thank you."

Instead of answering, Cedenye turned her regard on Kendra, eyebrows raised. When the girl did not immediately respond, a small, satisfied smile appeared briefly on the older woman's face, and she returned her attention to her meal.

Kendra took the opportunity to notice an empty platter and turned away to signal one of the serving girls.

Restraining his need for a sigh of relief, Cheynou went back to eating.

29. FARTHER NORTH

The next morning, life returned to its usual cycle in the Rochana Home. Cheynou was heavily involved with the trading and roadbuilding plans, and the days passed quickly, shortening as autumn approached. His status in the Home had taken on a new dimension. After his actions up on the Prairie, Cruzen and Maksa apparently decided he had the martial skills to deserve more training, and they began to include him in their Weaponless training. This bending of protocol was never discussed outside the training sessions. Cheynou knew when to keep his head down and take advantage of an opportunity, and he did his best to produce what the Masters demanded of him.

He and Maksa were relaxing in the latter's office after a heavy workout, enjoying a cup of chilled wine despite the cool breeze that fluttered the curtains on the open window.

"What's the weather like here, as winter comes on?"

Cruzen wrinkled his nose. "Rain and flooding, then bright sun, wind and bone-chilling cold. Then it rains again. Sometimes snow."

"Not good for travelling, then."

"Not very." The lord regarded him. "Cheynou, are you content here?"

"Content? Yes, you could say I am content here."

"Ah." Cruzen regarded him a moment. "But you are not happy."

Cheynou considered. "I am not unhappy. However, being content is not really what I am looking for, either."

"I see. So you are not interested in staying here."

Cheynou shook his head, not too sadly. "I am afraid I do not have it in my head to be a farmer. The contentment of sleeping under the same stars and rising to the sun on the same horizon does not appeal to me. It is a boon to stay in such a pleasant place with such wonderful people for a time. But some day, I must continue my journey."

"And where will that take you?"

Cheynou grinned. "That is part of the fun, isn't it?" Then he grew serious. "I can see no better course than to steer towards the centre of the Empire. Maksa and Faranos tell me there is much to be learned there. Also, there is another Sea. I would like to helm that water, to discover its mysteries."

Cruzen nodded. "In that case, I have a suggestion, if you are interested."

"Of course."

"I have business to be done in Kyabra, although I do not have the leisure to attend to it myself because of my work here, especially now that our trading opportunities have expanded. However, I am sending Maksa in my place."

"He did mention that possibility."

Cruzen grinned. "It was your arrival that interfered with those objectives. You set in motion other plans, sent us in new directions. Now our path is settled, but I am needed here even more to deal with all the new business we have created. So Maksa must go for me. He will be leaving soon because of the weather. I suggest you join him."

"That sounds good."

"Yes. Travelling with him will be comfortable, and he can ease your way once you reach Kyabra."

Cheynou sat straighter. "That sounds great. When do we leave?"

"Oh, it will take ten days or so to get organized. The party will be more than the two of you."

"I did not think Lady Miranra would miss the chance to reacquaint herself with the latest gossip and styles of the Emperor's Court."

"She would not. She would also like the boys to see their grandparents after a gap of three years."

"So it will be a slow trip."

Cruzen pressed his lips together. "I think you will be pleasantly surprised. Closer to the centre of the Empire the roads are much better, and a four-horse carriage can travel quite a distance in one day."

Cheynou nodded. "You can count on me for escort. I have enjoyed myself greatly here, but the opportunity you offer is exactly what I would wish. Thank you so much."

The lord grinned. "It is a pleasure to help someone with your potential. Perhaps you will remember us out here in the back woods when you have risen to great heights in the Empire."

"Hah! I am much more likely to cover great widths of the Empire than to scale its political heights."

"Perhaps you will be able to do both." Cruzen's face grew serious. "What about Lady Kendra? Will she continue your journey?"

Cheynou paused, unable to answer.

"I know it is your journey. Kendra may be the lady and you may pretend to serve her, but you are the leader. Perhaps she will follow."

"The lady will do what she will, as always." He grinned. "Was there ever any doubt?"

Cruzen's smile was a ghost of Cheynou's. "It is a matter of what she wills."

"The only way to find out is to ask her and listen to the answer." Cheynou shook his head. "Then wait a while and watch what she actually does. Only then will you know."

He found Kendra in the farmyard overseeing something to do with half-grown lambs. He watched for a while as she directed several men who seemed to agree with her mostly and only sometimes to dispute her choices. When this happened, a good-natured wrangle would ensue, usually ending up with Kendra getting her way, but not always.

Finally, she finished and came to stand beside him. "A fine drop last spring. These are strong and healthy."

"They're standing on four feet and they're breathing. I guess that means something."

She slapped his shoulder. "You know more than that. What brings you out here into the working world?"

He took her arm, turning her away from the chatting men. "We should talk, Kendra."

"All right." She strode along beside him, and he could feel the lift to her step.

"You're happy here, aren't you?"

"Yes. It's a thriving farm, and the people are so good to us." She stopped, looking at him. "Aren't you?"

He shrugged. "Yes, but..."

"But it wasn't what you came for."

"That's right. But you are happy."

"I am." She gazed around. "I could do well here."

"I think you could."

"Better than you think. Cruzen and Cedenye offered to adopt me."

"What?" His mouth gaped.

"Yes. It's not that unusual with the Kyabrans. They adopted Faranos to be their heir."

"Aye, but he's their nephew."

"Doesn't matter. They asked me."

"What did you say?"

"I can't. I thought about it, and it just doesn't seem right. In the first place, I have a family, and I expect to go back to them some day, not forever, but at least to visit. Getting adopted by someone else...it just seems disloyal, somehow."

He gathered his courage. "There would be another way."

"What do you mean?"

"Another way to stay here. Without being adopted." He stared at her uncomprehending face. "The usual way, Kendra!"

"What? Marry someone...oh." She stared at him. "Faranos?"

He held up his hands helplessly. "He's the heir. We have both noted that he's much more than he seems at first…"

She stared at him, arms akimbo. "Cheynou, do you remember how I spoke to Faranos after the stolen cattle incident?"

"Yes. You were quite strong in your opinions, as I recall. As usual."

"As usual. So I've done it again, haven't I? Just like with Orrick Bren. I couldn't marry him because of the way I cursed his offspring when he stole my horse. Can you imagine me marrying someone I trimmed down like I cut into Faranos that day?"

"Well…I suppose…"

"You suppose right. So, much though I love this place and the people who live here, I'm not staying, no matter how much they would like me to stay."

"They didn't ask me."

"Don't sound so pouty. They would have, but they knew you wouldn't. They know you're on a journey. Me, they weren't so sure of."

Cheynou swallowed. "So, what now? I'm happy here, but I'm going nonetheless."

"I'm happy here, too. It doesn't mean we stay here forever."

"Oh."

"Did you think I was going to let you go on with our journey and leave me behind?"

"Well, I didn't know. You came on this trip because you were looking for something. I thought maybe you found it here. Look at Cinders." He gestured towards the heavily-pregnant dog, lolling in the warmth of the fall sunlight.

"When I went south again, you said you were staying here until you figured out why you were here…I thought maybe…"

She shook her head. "No, not here. It's too soon, anyway. There's a half a continent out there we just discovered, and I want to at least get to the other side of it."

"Do you? When did you start thinking like that?"

She grinned. "Oh, it just came to me, one day."

His heart bounded. "So you're coming with me?" He held her upper arms and stared into her eyes, shining back at him. He couldn't stop himself. He kissed her.

Her arms went around him and, for a moment, her posture softened, melding with his. He tightened his hands on her waist, enjoying the feel of her lithe body against him.

Then she straightened and moved away, and it was over.

He raised a hand to his lips, and it looked like she did the same, although her back was turned. He glanced around, but the workers were studiously looking in other directions. His cheeks burning, he faced her. "Well...that settles it, then?"

She had regained her composure, her hands on her hips again, looking up at the warm stucco walls. "It does. When do we leave?"

"Ten days or so. Maksa and his family are going to Kyabra to visit and do some business."

"So we'll be travelling with them? That'll be fun!"

"And they can introduce us around when we get there."

"That will be good, too." She swung up on a fence rail and sat, looking down on him. "You know, Cheynou, this is all working out so well. I'm glad I brought you along."

He nodded. "Yes, it's a good thing you did. Otherwise, you'd still be hiking in circles up in the mountains somewhere."

She jumped off the fence, her arm snaking around his neck, and he found himself flying over her hip to land flat on his back in the dirt.

"Hey! Where did you learn to do that?"

She stood back, laughing. "I have brothers, remember?"

He scrambled up, brushing off a cloud of dust. "Next time, give me some warning."

She slapped at his back, raising more dust. "Nonsense. It's much more effective this way."

"Can't argue with success." He glanced at her as they walked back towards the house. "What was that all about? I thought you were finally learning some good manners."

She shrugged. "I've been trying to make a good impression, like you asked me to. I just realized that I've made whatever reputation I'm going to achieve and it's too late to try to fool anyone."

Miranra was sewing under an awning on the south patio. She looked up from her work as they approached. "Did I just see what I thought I saw?"

"If you saw it, you might have."

"I was afraid of that. Please don't do that sort of thing when the children are around, Kendra. They'll be expecting it of me."

Kendra laughed. "I doubt if you need to go to those ends to keep Maksa in line."

"You might be surprised. He can be quite stubborn."

"I gather we're going to get a chance to find out."

The older woman smiled. "Yes. I'm pleased you're coming with us. It will be such fun on the road, and once we get to the Capital, I will love showing you around."

"You mean showing us off."

"Oh, no. There isn't much shock value in a cultured lady like yourself, no matter where she comes from. Some will find you interesting, of course. The young men, for example." She turned to regard Cheynou. "You, however, have potential. We might dress you up and then let people get surprised."

"By what, my barbaric ways?"

"No, your good manners."

"You introduce me to a couple of adventurous sea captains and I'll play whatever court games you need, and with pleasure."

She regarded him. "Maksa and I were talking about that."

"You were?"

"Yes. Of course you would like to see the Capital, but you won't find what you want there. The Kyabrans are a land people. Oh, we have a coastline and a navy, but we think like land people, and Kyabrad City is inland. If you want the ocean and sailors, the Inner Provinces are much better."

"Can I arrange to visit there?"

"My family has holdings in Tenet, a large seaport at the mouth of the Kernegata River. Some of my cousins live there, and I would be glad of an excuse to visit. I think, Kendra, that you will find the Provinces more comfortable as well. Your Kyabran is improving, but you will find it awkward in social chat, not understanding the nuances. The Provinces speak your language, and your accent has almost disappeared."

"So I won't stick out like a wart on a pig's rear."

"Please, my Lady! A wildflower in a trimmed hedge, perhaps. But either image is accurate."

Cheynou nodded. "It sounds like an excellent idea. Thank you for thinking of us."

She smiled up at him. "We always try to maximize the potential of our resources." She bent once more over her sewing, then glanced up. "With an eye to our entertainment."

They laughed and continued into the house, Cheynou shaking his head. "Did you ever hear her end a conversation without a little barb, just to finish it off?"

"I believe that is the fashion at the Capital. Everyone tries to be witty and sharp."

"Miranra doesn't have to try."

"Actually, she doesn't do it all the time. Just with you, me, sometimes Cruzen."

"You mean she's nice to everyone else? Why not us?"

"I guess she thinks we can handle it."

* * *

The evening was taken up with planning and preparation, and it was late when they left the main hall in a haze of enthusiasm, laughter following them into the courtyard. They entered their little house, but as he started up the stairs, Kendra's hand touched his arm, holding him back. He turned to her with raised eyebrows.

"Cheynou, you kissed me today."

"I guess I did."

"It was the wrong kind of kiss for the wrong reason."

"Ah, yes. Caught up in the heat of battle. Forgot myself."

"I'm serious, Cheynou. It wasn't fair. Don't do it again."

"Never?"

"Never for the wrong reason."

He nodded once. "That's a fair request. I won't."

She echoed his nod. "Fine." She patted his arm. "Good night, Cheynou. It's a good beginning."

"It is. Good night, Kendra."

The soft brush of her feet on tile, and she was gone. He strolled up the stairs and crossed his room to the window, where he stared up at the stars for a long time, his heart light, his mind heavy with thought. *A good beginning...*

The End

For the moment

Here ends the second book of the Petrellan Saga. The third book, "Path of Water," follows Cheynou and Kendra as they journey to seek their destiny through the heart of the Kyabran Empire to the waves of the Inner Sea.

ABOUT THE AUTHOR

Brought up in a logging camp with no electricity, Gordon Long learned his storytelling in the traditional way: at his father's knee. He now spends his time editing, publishing, travelling, blogging and writing fantasy and social commentary, although sometimes the boundaries blur.

Gordon lives in Tsawwassen, British Columbia, with his wife, Linda, and their Nova Scotia Duck Tolling Retriever, Josh. When he is not writing and publishing, he works on projects with the Surrey Seniors' Planning Table, and is a staff writer for <indiesunlimited.com>

www.ingramcontent.com/pod-product-compliance
Lightning Source LLC
Chambersburg PA
CBHW051951240626
47153CB00005B/1717